MAR 0 0

Greco

more . . .

"A stunning novel of taut suspense, sensual romance, and intriguing characters . . . Snuggle down for an evening of cozy reading that will leave a smile on your lips, a glow in your heart, and a hunger to read the third book."

—*Under the Covers*

THE BRIDE OF ROSECLIFFE

"Rexanne Becnel creates a magical love story that compels the reader to stay up reading all night. Her three-dimensional characters and exquisitely detailed backdrop only add to the wonder of her lyrically told story."   —*Romantic Times*

"Ms. Becnel creates the most intriguing characters and infuses them with fiery personalities and quick minds!"

—*The Literary Times*

DANGEROUS TO LOVE

"Rexanne Becnel writes stories dripping with rich, passionate characters and a sensual wallop that will have you reeling!"

—*The Belles and Beaux of Romance*

THE MAIDEN BRIDE

"A master medieval writer, Ms. Becnel writes emotional stories with a deft hand."   —*The Time Machine*

HEART OF THE STORM

"Great characters, a riveting plot and loads of sensuality . . . A fabulous book. I couldn't put it down!"   —*Joan Johnston*

"Rexanne Becnel combines heartfelt emotions with a romance that touches readers with the magic and joy of falling in love. Destined to be a bestseller from a star of the genre!"
—*Romantic Times*

"Tempestuous and seductive, this winner from Rexanne Becnel will enthrall from the first page to the last."
—Deborah Martin, author of *Stormswept*

WHERE MAGIC DWELLS

"A passionate, compelling story filled with engaging characters."
—*Library Journal*

"Rich settings always bring Becnel's medieval novels to life."
—*Publishers Weekly*

"Enthralling . . . Another irresistible medieval romance from one of the best."
—*The Medieval Chronicle*

DOVE AT MIDNIGHT

"A master medieval writer. Ms. Becnel writes emotional stories with a deft hand."
—*The Time Machine*

"A non-stop read. Rexanne Becnel understands the medieval mind-set, and her beguiling characters' passions and adventures will hold you enthralled. Once more, Ms. Becnel demonstrates that she is a master of her craft."
—*Romantic Times*

The Mistress of Rosecliffe

Rexanne Becnel

St. Martin's Paperbacks

THE MISTRESS OF ROSECLIFFE

Copyright © 2000 by Rexanne Becnel.

ISBN: 0-312-97402-7

Printed in the United States of America

St. Martin's Paperbacks edition / March 2000

St. Martin's Paperbacks are published by St. Martin's Press, 175 Fifth Avenue, New York, N.Y. 10010.

10 9 8 7 6 5 4 3 2

For Pam, Deborah, and Barbara,
friends who go beyond the call.
Thanks for the lagniappe!

PROLOGUE

Those that made me were uncivil.
They made me harder than the devil.
Knives won't cut me, fire won't light me.
Dogs bark at me, but can't bite me.

—TUSSER

WHITLING CASTLE, ENGLAND
SEPTEMBER, A.D. 1153

RHYS AP OWAIN HAD THREE GOALS.

The first was to depart English soil forever and return to his beloved homeland of Wales. The second was to lay waste to the English who continued to encroach onto those lands—especially the FitzHughs—and thereby preserve Wales for the Welsh.

The third, and most urgent, was to unhorse the huge knight charging him at a thunderous pace.

He set his lance, aiming at the man's shield, a little left of center. His destrier gathered momentum. The tournament crowd roared. Another second only. Brace. Twist—

The shock of the collision was ferocious and almost unseated him. But he angled his body, and with a screech the man's lance slid past across his shield. He felt the solid contact of his own lance, though. Hard, solid contact. A jarring thud.

The other man's horse shied to the side. Then it was abruptly over.

Clouds of dust obscured the outcome of the joust. But Rhys knew the feel of victory. He knew the smell. He breathed deep of dust and sweat and horseflesh. Twenty-nine tournaments he'd competed in during the last three years, and he'd been unhorsed only four times and not once during the past season.

Even his warhorse sensed their victory, for the big animal's pace changed to almost a prance. The earth trembled beneath his heavy hooves, while behind them the other destrier came to a riderless halt.

Rhys circled the demarcated jousting ring, his lance held at a high angle while the fallen knight's men ran to help him. He knew what people said of him, the names that had begun to echo about him in recent years. He was known as Rhys the Ruthless, and Rhys the Wroth, and sometimes as Rhys the Enraged. It was because he fought not merely to win, but to crush his foe. To vanquish him.

To annihilate him.

Whether in the practice yard, at sanctioned tournaments— and unsanctioned ones—or on the field of battle, his purpose remained ever the same. It was always Englishmen he faced, and Englishmen he despised. So he fought them wherever he found them, and in England there were an infinite number of them willing to test their mettle against an upstart Welshman, a knight errant eager to sell his battle prowess to the highest bidder.

Along the way he'd become wealthy beyond his wildest childhood imaginings. But it was still not enough, not for what he had planned.

Across the yard, in the lord's pavilion, he saw a woman rise, but through the narrow slits of his helmet he could not be sure of her identity. Wife to Lord Whitling, or daughter? He could not tell. But she held out a length of red silk woven with white flowers and ribbons, and he rode to collect it. Silk and roses might symbolize the tournament champion, but the gold and silver coins that the defeated knights would pay him for the return of their horses and armor mattered far more to Rhys.

A good day's work, he decided as he paused before the elaborately draped and furnished viewing stand. He would collect a trunkful of riches for his work here.

He lowered the lance and the noblewoman wound the bauble around its tip. She smiled at him—it was the buxom mother, not the fair-faced daughter.

Rhys removed his helmet and the crowd of onlookers went wild, shouting, clapping, and stomping their approval. As four men fetched the last fallen knight away on a stretcher, their cheers for Rhys became whistles, and hoots of derision for the unmoving knight.

"I proclaim thee Champion of the Whitling Games, Sir

Rhys," the woman said. Behind her Lord Whitling lifted his goblet and drank, then belched. But she ignored her husband and stared steadily at Rhys. "You will join us at the high table this evening." *And in my bed later,* her half-lidded eyes silently added.

Rhys nodded. The daughter was prettier, but she would be a virgin and closely watched. The mother, meanwhile, was clearly eager and far more experienced. He'd bested seven English knights in this tourney. Tonight he would cuckold another—Lady Whitling's husband.

He grinned at the woman. Then he raised the lance and let her silken confection slide slowly down the long shaft of his weapon. Her small, greedy eyes widened at that, and a hot glow lit them.

Yes, she would give him a good ride, he decided. Then come the dawn, he would leave for the tournament at Gilling. Word circulated that King Stephen had come to terms with his youthful challenger, Henry, Duke of Normandy. Change was in the air in England, and with change came opportunity, if a man was ready to seize it.

He'd achieved one of his goals today. The time was fast coming when he would accomplish the other two.

BOOK I

Pretty mouth to sing a song, eyebrows delicate
*   and long,*
Bodies made for bodies' bliss, sweet smooth faces,
*   warm to kiss,*
Loving music, well they may, upon the lute or
*   tabor play,*
Swift in love and swift in quarrel, and deliciously
*   immoral.*

—FROM A MEDIEVAL *HAUSBUCH*

ONE

ISOLDE STOOD AMIDST THE CLAMOR OF WORKMEN SWARMING the chapel, her face puckered in a faint frown of concentration. The improvements progressed anon. But every task seemed to take twice as long as she anticipated. Still and all, the workers made headway. When it was completed, the chapel at Rosecliffe Castle would be truly magnificent.

Her father had been reluctant to approve any changes to Rosecliffe's simple chapel. But she'd been persistent, and eventually he had agreed. Now she meant to astound him with the transformation, and thereby ensure his cooperation in the other changes she envisioned for the castle.

Her frown eased into a smile as she visualized a series of continued improvements. A pleasaunce with a knot garden. An elaborate mantelpiece in the great hall featuring the wolf and rose motif her father had adopted. Tapestries framing the high table. More torchères—the new type with drip basins like those she'd seen at the mayor's residence at Chester.

At the moment, however, it was the plaster fresco of Saint John and the first baptism that she needed to concentrate on.

She backed up, staring at the entire wall, but not focusing on any one spot, so that the details blurred, and only the larger shapes and groupings of colors registered in her mind. It was a trick she often employed in her embroidery and her small illuminated pieces. But it worked even better on a large scale, she'd discovered. She extended one arm, sweeping through the air with her hand as if she were painting the wall with a giant brush.

"The river must grow broader as it courses down toward the altar," she said, more to herself than to the anxious artist at her elbow. "And the sun is too yellow. It should be a paler hue."

"I used this very color for the sun on the panel I prepared for the Abbot of Chester," the man retorted.

"But I want it paler," she insisted. " 'Tis not truly meant to represent the sun, you see, but rather, heaven in all its radiant glory." She took a thin pointed stick from its perch behind her ear and drew a faint line in the damp plaster. "Paler sun. Wider river. Like that."

She glanced at him sidelong, daring him to contradict her, and after a moment he nodded, albeit grudgingly. He did not like taking orders from a woman, especially such a young one as she. Were she not daughter to the lord and lady of Rose-cliffe, he would have dismissed her entirely.

But she was their daughter and this was her project, and he'd been hired at her behest. She meant to follow her own vision, no matter what the man thought. Besides, if he would not complete it to her satisfaction, she would do the task herself.

"How much longer until this final wall is complete?" she asked.

He shrugged and wiped his paint-stained fingers against his smock. "Another day and a half to paint. Two or three days to dry."

"Very good. I will have Father Clemson say a special mass on Sunday. And I would like you and your helper to sit in the family box," she added. "For this is to your credit, and I would have everyone recognize your talent."

He shrugged again, but he smiled a little at her compliment.

She needed to be more generous with her praise, she reminded herself. In her preoccupation with her myriad projects, she too often overlooked that simple courtesy toward others.

Once the artist and his assistant were back at work, Isolde scanned the room. The carpenters had built six elaborate benches and a heavy new altar. The stone masons had carved a fine rail and one older fellow had created a handsome holy water font from a marble block her uncle Jasper had obtained in Chester. Those items were now being installed. That left the crucifix.

She felt in her sleeve for the rolled-up parchment that held her sketch. Her mother wanted a Celtic cross to celebrate her Welsh homeland. Father Clemson wanted a classic design with the Son of God in his final agony, just before his resurrection. Isolde's father had refused to intercede, reminding Isolde that this was her project and she must resolve this issue herself. He'd chuckled as he'd thrown her own words back in her face.

So Isolde had girded herself to face the disagreeing pair alone. She did not like to contradict her mother; nor did she care to anger the priest who assigned her penance. Father Clemson could keep her on her knees many an hour if he decided she was not properly respectful of the Lord Jesus. She could only hope they would both like the compromise she'd contrived.

The solution to her dilemma had come to her in the soft moments when she was first waking, in the faint light of pre-dawn, before the lowing of the cows or the cock's first crow. A Celtic cross, taller and wider than any cross she'd ever seen. The Savior would be carved into the wood center, but beyond him symbolic Celtic designs would cover the ends of the cross. Heaven above him, the earth beneath his feet. And on either side, fire and water. Each of them a gift, given to man by God. And in the center God's greatest gift of all, his son, redeemer to all mankind.

Though her sketch had been hasty, she'd known at once that it was a good design, her best work yet. Still, she was nervous as she left the chapel in search of her mother and Father Clemson. She wasn't sure whether to present her idea to them at the same time or separately. But she needed to do it soon. Even so, the crucifix would not be completed by Sunday.

As she crossed the bailey she was preoccupied with thoughts of ocher and olive, and how to mix a vibrant purple shade. She made no note of the several knots of people standing with their heads together, nor the pair of strange horses that two lads attended just outside the stable. Only when she pushed into the hall and spied Gwen and her bosom friend

Lavinia arm in arm, twitching with excitement, did she drag her thoughts to the present.

"Whatever has you two in such a state?" she asked her younger sister. "Where is Mother? And Father?"

"In the office, receiving a message. From the Duke of Normandy. The Duke of Normandy," Gwen added dramatically. "Do you think he means to visit here at Rosecliffe?"

"Oh, but he can't!" Isolde gasped. "At least not until the chapel is complete!"

Gwen gave her a disgusted look. At thirteen she considered herself quite the lady and had little patience with her elder sister. "She cares more for plaster and paint than she does for the sad state of her hair," Gwen said to Lavinia. "And that gown." She shook her head.

"What you mean," Isolde countered, "is that I do not care merely for my hair and my gowns. We all hope you too will one day broaden your interests, Gwen. Until then, however, I suppose we have no choice but to tolerate your childish behavior."

She strode away, ignoring Gwen. If Henry, Duke of Normandy had sent a message to Rosecliffe, she wanted to know what it was about.

The castle office was a small space with a heavy damask curtain hanging across the arched doorway. It needed a proper door with a small window and shutter, and a metal knocker, she thought. Better for security and for privacy. At the moment, however, she was glad there was only a curtain, for by leaning near it she could hear fairly well.

"When will the coronation be?" she heard her father ask.

"In mid-December at Westminster Abbey," a man answered. "But he would confer with his barons before then and receive their personal pledge. Best that you leave within the next few days."

Her mother exclaimed, "That soon? But Rand, I cannot prepare—"

"Now, Josselyn," Her father said. "There is nothing to prepare. You will pack, and we will leave."

"But what of the girls? And Gavin is at Ludlow."

"We'll send word to him to join us in London."

London.

Isolde caught hold of the curtain with one hand. The entire family was going to London? To a coronation? Then the greater implication dawned on her. Earlier in the year Henry, Duke of Normandy, had been named King Stephen's heir. If he was to be crowned, that meant the old king had died.

Her father's voice drew her attention once more. "Mayhap my brother, John, will be there, for Aslin Castle is not so far distant from London. And if Halyard is there, we can discuss the matter of Isolde."

As quickly as that, Isolde's excitement fled. She'd never met her uncle, and a trip to London would be the adventure of a lifetime. But not if it would be used to wed her to Lord Halyard's eldest son, Mortimer.

Without thinking, she yanked back the curtain and pushed into the crowded office. Heads swiveled and a half-dozen sets of eyes focused on her. Besides her parents, there were two men she did not know, as well as Osborn, captain of the guard, and Odo, the steward.

"Isolde," her mother began in a chastising voice.

Her father pinned her with his glittering stare. "As you can see, I am occupied, daughter. Await me in the hall."

"But Father, I do not wish to wed Mortimer," she burst out. "You know that."

His jaw tensed and at once she realized her error, for his patience had never been vast when it came to her reluctance to wed. "Await me in the hall," he bit out.

The silence in the room was awful, yet Isolde could not relent, not on this subject. She sucked in a shaky breath and lifted her chin a notch. "I will await you in the hall. But I will never agree to so idiotic a plan."

Someone gasped at such impertinence toward the great Randulf FitzHugh, Lord of Rosecliffe. But she did not linger to find out who. Angry and fearful, all at the same time, she turned and quit the chamber. Forgotten were the chapel and her efforts there. Forgotten was the parchment in her sleeve with its daring design. Isolde hurried into the hall, worrying one of her fingernails, and consumed with one thought only. They were going to London to see the new king crowned and to finalize her wedding to that bumbling oaf of a boy.

How could a day which had begun so well have turned so utterly vile?

He kept her waiting on purpose. By the time the messengers left, Isolde was jittery with nerves. When Odo and Osborn exited, she almost pushed her way back in. But she knew that would not be wise, so she gritted her teeth, and sat on her hands to avoid shredding her nails any further. From her perch in a window ell, Gwen gave her a haughty look, then ignored her.

Finally her mother came out and, spying Isolde, made her way directly to her. "Will you never learn how to deal with your father?" she scolded. "That impetuous display has made your task infinitely more difficult."

"He is the one being difficult!" Isolde exclaimed. "He refuses to listen—"

"No more than do you! Have I not told you repeatedly that I will not see any child of mine unwillingly wed? Have you never heard me say that to you, Isolde?"

"Yes, Mama. But—"

"But you will not believe me and so you make the task harder still. Oh, Isolde." She threw her hands up in frustration. "Are Gavin and Gwen and Elyssa to be as difficult as you?"

Chastened, Isolde bowed her head and stared down at her knotted hands. A bit of dried plaster clung to one knuckle, and she picked absently at it. "Is he very angry?"

"Furious." Then her mother sighed. "You are fortunate that his anger with you is tempered today by his relief that after nineteen years, we will finally have a single, unquestioned monarch at the helm. But your sharp tongue has convinced him more than ever that you are in need of a husband's guidance."

"A husband's guidance?" Isolde made a rude noise. "Is that what you have, Mother, your husband's guidance? It does not appear so to me."

Her mother's lovely face softened with a faint grin. "I prefer to think of your father and me as a well-matched pair. He has his sphere of influence and I have mine. But I am his wife, Isolde, and you are his daughter. He is unable to view us in the same light. Indeed, he is hard-pressed to acknowledge that his daughter is of an age to assume wifely duties." Her eyes sparkled and her grin increased. "I think that may be why he has fixed his attention on Lord Halyard's son, Mortimer. Despite the great advantages of a match with the Halyard family, to your father's eye, the lad appears more a boy than a man."

Isolde digested that information for a moment. "Are you saying he wishes to wed me to a man—a boy—who cannot perform his husbandly duties?"

Her mother laughed, then sat down beside her and took her hand. "No. But still, I wonder if there is a part of him that cannot stomach the idea of any man taking his daughter's innocence."

Isolde was amazed. She'd known for many years how things worked between men and women. Her mother was straightforward about such matters and answered any questions put to her with complete candor. That her father might be squeamish about those same subjects had never occurred to Isolde. "If that is the case, why does he push me to wed at all? Why can I not continue as I am, until I find someone I truly wish to wed?"

Her mother shook her head. "Isolde, you attempt logic, when your father's reaction is not based on logic at all. He knows you must marry, and who you marry is vitally important to Rosecliffe. But in his heart he hates the idea, and so he welcomes Lord Halyard's offer."

Isolde crossed her arms. "Well, I don't care how wealthy and powerful the Halyards are. I refuse to marry Mortimer. He's slump shouldered, and skinny. And spotted. And he turns red in the face whenever I cast my eyes in his direction— which, I promise you, is not often."

Josselyn laughed. "He will outgrow all those flaws."

"But I don't love him!"

At once Josselyn sobered. "Yes. There is that."

Across the hall Isolde's father pushed the curtain aside and stepped out of his office. She looked up at him, and for once she regarded him, not as her father, but as her mother's husband, a man that a strong, intelligent woman could love.

Though she and her father often clashed, the truth was, she wanted someone just like him. A man who was strong but also gentle. A man who was confident—arrogant, even—but fairminded, as well. A man who was passionate, but tender.

Suddenly she was not afraid to confront him. She stood up while he continued to stare at her. "He may be stubborn," she told her mother. "But I am more so."

Truer words had never been spoken, Josselyn decided as she watched her firstborn child stride up to Rand. English arrogance and Welsh stubbornness had combined in Isolde to give her an utter fearlessness. It would take a very special sort of man to meet all the challenges the girl would present to her husband. Poor Mortimer Halyard certainly was not the right choice for her, nor were any of the several fellows who had made inquiries to Rand about her.

Josselyn fingered the ring of keys tied to her girdle. She wanted Isolde to choose a strong Welshman. Rand wanted to choose a mild Englishman. Somewhere between those two extremes was the right man for Isolde. Josselyn suspected, however, that Isolde would have to find him on her own.

Or he would have to find her.

"How many?" Rhys grunted as Linus fastened the gorget around his neck and shoulders.

"Sixteen knights in the tournament," the oversized squire answered. "That means . . . that means . . ." Linus stared down at his hands. He was counting on his fingers, Rhys knew, struggling with the simple computations.

"Eight matches," Gandy, his valet, said. "Then four. Then two."

"Eight matches," Linus repeated. "Then four. Then two."

"Bless me, but this shed has an echo in it," the quick-witted Gandy exclaimed.

"Leave the poor lad alone," said Tillo, limping into the shed.

"The poor lad? If he's a lad, I'm an infant."

"You're a dwarf, and an ill-tempered one at that," Tillo snapped.

"And you're a grumpy old cripple," Gandy retorted.

Linus looked up from his fingers. "Be nice," he rumbled in his deep, slow voice.

Rhys pulled his breastplate over his head. There were times, like now, when he regretted the motley group he'd somehow assembled. A foul-mouthed dwarf, saved from the stocks at

Pleshing. A giant, harnessed like a beast of burden, freed from the fields outside Cockermouth. As for Tillo, the old man had been hungry, and once fed, he'd refused to go away. Still, the odd trio was the closest thing Rhys had to a family. When other knights laughed at his strange, bedraggled entourage, he took great pains to defeat the boastful fools in the most humiliating manner possible.

Ignoring the bickering around him, he spoke to Tillo. "Is there news? You would not have returned so soon if there were not."

"News, indeed," Tillo said, hobbling over to a bench and lowering himself painfully onto it. "Word circulates that the coronation is planned in but a fortnight. All the great lords of the land have been called to attend."

"All of them?" Rhys went very still. "The lords of the Welsh marches, as well?"

" 'Tis what I am told. Young Henry wants them all there so that each of them may swear their allegiance to him. Methinks this boy king will hold his several kingdoms with a fist of iron. Pray God he will do better by the common folk than did that shiftless Stephen."

"He will not do better by my people of Wales," Rhys muttered. "A weak king allows his wayward barons to ride hard upon the land. A strong one will seek to solidify the gains they have made." He thrust his hands into the thick leather gloves used for the joust, then reached for his helm. "If I am to move, I must do so now," he continued more lowly to himself.

But Gandy had heard and the little man's eyes danced with excitement. "So we go to Wales, to this Rosecliffe Castle you despise so much?"

Rhys drew out the long sword from the sheath Linus buckled around his hips and stared at its finely honed edge. "We go to Rosecliffe. But only after I grind every knight in this tournament beneath my heels.

"Every English knight," he vowed.

TWO

ISOLDE WAS MISERABLE. SHE HAD HELD TO HER POSITION AND now she must suffer the consequences. But it was so hard—and so unfair!

Her father had given her two choices—both equally repugnant. Come to London and formally accept Mortimer Halyard's offer. Or remain in Wales and thereby insult her future husband and begin her marriage all wrong.

Despite Isolde's rages and pleading, her father would not relent. He was adamant that she wed the hapless Mortimer. He'd turned away three good matches already, he reminded her, good men of noble families whom she had disdained. He would not turn away young Halyard and his very powerful father. For the past three days Isolde and her father had barely spoken to one another. Even now she could not believe he would actually go so far as to force her to wed the man.

Her mother had kept apart from the discussion. Her only advice to Isolde had been that a woman, like a man, must stand by her convictions, no matter the consequences. And so Isolde intended to do.

"I will take up the veil before I agree to this," she now declared as her father mounted his favorite steed. She crossed her arms and stared balefully at him. "I mean what I say, Father."

He gazed down at her, a muscle ticking in his cheek. " 'Tis obedience the church expects of its servants. If you cannot be obedient to your earthly father, 'tis unlikely you'll be so to your heavenly one."

So saying he turned and the party started forward. If it hadn't been for her mother's small, encouraging smile, Isolde might have burst into tears, for she hated this estrangement from her father.

Still, her heart remained heavy as she watched the gaiety of her family's departure. Gwen and Josselyn rode their own palfreys, with young Elyssa riding before her nurse. Five knights, seven servants, six men-at-arms, and eight pack animals accompanied them, a considerable party for the month they would be gone. As one of the most powerful Marcher lords, however, her father would be expected to travel with a goodly number of retainers and to put on a handsome display.

Everyone remaining behind at Rosecliffe Castle envied them their grand adventure. Everyone but Osborn, Isolde amended. He was content to stay at home and maintain the peace, not that much effort was required in that vein. The English townsfolk revered her father and the Welsh ones respected him. As for her mother, everyone adored the Lady Josselyn, even the people of Carreg Du and Afon Bryn, the nearest Welsh towns. Except for the occasional petty grievance—mostly between English and Welsh—there was little enough peacekeeping to be done. Of late the greatest grievance, however, had been between father and daughter.

From her spot on the wall walk Isolde turned away from the view of the traveling party and leaned morosely against the solid stone crennels. Osborn shot her a knowing look.

"Having second thoughts, girl?"

Yes. "No."

"I see."

"I am far happier remaining here to finish the chapel and then begin my next project in the great hall. A visit to London would be interesting," she conceded. "But my father exacts too great a price."

She did not expect Osborn to concur. He was her father's oldest friend, and while they'd been known to disagree among themselves, she'd never once heard Osborn criticize his liege lord to another.

" 'Tis hardly a sin to want your daughter safely wed," he remarked after a moment.

"Did his father force him to wed a woman he did not want?

No," she answered her own question. "He wed Mother, a most unlikely choice, wouldn't you say?"

Osborn chuckled. "Unlikely on the surface, perhaps. But from their first meeting, it was clear they were destined for one another."

That drew a great heaving sigh from the depths of Isolde's chest. "That is precisely my point, Osborn. Don't you see? What I want is to meet the man destined to be my husband."

He leaned back against the wall beside her and studied her shrewdly. "Then you should have gone to London. The city will be crowded with noblemen attending the coronation. You'll not meet anyone new here in the wilds of northern Wales."

"But how could I go with him throwing me at Mortimer? My only hope is that his father will be so offended by my absence he breaks the contract—or that Mother can reason with Father."

Again Osborn chuckled. "Josselyn will no doubt prevail. Have patience, Isolde. This paragon of a fellow you seek will eventually find you."

"Humph," she snorted. But she was somewhat reassured. She shot a last glance over her shoulder. The travelers had passed the town gate, and were nearing the *domen,* the burial tomb of forgotten ages. Beyond that lay the old forest road. "A whole month?" she said.

"A month, mayhap more. Sufficient time, I suspect, for you to make enough changes to Rosecliffe to infuriate your father."

At that Isolde's lips curved in a small grin. Osborn had always known how to cheer her up. "Yes. A month will provide me with ample time for that. I suppose I shall simply have to take my pleasures where I can."

At the *domen* Rand paused. Newlin had not been much present of late, but he was here now, sitting atop the great stone slab as always. His voluminous green cloak settled around him in deep folds, disguising his deformed body and leaving only his grizzled head to identify him as a man. A very old man, Rand realized. Twenty years ago the bard had been an ancient creature. How old must he now be?

Rand flexed his hands, feeling the stiffness of age in his

own fingers. Perhaps it was as the Welsh folk believed. Newlin would outlive them all. If so, Rand hoped he gave the same sensible advice to Gavin and his heirs that he'd always given to Rand.

He waved the rest of the party on. They continued down the road, all except for Josselyn, who reined her palfrey beside his destrier.

"So. To London," Newlin said.

"To London," Rand echoed. "All of us, English and Welsh alike, pray that young Henry will do better by his people than Stephen did."

The old bard shrugged one of his bent shoulders. "Like all who would lead, he will not please everyone who falls within his shadow."

"Will he please us?" Josselyn asked.

Newlin smiled at her, a sweet smile that befitted a child more than such a gnarled and aged man. But Newlin was not like other men.

"Henry's desires are much the same as your husband's. Peace through strength, and prosperity for all."

"Doesn't everyone want that?" she asked.

"For the most part, yes. But one man's peace—one man's prosperity—they may be very unlike another's."

Rand's fingers clenched around the reins. He did not notice the pain in his knuckles. "Unlike one another's. Are you saying Henry's reign will bring a renewal of the conflicts here along the Marches?"

Again the bard shrugged. "Perhaps. Perhaps, however, it is only a different approach that may continue the bounty and accord of these past several years."

"What different approach? The people here have been—"

"Times change," Josselyn put in, laying a hand on his arm. "We cannot know what the future will hold when Gavin becomes lord of Rosecliffe."

"*If* he becomes lord of Rosecliffe," Newlin said. The words were soft, with no hint of threat in them. But Rand stiffened in alarm, as did Josselyn.

"Is Gavin in danger?" She urged her mount nearer the flat-topped *domen*. "Is he safe?"

The bard smiled. "Do not alarm yourself, child. Gavin will

forge his own future. But as with your other children, that future may not be the same one you envision. Their choices may not be your choices."

Josselyn's tense posture eased. "Do you refer now to Isolde and her father's foolish choice of a husband for her?" She shot Rand a sidelong look. He glowered back at her.

Newlin looked away, past them toward Rosecliffe Castle, resplendent on its hilltop site. It gleamed in the morning sun, impregnable and yet not intimidating. "Isolde will be mistress of her own fate. You have raised your children well. They must forge their own lives now. And you must let them." Then he settled into himself, subsiding like a drained wineskin, seeming almost to shrink as he pulled his thoughts back into the recesses of his remarkable brain.

He would speak no more, Rand knew, so he turned his horse away from the *domen*, and with Josselyn at his side, they regained the road.

"Good advice, don't you think?" Josselyn murmured.

"Perhaps," Rand conceded after a long pause.

"So you will not press Isolde further on the matter of young Halyard? Perhaps we should send a rider back for her. I hate for her to miss this trip to London."

He grunted. "You push too hard, woman."

"Do I?" She guided her palfrey closer until her knee bumped his. "Rand," she began in a cajoling tone.

"She stays where she is. She is too stubborn to suit any man and I want her to think on the error of her ways."

"But what of this matter of her betrothal to Mortimer Halyard?"

He shifted in his saddle. It was bad enough to suspect he was wrong on that front. It was harder still to admit as much to his wife. "I may reconsider that idea," he muttered at last. "But she still needs a husband."

He was rewarded at once by her warm hand on his thigh. "You are so wonderful," she said. "I hope Isolde can find a man as perfect as you."

"Perfect?" he scoffed. "Hah!"

"You were perfect last night," she murmured. "At least I thought so."

Their eyes met and Rand felt a surge of desire for his wife.

Twenty years since first he'd laid eyes upon her. Twenty years that they'd raised a family, constructed a mighty fortress, and built a life he would trade for no other. Twenty years and he loved her better with every passing day—and desired her as fiercely as ever.

He covered her hand with his and leaned eagerly toward her. "I know a green bower. Very private," he said. "We can rejoin the others later."

Behind them Newlin smiled and rocked himself forward and back. There were changes ahead and they would not come easy. But come they would, and with them the chance for great joy—and for great sorrow.

It proved to be a long day for Isolde. Despite her best intentions to complete the chapel, which project she had abandoned of late, her heart was not in it. By mid-afternoon the doldrums had settled heavily upon her.

"I believe I shall go into the village," she told Odo in the hall.

"Better tell Osborn—and take a maid with you," he added.

She took a maid, but she did not tell Osborn, for she knew he would want to send two guards along, and she was not of a mind for that much company. Between her and Magda they could bring the daily basket of extra bread for distribution to several needy households. Besides, Magda was unmarried and near to her own age, and was sure to understand her dilemma.

As they crossed the moat and started down the road to the village, Isolde looked over at the young maid. "Tell me, Magda. Has your father selected a husband for you?"

The pleasantly rounded young woman shook her head. "I'm one of six girls and four boys. My father hasn't the time for such arrangements as that. Besides," she added, emboldened by her mistress's frankness. "I've been walkin' out with someone of late, and Da' approves." The maid shyly smiled. " 'Tis plain your father loves you, miss. Is it so hard that he would pick a fine and wealthy husband for you?"

"I think I'm better able to make such a selection than he. Besides," Isolde grimly added, "you haven't seen Mortimer Halyard."

Magda chuckled. "I take it he does not appeal to you?"

Isolde grimaced. "Not at all."

"So. What do you want in a man?"

What, indeed? As they entered the village below the castle Isolde considered the question. "Young—or at least not old. And vigorous."

"Handsome?"

"Well, that would be nice. But it isn't essential. Rather, he should be manly, and fair-minded."

"And tall?"

Isolde grinned. "I suppose."

"With broad shoulders?" the girl pressed. "And a musician?"

Isolde laughed. "Are you describing your young man, Magda?"

The girl giggled and shook her head. "I was describing him." She pointed at a man standing near the smithy's shed.

Isolde paused and studied the fellow. She could see why he'd caught Magda's eye, for he was tall and broad shouldered, the very image of manliness. His back was to them, yet she sensed from his posture that he was young and vigorous. And he had some sort of musical instrument slung across his back. Whether he was handsome and fair-minded, however, was anyone's guess, as was the stranger's identity.

Still, he was nothing like Mortimer Halyard, and for a moment Isolde let herself imagine a man like that taking her in his arms, sweeping her off her feet, and making her his own. That he was no lord, but rather an ordinary fellow, only made her fantasy more appealing. Her father wanted a title, property, and power in a son-in-law, whereas Isolde just wanted passion.

A frisson of heat coiled in her belly at so impious a thought. But it made clear what she'd not previously realized. She wanted passion and drama in her life. She wanted a grand love with a man who would make her laugh and make her angry, and make her love him beyond all reason.

As if the man heard those bold thoughts of hers, his stance shifted, and before she could look away, he turned and caught her staring. At once Isolde averted her gaze. But she was shaken by the directness of his bold eyes.

Beside her Magda once again giggled, then caught Isolde by the arm and pulled her down the street. After a moment

Isolde laughed, too, but only to hide her sudden disquiet. Who was that man?

"Ooh, he's a fierce one," Magda whispered, glancing back toward the smithy's shed. "I wonder what he looks like beneath that beard."

Isolde did not respond, but she too glanced back at the dark-haired stranger. She did not recognize him, and yet there was something about him, as if she knew him—or *should* know him.

He was still staring after her, as well, as if he'd like to get to know her. Again Isolde looked away, and this time she forced herself not to look back. Staring at strange men in the street was not acceptable behavior by anyone's standards, her father's, her mother's, or her own.

But as Isolde ambled away, arm in arm with her maid, Rhys ap Owain kept his stare steady upon her. So that was Fitz-Hugh's daughter. He'd watched from the woods as the large party departed this morning. Since then he'd heard snippets of gossip about the eldest daughter's dispute with her father, and his mind had spun with the possibilities that presented to him.

Now as he watched her disappear around a street corner, those possibilities moved closer to reality.

The obnoxious little brat had grown tall and filled out most becomingly, he grudgingly admitted. No doubt, however, she'd also grown more disagreeable if her challenge to her father's authority was any sign.

He stroked his beard as he considered his plan. Her presence at Rosecliffe Castle changed nothing. In fact, it would probably aid him. Randulf FitzHugh had been a maudlin fool for his children ten years ago. Rhys had not been able to capitalize then on that flaw in his character. But he was ten years wiser now, ten years angrier, and ten years more determined to exact vengeance.

He would begin his conquest with Isolde FitzHugh, move on to the castle itself, then end it with the death of her father and uncle, and anyone else who stood in his way.

He stared up the hill toward Rosecliffe Castle within whose donjon he'd twice been confined. This time he would not be the prisoner. This time he would enter a free man and only depart when he had become its lord.

*   *   *

The next morning Isolde sat cross-legged in her bed brushing her hair in long strokes. She had awakened before dawn, alone in the bed she usually shared with Gwen and Elyssa. She'd often longed for the privacy of her own bedchamber, and this morning she'd stretched, then curled in the center of the bed, luxuriating in all the space. She'd not been able to regain her slumber, though, so she'd reached for her silver-backed hairbrush and begun the routine of the day. But she was aware of the different sounds on this particular morning. No muffled voices from her parents' chamber above hers. No footsteps on the stairs as the maids descended. With so many retainers accompanying her family to London, Rosecliffe felt strangely empty.

But she would stay busy, she told herself, refusing to let yesterday's loneliness return. For the next month she must perform the duties as the lady of Rosecliffe Castle, and first of all, she must look the part.

She parted her hair into two lengths, then sprinkled a few precious drops of oil of lavender on her brush and worked them through the heavy locks. She was proud of her hair, perhaps even a little vain, for she'd always thought the thick chestnut waves her best feature. She was of average height, with an average figure, neither too thin nor too buxom. Even her features were regular. But her hair was rather nice and so she always took special care with it, no matter what Gwen said.

By the time dawn crept up the narrow window of her bedchamber, her hair was dressed in two long plaits, woven with green ribbons and colored glass beads. She donned a pale green kirtle over her chemise and cinched it with a darker green girdle. Finally she slipped on short hose and work clogs.

She was ready for her first full day as lady of Rosecliffe, save for one important item: her mother's keys.

Isolde took the brass ring from where she'd placed it in her trunk, and hefted the linked keys. Simple lengths of iron and brass, adorned with fanciful ends and geometric designs, they yet conferred a considerable power to her who kept possession of them. Keys to the still room and the spice cabinet. Keys to the cloth stores and the granary. To the wine stores.

She tied the ring of keys onto her girdle and smiled at the beam of light slicing across the dim chamber. The others might be on their way to London and the coronation of the new king, but she was mistress of Rosecliffe, queen for now of her own castle, her own kingdom. By the time her parents returned they would hardly recognize the place, she intended to improve it that much.

But idle dreaming would not see it done. So she snatched up her apron and headed for the door. The neglected fresco and crucifix in the chapel first. Then she would tackle the hall.

If the servants thought to rest during their lord and lady's absence, by midday they were swiftly dispossessed of that notion.

Odo, the steward, retreated to the castle offices; Osborn fled to the stables. But for the others there was no escape. Her mother kept a good household, and Isolde could hardly improve on its cleanliness, its orderliness, or its organization. But its appearance . . . That was another matter entirely.

She had several bolts of cloth hauled up from the storerooms. Red damask, green kersey. A fine striped linen. The head seamstress, Bewalda, protested. "But your mother thought to make bedhangings for her daughters' weddings with this."

"Since there are no weddings presently planned, we will use it instead for new hangings in the hall," Isolde announced.

The older woman frowned. "What of this gold braid? 'Tis more like to adorn a fine new tunic for Lord Rand, or for your brother, the young lord."

" 'Twill dress new screens behind the high table most handsomely," Isolde countered.

Bewalda scowled and muttered her disapproval. But Isolde was adamant, and in the end, the seamstress did as she was instructed. By evening Isolde was exhausted, as much by arguing with balky servants as by her actual labors. But she'd made progress. She took heart that the changes were under way.

At supper she presided over a hall made quiet as much by its missing members as by the weariness of those remaining. Odo left the sanctity of his office only when hunger drove him out, and he approached her reluctantly. "You mother will not like such an extravagance," he muttered. "Do you know the cost of a full bolt of linen?"

"I do. Would you like oysters?" she asked, signaling a page to offer the platter to him. "Oh, did I tell you? I had cook prepare almond cakes."

"Almond cakes?" Odo's sour expression began to ease.

"Almond cakes?" Osborn echoed from his place on her other hand. Even the silent Father Clemson perked up. "Almond cakes. Mmm."

Isolde waved one hand airily, relishing her role as beneficent lady of the castle. "Everyone has worked so hard. I thought they would welcome the treat—though almonds do come dear," she added, with a sly glance at Odo.

He cleared his throat. "Aye, they do. But such generosity sweetens everyone and increases the diligence of the servants. Almond cakes are a good investment," he pronounced. "But not for every night."

Isolde grinned at him. "Every other night?"

She tempted him sorely; she could see that. But responsibility won out over his sweet tooth. "Every third night. Plus on Sundays," he conceded.

"Very good," she agreed. "Oh. I need extra candles for my chamber."

Osborn laughed at her unsubtle tactics. Odo frowned. "Why?" he asked, his mouth dripping juice from the baked oysters.

"I have decided to paint the crucifix myself. But I would do it in private, after supper."

"What's wrong with rush lights?"

"In a small chamber their oily smoke fouls the air. You know that."

He stared gloomily at his trencher but kept eating. "Your mother will have my head for allowing such extravagances."

"I have the keys." She jingled them beneath the table. " 'Tis my decision, not yours. Do not fret, Odo. I will report your reluctance to her. And Osborn will bear witness."

"That I will," Osborn said. "Is there cream for the almond cakes?"

"Yes." She smiled, sure of herself now. "And cinnamon, as well."

"Glory be," the old knight said. It was a sentiment echoed in various ways by the rest of the two score people that supped in the hall that night.

Afterward, while the tables were put away, several men played at dice, Odo and Osborn began a chess game, and Magda brought a lap harp to Isolde. It was often her habit to play the finely carved instrument in the evenings, and so she did tonight. But its lovely plaintive tones did not satisfy her as they usually did. Despite her weariness she was restless.

Perhaps she should have gone to London. Perhaps there she might have found a comely man, tall and broad shouldered, she thought, remembering the man in the village. She felt that same silly frisson of heat in her belly, then frowned and put the bearded stranger determinedly out of her mind. In a big city like London she would surely have met someone that she and her father could have agreed upon. Only she'd been too stubborn—though no more stubborn than him. Still, between her mother and herself, they might have prevailed upon him. But it was too late now.

She sighed. Where were the travelers spending the night? Probably at Buildwas Abbey, if they had made good time. Again she sighed and rested her chin on the carved crest of the harp.

"Can I fetch anything for you, miss?"

Isolde raised her eyes. "My thanks, Magda, but I am able to tend to my own needs. You may seek your bed now."

Magda curtsied and left. Near the hearth the fetching young maid was joined by George, one of the men-at-arms, and as Isolde watched, they left the hall together, strolling side by side. Isolde stared openmouthed at the door that closed behind them.

So that was Magda's sweetheart.

A surge of envy—for it could be nothing else—shot through her. Magda had a sweetheart while she had no one. And so long as she remained isolated at Rosecliffe, she was unlikely ever to find one.

Her mouth turned down in a frown, Isolde set the harp aside, then rose and made a final, restless circuit of the hall. When it was clear there was nothing left for her to do, she reluctantly turned for the stairs, trudging up to her room, trailing her fingertips dejectedly along the rough stone wall.

Despite her several projects she feared it was going to be a very long month.

THREE

THE COLORFUL MINSTREL BAND STOOD AT THE FAR END OF the bridge, awaiting permission to enter the castle. Osborn frowned and stared at the motley crew from high up in the gate tower. In truth, there was no need to refuse them entrance. It was common enough for minstrels and tumblers and mimes to beg a meal and a coin or two in exchange for an evening's entertainment. Not a week ago a fire eater had awed them all, and before that a pair of twin magicians.

But a week ago Rosecliffe had been fully manned. And a week ago Osborn had not been beset by this prickling sense of unease.

"Send out ale and bread and whatever the cook can easily spare," he told Eric, the guard at his side. "But turn them away. They may perform in the village, but we've no need of entertainments here in the castle."

"As you say, sir," the man answered. But his face reflected his disappointment.

From behind them Osborn heard a shout, and when he glanced down into the bailey, he spied Isolde. She had her hair tied up in a cloth—a paint-spattered cloth—and in one hand she still held a paintbrush. He shook his head, though fondly, God bless her, but she was a continuing surprise to him. Pretty as her mother; stubborn as her father; and more energy than the two of them together in their youth.

She waved up at him and he waved back. "Osborn!" she called. "Is it true there are minstrels begging entrance?"

Now how had the news traveled so swiftly to her ear?

"Aye," he called back. "But I am sending them on their way."

"Why ever would you do that?"

She disappeared into the gate tower, climbing the curving stairs up to the wall walk. "Why are you sending them away?" she demanded as she burst out of the dark tower into the hazy afternoon light. "I would welcome any entertainment they provide, as would everyone else. Let them in, pray, for there is no reason not to."

"They are four," he argued. "And strangers to me."

She leaned out between the crennels and stared down at the patient band. "I see an old man, and a child—"

"That's a dwarf."

"A dwarf?" She stared more eagerly. "A dwarf, and also a giant." She turned a pleading expression on him. "Oh, please, Osborn, grant them entrance. It will be ever so much fun. Can they do other than sing?"

The guard answered. "The giant, he wrestles all comers. The old man, he does magic, and the dwarf has a dog 'at does all sorts of tricks."

"What about the other man?" She stared curiously at the fourth member of the minstrel band. It was the bearded fellow from the village.

Avoiding Osborn's glowering stare, Eric answered her. "I believe he's a singer and master of the gittern."

"The gittern?" So that's what the instrument on his back had been. She turned back to Osborn, her gray eyes sparkling with excitement. "Now you must let them in, for I've long wished to learn to play the gittern. Please, Osborn. Everyone has worked so hard these past few days. They all deserve a pleasant evening's diversion. I see no harm in granting them entrance."

Osborn frowned and looked away from her and back at the foursome with their little dog and bony old horse. They were but four, and in truth, only two among them were men fully grown. What threat were they when Rosecliffe still had four knights, ten men-at-arms, and various tradesmen and servants, as well? Why was he so wary?

"Please, Uncle Osborn." She laid a hand on his arm and gazed up at him pleadingly. Osborn could feel himself giving in. She'd always been a favorite of his with her self-sufficient air and her winsome manner.

"All right. All right," he muttered. But try as he might, he could not suppress a faint smile. "I'll agree this time. But mind you, one night only. That big fellow looks like he could eat us out of house and home."

"Oh, thank you. Thank you!" On tiptoe she pressed a kiss to his cheek. Then she was off, flying down the stairs, trailing orders as she went. "Eric, guide our visitors to the kitchen. Louis, take their horse to the stable. Merydydd, tell the seamstresses the embroidery thread will be finished in the dye bath shortly. It should be dry enough to use tomorrow . . ."

Osborn watched her stride across the bailey gesturing with her hands as she went. Bemused, he shook his head, then turned back to watch the minstrels. The iron gate between the stone gate towers screeched open and the little band started forward. The giant led the horse with the dwarf and the old man astride. The fourth fellow followed with a pack tied across his back, a gittern hanging upside down upon it, and a spotted dog in his arms.

Osborn scratched the top of his head where his hair was thinning. The years were turning him into an old woman, he told himself. Wary. Jumping at shadows. He turned away and resumed his slow circuit of the wall walk that completely enclosed Rosecliffe Castle.

He did not see the minstrel with the gittern look up, his eyes dark and discerning as he scanned the wall walk, counting the number of guards. He did not see the man's shadowed expression as he passed through the enclosed gates. If he had, he would have slammed the gates closed and lifted the bridge against the man.

For beneath his cowl and frayed straw hat, Rhys ap Owain took careful stock of all he saw: soldiers, fortifications, everything. It had been ten years since he'd been at Rosecliffe. Ten years since the day he'd consented to let Rhonwen be nursed back to health in this English stronghold.

He'd lost her to the FitzHughs because of that one fateful decision. Then he'd been imprisoned and sent far from his homeland to the northernmost reaches of England, where he'd been forced to learn English ways. He clenched his jaw. Well, he'd learned their ways, and now he would use that knowledge to defeat them. And the first FitzHugh to taste his vengeance would be the spoiled Isolde.

So he walked and stared, though he kept his posture carefully nonchalant. But inside every muscle in his body remained tensed and ready. He had at last gained entrance to Rosecliffe, lair of his bitterest enemies, and it had been so easy as to be laughable.

He'd gained entrance to Rosecliffe, and now he would face death before he would give it up again.

The bells rang vespers, and Isolde grimaced. She should halt her labors now, for the next bell would be for supper. But work on the crucifix was going so well.

With shaved charcoal she'd marked the traditional Welsh designs at the ends of the cross, each one signifying the gifts God had given his people. The heavens. Earth. Fire. Water. She'd applied the blue and red paints; she had only the yellow and green and accents of black to add.

She sighed and stepped back to view her work. Her neck was stiff; her wrist ached from long hours gripping the brush too tightly. Though she would rather paint than eat, mayhap she should put her brushes and paint away until the morrow and prepare instead for supper. She'd been very careful to appear every day at both the dinner and supper meals, well groomed as any good chatelaine ought to be, though it was sometimes inconvenient.

At that moment Magda stuck her head in the door. "Will you be wanting a bath before supper, milady?" Then she ran her eyes over Isolde and answered the question herself. "Aye, you will. Hurry up, then. Remember, we've special entertainments tonight."

"Yes, the minstrels." Isolde plunked the goose quill paintbrush into a small jar of mud-colored water, eager now for the coming evening for she was undeniably curious about the well-built master of the gittern. "Yes, I'll bathe as soon as I clean my brushes. Lay out my blue kirtle, will you?"

By suppertime she was clean, with her hair freed of its wrappings and brushed to a sheen. She visited the kitchens briefly and glanced over the hall as she entered. Everything in order; everything prepared.

Her mother had trained her staff well, for they needed little guidance in the daily routine of the castle. It was in matters outside their normal duties that they required constant supervision, matters such as the various projects she'd undertaken.

Isolde stopped to inspect the new curtains in the pantler's cabinet. They looked very fine. She gazed up at the high wall where the new tapestry would soon hang displaying Rosecliffe's emblem—her father's wolf in a circle of roses. That would give a truly grand feel to the hall. Perhaps she should paint vining roses above the tall double doors.

She paused, staring at the empty space. She could paint wolf tracks among the blooms. Now that would be exceptional. Except Father Clemson would want saints, and her mother would probably agree with him.

Of course, if it was already completed before she returned . . .

She was preoccupied with her thoughts when she spied a boy scuttling across the hall with a dog trailing him. "Light two of the torchères now, would you please?" she called to him. "The ones on the far wall. And the rest later, as it grows darker."

He stopped and looked up. "Do you address me, miss?"

Isolde's eyes widened. "Oh. I beg your pardon." No boy at all, but a man. A very small man. "I mistook you for . . . well . . . for someone else," she finished lamely, feeling her cheeks heat with color.

He stared at her without blinking. "You mistook me for a child," he stated. " 'Tis no great thing. You are hardly the first to do so, nor are you likely to be the last."

She smiled at him, grateful for his understanding. "You are one of the minstrels. I am Isolde, eldest daughter of Lord Rand and Lady Josselyn."

"Ah, so you are the mistress of Rosecliffe, to whom we owe our welcome here." He swept low in an extravagant bow, complete with a flourish of his blue and white striped cap. "I am Gandy, at your service, milady. It will be my enormous pleasure to entertain you this e'en. To delight your ear and amuse your eye."

Isolde smiled at his grandiose manner. "I look forward to the performance most eagerly. I am especially interested in learning more of the gittern. I play the harp, but I would welcome the chance to learn something of other musical instruments. Do you play?"

"I regret to say the gittern is not my specialty. Rh—Reevius is a most talented musician, though." He watched her with small, clear eyes. "I will relay to Reevius your interest."

"How very good of you." Her eyes strayed to the dog that sat scratching one of his ears. "If you will remind me after supper, I will provide you with oil of pennyroyal to rid your pet of vermin."

"I thank you," he said with another grand sweep of a bow. "And Cidu thanks you." Another bow.

Cidu? She wondered about the animal's name. In Welsh *ci du* meant black dog. But the dwarf spoke Norman French, mixed with the occasional English word or phrase. Where were they from, these traveling musicians? And where had they most recently been?

By the time the hall began to fill and the pages to circulate with platters of roasted eel, pike in galantyne, and stewed boar, she'd half convinced herself that she could be happy traveling about as a minstrel. Were any women known to do such?

Father Clemson said grace and everyone set to the meal with a vengeance. Only Odo voiced any complaint. "Fish *and* meat, and enough to serve twice in one day," he scolded. "Lady Josselyn is sure to be displeased when she sees the state of the storerooms."

"I'm sure she and Father and the others are eating very well in London. They cannot complain when those of us left behind enjoy our meals."

"But it's not even a feast day," he muttered.

Isolde waved one hand in dismissal of his complaints. "You needn't fear you'll be held responsible, Odo. I'll freely admit that it was my doing."

On her other side Osborn had filled his trencher and was attacking his meal with gusto. "If it upsets you so," he said to Odo, "confine yourself only to bread and gravy at night."

Odo gave him a disgruntled look. "When you do that, then

so shall I. Until then, I see no reason not to dine as well as every one else at Rosecliffe."

Isolde did not listen as their bickering continued. Her eyes scanned the hall, searching for the minstrel band, eager for the evening entertainments and any news they might bring from distant lands. They sat at a table far removed from the high table, in a spot not well lit by the torchères.

She signaled the nearest page. "Light the rest of the torchères," she instructed him with a smile.

He bobbed his head and hied himself off to do her bidding. But Odo looked up. "So soon?" he said through a mouthful of roasted eel and bread sopped in gravy. "The sun yet lingers in the sky."

"Sweet Mary!" Isolde exclaimed. "Rushes and tallow can be replenished easily enough. Would you have our visitors eat in darkness?"

" 'Tis not dark," Osborn put in. "Besides, they are not visitors. They must earn their supper with the amusements they provide."

"Well, I, for one, am glad of their presence. And I will be glad," she added more tartly, "when the two of you cease this constant criticism of my decisions. Pretend I am my mother. You would never treat her so."

"Huh. Never had a reason to," Odo muttered. Osborn just shrugged and kept on eating.

Isolde turned her mind away from her two older mentors, and by the smoky light of the torchères she studied the foursome in question. The dwarf was a nervous, quick-witted little fellow, she saw. He sat beside the giant, emphasizing the difference in their sizes. They both had light brown hair cut straight across the brow and just below the ears, and both wore blue tunics with white sleeves showing through. One was a tiny echo of the other, she thought—or a huge echo, depending on your point of view.

The old man wore a cloak of purple with silver braid on the hood, and silver jewels on his hand, as if he were a mystic. How would he fare with their own mystic, Newlin? she wondered.

She signaled the same page. "Send one of the guards to invite Newlin to join us, if he is so inclined."

"Newlin?" Odo and Osborn said in tandem.

She ignored them, for her attention now turned to the fourth minstrel. The one with the bold eyes, who had carried a gittern and a little spotted dog with a Welsh name. Did she know him? she wondered again, for there was something familiar about him. Perhaps he hailed from Carreg Du or Afon Bryn. Or she might have seen him performing at a market or a fair.

But no, she was certain she would have remembered those wide shoulders. She squinted, trying to make out his features. His hair was dark, very nearly black, as was the heavy beard that covered his face. Was he young or old? It was hard to tell, but his bearing was youthful and his chest and shoulders were wide, not with fat, she suspected, but with muscles.

Without warning a row erupted among the dogs, and as she watched, the man sprang up from the bench, waded into the battling hounds, and scooped up his scrappy little dog. Once again Isolde felt some flicker of recognition. Reevius was his name. Reevius who played the gittern and took good care of his dog.

For a penny or two and an extra portion of sweets, he could surely be persuaded to give her music lessons. It would be pleasant to surprise her parents with a new skill upon a new instrument.

At the back of the hall Rhys stared slowly around the great hall of Rosecliffe. He was here. His plan was set into motion. Before the FitzHughs returned from the coronation, he would be in control of Rosecliffe Castle. It was a stroke of good fortune that Isolde, daughter of Randulf FitzHugh and the traitorous Josselyn ap Carreg Du, remained behind, for she would make an excellent hostage.

He quickly located her at the high table. In truth, she'd drawn his eye from the first moment she entered the hall. That she'd grown was no surprise, given the ten years since last he'd laid eyes upon her. But again he was struck by her changed appearance. He hadn't thought of her save as a nasty little brat. Though she was taller and more womanly, she was probably still nasty, and most certainly still a brat.

But she was also a beauty.

He squinted, taking in every aspect of her appearance, searching for a flaw. He found none. Still, beauty sat merely upon the surface of a woman. What counted with him was the content of the soul, virtues such as honesty and loyalty. Given her parentage, on the inside she could only be ugly and foul. The vile offspring of a vile people.

But she was his key to Rosecliffe.

Turning his gaze deliberately away from her, he ate, refilling his trencher twice. But all the while he scanned the hall with a careful, analytical eye. He'd counted only four knights, besides the aging captain of the guard, and no more than a dozen men-at-arms. Enough men to repel attackers come from without the walls, but woefully inadequate to protect against an enemy from within. Especially an unknown enemy.

A boy lit the torchères nearest them and Rhys hunched farther over his meal. She was staring at them. He could feel her eyes upon him. Did she recognize him? She hadn't seemed to yesterday in the village. Could she not see in him the same lanky lad who'd taken her hostage when she was but a young girl?

He lifted his head, chewing, and glanced sidelong at her. She stared with a pleased and eager expression on her heart-shaped face. No, she did not know him.

He scratched his beard then ruffled his hair, which he'd let grow wild and long. Once he took control of Rosecliffe—once he held her hostage to her father's and uncle's acceptable behavior—she would know him then. He would shave his face and cut his hair and shed the trappings of his minstrel disguise. Then she would know Rhys ap Owain. Then she would tremble with fear.

A warning growl should have alerted him but he was immersed in his dark and vengeful thoughts. Then a full-scale battle erupted among the dogs, with Cidu in the midst of it. He sprang up and in a moment snatched the feisty mutt from a pair of hounds each three times his size. He shoved one oversized hound back with his foot, and stared the other one down.

"Idiot animal," he muttered at Cidu as he placed the unrepentant cur on the bench beside him.

"No more idiot than his master," old Tillo muttered. "To attack a stronger enemy in his own home . . ."

"Methinks there is a poetic justice in it," Gandy put in.

"The small—the physically weak—are ever at the mercy of those bigger and stronger than they. But if they are clever, if they develop and use their superior minds, they can best their larger brethren."

"But sometimes you are glad that I'm your larger brethren," Linus rumbled. "This is good," he added, pointing at the food with his knife. He had two trenchers before him and showed no sign of slowing down on his consumption of food.

Gandy snorted. "Even an ass has its uses."

Suddenly the little fellow let out a yelp as he was enveloped in a huge hug that lifted him off the bench and practically smothered him in Linus's blue tunic. "You like to act mean, Gandy. But I know you love me."

"Let me down, you big oaf. You mountain of lard!" Gandy's feet flailed about, nearly oversetting his cup of ale. "You gargantuan imbecile!"

"Say please," Linus said, grinning down at the tiny head caught in the crook of his massive arm.

"Please. Please!" Gandy screamed.

"All right." But Linus pressed a fat kiss onto Gandy's brow before letting him go. And all the while his mouth turned up in an enormous smile. His entire being seemed to smile.

Gandy staggered backward on the bench, then leaped down, landing on one of the sulking hounds still eyeing Cidu. The hound growled then snapped, but the little man growled right back, knotting his fist threateningly. When the hound backed off, Rhys chuckled. Nothing Gandy could say or do seemed to alienate Linus. The slow-witted giant's loyalty to the ill-tempered dwarf, and to everyone he trusted, was unshakable.

By the same token, despite his insulting manner and antagonistic personality, Gandy was equally loyal to Linus. It showed in small ways, in little things easy to overlook. Though not of the same family, they were nevertheless like brothers, Rhys realized—not that he himself had any personal knowledge of brotherhood, nor of any aspect of family life.

His easy humor fled. Like his friends, he had never known the comfort of a family. He had no memory of his mother, and his father had been killed twenty years ago. His aunt had lasted another few years, but she'd been mad, and it had fallen to him, a mere child, to care for her.

No, he'd never known what it was like to be part of a real family. The FitzHughs had destroyed any chance of that.

He looked back at the head table, at FitzHugh's daughter, symbol of betrayal and dishonesty and all the misery visited upon him by her family. She'd never known hunger or hardship or the paralyzing fear of loneliness. She'd grown up cosseted and loved by her parents and the rest of her cursed family. Well, it would be his pleasure to separate her from her family, and from their ill-gotten gains. To overwhelm them all with some portion of the pain and loss he'd suffered at their hands.

She still stared down at him from her position at the high table. She was a pretty little bauble, a bored princess in a kingdom stolen from his people. *But I will end your boredom, Isolde FitzHugh. I will end it,* he vowed. *Although it will not be the ending you seek.*

He shoved his trencher away and pushed up from the table. "Time for the entertainments," he said to his friends. "Time to show the mistress of Rosecliffe our gratitude."

FOUR

ISOLDE CAUGHT HER BREATH WHEN THE MAN REEVIUS STOOD. What was it about his person that drew her interest so? Though minstrels were not an everyday occurrence at Rosecliffe Castle, they were hardly rare. She inevitably enjoyed their performances, no matter their level of talent. But tonight her anticipation ran higher than it ever had.

No doubt it was due to her role as mistress of the castle.

She grimaced and let her eyes scan the hall. It would be difficult to relinquish so heady a role. She would have no choice, however, once her parents returned. Perhaps she should give the matter of marriage more serious consideration—but not to Mortimer. The fact remained, however, that only through marriage would she ever be mistress of a home of her own.

For now, though, she did not want to think about that. The minstrels had taken up their instruments, they approached the high table, and she clapped her hands in delight. Before the evening ended she would force Osborn to admit she'd been right to grant them entrance.

The little dog scampered up first, barking. At once the castle hounds sprang up, but the pages caught their collars and dragged them from the hall.

As if celebrating his triumph over the hounds, the little dog suddenly made a complete back flip.

Everyone shouted with approval.

He did it again, then began to run in dizzying circles, chasing his own tail. Then he flipped backward again, and flopped down on his stomach, with all four legs extended. As laughter and applause exploded, the canny creature stared about, his pink tongue hanging as he grinned in dog delight.

Isolde clapped as vigorously as did the others, enchanted with the little animal. Meanwhile the four minstrels made a semicircle behind the dog. With practiced ease they began to play a gentle melody. Holding a small harp, the dwarf sang first.

> *You welcome us with victuals rare,*
> *We pay our debt with song and wit.*
> *The body needs one sort of fare.*
> *The mind and soul a rarer bit.*

The old man in his purple robes sang next, his voice high and thin.

> *From every place that is, we've come.*
> *To every other we shall go.*
> *—But for this ev'ning we shall hum,*
> *And mayhap play a song you know.*

Then the bearded man stepped forward. He strummed his gittern with the ease of long acquaintance, and stared straight at Isolde.

> *Unto a fortress on a hill*
> *The road has drawn us far and long.*
> *The seeds of truth are what we till*
> *In many ways, but first in song.*

His voice was strong and deep, a good contrast to the dwarf's strange sound and the old man's silver trill. *He* was strong and deep, Isolde decided, her eyes captured by his bold stare.

It was impertinent, the way he looked at her, yet it ignited a little flame deep in her stomach. Isolde forced herself to break the hold of his eyes, but it was only to examine the rest of his person. He was tall and straight, with good teeth and all his hair. Too much hair, she thought. What did he look like beneath that wild hair and bushy beard?

Suddenly he flew up into the air. She gasped, for she'd not noticed the giant come up behind him. In a moment he was seated on the giant's shoulders. The dwarf then ran straight at the giant who caught him and flung him high. Somehow he landed on Reevius's shoulders, standing proudly with his skinny little arms stretched wide. The dog followed in the same manner, tossed high and caught by the dwarf. Finally, the old man stepped onto the giant's outstretched palms and the giant raised him up. The gray-haired ancient stood there as easily as if on solid ground.

Everyone in the hall clapped and shouted, and pounded their cups upon the tables. But they silenced when the giant began to recite, unaccompanied.

> *The water cools, the fire burns,*
> *Earth sits below; the sky above.*
> *The days go by, the seasons turn,*
> *From birth to death, in war and love.*

Isolde listened and heard in their song more than merely words. Some minstrels sang of history. Others made pretty poetry with stories of myths and lovers and deathbed vows. But a few used their songs to address deeper subjects: politics, the church, the conditions of mankind.

She leaned forward eagerly, for she was certain this odd band was from the latter group. That meant interesting information from places far away, and fiery opinions about that information.

"You are most welcome to Rosecliffe, friends," she said. "Pray entertain our people this evening, then sleep you well among us and eat your fill once more, come the dawn."

The bearded fellow responded. "I hold Gandy above me, and he holds little Cidu. I perch upon Linus, who holds Tillo in his hands. I am Reevius, and we are but poor balladeers and tumblers who travel far and wide. We thank you for your welcome and bid you all to fill your cups, for it is our pleasure to entertain you." Though he spoke to the entire company in the great hall, his midnight dark eyes remained once more locked with hers.

Again Isolde felt that same odd reaction in her belly. A tickling sort of quiver. A hot, coiling knot. She sat back, nodding her approval, a little relieved when he finally looked away. But even as the four minstrels tumbled and sang and fought a mock battle in which old Tillo and little Gandy defeated the two larger men, to the great satisfaction of the audience—even then Isolde was conscious of a strange new awareness inside her.

A new sort of liveliness had infected her. The daily humdrum had peeled away to reveal a new excitement. She felt it. Did everyone else?

She glanced around her. Odo was grinning, thumping his fist in time with the giant's steady drumming. Osborn sprawled back in his chair, his hands laced across his stomach, and his face relaxed in a smile. Whatever concerns he'd felt about the minstrels had obviously faded.

A great whoop from the onlookers jerked her eyes back to the performers. Little Gandy chased Cidu back and forth between Linus's tree-trunk legs. The giant lifted one foot, then the other, nearly squashing the darting pair. Meanwhile Tillo and Reevius played a raucous tune in a speeding tempo that incited everyone in the hall. The tambourine pounded. The bells chimed, and the pipe filled the air with piercing notes.

Then in a crescendo Gandy caught Cidu, just as Linus collapsed on top of them both. The onlookers gasped in horror.

"Oh, no!"

"Get him off the poor lad!"

"They'll be crushed!"

Everyone leaped to their feet craning to see the terrible damage that had surely been done to the tiny man and his pet. Isolde and Odo were among them, as was Osborn, though he looked less concerned than they.

" 'Tis a trick," he whispered to Isolde. "No one is hurt."

But a loud wail made a lie of his words, and she gasped anew.

"Oh, no. Oh, no!" the giant rumbled from his place still flat on the floor. "I've killed them. I've killed them!" Reevius and Tillo ran over to see.

"Fetch the healer from the village!" Isolde cried, horrified.

Suddenly the dog crawled out of Linus's sleeve. He gave himself a good shake, barked, and began chasing his tail like before. Then Gandy crawled out of the other sleeve and clambered up onto the giant's broad back.

"Fetch the healer!" he echoed Isolde's words. "For I fear we've squashed poor Linus!"

Laughter erupted. Hands clapped, feet stomped, and mugs thumped the tables in deafening approval. Isolde was embarrassed by her gullibility, but charmed, nonetheless, by the clever act the minstrels had put on.

"You see?" she said to Osborn as she clapped along with all the others. "I was right to invite them in. Mother and Father will be sorry to have missed this night's entertainments." To Odo she said, "Fetch a silver denier from the offices. They deserve that much, I think."

It was a measure of Odo's enjoyment that he did not argue over her generosity. As he left Osborn stood. "I suppose it is past time when I must see to the guards and make my final rounds."

"Yes, do," Isolde murmured, only halfway listening as she watched the winded foursome gulp fresh ale. "I shall see to the hall. Good night."

But Isolde had more on her mind than overseeing the settling down of the hall. The maids cleared away the goblets and collected food scraps to distribute to the hounds. The pages wiped down the tables and stacked them along the walls. Isolde oversaw their labors, but all the while she watched Reevius with a surreptitious gaze.

"Go to the man Reevius, the one with the beard," she told a passing lad. "Bid him approach me, for I have a matter to discuss with him. Wait. Oh, never mind," she amended. "I'll do it." She owed the minstrels her compliments. There was no need to command their presence before her as if she were some exalted personage.

But as she made a circuit of the hall, giving instructions here and there, and bidding everyone a good-night, she was conscious of Reevius's eyes following her. Odo brought her the denier and she gripped it tightly in her damp palm. She was behaving like a silly child, she scolded herself. Like Gwen might. He was just a traveling minstrel—an impudent, bold-eyed one, to be sure, but a minstrel all the same—and beholden to her for his supper.

She raked the coals under a three-legged cauldron so that water in it would keep warm over the banked fire. Then she lifted her chin, turned, and approached the minstrels. Their conversation ended at her approach.

"My thanks, kind sirs," she began. "It has been many months since we have been so well entertained." She extended her open hand with the silver denier upon it. "Please accept this token of our appreciation."

Gandy grinned and bounced forward, the bell on his cap jingling. "Thank you, milady. Your generosity is much appreciated. I'm certain we can find a good use for this," he finished, snatching the coin and making one of his flourishing bows.

"You have more than earned it." She forced herself to look at the other minstrels, then drew a deep breath. "But I have a favor I would ask of you." She said this last to Reevius, staring at him and struck again by the oddest sense of familiarity. Where had she seen him before?

"A favor?" he finally echoed in a voice as dark and deep as his eyes.

"Yes." Her mouth went suddenly dry and she licked her lips. Why did this itinerant musician cause her to behave like such a goose? "I have long wished to learn how to play the gittern."

He nodded. "Gandy told me as much." Between his long hair, his heavy beard, and the failing light from the torchères, she could fathom nothing in his expression. "Do you play other instruments?" he asked.

"Yes. The lute, though not so well as Gandy. And also the pipe, but just a little."

"If you teach her to play the gittern," Gandy quipped, slanting his eyes at her, "she will not want our talents here when next we pass this way."

Isolde laughed. " 'Tis highly unlikely I could become that proficient. Even were that to happen, however, I would still desire that you return to Rosecliffe. My family would enjoy your entertainments so much."

"Would they?" Reevius asked. "Where are they now?"

"Gone to London, to attend the coronation of the new king, Henry."

His lips curved in a smile that showed in spite of his beard. "The coronation of England's new boy king. Now there's an entertainment, eh, Tillo?"

"Oh, aye," the purple-robed old man said. "But 'tis too far a distance for these old legs to travel."

"I will carry you," Linus offered.

"I am content where we are," Reevius stated, his gaze resting upon Isolde. "So, you wish me to give you instruction on the gittern."

She nodded. "If you are so inclined. I will pay you," she added.

"Will you?"

She nodded very slowly. "Of course."

He nodded also. "Very well, then. We can begin now."

"Now?" Isolde felt a flutter in her stomach. "Yes, I would like that, if it is not too late."

"Just a few minutes to teach you how to hold the instrument. Besides, musical instruction requires concentration. No distractions. In such a busy hall, night is often the quietest time." He glanced at his comrades behind him. "Seek you your beds. I shall join you later."

Like a lord dismissing his underlings, Isolde thought. He was neither rude, nor unkind, but the man had an air of authority sore at odds with his lowly station in life.

"Good night, then," Tillo said, shuffling away.

"Good night," the dwarf and the giant chorused as they departed.

Only the little dog Cidu remained, and he eyed Isolde as if to say "What are you up to with my master?"

In truth, she did not know.

Reevius picked up the gittern and strummed across the strings. "Where shall we begin?" He sang the words. "First we need a chair," he continued, one chord higher. "Then we need another, for the lady fair."

She smiled at his easy manner. "Two chairs. Or perhaps a bench." She led him to a bench beside the hearth and seated herself. Without waiting for an invitation, he sat next to her. Right next to her.

"How did you learn to play the gittern?" she asked, to cover the abrupt case of nerves that beset her.

He shrugged. "I was many years in service in a household. I learned from someone there."

"Have you been a minstrel ever since?"

"No."

At that short response she looked up at him. He met her gaze with no hint of apology. Indeed, his deep-set eyes seemed to probe hers. "I am a minstrel now. That is enough to know. And it seems you would mimic my craft. Is it so hard being mistress of a grand castle that you covet a life in the wildwood with only your lute and gittern and pipes to sustain you?"

"No. Not at all. Cannot a woman desire to make music for her own pleasure and that of her family?"

"She can." Their eyes met and held. He was so near that she felt the heat of his body and heard the rhythmic rush of his breathing. She could see the glint of torchlight in his ebony eyes. His was an overwhelming presence. She had to look away.

"Here," he said, and offered the gittern to her. "Tuck it under your right arm and grip the neck with your left hand."

She did as he said and strummed across the five strings, pleased with the harmonious blending of the tones.

"You press down with your fingers on the neck in order to shorten the strings and change the tones. Like this," he added. He leaned nearer, circling her shoulders with one arm and covering her left hand with his own. Heat rushed through her, burning wherever he touched her, then searing out to every other portion of her body. It was startling and unnerving, and more than a little thrilling.

" 'Tis the combination of strings that makes the different sounds," he murmured, very near her ear. Her heart beat a little faster. He moved her fingers into place. "Press down. Hard." Then he caught her other hand in his and said, "Strum."

She did. At the moment, Isolde suspected she would have done anything he told her to, she was that caught up in the spell he'd cast.

But the sound of the strings, still harmonious but in a dif-

ferent tone from before, brought her back to the moment. She
stared at the position of the fingers of her left hand. She had
done that? She was utterly delighted.

"You can also pluck the strings with your thumb or your
fingers to pick out a melody," he said. While still holding her
fingers in place on the neck of the instrument, he proceeded
to pick out a familiar Welsh lullaby with the other.

"Sweetly, sweetly in the night," she softly sang along in
Welsh.

Rhys froze at the sound of his enemy's daughter singing a
Welsh lullaby. He had not expected her to recognize the song,
though he realized now how foolish that assumption was. Her
mother was Welsh, so of course she would know it. Just as
she probably spoke Welsh as well as did he. But that did not
make Isolde FitzHugh Welsh.

He released her hands and pulled away from her. "That is
enough for tonight."

She remained bent over his gittern, fitting her fingers as
he'd shown her. She strummed, then hummed a little, going
back and forth between that one simple chord, and an open
one. She seemed completely oblivious to his presence.

He was not oblivious to hers, though. Unwillingly his gaze
traced the tilt of her head, the curve of her back. He frowned
and yet still noticed the silky sheen of her hair and the pale
skin of her nape, where the heavy length parted. He inhaled
and caught again the faint scent of lavender and had to force
himself to slide away from her.

She was young; she was comely; she was clean. Any man
would respond to a woman possessed of those traits, he told
himself. That explained his body's perverse attraction to her.
Still, explanation or no, the lust she roused in him was unexpected and he rebelled at the thought. She was a FitzHugh.
He hated her and all of her ilk.

But that did nothing to tame the demon beast of desire. She
was a woman and he'd been too long without the relief of a
woman in his bed.

She strummed and let out a soft chuckle. "This is truly a
wondrous instrument." She tilted her face up to his. "Where
did you come by it?"

Again desire struck, more fiercely than before. Her skin

looked so soft. Her eyes were a deep and lustrous gray, and her lips . . .

He took the gittern from her. "York," he muttered. He stood. "Enough. I am weary."

"But you will show me more on the morrow?" she asked as she stood.

He looked away, toward the stout oak doors and their heavy locking bar that leaned idly in a corner. "Yes. Tomorrow," he agreed.

She cleared her throat. "You and your comrades are free to linger at Rosecliffe a while," she offered. He did not respond and after a moment she continued. "If you have mending, the seamstresses will tend it. Or laundering. Or leather repairs." She clasped her hands in a knot at her waist.

Rhys's eyes narrowed. She wanted them to stay. That was to his advantage. "I am flattered that you enjoyed our entertainments so well. Perhaps we can delay our journey a few more days," he conceded. "Do you expect your family to return that soon?"

"No. Alas, they will be gone several more weeks. I do not expect them until just before the turn of the new year."

"I see." And so he did. Several weeks provided him more than enough time. "I can promise you no more than a few days."

She smiled at that, a smile at once innocent and alluring. The simple delight of a girl; the darker satisfaction of a woman. Which was she? Though it was madness, he wanted to find out.

So he stepped nearer, closing the distance between them, and offered the gittern to her. "You may have the free use of my instrument so long as we remain at Rosecliffe."

"Why, thank you." She took it carefully into her slender hands. "You must allow me to repay your generosity."

He gave her a short bow. "Your pleasure is payment enough," he murmured as he took his leave of her. But soon enough she would repay him, and very well, he told himself as he quit the hall. Three weeks to make Rosecliffe his own.

And the daughter of Rosecliffe? a sharp voice in his head prodded.

He heard the soft notes of the gittern and heard her humming once more. Mayhap he would make her his, as well. To take the innocence of his enemy's daughter would be to strike a mortal blow to FitzHugh's black heart.

And he'd been waiting to do that for twenty years.

FIVE

ISOLDE WOKE UP SMILING AND KNEW AT ONCE WHY.

Work on the chapel was complete and today she would finish the crucifix. The workmen would move on to the great hall, washing the walls, and painting them in the simple pattern of knots she had designed. By week's end the seamstresses would complete the new hangings for above the mantel and flanking the entry doors. Her labors were beginning to bear fruit.

More important than all of those, however, was one simple fact: Reevius had agreed to teach her to play the gittern.

She lay still in the deep feather bed, flat on her back, staring up at the heavy damask bed curtains she'd embroidered herself. Purple and a deep forest-green, the bedhangings were her favorite colors. Yet though she stared, she did not really see them. Her thoughts were elsewhere.

She tried to understand what had happened to her last night. A group of minstrels had played for their supper, a group not so different from scores of other such groups who'd come to Rosecliffe.

Yet to her they had been completely different.

A giant. A dwarf. A trained dog.

Then she groaned and closed her eyes, chagrined by her own dishonesty. It was neither Linus nor Gandy who made these minstrels different to her, nor the little dog Cidu. The truth was, it was Reevius. He was the reason she was smiling, even though she could not fathom why. But fathom it or not, she could hardly deny the truth. Not to herself anyway.

A simple minstrel of unknown origin, possessing nothing but a gittern, broad shoulders, and an enthralling voice, had captured her imagination. Skinny Mortimer Halyard had not done it. Nor had any of the several knights and lords' sons who had made their way to Rosecliffe over the past several years at her father's behest. But this man whose face she'd not yet fully seen, and who had not even behaved in a particularly friendly manner—he was the one who put this smile on her face and this eagerness in her heart.

She sighed and rolled onto her stomach, feeling twitchy all over. It was ludicrous, of course. An itinerant musician was hardly the sort of man that should appeal to a lord's daughter, like her. But he did appeal to her. And when he had sat down next to her and guided her hands . . .

A delicious quiver snaked down her spine and deep into her belly. No other man had ever made her feel that way before.

Then again very few men, save her relatives, had ever touched her hand for so prolonged a contact, and in so familiar a fashion.

She rolled onto her back again, and opened her eyes, staring blindly above her. Was that it? Was the confined life she led at Rosecliffe the reason she'd become so affected by this aloof, bearded minstrel?

She flung back the marten coverlet, dismayed by her own perversity. In truth, this was her father's fault. If not for his obstinance, she would be in London by now meeting the many important personages gathering there from throughout the kingdom. Had he not been so rigid about Mortimer, she might already have met several eligible young men, men as tall and broad shouldered and bold of eye as any traveling minstrel. Indeed, she might already have found one perfectly suited to her desires.

She sat up and slid her legs over the side of the bed, laughing at a sudden thought. Perhaps she should define her desires more clearly to her father. How would he react if she asked him to find her a man who made her stomach turn over, or one who made her skin prickle with gooseflesh? If her mother was correct, his voice would fail and his ears would turn red should she speak of such things to him. How amusing it would

be to embarrass her stern father with talk of her fleshly desires—desires she'd not even considered until the mysterious
Reevius had roused them.

Where had he slept last night? Where was he now? She
suddenly needed to know.

In short order she dressed, then hurried down the stairs.
The chapel bells pealed as if to announce her. But the hall
was empty save for Odo, who shook his head when he spied
her. "Morning prayers are about to commence. Father Clemson is frowning, and you know how he goes on and on when
he is put out."

"Yes, yes. I am sorry."

In the chapel she endured the longer prayers, unmindful of
Father Clemson's petulance. Her mind strayed from his endless sermon as she alternately admired the improvements she'd
made and worried for Reevius's eternal soul. It was one thing
to miss services when there were none to be had. But everyone
at Rosecliffe attended services, including their visitors. Everyone except minstrels, it seemed.

Afterward the hall was full and noisy as people ate gruel
and old bread soaked in goat's milk and flavored with honey.
Where was he? she fretted. Surely they had not left Rosecliffe,
not while she yet had his gittern.

The sun approached its zenith before she had any word of
Reevius, and then it was merely by chance, for she refused to
ask for him.

". . . a great bully boy he is," the alewife said as she directed the unloading of new barrels outside the butlery.

"And you know what they say of musicians," her sister,
Emelda, said as she muscled one of the barrels to the back
edge of the slat-sided cart. The woman grinned. "They have
the nimblest fingers and the cleverest touch."

The two laughed, then bobbed their heads respectfully
when they spied Isolde. She nodded and kept on her path to
the laundry shed. Inside, however, she fumed. Nimblest fingers? Cleverest touch? Did they speak of Reevius? Surely not.

But then, who else?

Isolde gritted her teeth. Had Emelda learned such things
about him firsthand? The woman was rumored to be less than

frugal with her reputation. Is that where Reevius had spent his night?

She marched blindly on to the laundry shed with the pouch of salt for spreading over stains. Afterward she stopped in the kitchen to collect the unused cooking herbs, then returned them to the spice cabinet. She should visit the weavers and the seamstresses, for they required daily exhortations and praise to keep up the quality and pace of their work. But she was hard-pressed to concern herself with any of those tasks.

She halted in the bailey and swept her unhappy gaze across the busy yard. She needed to be alone, to think and work out these strange and confusing feelings that beset her. But there seemed to be no place for solitude. The chief gardener toiled in the herb garden. The guards paced the wall walk. The armorer labored in his shed near the stables. Masons on their scaffolds. The dairy maid in her pens. Everywhere there were men and women, and even children, busy with all the tasks that kept Rosecliffe a safe and pleasant place to live.

She too had her own tasks awaiting her. But she simply could not concentrate on them now. Anyway, it was nearly time for the main meal. Surely he would appear for that.

But he did not. His three companions were there, gathered at the same table, in the back of the hall. But Reevius was not there. Nor was Emelda.

Though Isolde knew she was behaving like an addlepated fool, she could not repress either her anger or her disappointment, and immediately after the meal, she stormed up to her bedchamber.

Flinging herself upon the bed, she sat down cross-legged, her face set in a scowl. She'd felt these same unreasonable emotions once before, she realized, when she was a child and infatuated with her uncle Jasper. She'd fancied herself in love with him and even envisioned them someday wed. Then Rhonwen had come along and Isolde's childish dreams had been dashed. She'd behaved like a selfish little brat, as she recalled. Several years later she'd developed a similar tendre for one of her uncle Jasper's squires. As she remembered it now, she'd sulked for weeks when the cheerful lad had removed to Bailwyn Castle to serve Jasper there.

Now, as she sat in her silent chamber, she grimaced. She

was no longer a child of ten, or thirteen, but a woman of nearly twenty. Surely she'd matured at least a little during the intervening years.

Willing herself to be calm, she tried to understand why she was behaving so—and on account of an itinerant minstrel. She was frustrated by her father's attempts to arrange a marriage for her. That was the first thing. Then there was the frustration of being left behind while the rest of her family attended the coronation.

But that still did not explain her fascination with this wandering minstrel. Frowning, she planted her chin on her palm, determined to sort out her feelings.

Reevius was young and tall and fit. Very fit. So that explained one aspect of his attractiveness. Plus, he had a poet's heart, something no knight or young lord of her acquaintance possessed. The men she met cared only for politics and hunting, weapons and horses. But while they practiced their skills at war, Reevius practiced on his gittern.

She sighed, then looked over at the gittern lying upon her trunk. He had coaxed such lovely sounds from the instrument last night. And his deep voice had seemed to vibrate right through her.

She feared, however, that it was more than his physical appeal and his considerable musical talent that attracted her. From the very first time their eyes had met, something had happened. Some emotion she could not explain had passed between them. It was almost as if they had known one another, as if they were kindred spirits come suddenly face-to-face.

Or at least that was how she had felt.

Unfortunately, it was impossible to know what he felt, and so long as he remained absent from the hall, she was not likely ever to learn.

Again she sighed, no longer angry, but just as frustrated as before. Myriad tasks awaited her, but not one of them appealed. Nor, she rationalized, were any of them essential to the smooth operation of the castle. The fact was, the paint on the crucifix needed to dry and all her necessary chores had been accomplished earlier.

Her gaze moved once more to the gittern. Perhaps she would take Reevius's instrument and go down to the narrow

beach below the north wall. There she would surely find the
solitude she sought, and she could experiment with the gittern.
By the time Reevius finally returned to the hall to give her the
lesson he'd promised, she would already be more competent
than he expected. She would impress him, if not with her
talent, at least with her enthusiasm.

She slid off the high bed and picked up the hollow wood
instrument with reverent hands. Then, determined not to consider why Reevius and Emelda both were missing, and determined not to care if they were together, she made her way
down the stairs, across the hall, and through the bailey to the
postern gate.

No one stopped her, for the seaward side of Rosecliffe was
completely safe. So she made her way down the steep stairs
that had been chiseled into the dark cliff, holding Reevius's
gittern with one hand and gripping the rope railing with the
other. The wind buffeted her, playful then rough, heavy with
the salty scent of fish and damp and seaweed. The stairs let
out onto a rocky beach that gave way to gravel and occasional
patches of coarse sand. Three broad-beamed fishing boats lay
upended on the shore. A fourth bobbed far out on the waves.
Two men checking the fish traps. Otherwise, she had the beach
to herself.

She looked up at the castle, so high above the cliff. For no
logical reason, she did not want the guards looking down on
her, so she edged down the narrow beach toward a boulder
that jutted up at the sea's edge. As a child she'd clambered
up and over it a thousand times. Sometimes it had been a
mountain, other times a ship, and occasionally a terrible sea
monster or a fire-breathing dragon. Today, however, it would
be shelter, a protective wall keeping the world at bay and
allowing her to be the daughter of an ordinary man, instead
of a mighty lord. A woman unencumbered by birthright and
free, as all Welsh women were, to make her own choice
among men.

She removed her shoes and stockings, then holding her
skirts high, waited for an ebb in the waves before wading into
the ankle-deep surf. It took but seconds to gain the far side of
the rock, but even so, the bitter cold of the sea pierced her to
the bone.

"Sweet Jesu," she muttered as she hopped up and down, urging blood back into her poor feet. She settled on a dry spot of sand with her back to the rock, then glanced up in the direction of the castle. Nothing. Only rock and sand, water and sky. She was perfectly alone and satisfaction settled over her. Now to unlock the secrets of the gittern.

How much time passed she did not know. Shadows crept over her sunny cove, for the days were growing shorter. The waves came, stronger and higher, though she had no fear of becoming trapped. Curlews wheeled across the sky, their cries sharp and shrill as they hunted. When finally she looked up, there was no sign of the fishermen in the boat.

She ought to go back, and she would—as soon as she mastered the song she had finally worked out. She bent once more to the five-stringed gittern, grimacing when she formed the chord Reevius had taught her. She hadn't realized how sore her fingertips had become from the strings.

She pressed them down anyway, and began to hum, using the waves upon the shore for rhythm.

". . . like grains of sand or drops that fill the sea so wide . . ." The half-formed words to her song trailed away as her attention was drawn by a movement along the shore. Was someone there?

The fishermen, she reassured herself.

She bent again to the gittern, playing the notes and chords, and singing along. This time there were no false starts, no mistakes, and when she reached the final note, she held it an extra long time.

The measured clap of approval startled her. "Nicely done," Reevius said, stepping out from the shadows of an ancient twisted willow.

Isolde gaped at him, speechless. He was the last man she'd expected to see, though in truth he was also the one she *most* wanted to see. But faced with his unexpected nearness, her wits seemed to freeze.

Her eyes, however, did not. As he leaped down from a small boulder, they ran avidly over him. He looked different from last night, for despite the cold sea winds, he wore only a thin chainse over his braies. It was damp from the sea spray and so clung to him, outlining the wonderful breadth of his chest and arms. His hair was wet and slicked back from his face, and she realized that he was younger than she'd thought. Only a few years older than she. His eyes were more visible with his hair back, and even darker than she'd imagined.

He would be handsome beneath that beard, she decided, though in a harsh sort of way. Bold nose. Sharp cheekbones. Lean cheeks and a determined jaw. But his lips were full and well formed, she saw, and that thought sent color burning into her cheeks.

She sternly willed herself to be sensible. Her hands tightened around the gittern. "You startled me. I . . . I hope you do not mind that I brought your gittern down here. I did not let the water touch it."

He nodded, then he glanced up toward the castle. "You should not be here alone. No woman should."

"I am quite safe."

"Are you?" His midnight gaze fell back to her face.

Isolde swallowed hard and her skin prickled with excruciating awareness. It was not alarm, though perhaps it should have been, for there was something in his words, and something in his eyes.

"I am safe here," she repeated. "The guards are near and there are fishermen also."

"They beached their boat some time ago and are already up the cliff."

"They are?" She craned to see. "I must have been too immersed in the music to notice," she confessed, looking back at him.

For some reason that made him smile, a true and heartfelt smile not meant for an audience, but solely for her. Isolde's stomach did a flip-flop. Her heart lurched in her chest. Were she standing, she knew her knees would have buckled. As it was she found it hard to catch her breath. No wonder he was stingy with his smile. Were he to loose it indiscriminately, no woman would ever be safe again.

"When I play," he said, moving nearer, "time often fades away. There is something soothing in music."

He stopped before her, looking down as she gazed up the rangy length of him. What a truly fine specimen of a man he was, she thought. More manly than any of her father's knights.

For though he was as powerfully built as any of them, he wielded not a sword, but his music.

And that lethal smile.

This was the sort of man who could capture her heart, she realized with sudden clarity. That's why none of the men her father suggested had ever appealed to her. She wanted a passionate, yet gentle soul, not a coarse warrior. She wanted a sensitive poet, a minstrel, not a knight.

She wanted Reevius.

Aghast at such inappropriate thoughts, she thrust the gittern at him. "Would you play? Please?" she asked with lips suddenly gone dry. She licked them, then looked away from his keen stare. He could not possibly guess what she was thinking. Could he?

Rhys stared down at the woman who held his gittern up to him, and had to remind himself forcefully who she was. Isolde FitzHugh. Daughter to the hated Lord of Rosecliffe. Niece of the man who'd killed his father. She was his enemy, one he could use in his revenge upon her family. She was the leverage that would gain him what he'd dreamed of his entire life.

But at the moment, with the lowering sun glinting sparks off her rich hair, and her clear gray eyes gazing up at him, it was easy to forget those things. Her skin looked so soft and pale, save for the wash of color across her cheeks. Like pearls by firelight. And her mouth . . . When her tongue had swept across her full lower lip, he'd felt the unseemly rise of desire.

But he could not desire her. He would not allow himself to.

He took the gittern from her hand and she averted her eyes. Of course she did, he scoffed. She'd led such a protected life. Few men would have dared to stare so boldly at her. Nor should he, for it might alarm her and ruin the opportunity he'd been handed.

But it was impossible for him to look away from her. Her lashes were long and thick, and cast crescent shadows upon her cheeks. Her fingers were slender and long. Her waist delicate. Her breasts full.

"Taran!" he swore beneath his breath.

Her eyes widened in alarm. "Have I damaged it?"

"No. The instrument is fine."

"But you swore—" She broke off.

He swore again, but silently this time. He must remember that she spoke Welsh. She might be an English lord's daughter, and she appeared the epitome of English beauty, comparable to any of the ladies he'd known in the past ten years. But she carried Welsh blood in her veins. She knew the language and the customs, and if he were careless, she would guess his secret before he could spring his attack.

Clenching his jaw, he took a respectful step back from her. "My pardon for such thoughtlessness. You will want to return to the castle."

She rose to her feet and looked up the sheer cliff to the wall where a pennant flapped in the strong sea breeze. The breeze played in the loose curls around her face, and molded her full skirts against her hips and legs. She was taller than her mother, he noticed. The top of her head came even with his chin, and there was a dried petal caught in a curl near her brow.

He started to reach for it, then stopped. What was he doing?

When she did not flinch away from him, however, he could not resist. He caught the bit of pink between his finger and thumb, then slowly slid the dried blossom free.

He saw her swallow. He saw curiosity and fear and anticipation in the endless depths of her eyes, and again desire reared its demanding head. He wanted her. That she was a FitzHugh bore no weight. He wanted her.

"Will you be going now?" he murmured, at the same time demanding with his eyes that she stay.

"I . . . I thought . . . I thought we might have another lesson." She touched the gittern he held. "And I can show you what I have already learned."

Elation surged through Rhys. "As you wish." He glanced up at the wall again. No guard had yet looked down to see them together. He could as easily drown her or kidnap her— or ravish her—as give her musical instruction. Were those guards fools to have so little concern for her safety?

But that was good, he reminded himself. That was to his advantage, and he meant to make use of it.

"Let us sit," he said, lowering himself to the protection of the boulder. She sat, too, close enough to touch. But he did not touch her. Their legs extended side by side in the sand. Her feet were bare; her toes pink and soft.

He had to put the gittern across his lap to disguise the proof of his lust.

He cleared his throat. "You've put your first lesson to good use. Now I'll show you more, a chord to use in tandem with those others."

"My fingertips are sore," she admitted.

"Let me see."

She extended her hand palm up. He cupped it in his. It was the wrong thing to do.

Or perhaps it was the right thing. For though her touch lit a torch inside him and made him want to kiss her reddened fingertips and run his tongue in long, leisurely circles around her palm, it also gave him a brutal reminder of the vast chasm between them. Her hand was small and delicate and soft, the hand of the pampered daughter of a people who sought to rule his land. By contrast, his hand was big and hard, callused and coarsened by years of fighting.

He could crush her hand in his. He could crush her. He could force her to submit to him, and one day he would.

But there was no advantage in rushing things, he told himself. Indeed, there was pleasure to be had in discovering how far he could entice her. Just how good and obedient was this daughter FitzHugh had raised?

He ran one finger lightly over her sore fingertips. "Perhaps we should wait until tomorrow for the next lesson," he said.

"Oh, no. I can manage," Isolde said.

Across the short space that separated them he stared at her and raised her hand between them. "Are you certain?"

Had she looked away, he could have controlled himself better. Had she lowered her eyes and drawn her hand free of his, he would have picked up the gittern and begun the lesson she wanted. But she did not look away, nor seek to free her delicate hand from his.

And though she did not speak, he heard the request she made. There was a different lesson she wished to learn, on another subject entirely.

But he could teach her that lesson also, and very well. So, though it was madness, though it was not what he'd intended, at least not so soon, Rhys raised her hand to his lips. Then staring deep into her clear-water eyes, he pressed a kiss to her palm. Not a courtier's kiss. Not a suitor's kiss. But a lover's kiss, meant to arouse.

Meant to seduce.

SIX

At the touch of Reevius's lips to the center of her hand, Isolde thought she would faint. Her stomach lurched, curling into a knot, and every bit of her flesh tightened in response. Her skin prickled. Her insides melted, and her heretofore dormant nipples pebbled into taut nubs.

Her entire body seemed to strain toward him. And when his tongue moved in a small wet circle against her sensitive palm, she gasped, for every one of those sensations trebled.

What was happening to her? What was he doing?

Then he moved his clever mouth to her tender fingertips, and Isolde let out a little moan. He kissed each digit at the very end, one by one, a form of caress completely beyond her ken.

Lovers kissed, and they lay together, much as animals did, in order to procreate. That much she understood. But this . . . this unimaginable excitement . . . This fire in her belly caused merely by his lips upon her hand . . .

"Reevius." She breathed his name and he lifted his head.

"What would you have of me, lady. Music? Or something more?"

Isolde could hardly think, her mind was so completely muddled. He still held her hand. He still stared at her with eyes so dark she felt they might swallow her up. The very idea sent a new shiver of longing through her. What indeed did she want from him? Music lessons, or something more?

Both, she admitted to herself in a moment of total honesty. But she could not have both, not here. Not now.

Not ever, the voice of logic belatedly piped in.

She curled her hand into a fist, then slid it free of his strong, heated grasp, and looked away.

"I want . . ." She swallowed hard. "I want only a music lesson. That is all." She tilted her head and looked sidelong at him. She ought to rebuke him for the impertinence he had just displayed. But she could not. She swallowed again. "Perhaps we should return to the castle after all."

"As you wish." He rose easily to his feet then extended his hand.

Beset alternately by disappointment that he'd so swiftly agreed, relief that he would not press the issue with her, and a perverse longing for the same sort of kiss on her mouth that he'd given to her palm, Isolde stared up at him. Did she dare take his hand again?

She could not resist. She grasped his callused hand and felt at once the power he held in check. It thrilled her and alarmed her and convinced her more than ever that there was some connection between them, something meant to be. He lifted her to her feet as if her weight were nothing, but did not immediately release his grip. Instead he tugged her nearer, his eyes voracious. Intense.

"I want to kiss more than your hand, Isolde. Should you desire that also, you have but to ask it of me."

Then, on that utterly devastating note, he let her go.

Isolde stumbled back, reeling. Every step of the way—around the boulder, across the beach, up the steep stone steps, with him just behind her, she reeled from the impact of those few bold words. She slipped and he steadied her—no more than any gentleman would do. His hand caught her arm and curved around her elbow, courteous and impersonal. Yet she burned from the contact.

By the time they gained the narrow ledge at the base of the castle wall, her legs were putty, her face was flushed, and her conflicting emotions had her utterly confused. She was not one prone to such emotional upheavals, yet she seemed unable to pull herself together.

"Are you a'right, milady?" one of the guards called down, frowning when he spied her alone with Reevius.

"Yes. Yes," she repeated in a more carrying tone. The

guards would report this to Osborn, she realized. If she did not wish Reevius cast out of the castle, she must allay their suspicions.

She took the gittern from Reevius and raised it high for the guards to see. "I shall soon serenade the hall myself," she called up to them. Then, not able to meet Reevius's unsettling stare, she thrust the instrument at him, turned and fled through the narrow postern passageway to the safety of the bailey and the myriad people of Rosecliffe.

As the afternoon progressed Isolde made certain not to find time to continue her music lessons. She did not understand what had passed between her and Reevius on the beach and feared to put herself in the path of temptation too soon.

Temptation. As she made her late afternoon rounds of the weaving sheds, the dye vats, and the fresco painting, trying in vain to put Reevius and his wondrous kisses out of her head, she came to the unwelcome conclusion that what she'd experienced with him was not some special connection, but rather, temptation.

And also, the deadly sin of lust.

He'd tempted her. But she had been the one to feel lust—and what a powerful emotion she'd discovered it to be.

Could she keep it under control when next she saw him? She wasn't entirely certain. Did she want to keep it under control? In truth, no.

She groaned at her perversity, and abruptly changed direction. What did it matter the level of the honey stores if her soul were in mortal danger? Better to sit in the chapel and ponder Father Clemson's recent sermon on lust and fornication, the sermon she'd paid scant notice to.

So she knelt in the unlit chapel, empty now of workmen, and considered the dangers that beset her eternal soul. She clasped her hands and bowed her head and screwed her face into a frown of concentration as she prayed.

Let me not be tempted to sin with this man. Please, Lord, send me a sign. Send me the right man, the one I am to wed and make my life with. I know it cannot be him, for my father would never allow it. But please, Lord, send the right man soon, and save me from this fire in my belly.

She heard the chapel door open, but did not look up from

her prayers. No doubt it was Father Clemson. Should she confess her sins to him? Should she ask his guidance?

Then he stopped just behind her, and a jolt of sudden
awareness quivered up her spine. It was not the good priest—

"Do you pray for your immortal soul?" Reevius asked in a
husky whisper.

She leaped to her feet, bumping into him in her haste.

"Steady." He caught her by the arm but she jerked away
and stared fearfully at him. Was this the sign God had sent
her? Was it?

Was Reevius the man God sent to her? He'd come before
her prayer was scarcely done. Or was this only a test of her
moral fortitude? She stared at him, afraid to be wrong, unsure
of how to respond.

"Why are you here?" She gestured with one hand. "Have
you followed me?"

He spread his arms wide in a shrug. He'd donned a tunic
over his chainse, but it could not disguise his broad shoulders
and heavily muscled arms. "I came to the chapel to pray. Is
that so surprising?" He paused. "Would you prefer I leave?"

"No." Isolde wrapped her arms around herself and sternly
ordered herself to become calm. "No. You must stay, of
course. Stay and pray as you intended."

"I should not have intruded on your privacy."

"No. That is nothing." From behind him stray beams of late
afternoon light played in his hair, striking glints of gold against
the thick black of it. Almost like a halo, she thought.

Her mind spun with indecision. He'd come here to pray. It
must be a sign. Could it be that he was not just a temptation,
but instead the man God meant for her to find? Could that
have been God's purpose when her father made her remain
behind?

She took a deep breath, weighing all the evidence. God was
said to move in mysterious ways. Now, for whatever reason,
it seemed he'd sent a minstrel to her, not a man of war.

A minstrel.

A smile slowly lit up her face, and a strange sort of calm
settled over her. Her father would be furious, she realized. He
wanted a well-connected young lord for a son-in-law. A

knight, like himself. But eventually he would come around. He would have to.

Still smiling, she extended a hand to Reevius. "Let us pray together," she said, as happiness welled up inside her. "Let us pray together, for we are here in the chapel together. Come."

Rhys took Isolde's hand and he knelt beside her. It appeared he'd guessed rightly, that she'd slipped into the chapel to ponder what had occurred between them on the beach. If her smile and sudden calm were any indication, it seemed she might have come to some sort of conclusion, one that now welcomed his presence.

So he knelt beside her and considered his next move.

But it was hard to think. He was acutely aware of her, head bent, hands clasped in earnest prayer. Had he ever prayed so? Had he ever possessed such a faith?

He clenched his jaw in annoyance. Piety was easy for those with full bellies and time on their hands. It was easy for those who'd never faced the cruelties of life without the protection of family and stout stone walls.

No, he'd never prayed so, and he never would. But he would kneel beside this woman while she prayed, and lull her into complacency while he considered what next to do.

He forced himself to concentrate, to think ahead. He'd planned this campaign carefully, recruiting other discontented Welshmen to his cause. Glyn had assembled men in Afon Bryn, men from the Welsh strongholds in Powys. Even Dafydd, his old friend from ten years ago, had pledged himself and two others to taking Rosecliffe from the English. They were just waiting for Rhys to spring his trap. He would disable the guards on the north wall first, and bring his Welsh countrymen in through the postern gate. Then they would take the other guards and put them in the donjon—the donjon where he'd once resided.

And what of Isolde FitzHugh?

Uncomfortable with that thought, he shifted his weight from one knee to the other. By damn, but the floor was hard and cold. How long did she intend to pray?

Beside him she shifted and he immediately stilled. What was he to do about her? The answer was clear. He would seduce the pious wench. There was no reason not to and one huge reason why he should: he wanted her.

She'd heated his blood with her beauty, her innocence, and her unexpected passion. It was plain that she was ready for a man, and he was sore overdue the pleasures of a woman. She would do as well as any other.

Besides, what better way to gloat over the FitzHughs than to ruin their precious firstborn?

As she oversaw preparations for the evening meal Isolde kept her distance from Reevius. At the same time, however, she watched him constantly. She tried to keep her fascination with him to herself. But he would look up and catch her gaze upon him, and after a while she knew it was hopeless. He had to know what she was thinking, and she had a fair inkling herself of what he was thinking, too. That he might find her even half so appealing as she found him made her stomach giddy and her head spin!

An empty metal platter slipped from her hand, and she scurried to retrieve it. She glanced guiltily around. Did anyone else suspect the momentous change that had occurred to her today?

Odo was frowning, gesticulating with both hands as he harangued the hapless pantler. Osborn came into the hall with one of his knights, the two of them engrossed in conversation.

She let loose a sigh, thankful for that modicum of privacy, only to be startled by a tug on her sleeve.

"The fruits of prayer are many, and varied," an old familiar voice stated.

"Newlin!" Isolde gasped and again dropped the platter. "My goodness, but you frightened me. When did you arrive? Why was I not informed you were here?"

The ancient little bard looked up at her with his one good eye and his sweet, twisted smile. "I believe Odo did inform you. Do you not recall?"

"He did? Oh, yes. He did," Isolde admitted, feeling the heat of embarrassment creep into her cheeks. She turned away from Newlin's discerning gaze. "I have been forgetful of late. There are so many more details for me to attend while my parents are not in residence."

The old bard nodded. "Too many things on your mind, no doubt. I am told there is fine entertainment to be had after the evening meal."

"Yes. Minstrels." The color in her cheeks grew deeper. "They also perform acrobatics."

"And give music lessons. The gittern?"

He knew! Isolde gnawed one side of her bottom lip. "Yes," she slowly admitted. Had someone told him or did he, in the inexplicable way he had, simply know?

He smiled up at her. "Methinks these minstrels have a talent far beyond what we have yet to see." He started toward the low bench he favored, and Isolde watched the slow dip and sway of his peculiar gait. What did he mean by that? She hurried after him.

"To what sort of talent do you refer?" she asked.

"You would know that better than I, child, for I have yet to lay eyes upon these minstrels."

"Well . . ." Isolde hesitated. As usual, Newlin expected her to be completely honest with him. He would not share any portion of his mysterious knowledge with her if he thought she was being in the least deceptive. "He has a talent for . . . for attracting women," she said, embarrassed to discuss such a thing with the bard of Rosecliffe.

"He?"

"Reevius."

"Ah, yes. He calls himself Reevius."

"There are three others," she continued, twisting her fingers nervously. "Gandy and Linus and Tillo."

"Tillo," the bard echoed. "Another minstrel of surprising talents."

Isolde cocked her head. "What special talent does Tillo have?"

But Newlin seemed disinclined to answer. He sat on the bench and stared steadily at the minstrels—or at least that was the direction one of his eyes stared. Then he began to sway back and forth ever so slightly, and she knew from experience that he was unlikely to say any more on that subject.

In truth, Isolde was more than content to end their conversation. Newlin was too perceptive. She often feared he could read a person's thoughts. That would be bad enough under normal circumstances, but today her thoughts were far too unchaste for him to know. For anyone to know.

Except, perhaps, for Reevius.

By the rood! She had made the transition from complete innocence regarding men to urgent curiosity about one in particular awfully fast.

Yet hadn't she been given a sign in the chapel? She pushed a stray curl back from her brow. She had prayed to God for guidance, and at that very moment Reevius had come to her.

She stared at him across the fast-filling hall until he looked up at her. Only then did she look away, her heart racing. Oh, but this was getting out of hand! She needed to speak with someone about her confusing feelings for him. Not Father Clemson, though. She needed a woman's advice. Her mother's or Rhonwen's.

But her mother was gone, and Rhonwen and Jasper had left Bailwyn to go to the coronation. She frowned. No one else at Rosecliffe would dare be forthright with her regarding Reevius, because everyone owed their positions to her father. Even the most foolish among them would guess *his* opinion regarding a minstrel suitor for his daughter.

Again she thought of her mother, the one person who might understand how she felt toward Reevius, and who also would not fear to contradict the Lord of Rosecliffe. Osborn did not fear him, either, but he would be horrified by her fledgling love for a minstrel.

Love?

She pressed a hand to her chest and felt the fierce pounding of her heart. She'd recognized that he tempted her, and she'd recognized the sin of lust dangling before her. But was lust a sin if love was a part of your feelings? She'd never felt anything this strong before, not even for her uncle or his young squire. It must be love, she decided. What else could it be?

Oh, but this was so confusing! She did not know what to do.

Then her agitated gaze fell once more on Newlin and she realized that embarrassment or no, she would have to speak to him. He would understand the feelings that buffeted her and he had never feared her father's wrath. He would be honest with her if she were honest with him.

*   *   *

Rhys spied Newlin the moment the bowed and graying bard limped into the hall.

"*Taran,*" he cursed. Though Rhys had been ten years gone from Wales, though he stood taller and broader now, and wore a beard for disguise, he knew it would not fool Newlin. Once the wise man laid eyes on him, he would deduce the truth. "*Taran,*" he swore once more.

"What ails you?" Gandy asked as he clambered up onto the bench.

"The one man who can undo my plan has just entered the hall."

"Who? Who?" The dwarf craned his neck, staring about.

Tillo eased his aged frame onto the same bench and poured a cup of ale. "He will not do it except, perhaps, to avoid bloodshed."

"I don't like to see anyone bleed," Linus said. "I think it's wrong."

"Ah, he's thinking now. Beware," Gandy chortled. "The earth must soon come to an end."

With one huge hand Linus ruffled Gandy's head good-naturedly. "Don't worry, my little friend. I will keep you safe."

Gandy ducked and cursed, but Rhys ignored them and focused on Tillo. The skinny old minstrel sat leaning on the table, enjoying a cup of ale. "Why do you think he will not reveal my identity to Osborn?"

"Or to Isolde?" Tillo cackled. "Because he is wiser than you or I. Much wiser," he added under his breath.

Rhys took a seat between feisty Gandy and complacent Linus. Tillo's remarks eased his concerns but did not banish them. He knew less of Tillo than he did his other two companions, for Tillo spoke little of his past. Not of family, or place, or even of memories. For that reason Rhys had been slow to trust him.

But Tillo had reminded him of someone—of Newlin, he now realized. The two of them were old and crippled and seemingly ageless. Though Tillo had never displayed any of the powers credited to Newlin, he was nonetheless sensible and practical. Through the years his advice had proven itself over and over again. If Tillo felt Newlin would keep his own counsel regarding the minstrel Reevius's true identity, then he was probably right.

But Rhys was cautious about trusting Newlin for too long. He would have to move swiftly.

He sought out Isolde with his eyes, and caught her once again staring at him. She averted her eyes at once, as she had every other time their gazes had connected. And like all those other times, the muscles in his groin tightened in response.

She wanted him. That was plain. And he wanted her. But while she did not know that he was her enemy, he did not have the excuse of ignorance. He knew exactly who she was. That's what made his desire for her so hard to accept.

But he had decided to accept that burden.

Now that Newlin was here and the threat of exposure hung over them all, the urgency of his mission had increased tenfold. Tonight he would entertain Isolde and her retainers after the evening meal. Perhaps he would even seek out Newlin and determine his intentions. But after that he would find Isolde and see what sort of lesson she wanted more. He could teach her songs to play on the tautly strung gittern. Or he could teach her the special music of desire, played on the taut places of her young body.

An image of her, smooth and pale and naked, rose in his mind, and his own body grew taut. He grimaced and looked away from her. Why could he not be drawn like this to the dairy maid, or the freckle-faced wench in the laundry? She'd offered to bathe both him and his clothes.

But it was his enemy's daughter he wanted, and his enemy's daughter he would have.

And once he had her, once the conquest was made, he would be content. Whether English knights on the field of battle, or English women on a field of linen bedsheets, his joy in life was to best his foes, then move on to the next of their ilk.

Isolde FitzHugh would be no different.

SEVEN

Isolde waited near the hearth in the great hall. She was behaving like a simpleton. Waiting for Reevius. Afraid he would come—then afraid he would not.

He'd entertained the entire company after the meal. This time the performance of the minstrels had been more boisterous than before, with tambourines and drums in lieu of gittern and lute. It had also been more bawdy. Osborn had howled with laughter when the giant Linus donned an apron and *couvrechef* and minced around, with little Gandy strutting in ardent pursuit. Isolde, however, had focused more on Reevius and the stirring song he'd sung. He had such a beautiful voice, especially when he sang of Paris who pined for his Helen, and David who had lost everything because of Bathsheba. Of Samson, the strong man of legend who'd been brought low by a woman.

But his songs of warning had not prevented the swaggering Gandy from pursuing his gigantress love, and in the end Gandy had been crushed by his lover's passion—and her weight.

It had been hilarious, but for Isolde, it had also been sobering. Did Reevius imply that women always destroyed the men who loved them? Did he believe the warning he sang in his humorous tale?

So she waited now, doing the final check of the new cloth tapestry by lanternlight. It wanted sunlight to do the task properly, she knew. Then again, it wanted her complete concentration, as well.

She sighed. The hall was quiet. Only a few lingered still. Three men playing at dice. Gandy doing sleight-of-hand tricks for two amazed boys. Newlin and Tillo sat opposite one another conversing quietly while Reevius looked on. If he did not mean to approach her, then she must take the initiative and go to him. If she hesitated much longer for her lesson, the torchères would be spent. Besides, it was useless to pretend she was accomplishing anything. So she folded the heavy wall hanging to the side, and went up the stairs to her bedchamber to fetch the gittern.

When she returned to the hall Reevius was waiting for her at the bottom of the stairs, one foot propped on the second step. Her heart skipped a beat when he looked up at her, and she would have stumbled had she not caught one hand on the wall.

"You are ready for your musical instruction?" he asked, his eyes burning into hers.

She nodded, then looked away. His intensity frightened her, and yet it also thrilled her. Beyond him the hall was quieter than before. Only Newlin and Tillo remained.

"Come," Reevius said. He extended a hand to her.

It was a courteous gesture—for a nobleman. For a mere minstrel it would be considered excessively bold. But he did not look like a minstrel, not with those broad shoulders and thickly muscled arms. In her eyes he appeared as noble as any knight or lord her father might push at her. In her eyes he was everything her father could want for her. Certainly he was everything she wanted.

She took his proffered hand, watching as it swallowed hers up. That was how she felt: swallowed up by him, overwhelmed. Consumed. And he'd only touched her hand. What would happen to her should their touch become more personal, more intimate?

The very thought left her short of breath, and even at the bottom of the steps when she pulled her hand free—when he let it go—it seemed an intimate act merely to walk beside him.

They settled on a bench away from the two old men.

"Have you practiced further?" he asked.

She shook her head. "I have been busy with other tasks."

"But now you have time."

"Yes."

He positioned the instrument in her hands and after a few shaky minutes she relaxed. It was only music instruction. Why was she behaving like an infatuated girl?

She gnawed on her lower lip. Because she was infatuated. Because God had sent her a sign—maybe.

She bent over the instrument, trying to concentrate on her lesson. She was working to fit her fingers to a particularly difficult configuration he'd shown her when he sighed. She looked up. "Is this wrong? I'm sorry I am so slow to understand."

"You learn remarkably well."

"I do?" She warmed to his compliment.

"You do." Their eyes held a brief moment before he looked away. "This must be your last lesson."

"The last one? But why? You need not leave Rosecliffe so soon. You are welcome to linger—"

" 'Tis too hard to stay."

"Too hard?"

Slowly he turned his head until their gazes once more met and locked. " 'Tis too hard to be this near to you, Isolde."

Though beyond earshot, across the hall Newlin looked up. So did Tillo. One of the hounds jerked alert, then seeing no cause for alarm, flopped down again in canine weariness.

Isolde saw none of it, however. All her senses, every one of them, focused upon Reevius and those few momentous words he'd uttered. "But . . . But I want you to stay." She said the words fainter than a whisper. "Please don't go."

He shook his head. "To be near you and not have leave to touch you . . . 'Tis too hard a thing to ask of me."

"You can touch me." The incendiary words were out of her mouth before she knew it, heaping fuel on the fire that burned already in his coal-black eyes.

"Your hand?" he mocked. "Your shoulder when we sit together, or mayhap your elbow?"

Isolde swallowed. She knew what he meant by touching. But what did she mean? "Perhaps . . . Perhaps in time it could come to more than that. More than my elbow or my shoulder," she clarified.

He shifted a little nearer so that the length of his hard thigh rested against hers. He circled her shoulder and covered her hand that held the neck of the gittern, much as he'd done that first time. She glanced in alarm at Newlin, but he appeared preoccupied by Tillo, and there was no one else in the hall.

Then Reevius spoke, a husky whisper very near her ear. "I asked you earlier today what you want of me, Isolde. Tell me now. Do not leave me in this misery of unrequited love."

Love.

It was the magic word that moved her like no other. Not unrequited desire. Not unrequited passion. But unrequited love.

She leaned her weight fully against him and let her head fall back against his arm. "It is not . . . unrequited."

At once his hand tightened over hers. The other lifted and he brushed his knuckles lightly down the curve of her cheek. Had they been anywhere but in the great hall, Isolde feared she would have succumbed to him on the spot, the effect of that gesture was so profound. That she wanted to do such a thing was terribly disconcerting. That she could not do it was unbearably frustrating.

She closed her eyes and let out a groan at the perverse tug-of-war inside her. He muttered an impatient curse, then released her and shifted, breaking all physical contact between them.

Bereft of his touch, Isolde stared longingly at him. She wanted this man in the way a woman was supposed to want only her husband. And he wanted her in the selfsame way. Did she dare act upon those feelings? Did she?

His eyes ran darkly over her and he seemed to read her mind. "Where can we be alone?"

The breath caught in her throat. She averted her eyes, and her hands tightened on the gittern. "My . . . my private chamber is but one floor above us."

"What of your maid?"

She thought of Magda and her sweetheart, George. "She went off earlier."

"Will she return?"

Isolde hesitated. Was she mad to consider such a meeting with him? At the moment the answer seemed very clear: she *was* mad. Mad with desire. Mad with love. Mad with all the pent-up passions she'd discovered seething within her belly. What if her parents should hear of this?

Then she recalled a fact, well-known around Rosecliffe, but little discussed within their family. She had been born long before her parents wed, a child of their hard-fought passions. Though avowed enemies, they had fallen in love despite every obstacle. How could they blame her now for behaving as they themselves had done? At least she and Reevius were not enemies.

She took a deep breath. "No. She should not return before dawn. To be sure, we can go to the third level."

His brows arched in surprise. "To your parent's chamber." Then he smiled.

Without further discussion Isolde rose and, on wobbly legs, marched toward the stairs. She'd done it now. Sweet Mary, but she'd really done it now.

From across the hall Newlin watched Isolde disappear up the stairs. Although her young man remained upon the bench, it took no great insight to foresee where this evening would lead. Ah, well, he thought. It was inevitable. Perhaps it was even to the good.

Opposite him Tillo smiled thinly. "Young love. 'Tis a fine thing to see, but painful to live through."

"I fear that the pain of this young love will rain down on all of us at Rosecliffe," Newlin responded. Then his faded eyes focused, both of them at the same time, upon Tillo. "He has returned to exact his revenge. You know this."

Tillo looked away. "I have heard his tale and so cannot fault him for wanting revenge. It is hard, though, to look into your enemy's eyes, to get to know him, to sit at table with him and understand his humanity, and yet remain enemies."

"As we sit?"

Tillo smiled. "We are not enemies."

"No. Nor need they be."

"Perhaps they will learn not to be enemies," Tillo said, shrugging. "Perhaps this night will teach them that."

Newlin's eyes once more went their separate unfocused directions. "So long as he chooses to keep his secret there can be no trust between them. Secrets have a way of undermining friendship. Do you not agree?"

Tillo frowned, then pushed abruptly away from the table.
"Those two will do as they see fit. He should not pursue her,
but he does. She should abide by her parents' wishes, but she
does not. They are too young and too impulsive to do the
things they ought."

Newlin studied Tillo's creased face. "You are angry now.
Why is that?"

Tillo stared back at him with wary eyes. "Methinks you
already know the answer to that." He paused. "Do you?"

Newlin began slowly to rock back and forth. "I know many
things. I know many secrets."

"Mine? Do you know mine?"

After a long moment Newlin answered. "Yes."

Tillo pulled his purple cloak tighter around his thin, aged
body. "Then you know why I am angry."

"No," Newlin said. "That I do not comprehend."

Their eyes met and held. Tillo was the first to break away.
"Men," the old minstrel muttered, hobbling away. "They are
a troublesome lot, no matter their age."

Newlin watched Tillo's departure in bemusement. There
were times when he grew weary of the special knowledge
given him. Now he had this new surprise of Tillo's. More
importantly, however, he now had this new worry.

Though he'd always known Rhys would one day return,
how matters would resolve themselves remained a mystery to
him. For the several people involved possessed strong wills,
and he could not be certain what decisions they would make.
What actions they would take.

An echo of a long-ago conversation returned from across
the years. Twoscore years, yet it seemed only yesterday. "Winter's end is nigh." Josselyn had repeated the phrase in Welsh,
then French, and finally in the Saxon English. She'd possessed
a quick mind, that Josselyn, and her daughter Isolde was just
as quick.

And just as impulsive.

But perhaps winter's end was nigh, he reasoned. Perhaps
the third portion of the children's chant would soon be ful-
filled, and with it the true blossoming of spring upon this oft-
buffeted bit of Wales. He began to rock and the voices of a
hundred children—a thousand—echoed in his head.

When stones shall grow and trees shall no',
When noon comes black as beetle's back,
When winter's heat shall cold defeat,
We'll see them all 'ere Cymry falls."

'Ere Cymry falls. But perhaps it would be Cymry's rise.

He gazed at the stairway. Rhys would soon mount those steps and seek out his enemy's daughter. What route would those two follow? The world would turn. The future would come no matter what choices they made. Soon enough that future would be revealed.

Meanwhile, there was Tillo's secret to ponder.

EIGHT

RHYS SAT VERY STILL, LOOKING AT THE STAIRS AND THINK-
ing. He saw Tillo leave, shuffling along, bowed over more
than usual, as if beneath a heavy weight. This journey had
been hard on him, Rhys knew, but the old man had insisted
on coming.

Next Rhys watched Newlin depart, hobbling along with his
peculiar sideways gait. Tomorrow he would find out from
Tillo what they had discussed. Newlin must surely know the
truth about who Reevius the minstrel was. But he'd chosen
not to reveal it. For what purpose? Rhys would not allow his
fate to be controlled by so unpredictable a creature as the fey
Newlin.

But at the moment Newlin's threat was of lesser import
than another urgent matter. The hall was empty. The stairs
beckoned. Rising, he responded to its call.

Twenty-five wide stone steps up to the next level. Fifteen
more carried him up to the floor where Isolde awaited. The
part of him that hated the English and had plotted all his life
to overthrow the FitzHughs took note of everything: the number of steps, the placement of windows, and even the position
of the torchères along the way. He saw and noted all the conditions he might need to know should he ever have to fight
his way in—or out—of the keep.

But the part of him that was a man, hungry for a woman—
that part noted that there were no maids straying about, that
the door to her parents' chamber stood ajar, and that a single
candle flickered pale golden light across a massive raised bed.

The bed hangings were of rich blue silk and they cast dark shadows across the half-hidden mattress.

As Rhys came into the chamber and closed the door behind him, all he wanted was to lay Isolde, pale and naked, upon those silken bedclothes and to know she was his for the taking.

He looked around, searching her out, for he was aroused and ready for her, and more than tired of this game of cat and mouse. She was ripe for seduction and he was willing to do the seducing. But where was the tempting little wench?

The door latch clicked and he spun around. The hinges creaked as the door leaf swung in, and he slid his dagger from the sheath at his hip.

She'd set him a trap!

He braced for attack. But it was not Osborn or any of his men-at-arms who advanced into the room. Instead, Isolde peered cautiously around the door, her rich hair glinting in the single candle's flame. She blanched when she saw the weapon in his hands.

"What's wrong? Why do you—"

" 'Tis nothing." He sheathed the dagger then caught her by the shoulders and pulled her roughly into his embrace. His heart was still pounding.

"But why—Wait—" She struggled, pushing against his chest.

He would not release her, however, and held each of her arms in a firm grip. "I did not see you," he explained, staring deeply into her eyes. "Then the door opened and I feared your watchdog, that captain of the guard, might have followed me. That's all. But happily I was wrong. And now we are alone— as we have wanted to be. Come, Isolde. You need not fear me," he said, pulling her nearer. "Come," he coaxed when he felt her firm young breasts pressed against his chest. "Kiss me, for I am in dire need of your kisses."

Isolde felt herself relenting, and yet a part of her was troubled. Something was not right. Something about Reevius's words did not ring entirely true.

But then his mouth came down on hers, and it became impossible for her to think. His strong arms encircled her, his clever lips moved over hers, and his will sucked any protest out of her. Gone was logic and reason and any thought of propriety. In their stead came a powerful aching desire. It was fearful and fierce and she gave herself up wholly to it.

He took possession of her mouth, nibbling on her lower lip, then creating a breath-stealing friction when he slid his lips back and forth over hers. She wound her arms around his neck and mimicked the action of his mouth. But he knew so much more of lovemaking. She could hardly keep pace with him.

Somehow he parted her lips—or she did it herself—and his tongue found entrance. At once he lifted them to a whole other plane of desire. He devoured her mouth, deepening the kiss, and awakening an inferno deep inside her. He slid his tongue in, then drew hers out, and tremors of excitement began to build in her belly.

Without her understanding how or when, she found herself on the bed, lying on top of him. And still the kiss went on, robbing her of everything but her awareness of him. Then he rolled them over and she was beneath him and finally he ended the kiss.

In the quiet room with only the one candle she'd lit, all was in shadows. He was a dark looming silhouette over her, and were it not for the feel of his hard body pressing onto hers, she would have thought him a phantom lover, a wicked dream come to her at the hour of midnight. But he was real and they were in her parent's huge bed, and doubt suddenly assailed her.

"We cannot," she began.

"We can." He kissed her again, urgently, stroking in and out of her mouth in an arousing rhythm, until she melted beneath him. "We can," he murmured, moving his kiss down her cheek to her ear, to her neck and throat, and along her collarbone.

"Yes, but . . . but not in here," Isolde managed to say. As protests went, it was meager, for her hands urged him on even as her words bade him stop. "Not in here."

"Why not?" With one hand he tugged the neckline of her kirtle down past her shoulder. " 'Tis a big bed, and soft. Perfect for what I have planned."

"But Reevius," she said, then gasped when his mouth closed over her nipple. Even through her chemise and kirtle she felt the erotic nip of his teeth and she arched in an agony of new sensations.

" 'Tis a fine bed," he said, drawing her skirts up and sliding one hand beneath her thigh. "I've always wanted to possess a bed such as this one."

"But . . . but 'tis my parents'."

He did not answer that, at least not with words. But his body had an answer. His lips and fingers gave an answer, and her protests were silenced by what they said. He caressed her everywhere, sliding his hard torso against her, abrading her inner thighs with the rough wool of his braies. One of his hands teased her breasts, rubbing across the incredibly aroused peaks. And though he did not kiss her mouth this time, he found every other sensitive spot with his lips: Her earlobes. The hollow of her throat.

Her fingers threaded through his hair as she clutched his head to her. Something wonderful was happening to her. Something momentous. Something so intense she could not bear it. But she could not bear to end it, either.

With an effort she forced him to look at her. "Reevius . . . Wait. I . . . I have prepared a different place for us. That's where I was, up in the tower room."

She thought he had not heard her, for passion ruled his features. His eyes burned with it and perspiration beaded on his brow. But he did hear and after a moment he rubbed his thumb across her lower lip. "Very well. We will go to the little nest you have prepared for us. We will go just as soon as I finish one small task."

So saying, he slid slowly down the length of her. His weight flowed over her, heavy, wholly masculine, and arousing her with the very possessiveness of the movement. When his face hovered above her breasts she began to breathe even harder than she already was.

What was he going to do to her now? Her body tensed in anticipation. Oh, God, let him do it soon, else she would surely explode!

Then she felt his hand between her thighs, touching her where no one had ever touched her—where she hardly touched herself! She tried to clamp her legs together, and failed. She grabbed his shoulders and tried to dislodge him, but he did not budge.

"Reevius, wait—"

"Shh," he answered, as his finger began to stroke her down there.

"Oh . . . Reevius." This time it was more a sigh, for her body was melting into the bed. "What . . . What are you doing?"

"Showing you how good it can be when a woman gives herself up to the right man."

"Yes. Yes." She panted the words as the rhythmic motion of his fingers became the center of her world.

"This is but the beginning," he whispered in a low, rough voice. "There's much more to come, Isolde."

If there was more, it surely would destroy her. That was the last sensible thought she had. For once again Reevius lowered his head to her breasts, and when he took one in his mouth, something broke inside her. He'd pushed her too far, too fast, and something gave way. Like a storm-driven wave breaking upon the rocks, she crashed and burst apart, wave after wave after wave.

And when it was done, she was left utterly destroyed, dead, perhaps. He had killed her with the violent pleasure he'd given her.

She was revived only when he slid down her body further and pressed his face against her belly, breathing hard, as if he could draw in the very essence of her. The part of her that she feared had been broken flickered again to life.

What was it he'd done to her? She knew how men and women joined together, how a man's seed was planted in a woman's womb. But what he'd done, touching her so . . . Her mother had never explained anything like what had just happened to her.

Did her father do that to her mother?

Isolde did not want to think about that. Suddenly she gasped. They were still in her parents' great bed.

She pushed up onto her elbows, staring wildly about. "This is wrong. We weren't supposed to—"

"Wrong?" Reevius looked up and his eyes scorched her with the power of his desire.

"No, not that. That was . . ." Words failed her. "I mean here. This bed."

"I think it's right, what we did here. And this bed is the right place for us to finish what we've begun. The fitting place." He came up over her and she felt the heat of his thick arousal. He drew the hem of her gown up to her waist and loosened the ties on his braies.

But though Isolde's body desired him still, her belated sense of right and wrong persisted. "Not here, Reevius. Please. Let us go up to the tower room."

He paused. "It bothers you that your parents sleep in this bed?"

She nodded.

He grunted. "More reason to use it, then."

Her brow creased in confusion. "What do you mean—" She broke off when his arousal slid against the excruciatingly sensitive place his fingers had touched before. He moved his hips, rocking them back and forth against her, and the fire in her belly leaped back to life. Yet something troubled her still. "I don't understand. My parents have nothing to do with this—with you and me."

He did not answer but shifted his hips so that he was poised at the entrance of her femininity. Something was not right, she realized. Something, only she did not know what.

But she did know. She lay in her parents' bed with a man who was not her husband, a man she'd known but one day. Though she was drawn to him in a way she could not understand, she had succumbed to him too fast. Much too fast. In truth, what did she know of him as a man?

Nothing.

"Wait." She pushed at his shoulders.

"No." He pressed further, entering her.

"Wait!"

Their eyes met and held. His were so dark—deep set, long lashed, and completely black save for the tiny reflection of candlelight. They looked so familiar.

"I can wait no longer," he said in a strained voice. Then with a swift thrust, he was inside her.

Isolde gasped at the quick stab of pain, and held her breath in alarm. She'd done it now. Dear God, but she'd really done it now.

Then he began to move inside her, and her doubts burned away in the exquisite friction he created. His breathing was harsh as he built the movements, slow and shallow at first, then deeper and harder when she began to moan her pleasure.

"By damn," he swore. "By damn."

"Reevius." She panted his name mindlessly.

"Reevius." He repeated his own name and the expression on his face grew grim. At once his movements grew harsher, more demanding. She was suddenly afraid of him, yet on fire for him, too.

"Ten years," he muttered, saying the words in Welsh. "Twenty."

She blinked, not understanding what he was talking about. "Ten years? Twenty? What do you mean?" she asked, speaking Welsh, as he had done.

He did not cease the furious pace he set. He came in and out, in and out. On his face was the evidence of his arousal as he strained toward his own completion. But in his eyes . . . in his eyes she saw pain and also anger. Though her body responded to his with rising passion, her mind spun. What was wrong?

What was wrong?

Then the awful truth struck her. A truth too hideous to face, but impossible to ignore.

"Rhys!"

She didn't realize she'd said that hated name out loud. She was that horrified by her suspicions. She lay beneath him in the final throes of their joining, overwhelmed by rising pleasure and sickening guilt. "Rhys ap Owain!"

He looked at her then and she saw the confirmation in his black eyes. But it was too late. She'd cried out his name and in the next moment he plunged deep and spilled his seed within her.

The seed of the one man in the world she despised.

Rhys exploded in Isolde with a release that was both physical and emotional. He plunged in and out, never slowing, though he was drained, though his muscles trembled with exhaustion. But he could not stop. It felt too good to stop.

Beneath him she tried to fight her own passion, for she knew him now. She knew it was Rhys ap Owain who'd brought her to such shattering pleasure. She knew it was her enemy who'd taken her innocence. But she still could not silence her desires and so he pressed on, determined to bring her to fulfillment. He'd done so as the minstrel he pretended to be. He would do so now as the Welsh rebel he truly was.

He moved within her in long, slow strokes. Deep, persistent strokes. He caught her hands that tried to push him away, holding her knotted fists within his own. When she turned her face aside and squeezed her eyes shut, he kissed her ear.

"Give yourself up to me, Isolde. Feel how good it is between us," he urged in a hoarse whisper. "Feel how good it is and how good it can continue to be."

She shook her head no, but he saw the flush of rising passion on her chest and throat and cheeks.

"You were meant for this," he continued, feeling the return of his own passion. "To receive pleasure from me. To give it back."

Her breath came in quick, shallow pants, a sound that unaccountably affected all his senses. Damn, but she was pushing him again to completion! He buried his face in the thick silk of her hair, fighting to maintain some level of equilibrium. He had not meant to want her so fiercely. She was the last woman he should want in this way. But he did want her and everything was fast spiraling out of his control.

Then she began to meet his thrusts, raising her hips and granting him an even deeper entrance than before. Her body was slender and shapely, soft and strong, and she was making the most erotic sounds. Sighs and whimpers. Groans.

It was too much for him to take. With a groan of his own, he began the mad rush to completion, to hers as well as his. And when she cried out, then tensed and arched up beneath him, he let loose a cry of his own. *"Fi Duw!"*

He felt the spasms that shook her, and in turn, they wrenched something powerful from him. He plunged in, giving her everything he had, then collapsed over her, well and truly spent.

If he wondered at the enormous satisfaction he felt at that moment, at the stupendous sense of well-being, he rationalized that it was simply the incredible feeling of victory. As at the tournaments or on the field of battle, he'd proven himself once more the victor over his English enemies.

But the woman beneath him was like no enemy he'd ever faced before.

He rolled to one side, careful not to hurt her. Then he wrapped her in his arms, holding her close, savoring his triumph as he contemplated his next move in the deadly game he'd just put into play.

BOOK II

And when he came to the castle gate
He let not to clap or call,
But bent his bow against his breast
and lightly leapt the wall.

—HENRY OF HUNTINGDON

NINE

ISOLDE COULD NOT LOOK AT HIM. SHE COULD NOT LOOK AT the man who held her in his arms upon her parents' bed.

What had she done?

She squeezed her eyes tight and tried to blot out the impossible reality of it. But she could not. His heart beat fiercely in her ear. His chest rose and fell in the same cadence as her own. And they were locked together in a lovers' embrace, damp and sticky with sweat—and more. He was her enemy, yet she'd given him her virginity! Worse, she had liked it.

She had reveled in it!

"Dear God," she whispered in abject despair. "Dear God."

The muscles of his arms tensed and he took a deep breath, then slowly exhaled. " 'Tis too late for prayers, Isolde."

With a cry of anguish she shoved away from him. To her surprise he did not grab at her but let her go, and she scrambled backward. Her legs were bare and weak, and when she slid down from the bed, they nearly gave way. Her kirtle was in complete disarray. The neck was loose and caught over one shoulder. The skirt twisted and tangled with that of her chemise.

She tugged and yanked, trying to right it, then caught sight of the damp spot on her bodice where he'd caressed her breast with his mouth.

"Oh, sweet Mary!" she cried out, backing toward the door.

In the bed he rolled to one side and propped his head up on his hand. "Are you going out among your people in such a state as that?" he asked. "With your hair loose and flowing about your shoulders and your clothing all awry, anyone you come upon will know precisely what it is you've been up to. Your lips are still red from kissing me, Isolde. Your face is flushed. And you carry about you the unmistakable scent of passion. Lust," he added with a mocking grin lifting one side of his face.

One of her hands went to her tangled hair, the other to her swollen lips. It was true. And between her legs she was warm and wet.

"Oh, sweet Mary," she groaned again, unable to think of anything else to say. What was she to do? What?

Then thankfully—miraculously—her common sense took hold. This man was her enemy—her family's enemy. And he was inside Rosecliffe Castle. No matter the cost to her reputation or her pride, she must alert the guards.

She whirled and darted for the door. But though she was closer, he got there first. "Oh, no you don't," he muttered, catching her around the waist and swinging her off her feet.

"No—"

His hand cut off her scream before she could form it. Though she kicked and fought and flailed wildly at him, he was unrelenting. He threw her back onto the bed, holding her down with his greater weight, in a hideous parody of what they'd just done in this very spot.

"You will not sound the alarm against me," he taunted as he ripped a strip from the hem of her kirtle then gagged her with it. "You will not thwart me no matter how hard you try," he continued, flipping her onto her stomach. He caught her wrists behind her back and bound them together, then did the same to her ankles. She bucked and fought against him, but it was all for naught, for he just sat back on his heels and waited until exhaustion brought her to the point of collapse. Only when she lay gasping for breath, her every limb shaking with rage, did he speak.

"I am not averse to killing Englishmen."

Fear cast its chill over her rage. He meant to kill her people! Terrified, Isolde sought to control her breathing, to hear the entirety of his softly spoken threat.

"I am not averse to killing Englishmen. However, I prefer to avoid bloodshed when I can."

She twisted her head to see him, but could not. Then he caught her shoulder and rolled her onto her back, and she wished she did not have to see his deceitful, hateful face.

While she watched in terror, he unwound a thin chain from within his boot, then fastened one end around her waist and the other to one of the bedposts. In the guttering candlelight he looked more a demon than a man—the devil taken the form of a man. And she'd taken him for her lover!

Was she cursed? Had God abandoned her entirely?

He stood beside the bed, examining his handiwork. His black eyes ran slowly over her, and she shivered as if he touched her. But those eyes revealed nothing, neither desire nor disgust, neither passion nor hatred. Isolde feared, however, that her own eyes were not as shuttered, and so she closed them and looked away.

"You will remain here," he said into the awful darkness. "It is pointless to seek escape, though no doubt you will try. But it will do you no good. When next I return to this chamber, Rosecliffe Castle will be mine, claimed for Wales, as is only right."

When she looked back at him, her eyes wide with fear, he added, "I will decide then what to do with you, Isolde, and with the rest of your people." Then he was gone.

Isolde lay alone in her parents' bed, helpless and terrified by everything that had happened. What of Osborne and the others who would fight for Rosecliffe? Would Rhys kill them all?

She fought the bindings at her wrists, twisting and pulling until her skin was raw and painful. Then the candle guttered out and she was cast into total darkness. Only then did the first tear leak from her eyes. Only then, as the utter futility of her situation struck home, did fear overwhelm her. She strained to hear what was happening elsewhere in the castle, but her own harsh breathing and occasional choked sobs were all that broke the utter stillness.

Rhys ap Owain had returned to exact his revenge and only God knew how it would end.

As he crossed the darkened great hall, Rhys was both exhausted and exhilarated, and he trembled with anticipation. He'd not meant for matters to come to a head tonight. He'd been a lunatic to allow his physical desire for his enemy's daughter to alter his carefully worked-out plan. But she'd been so willing, and his desire had been so great. He straightened the collar of his tunic. What was done was done. With a little luck there would be no serious repercussions, for his old friends Glyn and Dafydd and the others they'd gathered camped now in the forest beyond Carreg Du, awaiting his signal.

In short order he found Gandy and Linus asleep in the stables in an empty stall. One shake and a nod, and Gandy understood. He melted into the darkness, heading for the postern gate and then for the hidden woodland encampment where the other rebels waited. Linus followed Rhys, and together they crept up to the wall walk.

The first guard fell with one blow. The second and third, as well. Rhys tied them up; Linus carried them down to the postern gate and left them outside. Then they headed back to the stables. One by one, the stable master and the several lads in his care were dragged from their pallets, gagged, bound, and locked inside the laundry shed. Next, the cook and Odo.

Odo put up a greater struggle than the others, but he quieted when Rhys held a dagger against his throat. "If you wish to keep your mistress safe, you will cooperate."

By the time the moon crossed the night sky and dipped near to the horizon, Rhys and Linus had overpowered all but the several knights and men-at-arms who still slept in the barracks. The armorer lived in the village, as did most of the masons and carpenters, so they were not an immediate concern.

"Where is Gandy with Glyn and the others?" Rhys muttered as he locked the storeroom behind Odo.

"Perhaps he lost his way in the woods," Linus suggested.

"Perhaps he had a change of heart," said Tillo.

Rhys whirled to find the stooped old man standing in the open doorway of the stables. His eyes narrowed. "It sounds as if perhaps you're the one with the change of heart."

The old minstrel shook his head. "It matters nothing to me who rules within this careful pile of stones."

Rhys clenched his jaw. There was something odd in Tillo's manner tonight. "You knew what I was after when you came here. All of you did. Gandy will not betray me," he stated with confidence. "But tell me, old man. You spoke a long while with Newlin. What did he have to say?"

Tillo lowered himself slowly onto an overturned bucket. "He is tired."

"And so he removes himself from these matters?"

"He trusts you to do no harm."

Rhys did not respond to that, save with a snort of disbelief. So Newlin had finally accepted the inevitable. Or more like, he'd decided to cast his lot with the victor. That's what he'd done twenty years ago when the FitzHughs had first arrived. He'd given no aid to his Welsh people but instead had befriended the stronger English force. He was doing it again now, not actually giving aid to Rhys, but not opposing him, either.

A surge of elation chased the weariness from Rhys's body. He would be victorious this night. He'd been sure of it, but Newlin's defection confirmed it.

He grinned into the darkness where Tillo sat. "Take heart, old friend. After this night you will never have to traipse the highways again. No tournaments, no performances. You will have a home here, Tillo. To live out your life in comfort."

Tillo lifted his head. "I thank you for that, lad. But I begin to wonder whether I am suited to such places as this."

A movement in the bailey caught Rhys's eye and he tensed. But it was Gandy, skipping across the open yard with a column of well-armed Welshmen trailing warily behind him. Rhys strode out to meet them.

"What happened?" Glyn whispered. "Did someone find you out and force your hand?"

"Aye," Rhys answered, but he was not of a mind to elaborate. "We've taken nine men prisoners. There are eleven more, all fighting men, all still abed in the barracks. Once we capture them, the castle is ours."

He divided the Welshmen into three groups. Dafydd's group took charge of the gatehouse and wall walks. Another group held the bailey against any escape from the barracks. Meanwhile Rhys and Linus made for the main door of the barracks, while Glyn and his men took the back entrance. Three minutes to take their positions. Then with an earsplitting whistle he signaled attack and burst into the barracks.

In the dark it sounded as if hell had erupted through the

floorboards. Welsh battle screams; crashing furniture; the deadly ring of steel striking steel.

The Englishmen sprang up, alarmed, confused, and fumbling for their weapons. But the Welsh were ready. They'd been ready a very long time. They swarmed the English warriors from both ends of the low-ceilinged barracks, forcing them to the middle, striking them down and taking prisoners as they went.

Rhys had given orders: kill no one save in the protection of your own life. His reason for that was twofold. He wanted to prove to the Welsh citizenry that he was not the pitiless monster his reputation made of him. He wanted also to take Rosecliffe in a bloodless revolt and thereby embarrass the FitzHughs with his prowess—and their ineptness.

But he heard the grunts and cries of pain, and he knew that in a war nothing could be predicted. And this was a war.

He shoved one Englishman down, and with the hilt of his sword, smashed another over the head. "Bring the torches!" he yelled, and in a moment harsh light flooded the room.

It was a shambles. Five Englishmen lay in a heap. Six others huddled back to back, facing the Welshmen who surrounded them. They held swords and daggers, but they were no match for the invaders and they knew it. Rhys spied Osborn among them, his gray hair disheveled, his legs bare beneath the loose shirt he slept in.

He addressed the captain of Rosecliffe's guards. "Surrender, Osborn de la Vere. Surrender your men and this castle to Rhys ap Owain. Surrender or die."

The man's eyes whipped around to Rhys when he spoke. Now they narrowed in disbelief. "Rhys ap Owain? You come to us as the minstrel Reevius—" Then he broke off. "Where is Isolde?" He pointed his weapon at Rhys and in his face his worry outshone rage. "What have you done with her?"

Rhys grinned. "You can ask her that yourself, if you lay down your weapon."

Osborn glared at him. "Is she harmed? If you have harmed her in any way—"

"You will what? Have no fear, old man. I have not harmed the wench—not that you could prevent me doing so," Rhys taunted. Then his expression grew fierce. "Lay aside your sword. Surrender to me. Only then will I allow you to see her."

The old knight glanced swiftly around. There was no escape, and no hope for defeating the men who had surprised them. After a long, tense moment, Osborn lowered his sword. Behind him his men slowly followed suit.

Rhys jerked his head and Linus lumbered up to collect the weapons. "Put them in the donjon," he instructed Glyn. "Linus will show you where it is."

"What of Isolde?" Osborn demanded as one of the Welshmen shoved him along with the others.

"I will bring her to you," Rhys said. "Once the castle is secured and I have had my first meal as lord of Rosecliffe, I will bring her to you."

"You bastard!" Osborn lunged at him, but three men held him back. "You lying whelp! Rand should have hung you ten years ago when he had the chance!"

Rhys gave him a dark, satisfied grin. "That he should have. But that was his mistake and now he will pay dearly for it. Take him away," he ordered, sheathing his sword with a show of disdain.

Osborn fought his captors the whole way; Rhys heard him. But when the others left, Rhys remained behind in the empty barracks and let the truth of what he'd accomplished wash over him.

He'd done it.

Against all odds he had taken Rosecliffe Castle, imprisoned its English guard, and replaced it with Welsh loyalists. And he'd done it all while the rest of the castle populace remained blissfully asleep. If he believed in God, he would believe he'd been blessed this night. First a tumble with a delectable little wench, then a good fight and a clean victory.

But God had played no part in his triumph.

Rhys raked a hand through his hair. He had paid for tonight's success with his sword, with his blood, and with twenty years of misery. But as he stared about the barracks, so like the one he'd lived in at Barnard Castle, he could not dredge up the joy he'd expected, the fierce satisfaction. His whole life he'd plotted for this moment. Why wasn't he elated?

Again he raked a hand through his hair, then ran it over his beard. He was still Reevius the minstrel. That was the problem. He needed to be Rhys ap Owain again—and he needed to lord his victory over a FitzHugh.

He squared his shoulders and grinned into the shadowy room. A bath, a shave, and an audience with the only FitzHugh currently in residence. Yes, he was eager to see Isolde FitzHugh again, for he had much to lord over the troublesome English wench.

Isolde had heard very little, a dull thump from far away, a hushed voice on the nearby wall walk. She strained to hear better. Was it an English voice or a Welsh one? She'd not been able to tell. So she had lain there in the dark, cursing Rhys ap Owain, beseeching God's help, and bemoaning her own stupidity.

How could she have been so blind? How could she not have seen the resemblance? The same black eyes. The same arrogant manner. She should have recognized him. She should have guessed.

She should have listened to Osborn.

He had not wanted to let the minstrel band inside the castle at all. But she'd been so sure of herself, so heady with her own power. Just look where it had brought her.

In the darkened chamber she silently raged and fought her bindings. But it was a futile battle, as futile as her vain attempt to put the worst of her many errors out of her mind. She'd given her innocence to a man she hated, one she'd loathed since she was but a child. Like the green girl she was, she'd been completely taken in by him, besotted by his fine physique, his deep voice, and his intense gaze. And to think she'd been fool enough to believe he possessed the heart of a poet.

Once more she fought her bindings, chafing her already scraped wrists and ankles. Tears stung her eyes and slipped down her cheeks. Had she truly been so stupid as to think love was a part of her feelings for him? She groaned in shame. Bad enough that he'd evoked those incredible feelings from her body, traitorous creature that it was. But for a few moments she'd actually thought she loved the odious wretch!

Outside a voice sounded and she went still. Laughter. Had

Rosecliffe's guards foiled Rhys's plans? Had they captured him and cast him into the deepest hole in the donjon? She prayed it was so. She prayed desperately that it was so.

But then a voice came more clearly through the window, a jovial Welsh voice. "Ho, Dafydd. What a night, eh?"

"Aye. A good night to be Cymry. A bad night to be a FitzHugh," the man added with a coarse laugh.

Isolde's hopes died a swift, brutal death. He'd won!

She'd hardly had time to digest that awful fact when footsteps echoed in the stairwell, heavy footsteps rising nearer and nearer.

She twisted her head to see the door and shuddered when it opened, for the figure silhouetted there was tall and broad shouldered. It was him. She knew it though he did not speak.

He closed the door and moved deeper into the room. Steel struck against flint, and each time she jumped. Once. Twice. The third time a tiny spark caught the bit of charred cloth in the bowl beside the bed, and with that he lit a fresh candle.

But as light filled the chamber, as he lit two more candles and stood them in the candlestand, it was a different man who turned to face her. He'd abandoned his rough tunic for a warrior's leather hauberk, and his worn brogans for tall boots. A sword hung at his side, heavy and ominous, and a thin dagger dangled at his hip.

This was a man of war, not a minstrel. How had she not seen that before? Those thickly muscled arms came from wielding a sword, not a gittern. The wide shoulders and thick chest were built through years of battle and exercise, not through strumming and singing.

Then he raised the candles higher and she saw his face and gasped. Gone was the long wild hair and woolly beard. In their stead appeared a face she would have known. He was ten years older—and ten years harder—but he was the same Rhys ap Owain who'd kidnapped her so long ago. He was her enemy no matter how comely his features and how manly his form. That his teeth were straight and his lips well formed only drove home to her the depths of her terrible mistake. He could have the face of an angel, yet still he was the devil's spawn.

Isolde's chest hurt, her heart pounded so violently. She

should have been more wary. She should not have been so smug. She should have done as her father wanted and agreed to a marriage with Mortimer Halyard. Because of her vanity and stupidity, she'd been ruined. But far, far worse, she had opened wide the door to her family's ruin.

As if he guessed her thoughts, he grinned down at her, the awful, beautiful grin of a predator who toys with his victim, knowing full well she has no escape. He crossed to the bed, then set the brace of candles on a table near her head.

" 'Tis a great day at Rosecliffe, Isolde. The Welsh have regained what was stolen from them."

She closed her eyes against the wolfish triumph in his face, then jerked them open again when he sat beside her on the bed. "I am victorious," he continued in a huskier tone. "And you know what is said of the victor. To him go all the spoils."

TEN

SHE WAS TERRIFIED OF HIM. HER GRAY EYES WERE HUGE IN the golden light, and half-dried tears sparkled in her thick eye-lashes. As Rhys sat beside her, she stiffened and tried to roll away.

Yes, she was terrified, and he took a certain pleasure in that. But not as much as he'd expected to. When he pulled out his dagger, her eyes turned nearly black. As he raised it near to her cheek, all color fled her face.

"Rest easy, love," he murmured, pushing a damp tendril of bronze-colored hair from her cheek. "I've come to release your bindings, nothing more."

He slid the knife along the curve of her jaw, catching the tip on the cloth that gagged her. With a tiny jerk he cut it and she sucked in a great, gasping breath. But even before she'd fully caught her breath she demanded, "What have you done to my people? Have you hurt any of them? Have you killed anyone?"

"They are my people now, not yours," he answered curtly. "Better that you concern yourself with your own well-being."

Her eyes narrowed in angry disdain. "You think because you take control of Rosecliffe that the people in it will become your people?"

"They will, or they can leave this place. 'Tis a very simple solution." Annoyed by her temper, he rolled her over. He cut her wrists free and her ankles, and released the locked chain around her waist. And all the time he cursed his own perver-sity. Though he should not care how she felt, he did not like

it when she looked at him with fear. He liked it even less
when she viewed him with contempt.

Sheathing his dagger, he yanked her to her feet. "Best you
mind your manners with me, woman. I am lord of Rosecliffe
now and you merely another castle wench whom I may command as I see fit." When she tried to pull out of his grip he
tightened his hold. "Osborn wishes to see you. He doubts my
word when I say you have not been harmed."

She swallowed. He saw the smooth undulations of her
throat. "Is he all right? Is anyone hurt?"

Rhys shrugged. "A few knocked heads. Very little blood
spilled. They will all recover well enough." Then he laughed.
"Not a particularly good showing by your noble English fighting men."

"There is nothing like the betrayal of a friend to take a
person by surprise," she retorted.

He deflected her disdain with a disdain of his own. "Yes.
I know all about betrayals."

"Your specialty, I should guess."

This time his eyes narrowed in warning. " 'Tis in your best
interest to guard that sharp tongue of yours, Isolde."

She blanched at the threat he implied. But her chin went
up a notch. "Oh? Will you punish me when I but speak the
truth?"

She was brave. He would give her that. That sort of un-
thinking bravery could be dangerous, though. But she knew
nothing of the world and the dangers it held. It was time she
learned. "I may do any number of things to you. Or with you,"
he added. He pulled her up against him and, with one arm
around her waist, trapped her at his side. "Or maybe that is
what you want."

"No!" Panic filled her eyes as she strained away from him.

But that only fueled Rhys's temper. If she thought she
could deny the desire she'd felt for him only hours ago, she
was more than mistaken. He would not allow it.

"Is it the beard?" he taunted her. "Your minstrel lover had
a beard. Shall I grow it back?"

"I don't care about that. I despise you no matter how you
look. Let me go!"

"Aha, but you did not despise Reevius. Mayhap I should

play you a love song on my gittern. Then will you soften for me, Isolde? Then will you open your arms for my pleasure? And your legs?" he added, being deliberately coarse.

She flinched at his words, and he could feel her body trembling in his rigid embrace. But it was not from passion, and he was suddenly repulsed by his own behavior. He abruptly released her and she collapsed back against the bed. She found her legs quick enough, though, and scrambled to the far side of the room. Then she stood, breathing hard, watching him with a wary eye and glancing uncertainly at the door.

He was breathing hard, too, and as he stared at her, he was conscious of a fledgling arousal. She would not easily be mastered, he realized. She'd succumbed to the minstrel Reevius with surprising haste, and surprising passion. But for Rhys ap Owain, the rogue Welsh knight, she would be a challenge.

He liked nothing better than a challenge, however. Rosecliffe had fallen too easily. That must be the cause of this vague dissatisfaction he felt. But the daughter of FitzHugh . . . Mastering her would be a much greater challenge.

He thrust one hand through his hair. "Enough of this. I am lord of Rosecliffe now, and you but one of its citizens. You will obey me or suffer the consequences. Do you understand what I say?"

Her eyes narrowed with fury. "Oh, yes. I understand very well. I wonder, though, whether you understand the consequences of what you have done."

He snorted with laughter. "I understand that this chamber is now mine."

"My father will make you pay," she threatened. "He will not rest until he has bested you. He will go to his grave before he allows—"

"Then he will go to his grave." He advanced on her. "It will be my greatest pleasure to put both him and his jackal of a brother in a common, unmarked grave."

He meant every word he said, and yet, could he have taken them back, at that moment he would have. For she stared at him with such horror, with such hatred and contempt, that he felt an uncomfortable flush creep into his face. Damn the bitch for twisting his emotions around now, when he finally had what he'd worked so long to achieve.

"I always knew you were despicable," she said, so faintly he had to cock his head to hear. "And I always knew I hated you for it. I just never suspected how completely without redeeming qualities you were—and how completely I could despise another human being."

He stiffened, and before he could think better of it, caught her arm in a harsh grip. "Hate me, Isolde FitzHugh. Hate me all you want. It changes nothing. For we both know I can make you want me. I did it once," he hissed in her ear. "I can do it again."

When she looked up at him, a stricken expression on her face, he thrust her toward the door. "Unless you wish me to prove my words now, I advise you to get moving. Time to visit your countrymen in their stout Welsh prison." Then, guiding her with little shoves, he forced her to leave the lord's chamber and travel down the stairs, through the hall where English citizens would soon serve Welsh loyalists, and toward the narrower stairs to the donjon.

Once upon a time he had been a prisoner in that dank place. Now he was master of the keep. His transformation would be easy. In truth he'd already made the change, for he felt like a lord this morning, not a hunted rebel.

For the cosseted daughter of Rosecliffe, however, the transformation to villein, or even serf, would be much harder to accept. But she would accept it. He would make certain of it.

Isolde kept her teeth tightly clenched and her lips pressed together. It was either that or risk sobbing out loud, and thereby revealing the terror and panic that filled her soul. Everything had been turned upside down. Everything. In one short night her entire world had shredded apart.

But so had everyone else's. She was not the only victim of this treachery.

She passed Magda in the hall and met the girl's tear-swollen gaze. Had they hurt her? Then she remembered Magda's sweetheart, George. Was it for him she wept? Had he been felled in the attack? Or did the girl even know his fate at all?

It suddenly occurred to Isolde that she was the only FitzHugh in residence still at Rosecliffe. She was the only

FitzHugh and she had a responsibility to her people.

She took a shaky breath. What would her father do? Then she thought better of that. She must not try to think like her father, for she was no warrior. Rather, she must think more like her mother. How would Josselyn FitzHugh, née Carreg Du, handle such a disaster? She would weigh the situation and she would find some way to send for help.

Isolde squared her shoulders and vowed to do just that. She looked around, studying the hall, noting every change. Odo was not in his usual place. The old minstrel Tillo sat in Odo's corner, his head bowed as if in prayer. He did not look up at Isolde's passing. Three heavily armed men she did not know lounged near the doors. They stared boldly at her; she glared contemptuously at them, then looked away.

She would not be beaten, she vowed, as Rhys caught her elbow and directed her to the stairs that led below. He might think he had beaten her, but he had not.

"Where is Odo?" she asked as they passed the cold storage rooms. "He is not a man of war, so why is he not in his office?"

"I no longer require his services."

"Where is Newlin?"

He did not answer.

At the bottom level of the keep they halted before a heavy steel gate. Inside several men crowded the two small cells. Isolde rushed forward. At the same time Osborn rose and met her. He caught her hands and they stood together, separated by the fearsome bars her father had designed for criminals.

"How fare you, child?" Osborn spoke quietly, but his words nonetheless carried throughout the cramped, low-ceilinged chamber. "Has he hurt you, Isolde?"

His eyes were sober and intense. She knew what he meant and she swallowed hard. "Do not fear for me, for I am unharmed," she stated as firmly as she could.

"And she will remain so," Rhys interjected, "just as long as you and your men follow my orders."

Osborn shot him a narrow-eyed glare. "You have no cause to lay a hand on her then, for we can do nothing from the donjon."

Isolde rounded on her hated captor. "You cannot mean to keep them in here."

Rhys crossed his arms. "I can and I will."

" 'Tis too small for so many."

"Those wishing to leave have only to swear fealty to the new lord of Rosecliffe."

"You? Hah! You'll never be the true lord of Rosecliffe," she hissed.

"There's no one to stop me," he gloated. Then he addressed Osborn over her head. "You have seen her. She is safe and will remain so." He signaled the guard. "Take her to the hall. Seat her at the high table." To Isolde he said, "I will join you shortly."

"Wait. No!" She tried to evade the guard, but he was unyielding and he dragged her up the stairs.

In the wake of her departure, Osborn and Rhys stared at each other. The English prisoners shifted around the cells uneasily. Angrily.

"Son of a bitch—"

"Welsh bastard!"

Osborn held up a hand and their muttering ceased. His gaze never veered from Rhys's. "How long will you keep her—and us?"

Rhys grinned. He was enjoying this. "That depends on her father."

"Someone from the village is sure to send word to him at the coronation."

"I am counting on it."

Osborn's eyes narrowed. "He is in London. He will have no trouble raising a mighty army against you."

Rhys shook his head. "I fear you have been too long away from London, Osborn. In these unsteady times your noble English lords are not likely to spare their own men for someone else's cause. They have their own troubles. They know Henry D'Anjou is not Stephen of Blois, and he will be a very different sort of king. They fear he will close his fist on his restless barons and so they must be at the ready. Your liege will return with little aid from his friends. Then he will have to face me."

"What do you hope to gain from this?" Osborn demanded,

his fists taut upon the iron bars. "You cannot hope to win."

"To the contrary, so long as I hold his daughter, I cannot help but win."

That confident statement enraged several of the Englishmen, and Osborn had to raise his hand to still his furious men. He stared at Rhys as if he sought to ferret out the secrets in his head. "You cannot hold her forever."

"Who's to stop me? I am no different from your liege lord. He took lands claimed by others. And their women, too."

Osborn lunged through the bars at him, but Rhys deflected his fist with a swift, defensive move.

"Touch her and I'll kill you myself!" the old warrior vowed, his voice harsh with emotion.

"I will make you one promise only, old man. If I touch her—*when* I touch her—it will be because she wills it."

"So you say," Osborn snapped. "But I remember your father." His lips curled in disgust. "And you are his son."

Rhys's humor fled. "I too remember my father, a man who died the noblest of deaths, fighting for his country."

Osborn spat on the floor. "Your father was no hero, but rather a coward, a gutless bully who—" He broke off when Rhys whipped out his sword, and fell back, along with all the others in the cell.

"Shut up! Shut up or by God I'll slice out your tongue!" Rhys threatened, enraged by the man's gall.

The sudden silence was deafening. The Englishmen stared fearfully at Rhys and the vicious edge of his raised sword.

But Rhys knew he'd made a grave error. For in his anger he had revealed his weakness to Osborn. He had shown him the tender sore that festered in the place where his heart was supposed to be. His father had been a man without fear. No one disputed that. He had died at the hands of an Englishman. But he had also been a cruel man, cruel to his women, cruel to his son. Cruel to anyone smaller or weaker than he. Rhys remembered little of the man, but he remembered that. Still, Owain had fought the English invaders when no one else would do so, and Rhys had vowed on his father's grave to do the same.

Though he trembled now with rage, he forced himself to sheathe his sword. "Best you guard your words in the future, old man. My intentions are not to draw blood, but goad me enough, and I might forget those intentions."

Rhys quit the donjon after that, dissatisfied by the confrontation, and for the first time disheartened by the task he'd set himself.

Osborn watched him go, and though the other men in the two cells began to mutter and curse and make boastful threats against the Welshman who'd deceived and imprisoned them, Osborn kept his own counsel. He scrubbed his hands across his face and tried to think. It was not possible that the man would keep his distance from Isolde. She was too winsome—and she was a FitzHugh. He feared also that with her temper and outspoken ways, she would goad Rhys quickly to fury. "Sweet Jesus," Osborn muttered. If Rhys was even half so cruel as his sire, Isolde's future looked grim, indeed.

He had to do something. But what?

He tried to remember her face as she'd vowed she was unharmed. Had she lied? She had shown an unusual interest in the minstrel Reevius, but Osborn had assumed it due to the man's gittern. She had wanted desperately to learn how to play it. But had there been more to it than that?

But even if there had been, he consoled himself, once she learned his true identity that would have changed everything. For Isolde hated Rhys ap Owain. Neither Josselyn's nor Rhonwen's defense of him in the past had ever carried weight with her. Josselyn recalled the motherless boy he'd been. Rhonwen recalled the loyal friend he'd been to her in their youth. Rand and Jasper had seen potential in the lad, and so they'd sent him away for a proper education in England.

But Isolde had seen nothing but hatefulness in Rhys, for he'd kidnapped her when she was but a child. Ever since then she'd hated him with a passion rare in so young a person.

Osborn grasped the cold iron bars that held him in and heaved a sigh. They'd all been wrong: Josselyn and Rhonwen to see the good in the wild boy; Jasper and Rand to believe he had any potential for the future. He too was guilty for ignoring his instincts and granting the strange minstrels entrance to Rosecliffe.

But Isolde had been right. She'd been right to hate and fear Rhys ap Owain, and not to believe any good of him. She'd been right, but she was now the one who would suffer for everyone else's error in judgment.

"God help her," he prayed, his brow pressed against the iron gate. God help them all.

ELEVEN

Isolde presided over a morning meal unlike any previously served at Rosecliffe. There were no morning prayers preceding it, and no easy hum of conversation as the boiled oats, honey, and milk bread were served. At the high table she sat alone with a shifting cadre of rough Welsh men-at-arms lounging at the table nearest her. They were loud and boisterous, elated by their victory, and they ate and drank as if they'd never before had a completely filling meal.

Meanwhile, she sat there, sick at heart, unable to eat at all. Unable even to stomach the idea of food. The serving women scurried about, their shoulders hunched in fear. The cook's helpers and the several pages performed their tasks as usual, albeit silently. But the absence of the male servants was unmistakable.

Rhys was taking no chances, she realized. But where had he put them all? They hadn't been in the donjon. Were any of them wounded? The very thought made her chest hurt.

She spied Magda refilling ewers of ale and, when the girl glanced up, signaled her over. One of the soldiers leered and said something to the serving girl. He laughed uproariously when she shied away from him, but he did not prevent her passage.

Magda's hand shook as she bent to refresh Isolde's untouched ale, and Isolde glared at the oaf who'd deliberately terrified her. "Rest easy," she whispered to the distraught maid. "I have seen George and he is unhurt. But he has been imprisoned along with the other men-at-arms."

"He is not hurt? You are certain?" The girl's eyes glistened with worried tears.

"Yes. They are held in the donjon, but otherwise they look unharmed."

"Oh, thank you, miss." She pressed Isolde's hand fervently. "Thank you."

Isolde gave her a bittersweet smile. "Does your young man love you as much as you love him?" The question slipped out before she could prevent it.

"Oh, yes," Magda answered, bobbing her head. "He meant to speak to my father this Sunday coming, and then, upon Lord Rand's return, to ask his permission for us to wed."

It hurt to look into the maid's brown eyes and see how deeply she loved, and was loved in return. For a short time, fleeting but intense, Isolde had thought she might find such a love. But it had all been a lie, a huge deception.

She smiled grimly, then looked away. "I know our plight appears hopeless, but when my father learns of this, he and my uncle will come to our rescue."

"D'you think so?" Magda asked hopefully. "D'you think they can chase these thugs away?" Then fear crept back into her voice. "What of the village? What of my mother and father and all the little ones?"

Isolde clasped the maid's trembling hand, as worried as she. "I don't know but I'll try to find out. Meanwhile be very careful and try not to get caught alone with any of these—" She broke off when Rhys strode into the hall.

Spying him, Magda let out a squeak. "You be careful of that'un, miss. Be very careful." Then she scurried away, leaving Isolde to face her enemy alone.

He saw her at once. Their gazes met with an unsettling jolt—at least it was unsettling for Isolde. For him it seemed of no particular moment, for his eyes moved on, scanning the hall with a proprietary air.

The unconscionable wretch!

She bent to her food, determined to conceal her distress. But every bite tasted like congealed lard. She had to force herself to swallow.

He wended his way through the hall, shaking hands, slapping backs, and exchanging congratulations with his men.

"Good work last night, Glyn. Good work."

The other man laughed. "They didn't put up any kind of a struggle."

"They sure didn't," the man who'd accosted Magda interjected. "An' you promised us a good fight."

Rhys grinned and shrugged. "I expected a fight from them, Dafydd. But then the English have ever been a disappointment to me."

Isolde's nostrils flared with anger and the boiled oats stuck in her throat. Miserable cur. Lying snake. Unholy bastard! She shoved the food away and lurched to her feet. How dare he boast of his triumph in front of her!

He looked up when she stood, as did all his men. At once the hall went quiet, and for a long, frozen moment, their gazes clashed.

"Sit down," he ordered. "I'll be with you shortly." Then he turned his attention back to his men.

Pitch kindling tossed upon glowing coals could not have been more incendiary than were those few dismissive words. Isolde did not consider how to react, she simply reacted. She pushed her chair aside, and with her back rigid and her chin jutting forward, she left. She marched across the wide hall toward the doors, holding her skirts high enough so that her strides were long and steady. He would not let her leave, she knew that much. But he would not cow her, either, and he would have to learn that lesson now.

She reached the doors and yanked one of them open. She crossed the threshold and stomped down the steps. Then across the bailey—to where? she wondered. The gate was closed but it was not barred, so she headed in that direction.

"You cannot leave the castle grounds," a guard called down in Welsh. "No one can."

"Go to the devil," she muttered. Her heart had started to race. Was Rhys letting her escape? She was confused as she put her shoulder to the mammoth gate.

"You cannot leave," the guard repeated as he exited the gate tower stairwell and hurried over to her.

"Touch me and I'll have your hand sliced from your wrist," she spat. Where such a vile threat came from she did not know. But at that moment she meant it with every fiber of her being.

He wiped one dirty hand across his mouth. "I cannot let you go," he insisted, shaking his head.

The gate shuddered open a crack. Emboldened, Isolde shoved harder, throwing her entire weight against the thick oak. The guard grabbed it and pulled back.

"Get away! Get away from me!" she screamed like a madwoman. A few more inches and she could slip through.

"Get back to your post, Tadd. I'll handle this matter."

Isolde flinched at the sound of that hated voice. When the guard released the gate, however, she did not look at Rhys, but instead renewed her efforts to push it open.

"Perhaps I should have the same conversation with you that I had with Osborn," he said, his voice cool and controlled. Smug.

Isolde swallowed hard but kept pushing. The gate eased open. One inch. Another. The space was nearly wide enough. Then he reached over her shoulder and shoved it wider still. "I told him your safety depended on his good behavior," he said, practically in her ear.

Isolde froze. Beyond the gate the bridge was open. The road led down the rocky hill to the town square. She could see the well and the small green. The thatched roofs of the half-timbered cruckwork houses looked as they always did with the morning sun gleaming on them. Smoke puffed from twoscore chimneys. It was all reassuringly familiar, and the temptation to flee was overwhelming. But his words stopped her, for the threat they implied was unmistakable.

"Are you saying you would punish him for something I might do?"

"I would. 'Tis the nature of hostage-taking," he added. He pushed the gate all the way open. "Your choice."

"My choice?" Slowly she turned her gaze away from the village until she was staring at him, this man who had tricked her and used her and stolen her innocence. " 'Tis plain I have no choices here. You have no intention of allowing me free passage from Rosecliffe."

He waited a moment before responding. "You mistake me, Isolde. I will indeed allow you to choose, if only to satisfy my curiosity. Will you stay and suffer the same fate as your people? Or will you flee and leave Osborn and the others to bear the extra burden of your desertion?" He gestured with his hand. "Go. Go, if that is your will."

How she wanted to do just that! How desperately she wanted to flee his presence. But she did not trust him, and anyway, something in her could not abandon Osborn to any additional cruelties beyond those he already suffered.

"What will you do to him?"

He smiled. His teeth were straight and white in his shadowed face. His eyes were black as sin. "Why should you care?" His eyes slipped lower and moved over her with casual insolence, and her resolve nearly broke. She almost ran. His look was so possessive, so knowing, that she shivered with the most perverse awareness. This was the same man she'd lain with last night, the minstrel she'd been so enamored of. The man she'd sacrificed her innocence to. But he was a Welsh rebel, someone she'd always hated. Now she hated him more than she ever had before.

She turned away, away from the village and its beckoning freedom, and faced instead the castle yard. For the first time in her life it was a strange place to her, her home and yet her prison.

Drawing a steadying breath, she cast him a sidelong look. "I am no coward to abandon my responsibilities. Besides," she added in a bitter tone, "you have no intention of letting me go. I am too important a hostage, too important to this mad plan of yours."

He shrugged, and half of his mouth turned up in a smug smile. "Perhaps you are right. But now you will never know."

She did not want to hear anything further of his hateful words, so she started back to the keep. But he caught her by the arm and swung her around to face him.

"I want life in this castle to continue in its normal manner."

"Normal? 'Tis hardly normal to—"

He cut her off with a hard shake. "Everything is to proceed as it did before. The kitchen work. The gardening. The laundry and candlemaking and alehouse."

"You are mad to believe that *anything* can go on as it did before!"

"You will do as I say, Isolde. I saw how you managed this place. You did it before. You will do it again."

"Without any menservants? Who is to check the fish traps and clean the catch? Who is to chop wood and carry in water? What of the fowler? And the stablemaster?"

"You will have them again, soon enough."

"When?" She glared furiously at him.

"When they swear fealty to me."

"Hah! That will never happen." She tried to twist out of his hold but his powerful hands tightened on her arms.

"It will happen," he vowed, his voice low and menacing. "When the people see your calm acceptance of me, they too will grow calmer. One by one they will come around."

"Then it will never happen," she repeated. "For I will never accept your presence here."

He met her furious glare with a confident grin. "So you say. My experience with you tells me otherwise. It seems you can be persuaded to just about anything. Surely you have not forgotten last night."

She wanted to scratch his eyes out! She wanted to hang her head in shame. Yes, she remembered last night. If only she could forget.

Though her face had gone hot with color, she met his mocking gaze. "Last night I made a fatal error in judgment about you. Last night I believed what I saw on the surface, and was too foolish to look any deeper. But now I have discovered your true self, and I will never, *never* be persuaded to make that same mistake again."

His left hand clenched, just a little. For a moment she thought she had wounded him with her words, for something flickered in his eyes, some emotion too fleeting for her to decipher. But then he grinned, the cold half-grin of a predator, and she knew she was wrong. Her words had meant nothing to him. Less than nothing. For words did not count with men of his ilk. He was a man of war. He'd thrived on hatred his whole life; he was glutted on it now.

He released her arms, but before she could gather her wits to back away, he caught her chin between his thumb and forefinger. "Do not judge yourself too harshly, Isolde. You would like to hate me. I know that. The day will come, however, when your natural passions will overcome that hatred."

"Never!" She flinched away from his touch.

"Soon," he contradicted as she hurried back through the bailey.

Soon.

She had escaped his presence for now. But that single word haunted her as she fled. Soon.

But he was wrong about that, she vowed. Completely wrong.

Rhys watched as Isolde fled across the yard, her hair long and tangled, streaming like a pennant in her wake. He frowned as she disappeared into the keep.

He was enjoying this far too much.

To taunt a FitzHugh and take pleasure in it—on the surface there was nothing wrong with that. It was one of the rights of victory. But she roused more in him than he wanted.

He rubbed one hand across his chin, startled at first by his missing beard. To lust after the enemy's womenfolk was also a right of victory, he reminded himself. He'd taken his pleasure of many an English noblewoman in the past ten years. There was no great novelty in that. But something about this particular woman made it different from all those other times.

It was because she was a FitzHugh, he told himself. That made her different in his eyes, more contemptible.

He stared at the keep, at the doors closed and sheltering her within. This was his castle now, not hers. His fortress. He'd taken it and he would hold it fast against his enemies.

He would take her, too, if he so desired. And he would keep her so long as she roused him to lust. But she was no more than any other wench to him. Even less. The day would come when he would send her away from Rosecliffe. But only after her father and uncle lay dead by his hand.

Then he would be done with the FitzHugh family once and for all.

The day passed in an obscene blur. Isolde knew her duty. She was of the lord's family, and when their people turned to her she must be brave and confident and reassuring. So, as much as it galled her, she did as Rhys ap Owain bade her do. With that odious man Dafydd trailing her like a slovenly hound, she circulated among her people. She put them to their work, cleaning, cooking, washing. It was mostly women's work. No men came up from the village to repair leather harnesses or weave stout ropes of shredded reeds and coarse flax. No one shaved barrel staves. No one worked the bellows. But the meal was cooked, and when the bells rang sext, the midday meal was served.

She wanted to stay away from the hall during dinner, for she did not wish to sit near Rhys. But the barrel-chested guard would not cooperate.

"Get you to the hall," he ordered. "Your parsley plants will still be here after dinner is done."

"I'm not inclined to eat," she retorted, continuing down the straw-covered garden path.

"Well, I am." Dafydd caught her arm in his ham-sized fist. "Come along—"

"How dare you! Unhand me, you vile cur!"

"I'm hungry," he snapped, hustling her along despite her struggling. "Move your arse!"

He dragged her to the garden gate but not through it. For propped against the fence was a spade, and Isolde did not think twice. She snatched it up, and with a wild, desperate swing, she caught him below the knee with one edge.

"Ow!" he yelped and let her go. "Uff!" The burly brute went down like a felled tree when she slammed him on top of the head.

From a distance someone shouted—one of the guards in the gate tower, she vaguely realized. But Isolde simply stood there, gaping at the crumpled Welshman, filled with righteous anger—and then with a sickening fear. Had she killed him?

She threw down the spade and leaned over the man.

"Damnation!" Rhys bellowed from across the yard.

Isolde's head whipped up and she sucked in a sudden breath as he bolted across the bailey. Dear God, but she was in for it now!

"Damnation!" he swore again, shooting her a black look before crouching over the fallen guard. "Dafydd. Dafydd! Can you hear me?"

A low groan answered and, in spite of her fury, Isolde felt an immeasurable relief. She hated these men who'd taken

Rosecliffe, but she wasn't quite ready to kill any of them herself.

The man groaned again as he sat up, and raised a hand to the top of his head. "Ow. Oh, I'm bleedin'!" He held out a bloody hand to show Rhys, while he sent her a damning look. "She cracked my head open with a spade—an' for no good reason."

Rhys stood and looked at Isolde, too, as did the other men who had come to investigate the row. "If it is your plan to take us down, one man at a time, Isolde, heed my advice. You will succeed far better with your attacks at night than during midday when everyone can see you."

His men guffawed with laughter, all but the one she'd felled. Isolde glared at Rhys. "I will not be strong-armed by your thugs."

"Strong-armed?" Rhys's attention turned abruptly to the guard.

"I didn't do nothin'!" Dafydd protested, lurching to his feet. "It was dinnertime an' I was hungry. That's all."

A muscle ticked in Rhys's jaw. Despite her own fears, Isolde noted that subtle movement, and noticed also that his anger was focused on the unpleasant Welshman now, not her. As if he sensed the danger he suddenly was in, the guard took a step backward.

Isolde's mind spun. This was not at all the reaction she'd expected after such an act of insurrection. She was the prisoner, yet it was one of her jailers being accused by Rhys's night-dark stare.

Then those eyes turned upon her and the incident was finished. "Enough of this," he snapped. "Bandage his head then return to the hall and preside over the meal in your usual fashion." To Dafydd he said, "Go with her then get your dinner."

With one stern glance he sent the onlookers on their way. Then he too left, and Isolde and the disgruntled guard were alone in the kitchen garden once more. Isolde watched Rhys stride away, confused by what had just occurred. What was she to make of that?

The Welshman took the spade and heaved it across the garden. Despite her distrust of him, Isolde knew just how he felt.

"Come along," she muttered.

"I don't need nothin' from you." He growled the words at her. "But I owe you something' for this, an' I won't be forgettin' it."

Isolde's nostrils flared at the threat in his voice and she turned away, heading for the stillroom. She'd made an enemy of him, that was certain. But then, they were all her enemies. When the man nevertheless appeared in the stillroom a few minutes later, Isolde understood two important things.

One was that Rhys ap Owain ruled men with an iron hand. It took but one look, the raising of his brow, or a mildly stated command to make them react. The threat he made, though not overt, was nonetheless real: do as I tell you or suffer the consequences.

The second was that she must watch her back with this Dafydd. His narrow eyes watched her with an avidity that made her skin crawl. She glared back at him, but her hands shook as she assembled powdered alder bark and dried woundwort in a small crockery bowl with a small amount of oil and melted beeswax.

"Here." She thrust it at him. "Clean the wound first, then put this on it."

He gave her an ugly grin. "You do it."

"Not bloody likely," she swore. She set a bowl of water before him and a small cup of soft soap. But she had no intentions of touching the unsavory brute. After a moment he began the task himself, and when he winced at the sting, she felt an unwonted glimmer of regret.

"I'm sorry," she said, though with less sincerity than she hoped. He was a despicable example of Welsh humanity; however, she did not need his enmity.

He scowled at her.

"I said I'm sorry. Did no one ever teach you manners?"

His eyes swept over her, lingering insolently at her breasts. "You're sorry, are you? Then whyn't you make it up to me?"

Giving him a disgusted look, Isolde yanked open the door. "I hope it festers and turns putrid and that your head rots off." Then she swept from the stillroom, her head high and her jaw clenched. Inside, though, she shook with impotent rage. She hated him. She hated all of them, most especially their wretched leader!

But she could not reveal her fears, she reminded herself. She could not reveal her exhaustion, for that's what they all wanted. She must be brave and fierce. And she *must* control her emotions, for her people were depending on her.

Easy to say; infinitely harder to do. For when Isolde entered the hall, the sudden silence was deafening. Dozens of faces turned her way and watched her progress through the hall. The castle folk were bewildered and fearful. The Welsh invaders, cocky and watchful. And the most cocky was Rhys ap Owain.

She strode between the tables, ignoring him. Instead, she stopped here and there, forcing herself to behave as if it were any other midday meal. She spoke to the pantler's stand-in, a twelve-year-old lad pressed into duty, and to the woman who was performing the butler's chores. She checked the ewers and nodded to the pages to pour. The serving maids paraded their trays before her and she gave approval for each of the dishes. Slowly sounds filled the hall: low murmured voices; mugs thumping softly against the tabletops. The Welsh voices were louder, but there were more English, and eventually their voices dominated.

Only then did Isolde take her own place. Only then did she acknowledge Rhys's presence. For he stood and pulled out her chair, and she was compelled to mutter a reluctant thanks.

"You did that very well," he said, filling her goblet with wine and offering it to her.

"I hardly require your approval for behaving as my parents would expect me to behave."

"Nonetheless, I approve." He signaled a page. "Serve your mistress the best portion of the bird. A tender piece."

"I am not of a mind to eat."

The serving lad halted and glanced from Rhys to her, then back to Rhys, his eyes round with worry.

"Nonetheless you shall eat," Rhys said, serving her himself.

"Will that be your answer to every objection I make?" Isolde erupted in anger. " 'Nonetheless you shall do it.' "

Rhys waved the boy away. Then he propped his elbow casually on the arm of her father's chair and leaned nearer to her. "You can choose to oppose me, Isolde. No doubt you would like to do so at every turn. But in the end you shall obey me—from the smallest task I set you, to the greatest. You may fight me all you want, if that is your will. But know this: I will be the victor in our every confrontation." Then he speared a piece of meat with his knife and began to eat.

Isolde forgot her promise to hide her emotions. He went too far! She jerked to her feet. "You will rue this day for the rest of your very short life," she swore.

He grinned up at her. In the suddenly quiet hall his voice carried too well. "Do you think so? One thing I shall never rue . . . the night just past." He yanked her arm, forcing her once more to sit, then added in a lower voice for her ears only. "Nor will I rue the ones to come."

TWELVE

RHYS KEPT ISOLDE WITHIN HIS SIGHT THE REMAINDER OF THE day. It was a foolish decision, he suspected, but one he could not undo. Because he did not like the way Dafydd's resentful gaze followed her, he set Linus and Gandy to guard her, with strict instructions that no one was to manhandle her. Then he ordered the steward and the former captain of the guard to be brought up from the donjon. He meant to review the castle record books with the former. As for Osborn, he wanted the man to witness the smooth transition Rhys was making at Rosecliffe, from English rule to Welsh.

He watched through the open door of the castle office as the two men entered the great hall, shepherded by three guards, and he saw Isolde's glad response. She threw down the needlework in her lap and rushed to their side, and when Osborn opened his arms, she flew into them.

Rhys rubbed his knuckles against the slight bristle along his jaw and stared at the three prisoners. No one could ever accuse her of being dispassionate, nor of lacking empathy with her people. He watched her reunion with the old knight and the fidgety steward, and knew the affection they shared was real.

She was no cold English bitch, he conceded. In her volatile emotions, at least, she revealed some portion of her mother's blood. But she'd been raised as English nobility, and the men she huddled with now were English invaders in Welsh lands. The blood of dragons might run in her veins, but she'd long ago turned her back on Wales.

Could she defeat him, she would do so. It behooved him never to forget that fact.

He strolled out of the office, cognizant of the precise moment the threesome became aware of his approach. Osborn stiffened first, then the other two turned to look. Rhys had to suppress a spurt of anger when Isolde leaned back against the old knight and the man circled her shoulders protectively.

"You have had your time together," Rhys said. "Now we have business to discuss."

"What sort of business?" Isolde demanded to know.

He had originally addressed Osborn. Now he looked directly at her. "Men's business."

Her chin tipped up belligerently. "Whatsoever occurs in this castle is as much my business as anyone's."

The steward groaned. Osborn tightened his hold on her. "Be still, girl. Odo and I will deal with him."

"Yes. Be still, girl," Rhys echoed, enjoying her frustration. "You have work to do. Get you to it."

She was a study in seething fury. Her gray eyes sparked with it, her porcelain skin fairly glowed with it. Her hands knotted into fists, yet somehow she controlled her temper. Osborn murmured in her ear, and Rhys saw her grit her teeth. But when the man patted her shoulder and gave her a little shove, she went.

Rhys wanted to watch her go. He wanted to watch the natural sway of her hips and see the flicking back and forth of her long plaits as she moved. She was the epitome of femininity: small but strong; slender yet shapely; soft, yet possessed of a core of steel. But he had other matters to tend, so he cut his observations short.

Osborn too had watched her walk away. When he looked at Rhys his eyes were narrowed. "Only a coward attacks his enemy through his child—especially a girl child!"

"She's hardly a child," Rhys drawled, then smiled at the black look his words drew from the man. "But enough of that. We have business."

"Ransom?" the old warrior muttered.

"I am not in need of your English coin. I've plenty enough of that. Earned honestly," he added.

Osborn studied him a moment. "Yes. We've had word of your prowess, both in battle as well as in tournaments. You are a mercenary and come at a high price. Have you never thought to whom you owe a debt for the training you have received?"

"A debt?" Rhys laughed, though with little mirth. "Your liege sent me to Barnard Castle to separate me from my home-land. He sent me there to suffer at the hands of Englishmen because he did not have the fortitude to punish me himself. He sent me there in the hope I would not survive. That I did so—that I have prospered and grown rich—is not to his credit. I owe him no debt, nor his brother, save one. The debt of revenge. And that I will have!"

Osborn did not shrink from his bitter words, but Odo did. The three guards who accompanied the English prisoners also shifted nervously. Linus and Gandy were near Isolde, close enough that all of them heard his threat. With a slight frown on his broad face, Linus stood and crossed the hall.

"A ship is sighted," he said to Rhys, breaking the tense silence. "Glyn saw the sails."

Rhys shuddered as he beat back the rage that threatened to engulf him. "Right on time," he muttered. Then he stared at the two Englishmen. "Ransom is of no interest to me. I am casting you out of Rosecliffe, casting you out from this castle and from this country."

"What?"

"You're letting us go?" The steward spoke at last, and relief was evident in his voice.

"You and all the others not born of this land will go," Rhys said.

"But you can't just put us out," Odo began.

"I can. Those among you with Welsh wives may choose to stay, but only if you swear fealty to me. Even now the ship comes. Tomorrow you go."

To his credit Osborn considered this startling information a long moment before reacting. "Where do you send us?"

"Tintagel."

"Tintagel!" Odo exclaimed. "But that's so far!"

"Who's to go?" Osborn asked. "All of us?"

There was no reason for evasion, for Rhys knew to whom he referred. "She stays."

Odo instinctively grabbed Osborn's arm, but there was no need. For instead of erupting in fury, the old knight cocked his head. "Why do you keep her?"

Rhys crossed his arms. "Why do you think?"

Osborn studied Rhys for a moment. "I am not certain. Mayhap it is more than the obvious. Why Tintagel?" he asked, changing the subject.

"FitzHugh will not expect it. He will arrive here with few men and then find no reinforcements. I will defeat him," he vowed. "I will defeat him and his brother."

Osborn crossed his arms, mirroring Rhys's stance. "What will you do with Isolde, then?"

Rhys stared at the man. He was a cagey old fellow, wise enough to see past the surface of his own situation to the deeper implications. He was also loyal to FitzHugh and FitzHugh's children. Rhys shrugged. "She is partly Welsh. If she can throw off her English upbringing, mayhap I will wed her to some good Welsh fellow. One who will beat the pride out of her," he added, trying to provoke Osborn.

But even that did not rouse the man's temper. Osborn studied him thoughtfully, then heaved a great sigh and scanned the hall with his faded eyes. "You have taken charge of a good fortress, a good home." Then those eyes fastened on Rhys's once more, sharp and fierce again. "Learn something from this. Learn that it is better to build up than to tear down."

Rhys laughed. "So you concede to me. You give up, and without any show of opposition." He paused. "I expected better from you."

Instead of anger at his taunt, however, Osborn reacted with a long look, as if taking Rhys's measure. "Enjoy your victory, son. While it lasts." Then he turned on his heel and headed back to the donjon.

Rhys stared at him, reluctantly impressed. The aging knight bore himself well, even if he was wrong. He gestured for the guards to follow Osborn. To Odo he said, "Go to the office. I would review your books." But as the steward scurried to do his bidding, Rhys's eyes followed Osborn.

He knew something. He must. Otherwise he could not be so complacent. But what could it be? And why was he not more concerned about Isolde?

Rhys looked around and spied her pacing before the hearth, casting damning looks in his direction. Above her a wolf tapestry hung, the immense beast surrounded by roses. That would be the first thing to go. He started abruptly toward her and she ceased her pacing. Linus sat on a stool, calmly watching with Gandy beside him. But for once Gandy kept quiet. When Rhys drew near, however, Isolde snatched up a poker from the hearth and held it before her like a weapon.

"What kind of man sends people away from their homes!" she cried in agitation.

"What kind of man steals other people's homes?" he countered.

"If you allude to my father, he stole from no one! He has built a new village that welcomes everyone, and a fortress that protects Welsh and English alike."

"We did not need any of it!" He ripped the poker from her hands and flung it across the hall. Startled, a hound scrambled up from its nap and began to bark. A cat leaped onto one of the trestle tables, its back arched, its tail thick with fright.

Isolde felt like the cat did when Rhys stopped not an arm's length from her. Terrified. Furious. She was prepared to fight him, but she really wanted to flee.

"That hanging." He pointed above her head. "Rip it down. Burn it. Then make me another with a dragon on it. That's the emblem of Wales," he added caustically. "In case no one has ever told you."

"I know as much of Wales as you do," she swore, forgetting to be cautious. "Probably more."

"Probably more." He laughed. "If you are so well versed in the history and lore of our noble land as you say, then I can trust you to do a creditable job of it."

"A tapestry takes a long while to create. You will be gone from here before I am barely begun," she taunted.

"Paint the dragon, then. And while you are at it, paint another in the master's chamber. Above the bed."

The sharp reply she intended died at the mention of the

master's chamber and the bed. It didn't help matters that his eyes burned with hot knowledge of what had occurred in that very bed. Had it only been last night?

"In the master's chamber," he continued. "I would have you paint a dragon besting a wolf."

"You will never best my father," she vowed.

He grinned. " 'Tis not your father that painting will serve to remind me of."

Color flooded her face and her cheeks stung with it. Her chest hurt, her heart pounded so fiercely. "I . . . I will paint no such thing," she stammered.

"Ah, but you will, Isolde." He advanced on her, still grinning triumphantly, and she fell back. "The dragon above; the wolf prostrate below it."

"Does the dragon breathe fire?" Gandy piped up.

In utter relief Isolde turned to him. Anything to avoid Rhys's devouring gaze. "That's just a legend."

"Dragons are just legend," Rhys said.

"But the ship, that is real," Linus reminded them.

Isolde could have kissed the gentle-mannered giant. And Gandy, too. In their own way they seemed set on distracting Rhys.

Rhys just glared at his two friends. " 'Tis tiring enough when Tillo acts the part of my conscience," he said, a warning tone in his voice. "I have no need for either of you to assume that role."

Chastened, they fell silent. But they did not depart, and Isolde took what comfort she could from that. To be alone with Rhys was her greatest fear. Yet it seemed he meant to isolate her if this ship did indeed come to take the English residents away.

She girded herself for further battle with him. "That you have any conscience at all comes as a complete surprise to me," she stated. "If you seek to rid yourself of those who oppose you, I should be the first to board that ship."

"You had your chance to leave this morning. Remember?" He touched her chin with one finger.

She jerked away. "I stayed to ensure Osborn's safety. Had I known you already planned to send him away—"

"You are staying."

"Why?" she cried.

He caught her by the arms and leaned down so that his face was level with hers. "Because I want you to."

"But why?" The question was out before she could prevent it. Then, "No." She shook her head, not wanting him to answer.

He straightened and she felt his hands tighten. He pulled her closer, just an imperceptible distance. But the danger level increased tenfold. "Paint the wall in my chamber, Isolde. Begin now," he ordered. Then he let her go and gestured toward the stair. "Fetch your paints and brushes, and go."

She went.

She didn't do it to obey him, she told herself, but rather to escape. Once hidden by the curve of the stairwell, though, she stopped and chided herself for such a foolish reaction. She pressed back against the solid stone wall, breathing hard. It was hopeless! She could never escape him. Not now. He meant to send everyone who was dear to her away, and while part of her rejoiced for their safety, another part of her feared for herself. What would she do now?

What would he do to her?

A little sob caught in her throat, but she beat it back.

She could not afford the luxury of weeping, she berated herself. She must remain in control of herself, for there was nothing else here she could control.

Except the painting.

She pushed away from the wall and forced herself to consider the possibilities. She looked up the stairs, then down. No matter which direction she chose, she was trapped. Likewise she was his prisoner whether she opposed him or did as he bade her.

She pressed the heels of her hands against her temples and tried to think. While the urge to contradict him at every turn was enormous, perhaps it was not the wisest choice. He thrived on conflict. He enjoyed bending her to his will. Only by meekly acquiescing to his demands could she rob him of that pleasure.

But there were some things she would not agree to, some things she would never agree to do again.

She turned and began to climb the stairs. She retrieved her box of charcoal from her bedchamber, then climbed further, up to the third level where she'd spent the last night lying half-naked in his arms. She trembled as she entered the room and saw the rumpled bed linens.

"Oh, God," she moaned, as erotic memories washed over her. She'd been falling in love with Rccvius, both her mind and her body. But although she now knew he was not the man she'd thought, her body seemed unable to understand. Some wickcd part of her trembled with remembered passion every time she thought of last night.

She clenched the ashwood box against her chest and stared wildly around the room. She could not do this. She could not paint the images he wanted on the walls of this room.

Flinging down the box, she shoved the door open and fled the chamber with its oppressive atmosphere of lust and sin. She needed to confess what she'd done, she realized. She needed desperately to confer with Father Clemson. But she could not risk running into Rhys again.

With no other choices left to her, she trudged up the last narrow run of stairs to the tower room. The fur pelt she'd dragged up just yesterday still lay as she'd arranged it. The pillows were there, and the two candles, though they'd burned down to nubs.

What a fool she'd been. What a reckless child. She'd played at love and seduction without the least inkling of the serious ramifications that must follow. How much wiser she'd become in less than one arc of the sun across the heavens. How much older she felt.

Miserable and angry, she pushed open the one door in the little room and burst out into the fresh air, then slammed the door closed. If only she could bar it against everyone. She took a deep breath, then closed her eyes. If only she could go back to yesterday.

But she couldn't. A gull cried and wheeled across the sky, and she opened her eyes. She could only go forward and make the best of her future. She knew that in her mind; now she must accept it in her heart. So she knelt and bent her head in prayer and vowed to be brave during the ordeal to come, to be stronger than her adversary.

Strong enough to endure whatever he did to her.

Strong enough to resist him.

THIRTEEN

RHYS DRUMMED HIS FINGERS ON THE TABLE. HE DID NOT like what he saw. The books the steward showed him were clear and up-to-date, carefully inscribed with a neat hand. Rosecliffe Castle appeared to be well run, providing adequate foodstuffs for both castle and village folk. The workers were paid every quarter day, the same rate for Welsh and English alike, and comparable to wages paid in England. It seemed also that the labor days FitzHugh required of his vassals were fewer than what was the norm in other places Rhys had traveled.

Annoyed, Rhys flipped the painstakingly lettered page back to stare at the figures for the previous year. The steward, Odo, shifted uneasily from one foot to the other.

Rhys stabbed his finger at an odd symbol in the ledger. "What are these expenses?"

"New hives for the bees. Ten of them."

Rhys scowled as his eyes skimmed down the page. "And another ten here? Is this not a steep price to pay for beehives?"

"They're special hives. Lord Rand pays some of the old men of Carreg Du to make them—" He broke off at Rhys's sharp look.

"Old men?"

"Yes." Odo cleared his throat. "The ones too old to work in the fields or do heavy labor. They make hives and twist rope. Sometimes they repair leather harness. It's a way for them to make a living, you see, despite their infirmities."

Rhys frowned, understanding now about Glyn's caution

that the elders at Carreg Du were not likely to support insurrection against Rosecliffe. Rhys had laughed it off to cowardice and had not worried. Old men would be little help in a battle anyway. In truth, they would be a hindrance.

That had not changed; except he saw now that it was not cowardice holding them back. It was complacency.

Did they truly think that he, a Welsh loyalist, would not take better note of their needs than did an Englishman? Gaining possession of Rosecliffe Castle was not just an act of personal vengeance. He did this for his Welsh countrymen. His people.

His fingers drummed in agitation. Once he purged the place of Englishmen, everything would be better than it was now. Even the old men of Carreg Du would eventually see the improvements. Then they would celebrate the return of Welsh rule—and the return of Rhys ap Owain—to the lands of northern Wales.

He focused back on the ledger. "What is this?" He jabbed at a series of listings.

"That?" Odo bent forward and squinted to see. "Oh, that is the new births."

"He charges a tax on new births?"

"This is an expenditures column, my lord, not collections," Odo explained. "He makes a christening gift for each babe born at Rosecliffe or Carreg Du."

Rhys snorted. "I've never heard of such a thing."

" 'Twas milady Josselyn's idea—"

Rhys cut him off with an impatient gesture. "What is this?"

And so it went. Good management, fair treatment, and a tidy profit that went to improving both the castle and village. Rhys had not wanted FitzHugh to be a good lord to his people, but the facts were clear, both in the ledgers as well as everywhere Rhys looked.

Still, that excused nothing.

He slammed the book closed and Odo jumped. "Bring the strongbox," he ordered.

" 'Tis . . .'Tis there." The man pointed to a squat cupboard.

"Open it."

"I . . . I cannot."

"You cannot?" Rhys lowered his brow in a menacing manner.

"It requires two keys!" the fearful steward yelped.

"Then get them."

"I have only the one."

Rhys was beginning to tire of this. "Then get the second one. Who has it?"

The man swallowed hard. "Lady Isolde."

Rhys found her on the topmost floor of the keep, but only after rampaging through her chambers, her parents' chamber—now his—and then the rest of the hall. She was on her knees when he stormed through the tower room and yanked open the door. On her knees, but not praying. She did not so much as flinch when he burst out onto the parapetted overlook.

He exploded with anger. "Your orders were to paint a dragon, not to daydream!" He knew there was no need for such venom in his tone, but an unreasoning panic had taken hold of him when he had not immediately found her. So he shouted at her and felt the quick return of his sanity. "It might have been your way to waste time when you were mistress of this castle," he went on more coolly. "But you are no better than any household drudge now, merely a commoner. A wench like any other, and subject to the orders of your liege lord." He stifled the urge to add, "Look at me!"

Slowly she turned her head. Her eyes were an icy gray, her expression filled with contempt. "I am considering how best to carry out your orders, *my lord*. It takes time to create a design. Thinking time. Unless, of course, you do not care how your dragon looks."

He chose not to reply to that and instead extended his hand. "Give me the key to the strongbox."

"Ah. The strongbox." She rose to her feet. "I should have known you would eventually come round to that." She lifted the circle of keys that dangled from the end of her girdle. "Here. Take them all. That way you need not confine yourself only to gold, but can also plunder the rest of Rosecliffe's stores."

He took the keys she thrust at him and tied them to his own girdle. "You misunderstand my purpose," he answered, raking her slender form with his eyes. "Plunder has never been my aim. The people of these hills are my people. I would never do them harm. I have taken charge of Rosecliffe as my home. I plan to make it a Welsh stronghold and to hold it for Wales."

She made a rude noise. "To hold it for yourself, more like."

"No more so than did your father."

She shook her head. "You have no inkling of what life at Rosecliffe is like. You hate my family and so you justify ruining everyone's lives. But it is a misguided revenge you seek. You cloak it as justice for your Welsh countrymen, but it is not they who are filled with hate for us, only you. 'Tis not justice you seek here, but revenge."

Rhys withstood her contemptuous words stoically. She had no weapons but sharp words and they were harmless enough. But something in him wanted her to take them back.

"Time will prove you wrong, Isolde. Soon enough you will see the truth."

She turned away from him and stared back out at the horizon. Only then did he notice what she had been watching. The ship drew inexorably closer. Soon it would set anchor and take on its human cargo. She was afraid, he realized, afraid for those who must leave, and afraid also of being left behind. For him, however, the departure of the English could not come soon enough.

He strolled the perimeter of the tower, circling the small tower room that stood in the center of the overlook. The crennels were not as high and deep here, for this was more an observation post than the position for men at war. The walls fell away, straight down to the bailey fifty feet below. She would find no escape here.

His eyes swept the horizon, noting the mountains to the west, and the open sea north and east. Yes, the tower room was well suited to her. Close to him. Private. That privacy was why she'd prepared a place for them here last night. He'd little noticed that nest when he'd stormed through searching for her. Now, though, despite her disdain for him, the very thought of her making such preparations heated his blood.

He made the full circuit of the overlook and found her as she had been before, staring out at the ship. The wind blew in from the sea, cold erratic gusts. Winter would soon grip the land, making it harder still for FitzHugh to mount any sort of attack.

But the threat of the FitzHughs faded in Rhys's mind as he studied his enemy's daughter. Her hair streamed behind her, a rich, windblown tangle, as she faced down the wind. Her blue gown and soft gray mantle molded against her, revealing her feminine curves. She was like a beautiful wild bird that might at any moment spring out and fly away from him. He shuddered and something in his gut tightened.

He wanted her.

He wanted her, and he would have her. What worse blow to Randulf FitzHugh than that? What better reward for himself?

He caught the flailing end of one of her waist-length locks and rubbed the silky strand between his finger and thumb. She stiffened and quickly swept her hand across the back of her neck when she sensed his touch, gathering her loose hair in her fist. Then she took one step to the side, away from him.

He followed. A part of him knew he should not torment her so. He was not a man roused by an unwilling woman. He'd never needed to be. But something about this particular woman drove him in directions he'd never before gone.

"You will be confined to the tower room," he said. *Look at me.*

Her jaw jutted forward but she did not turn toward him. "Better here than other places," she retorted. "If my people are to be sent away, I'd rather bear my imprisonment in solitude."

"These upper floors will be forbidden to all but you and me," he continued.

That drew her gaze from the ever-approaching ship. She whipped her head around and glared at him, furious and yet also afraid. "I will fight you at every turn," she vowed.

He smiled at that. "My life has been but a series of battles, Isolde. First I fought merely to survive; later to prosper. Now I fight to dominate my enemies. So fight me, sweetling. Use your feminine wiles, all the weapons a woman employs." He cupped her face with one hand. "Mayhap you will kill me with pleasure, mine and your own."

She jerked away, but he saw her eyes darken and he went on. "Yes. Your pleasure, Isolde. You found it last night in my arms. Why do you pretend now to be repulsed?"

" 'Tis no pretense," she snapped. "I *am* repulsed."

"No," he countered. "You are not. You believe you should be, but given the opportunity, you could easily quiver beneath my hand again. Shall I show you?"

Isolde let out a squeak—it could only be described as thus—and scuttled back from her hated captor. Why was he doing this? Was his victory not already assured? He'd deceived her—ruined her—and stolen her family home. What more did he want?

And how could she prevent him taking it?

She crossed her arms over her chest and tried to calm her racing pulse. "You have already shown me more than I wish to know of my frailties. That I have committed a grievous sin with you is something I acknowledge. That I took . . ." She faltered. "That I took pleasure from it is a . . . a shame I will carry forever."

"Ah, yes. The shame of it." He grinned, a confident grin, wholly masculine and perversely attractive, and the quiver he'd spoken of sprang to life inside her. He went on. " 'Tis a hard thing to desire most what you know you should despise. Isn't it, Isolde?"

She swallowed the lump of guilt in her throat. "Is that how you feel?" she flung back at him. "You want what you know you should hate?"

"Yes."

The power of that simple response made her gasp. He held her gaze captive and in his eyes she saw the truth in his words. He wanted her, even though he despised her. He desired her body even as he hated the blood that ran in her veins. The English blood.

"How can you?" she whispered, hardly aware she'd said the words. "How?"

To her surprise, the taunting expression fled his face. When he spoke his voice was bitter. "When I hunger, I eat. As do you. And if I am starving, I will eat whatever I must in order to survive. You have never been hungry, so you have yet to learn that lesson. A man's need to find physical release with a woman is no different from his need for food. He will take what he can get." He laughed, a cold, mirthless sound. "I suspect women are much the same. You sated my appetite last night, Isolde. Very well. But I will be hungry again, and so will you. So I will keep you close, here in this tower room. You will sleep above me; I will lie below you, just a few steps away."

Horrified by his crude assessment of what they'd done, Isolde backed away until she came up against the stone wall of the tower room. "If any wench will sate your vulgar appetites, then you'd best find yourself another. For I will never come down those stairs to you. Never!"

"You know your task," he said, ignoring her impassioned words. "Paint the dragon with the wolf prostrate beneath it. You will have the freedom of the tower room and my chamber. Do not try to descend further, for a guard will be posted on the stair."

She wanted to fly at him and hurt him, to claw his face and inflict upon him the same sort of pain he was inflicting upon her. But he would welcome just such an attack, she feared. He would easily overpower her and she could not allow that to happen. So she threw at him the only weapon she had, bitter words and her utter disdain.

"You send away everyone I hold dear. What reason have I to seek the company of the hall? I would rather my own lonely company to that of you and your ilk. I will stay in my tower prison and paint your puny dragon, and I will wait for my father's return. Then we will see who will dominate, dragon or wolf. Then we will see!"

She whirled and yanked the door open. But he slammed it shut, tearing it from her hand so fast her palm stung. Then he jerked her around and thrust her ruthlessly against the rough door.

"We will see, Isolde. *You* will see."

"I hate you!"

"But is that all you feel for me?" He leaned nearer. Already her heart thundered, but panic added now to its plight. His face lowered to hers, but she twisted her face away to avoid it. Then his hard thighs bumped hers; his hips pressed against her hips, and his chest brushed her breasts. "Tell me true, Isolde." His voice was a hot, hoarse murmur in her ear. "What do you feel now?"

"I hate you," she insisted, but breathlessly. "You are as awful and black-hearted as you have always been."

"But I am wiser than I was all those years ago." He paused a long moment before adding, "And you are no longer a child."

Then his weight came fully against her and his lips moved in her hair, and Isolde knew she was in fearful circumstances, indeed. For it was not repulsion she felt when his strong male body molded against hers. Something in her—some base part of her that she utterly despised—responded as if he were still Reevius. Her body recalled the pleasures a young and earnest musician had taught her, and blotted out her mind's protestations that he was an impostor, that he was, in truth, her most hated enemy. He'd left some mark on her last night, and now she was vulnerable and weak.

Oh, so weak!

She tried to avoid his mouth but she could not. He kissed her neck, nuzzled her ear, and when she bowed her head against his chest in defeat, he kissed the crown of her head.

"Mayhap I will keep you here forever," he murmured. "Away from the light. Away from the company of others. If I bring you your every need, food, water, your comforts— your only company, your only pleasure—will you confess then to the passions you feel for me? Tell me, Isolde. Will you admit it then?"

A sob caught in Isolde's throat. It would take far less than that to make her admit it, she feared. She was very near to confessing it now.

"No!" She thrust him away, and with a muffled curse he let her go. She rushed to the parapet and gripped it, leaning out as far as she could, anything to put some distance between them. "Go away," she sobbed. "Go away!"

"Isolde—"

"Go!" She was nearly hysterical.

He let loose a foul curse. But after a long moment the door creaked open, Then it closed with a dull thud and he was gone.

Only then did Isolde's hysteria burst forth. Unable to restrain her tears, she slumped against the parapet, then slid down against it and succumbed to her rampaging emotions. How could she have responded to him that way? How could she!

In the courtyard below, standing near the laundry fire, Tillo stared up at the tower overlook. He saw Isolde's bowed head and sensed the heartache she suffered. It had ever been thus for women, the old minstrel bemoaned. Men took what they wanted while women adjusted their disrupted lives accordingly. But Tillo had thought Rhys a better man than that. Until now.

By nightfall the ship had struck anchor. By dawn the exodus had begun. The narrow beach below the castle bustled with activity. Two boats ferried passengers and supplies back and forth to the ship anchored in the little bay.

Isolde could not see everything that occurred. But she saw the parade of men who made their way to the postern gate. She saw their weeping wives and anxious children following behind, along with their bundles of belongings and kegs of supplies. Then they all disappeared down the steep cliff path.

She saw them again once the boats struck out from the beach. She watched until they reached the ship and boarded, and were lost completely from view. Then she watched the boats return for the next load. How many were leaving? She was afraid to know.

At least they were allowed to carry their possessions with them, she consoled herself. They had their lives and their families and their goods. She supposed he could have killed the men. There was at least that to be thankful for.

But he sent so many away. Odo went, along with all the knights and men-at-arms, including Osborn. She bit her lip to stifle her tears when her father's closest friend looked up, searching for her. He raised a hand in a farewell salute when he spied her peering down from the overlook, and she raised her hand in return. Then he was gone.

All of the Englishwomen left, and a few Welsh ones who'd married Englishmen. Magda was among them, and that depressed Isolde further. Magda would follow her sweetheart and marry him. They would build a life together, whether in Wales or England would not matter to them, so long as they had one another.

But what sort of life was *she* now to have?

Father Clemson was the last to go, stomping angrily across the yard. "Say a prayer for me," she whispered to his black-robed figure in the boat as minutes later it bobbed across the dark, choppy sea. She watched the last boat unload, then return for shore as the ship pulled anchor and its sails unfurled. Then it began its slow crawl across the horizon, heading west, and she watched until it was gone.

Only then did she turn away and contemplate the terrible fate she'd been given. Imprisoned in her own home with no allies left to turn to. She was completely surrounded by enemies and subject to the whim of the devil himself.

She swallowed hard to think of Rhys. Their confrontation yesterday had been bitter, indeed, a bitter realization of how weak-willed and perverse she truly was. Thank God he'd not come back last night, for she was not certain what she might have done. Instead he'd left her alone to worry and fret and toss restlessly the whole night long. Food had been left with a knock at her door. There was no lock to prevent her leaving and no guard visible. But the threat of confronting Rhys had kept her hiding in the tower room like the pitiful creature she was.

She could not stay here forever, though, if only because she would go mad. Her art supplies were in her bedchamber. She had neither pen nor parchment, nor books nor lute to entertain herself. It was but mid-afternoon of the second day of Rhys's takeover and she'd had nothing to do but rage and weep and plot one revenge after another. But she could accomplish nothing from her tower prison.

Perhaps it was time for her to test the limitations of her prison and see just what liberties he meant to grant her.

The stairwell was empty. Likewise, no one occupied her parents' chamber, though she saw every evidence that he had made it his own. A maroon tunic hung from a wall hook. A soiled chainse had been flung over a stool. A half-filled ewer of water and soiled toweling indicated that he'd bathed himself. The rumpled bed showed where he'd slept.

And where they'd lain together.

A fit of trembling seized her, and she nearly fled. But that would gain her naught. So she retrieved her charcoal and brushes and paints from her own chamber and stowed them on the stairs. Then she took a deep breath, smoothed her rumpled skirts, and began her descent to the hall. She spied a guard on the steps just below the second level. He slouched against the wall and she guessed he was asleep. Carefully she stepped past him. On impulse she prodded his knee with her foot. He jerked awake, but she leaped out of his reach.

"Hey!" he cried. "Come back here."

But Isolde flew down the last stretch of stairs triumphant, with him in belated pursuit. And when she entered the hall, she kept going.

Three maidservants labored there, all Welsh women from the village, and familiar to her. Two men she did not know lounged at a table, and a boy played with a dog. No, it was the dwarf, Gandy, with his little spotted dog. The tiny fellow jumped up, smiling when he spied her. But she gave him a haughty glare. Deceitful wretch!

"Good day, Lady Isolde." He made his grand, trademark bow.

"Here, you!" the guard said at the same time. He grabbed her arm. "You're to stay abovestairs."

"Remove your hands from me at once!" she cried, trying to jerk free of his hold.

"Best that you do not touch her again," the dwarf warned. "She belongs to Rhys and everyone knows he's possessive of her. Can't abide another man laying a hand upon her."

"But I have me orders—"

"I don't need your interference," Isolde told the tiny minstrel.

Gandy spread his arms. "I'm only trying to help both of you."

Ignoring him and the now hesitant guard, Isolde poured herself a cup of ale and tore a piece of bread from a trencher not used during the midday meal. She'd not been hungry and had disdained the food sent up to her. Now, though, she was ravenous—and angry. This was her home and she would not relinquish it without a fight, no matter how great the odds against her.

She looked around. The people in the hall were all watching her. Soon enough Rhys would be summoned. Until then, however, she must make the most of this opportunity.

"Who is managing the kitchens?" she demanded to know.

One of the maidservants, Bettina, stepped forward. "Gerta, Miss."

"And who has charge of the keys to the spice room, the wine stores, and the stillroom?"

"That would be me," Gandy answered.

"You?" She stared down her nose at the odd little fellow and bit off another piece of bread. "What know you of wines and spices and medicines?"

"I worked in the kitchens at Barnard Castle for many a year."

Barnard Castle. Isolde's eyes narrowed. Barnard Castle was where her father had sent Rhys to foster all those years ago. It was all beginning to make sense. "You've known him a long time, then."

He smiled. "Long enough to know that he is a man of his word. He'll have his head—" he indicated the guard—"should you escape."

"Escape? I hardly call this escape."

"C'mon, miss. You must go back," the guard implored, flapping his hands encouragingly, but careful not to touch her.

"No." She quaffed her ale then bent nearer the fire. "You're nearly out of wood, Bettina. Send a boy to fetch more."

"Yes, miss."

"And the rushes need replenishing." She eyed the dog, Cidu, as he scratched his head. "Be sure to sprinkle the crushed leaves of black alder among them to discourage vermin."

"How kind you are to see to our comfort," Gandy remarked.

Isolde made a rude sound. "Your comfort means nothing to me. Less than nothing. I seek only to maintain Rosecliffe as it is always maintained, so that when my father drives all of you out, our lives will not have been excessively disrupted."

"What a good daughter you are."

Isolde whirled around at that deep, sardonic remark. "Yes, I am," she said, as confidently as she could manage in the face of Rhys's sudden, overwhelming presence.

"Then you will understand my actions here, for I behave only as any good son would do."

As if from an unspoken command, the several onlookers melted away, leaving Isolde alone with him. It was precisely what she should have expected of them, but still a quiver of fearfulness marked its way down her spine.

"You are not yet granted the freedom of the hall," he stated.

"Why?"

" 'Tis a privilege you must earn."

She crossed her arms. "Earn how?"

He gave her a considering look. "Any number of ways."

That drew a hot response from her. "If you think—"

"Have you begun the dragon mural on the wall in my chamber?" He cut her off. "I did not see any evidence you had started sketching on the wall last night."

She did not answer but stared at him with scathing eyes.

"I see." Without warning he wrapped his hand around one of her arms and started for the stairs, dragging her along. "When that task is done to my satisfaction," he bit out, "then I will consider letting you leave the tower. Until then you are forbidden to descend below my chamber. Do you understand me, Isolde?" he finished with a little shake. Then he released her with a shove up the stairs.

"What do you think to gain from this!" she shouted as he spun on his heel to depart.

He paused and faced her once more and she was suddenly struck by the fact that he was dressed in much finer garb than she had previously seen him wear. A closely woven kersey tunic of Welsh green, trimmed with braid around the neckline and sleeves, and amber-colored braies of a fine, soft wool. His boots were tall, the leather burnished with oil, and he wore no weapon save a short dagger at his hip. Were it not for the fierce light in his eyes, no one would take him for other than a prosperous gentleman, a noble English lord at ease in his own abode.

But the light in his dark eyes was fierce, and it revealed his true nature. "What do I think to gain? Complete victory," he stated, speaking in his native Welsh now. "Complete domination. And in your case, complete submission."

FOURTEEN

ISOLDE WORKED WITH A SPEED AND INTENSITY FUELED BY all consuming rage. He expected complete victory? She would show him. He thought he could dominate the FitzHughs? He was a fool!

He meant to make her submit?

Her hand trembled and the charcoal veered wrong on the rough plaster wall. "By the saints!" she muttered, then was appalled at how easily the curse slipped from her tongue. It was all his fault!

A soapy cloth corrected the charcoal error and she quickly completed the dragon's arched tail with its march of jagged scales. But her anger did not abate. He thought she would submit, and it might appear to some that she was doing so. But she had her reasons for painting the mural he demanded. The ultimate defeat of her enemy, she reminded herself, far outweighed any urge she felt to defy him at every turn. She must force herself to make her decisions based on logic, and not be sucked into an emotional reaction to him.

She had reasoned out that it would take at least a week for her father to hear the dire news of Rosecliffe's fall, and another for him to return home. That meant she had at least a fortnight to suffer like this. It also meant she had a fortnight to learn Rhys's plans and to determine his weaknesses. A fortnight, less two days.

Surely she could bear to demean herself for such a short period of time.

So she drew the dragon with its fierce claws and vicious

fangs. And she sketched the wolf, prostrate beneath it, though not yet defeated. Soon enough the tables would turn, she reassured herself as she worked. Soon enough. Then she would wash down the thin water-based pigments she meant to use on this temporary mural. She would paint a new image over it using more binding paints, and in that scene the dragon would succumb to the wolf. The dragon's blood would drench the lower portion of the painting with bold streaks of red, she decided. Its foul spirit would drift across the top of the scene in a faint haze of blood-gray smoke.

She stepped back from the wall, viewing this hated sketch, but in her mind's eye seeing the final version. It would be her best piece yet.

Her mother would not like it, though.

Isolde frowned. Her Welsh mother would never countenance such an insult to her homeland. How often had the Lady Josselyn preached that the strengths of both Wales and England came together in her children? She believed the union of the two cultures would build an even better tradition, banishing Welsh divisiveness and English aggression, and creating a strong, contented people—and thereby a strong, contented land.

Unfortunately her mother had not counted on Rhys ap Owain's return or on his deviousness. Or his cruelty.

Isolde continued at her unhappy labors until she heard footsteps on the stair. At once she rushed from the chamber, leaving the charcoal and rags strewn about the place. She had no intention of becoming trapped in that chamber should her hated captor decide to press the issue of her submission to him.

But it was only Gandy she found in the antechamber, and she pressed a hand to the pulse racing in her chest.

"What do you want?" she snapped.

He spread his arms wide in an innocent gesture. "Ah, kind mistress, I am in need of your assistance. That woman in the kitchen is sorely testing my patience with her endless tears. I thought you might be inclined to come and calm her."

Isolde eye him warily. "Gerta is a hard worker and exceedingly competent. But she is a timid soul. No doubt she is terrified by the horrid goings-on of the past two days."

He made a face. "She burned the bread and salted the fish stew twice."

"Oh, dear," Isolde replied, pressing her palms to her cheek in mock horror. Then with a sniff she brushed past him and returned to her mural.

"You gloat," Gandy said, following her. "But 'tis your meal she ruins as well as his."

"I don't care."

"But you said you meant to maintain Rosecliffe as it always was. Please, Lady Isolde. Just a short visit to reassure poor Gerta. You owe your people that much."

"I am forbidden to leave the upper floors of the keep."

"Linus and I will accompany you. It will be all right."

"What of your master? What of Rhys?"

He smiled and gave her a sly look. "He has ridden down to the village. And besides, in Wales no man is master of another. I am not bound to him save by my own choice."

Though she did not believe anything the little man said, in the end, the chance to go against Rhys's orders was simply too hard to resist. When they arrived in the kitchens, everything was in complete disarray and the sudden appearance of the giant and the dwarf sent another wave of panic through the overheated chamber. Gerta flung her apron over her head and huddled in a corner, her face hidden. Only when Isolde spoke did the woman peep up through her fingers.

"Do not worry," Isolde reassured her. "Come, Gerta, there is no reason to fear."

"Oh, miss, you are safe!" the older woman cried, enveloping Isolde in a fierce hug.

"I am safe and so are you. Come now, let us put this kitchen to rights."

She spied Gandy grinning at the success of his plan, and Linus grinning simply because he was happy. None of this seemed quite real, and yet Isolde knew it was. Though it galled her to fall in with their plans, if she were to find any order in the world, it seemed she would have to create it herself.

She surveyed the kitchen, her fists planted on her hips. "Linus. Fill the wood bin with enough fuel for tonight and tomorrow. Gandy, round up at least three lads to fetch and serve the meal. And do not balk at my orders," she said, anticipating the dwarf's opposition. "This was your idea, so you will now do as I say."

When Rhys rode into the bailey just before sundown, he was met with a strange sort of calm. The gatehouse was guarded by his men. In the yard a few chickens scratched. Three half-grown pups romped, and outside the stable two lads groomed a horse.

He dismounted and tossed the reins of his destrier to one of the boys, and though there was a wariness in the lad's eyes, he was quick to do his duty.

All in all, the peaceful sort of homecoming any lord might expect at the end of a long day in the saddle. Then he sniffed. Apples. Stewed or baked or whatever, they smelled wonderful. He sniffed again and his mouth watered. "Smells like a good supper for us tonight," he said, grinning at the two boys.

"Yes, sir."

"Yes, milord."

They bobbed their heads respectfully, but one of them smiled slightly, and Rhys felt a wave of relief as he crossed to the hall. There was no visible sign of the recent turmoil. The evening fell soft and lavender over the mighty stone walls. The night cry of a hunting falcon echoed over the castle as easily as it might over forest and fields. He'd taken Rosecliffe Castle, he exulted as he pushed open the door and entered the hall. He'd taken the English stronghold and driven his enemies out, just as he'd always planned.

But his satisfaction dimmed as he progressed into the hall. Something was not right.

His gaze swept the hall, scrutinizing it, searching for the problem. But he found none. A hearty fire blazed in the wide hearth. The torchères attached to the walls at regular intervals cast a warm golden light throughout. Four maids shuttled groaning platters of foul and fish and steamed vegetables from the kitchen into the hall, while a trio of lads labored under the new butler's tutelage, filling ewers with rich brown ale and clear red wine. Gandy sat on a little carved stool, plucking on a lute, while two Welsh soldiers rolled dice in the corner as they awaited the meal. A peaceful scene.

Too peaceful.

When he'd left this morning, the household had been chaotic. The servants had been jumpy and frightened, and no one had known who to answer to or what to do. How had everything changed in just a matter of a few hours?

He gritted his teeth. The answer was obvious. This was Isolde's handiwork. Isolde, with the assistance—or at least the compliance—of those he'd left in charge. He speared Gandy with a sharp eye, but the little man smiled with feigned innocence.

"Welcome home, my liege. Your people await your return. We are all hungry," he added with a smirk. "And you are late."

"Where is she?" Rhys growled. "And spare me your performance. I see what is going on."

The dwarf's expression did not alter one whit. "She is abovestairs, I am certain. Was that not your wish?"

Rhys did not respond. Though he'd vowed several times during the long afternoon not to allow her to influence his actions, the urge to see her now was overwhelming. He glared at Gandy. "Once I make my ablutions the meal may begin."

He did not see the clever little man's knowing look follow him across the hall. Nor did he see the grin that passed between Gandy and Linus as he took the steps two at a time. Near the second-floor landing, however, he did spy Tillo sitting on the stairs. The old minstrel's lined face turned down in a scowl when Rhys approached.

Tillo rose to his feet. "You play with fire, Rhys. You do not see the drastic changes you have put into play."

"What cause have you to complain? You knew my intentions when we set out from Gilling: to take Rosecliffe Castle. Have I not stayed true to my word? Can you recall another coup so bloodless as this one? Even a melee, a mere game of war, involves more loss of blood than did my takeover here."

But Tillo appeared unmoved. "You sent the other English away. Why did you keep her?"

"Why should you care?" Rhys countered, growing impatient now. He stared past Tillo up the stairs toward his third-floor chamber where Isolde might yet linger at her work."

"You play with fire, Rhys. But you may find that you are the one who will be most burned."

Rhys cut the air with one hand. "Enough of this. My plan

remains as it has always been: to take possession of Rosecliffe, then to engage the FitzHughs in battle."

But Tillo stood his ground. "You said nothing of battling against women."

Rhys could not believe this. " 'Tis not my intention to battle with her." Then his voice turned silky, and smug. "Seduction is far easier, and far more satisfying."

He did not wait for a response after that, but sidestepped his old friend and continued up the stairs, to the chamber he'd claimed for his own. Dismissing Tillo's accusations, he jerked the door open. A quick glance told him Isolde was not there. But she had been, for a charcoal sketch of a giant dragon and an oversized wolf dominated one entire wall. Mollified by her cooperation, he tossed his leather gloves onto the bed and pulled off his hauberk. Then he returned to the stairs, heading up the final flight to the tower room.

Tillo's words briefly echoed in his head. But playing with fire was not something to avoid, not when it was the fire of passion he toyed with. The carnal burn of lust.

And burn he did. By the time he reached the tower room he was already aroused, and he had to pause outside the door to compose himself. He straightened his girdle and brushed the hair from his brow. This inappropriate desire he felt for her gave her too much power over him. He could not let her see how intensely he wanted her in his bed again.

He found her outside on the overlook, staring out at the sea. Her head was bare, her hair coiled neatly and held in place beneath a silver caul. She was dressed simply, in a green wool kirtle that looked soft as down. Across her shoulders she had wrapped a shawl, for it was bitterly cold and damp from the winds that ripped unimpeded across the northern sea.

She glanced sidelong at him when he appeared, then away, never meeting his gaze.

"You have my thanks, Isolde," he began.

She stiffened and he saw her blink. But she kept her eyes trained steadily on the cold winter seas. "I take it my sketch meets with your approval?"

"It exceeds my expectations. I did not realize the depths of your talent."

She blinked again, and her hands tightened on the rough

stones of the ramparts. He saw her knuckles whiten and he suppressed a chuckle. She was vain about her art. How it must gall her to receive praise from her enemy—and for a work she must despise. He folded his arms and leaned his back against the parapet.

"I've traveled the length and breadth of the British Isles," he said. "And I've been in many a grand hall, ornamented with frescoes and carvings and handsome tapestries. But it is clear that you have the skills to make Rosecliffe outshine them all."

This time she swallowed and compressed her lips in a line. " 'Tis but one wretched dragon and only a sketch."

"Precisely. That you can convey such strength and emotion in only a sketch requires a rare talent. I am eager to view the completed work. 'Tis sure to be a masterpiece."

He stared at her profile, at the straight, slender nose and full, curving lips. He wanted her to look at him. He wanted to stare into her eyes and know all her thoughts. But her lashes swept down over those eyes, long and lush, and she turned away.

"I know nothing of what you may have seen in other places. All I know is my own work. That sketch I did today was created under duress. In my mind it possesses neither strength nor emotion—save, perhaps, hatred," she sarcastically added.

"Ah, but hatred is a powerful emotion. A passionate emotion," he added, deliberately taunting her.

But she did not rise to his baiting. He wanted to turn her around and make her face him, to take hold of those slender shoulders and draw her up against him. Instead he restrained himself, only catching her by the elbow. It did elicit a satisfying gasp of alarm from her, however, and he steered her to the door. " 'Tis time for dinner. I would have you enjoy the fruits of your other efforts today—those in the hall."

She looked up at that remark, a wary expression on her face.

"Yes, I am aware you have taken matters in hand below-stairs, despite my orders to the contrary. The hall was not so calm when I left this morning."

"Mayhap it is your absence that restored the calm," she

snapped. Then she yanked her arm from his hold and hurried ahead of him to the stairs.

Rhys watched her go, grinning at her angry strides. Angry or no, she exuded some sort of seductive aura and he acknowledged to himself that he was not immune. He'd had the entire day to consider her and his perverse attraction to her. He still did not entirely understand it. He'd known women with features more exquisite than hers, women with more curvaceous bodies who were far better versed than her in the pleasures of the flesh. But this woman . . .

He shook his head. Though he did not understand his desire for her, he was wise enough to accept it as fact. He wanted her; he would bring her to heel; and he would have her.

Perhaps it was only that he possessed Rosecliffe now and so had no other challenge save the one she presented. Whatever the reason, he meant to master Isolde FitzHugh. It would be an entertaining pastime and would help speed the days until her father and uncle returned, and he could take up his sword once more.

She had seated herself below the salt when he descended to the hall. Every eye in the vast chamber turned toward him when he entered. Everyone in the hall waited to see what he would do.

"You will sit beside me," he said as he strolled past her.

"No."

He stopped and turned on his heel. "I am lord here. You will obey me or suffer the consequences like everyone else."

She jerked upright, glaring at him. "Then I will suffer the consequences." She started for the stairs, but he caught her wrist and spun her around. With a cry she swung her free hand wildly, and with a sharp crack, her palm connected with his cheek.

The entire company gasped at her recklessness.

Isolde heard their gasps, and heard also her own quick intake of breath. What had she done? And to what end?

She faced her nemesis, the man who controlled her fate, and felt his hand tighten around her wrist, almost to the point of pain. How could she have forgotten the vow she'd made? If she could not control her temper for even a few hours, how would she ever control herself for two weeks?

Though she hung back, he pulled her closer to him, so close that when he bent down their faces were but inches apart. She heard the hiss of the fire in the hearth behind her, and the nervous clearing of someone's throat. A chair scraped back and footsteps sounded. But her attention was riveted upon Rhys.

"Your heart is racing," he said, too low for anyone but her to hear. "Are you afraid?"

How she wanted to say no. But at that moment she was terrified, and she knew he could see the truth.

"Yes," she managed to say, through lips gone completely dry.

"Good. I am reassured that you retain some remnant of self-preservation."

"I may be afraid," she rashly went on. "But I will not be cowed by you. And I refuse to sit beside you and share a meal while you pretend to be lord here!"

They were words intended to prick his pride, and they worked very well. She saw the burn of fury in his night-dark eyes. But his voice maintained an icy calm.

"You will share a meal with me, here in this hall, Isolde. Or else we can dine together in private." He pulled her so close she could feel the heat of his body. "Is that what you desire?"

"No—"

"I think that is enough," a voice said from beside them.

Isolde turned gratefully to see Tillo standing there. At least someone was brave enough to challenge Rhys. But one glimpse at the cold fury on Rhys's face banished that brief glimmer of hope. The old minstrel was twice Rhys's age, and half his size.

"Did you want something?" Rhys bit out in a dangerously quiet voice.

"Do not fault him for his concern." Isolde spoke before Tillo could. "It takes an exceedingly brave man to interfere when his only weapon is reason."

Rhys turned his black stare from Tillo to her. To her surprise, however, her words seemed somehow to have calmed him. He scrutinized her face. "You need not defend him to me. I have a great respect for his bravery—and his loyalty.

Take your place," he added to Tillo, without glancing at the man. "She will come to no great harm at my hands." Then he swept the silent hall with a sharp gaze.

"Since you will not deign to sit at the high table, nor will you willingly dine with me in private, you leave me but one option. No," he said, interrupting her sigh of relief. "You will not be allowed to return to the tower. Not yet."

Isolde regarded him warily. "What do you mean?"

"If you will not perform the role of mistress of Rosecliffe, then you must perform the role of servant."

"I've been doing just that all day," she muttered.

"*Personal* servant," he clarified. Without warning, he started for the high table, dragging her behind him while everyone gaped at them. He released her, then seated himself in her father's chair and fixed her with a stern look. "Serve my meal; pour my wine. Mend my garments; clean my boots. You will perform all those tasks for me. Unless you prefer to dine at my side." He gestured to the empty chair.

Isolde frowned and unconsciously rubbed the wrist he'd held so warmly. How had it come to this? She'd not intended to confront him, certainly not in full view of all the castle folk. Now everyone stared expectantly at her, awaiting her response.

What should she do?

To serve him would be galling. But to acquiesce to his demands would be more so. She should not have tried to annoy him by sitting below the salt. Now she was in a worse position than ever And if she refused to accept either of the choices he gave her now . . . She did not want to think about spurring his temper that far.

She swallowed her pride, though with exceeding difficulty, and lifted her chin to an arrogant level. "Very well, then. I suppose I will serve you your meal."

He smiled then, a slow grin that sent waves of alarm skittering up her spine. There was triumph in that smug smile. But worse, there was knowledge in it. Had he guessed what she'd been up to, that she had meant to go along with him but in a fit of anger had forgotten her plan? Surely he could not know that. Yet it was clear he did know how to play on her volatile emotions, and thereby ruin any plan she mounted. He had simply to rouse her temper.

Isolde swallowed and looked away from him. She must maintain a better hold on her emotions. Then, angry, she snatched a ewer from a gawking page and began to fill a goblet of wine. She would show him that she had a stronger will than that!

Slowly the great hall came back to life. The servants carried in their platters of food; those seated began heartily to eat. As if her dilemma were ended, everyone assumed their normal places and performed their normal roles.

But there was nothing left of normalcy at Rosecliffe. Not really. Throughout the long meal she picked out his food: tender slices of guinea hen and eel; a bowl of stewed vegetables; a generous slice of white bread slathered with salted butter. Her own stomach growled, for she was hungry. But she would eat later, with the other servants.

When Linus and Gandy took up their instruments to begin the evening's entertainments, Isolde stepped back, hoping to escape to some private spot. But Rhys spied her movement and, with a crook of his finger, halted her.

"Fetch me my gittern," he told her. "You have not had a lesson in several days."

She stared at him dumbfounded. "The gittern?" Her expression turned bitter, for they both knew he had used her interest in music to seduce her. Outraged that he could bring that up now—outraged and humiliated—she glared at him. "I no longer have any interest in learning to play the gittern."

His expression did not alter, unless it was to grow more smug. "So you say. But just as a passionate anger can fire great art, so can it fire great music. Fetch the gittern, woman. I would hear you sing and play 'ere I seek my bed this evening."

"I am hardly in a mood to sing," she snapped, balling her hands into fists.

He shook his head as if he were forced to a great patience by a recalcitrant child. "Have you not yet learned the futility of opposing me? I will hear you sing and play in the hall, in this company." His voice lowered. "Or else I will hear you moan and sigh, in private with me. Which will it be?"

Isolde sucked in a harsh breath. She wanted to scream her frustration at him, but her shame was too great. She glanced around, horrified that others might have heard his wicked words. Thankfully no one was near enough. But her face nonetheless flamed with color to imagine herself once more moaning beneath him. Better to fetch the gittern, she consoled herself as she made her way on shaky legs to his chamber. Better that than the alternative.

In the dimly lit chamber, however, the dragon she'd sketched on his wall mocked her, as did the wolf prostrate beneath it. She stared at the design she'd drawn so angrily, and to her chagrin, she saw what Rhys had seen: fiery emotion. Erupting passion.

"*Taran,*" she muttered, turning away in despair. How had that happened? But tomorrow she would change the design to something milder, something not so potent. This painting would *not* be a masterpiece, she vowed.

And he would not manipulate her any more.

FIFTEEN

THE LITTLE DOG, CIDU, DID HIS TRICKS. GANDY SANG, ONCE more wooing his gigantress love, and well sated with food, the subdued people of Rosecliffe slowly relaxed. Two of the young pages performed a tumbling routine Gandy had taught them.

They were upstaged, however, when three of the hounds chased Cidu through the hall, under tables, over benches, and knocked down one of the maids. It took three men and both of the lads to drag the beasts away from the cocky little dog, and everyone was still chuckling when peace was at last regained.

Everyone but Isolde.

She stood behind Rhys with the gittern clutched in her damp palms, waiting, as good servants were expected to wait, until her master bade her come.

Her master. How she despised the idea of serving him! But there was little she could do to alter her fate—her *temporary* fate. So she stood there amidst the other gaiety of the hall, and she waited, and she glared her hatred at the back of Rhys's head.

He seemed, however, impervious to the force of her emotions. Her dark, menacing looks only deflected off him, repelled by the arrogant set of his wide shoulders, and glanced off his rich, shining hair. His hair was pure black, she noticed as the entertainments progressed, and still a little too long, as befitted a ruffian. But it was clean and thick, and it glinted in the golden light of the torchères, appearing blue-black and golden, all at one time.

His eyes were like that, too, she resentfully recalled as he kept his interest focused elsewhere. They were black as midnight, yet there was a light in them that burned.

She clutched the gittern to her chest as her mind ranged into dangerous territory. Why could he not have remained Reevius, the beguiling minstrel who had captured her heart? The compelling poet who'd stolen her innocence.

Not stolen, she admitted. She'd been a more than willing accomplice, until the very end. Yet even then he'd seduced her into willingness. Even when she had known his true identity, she still had found pleasure in his arms.

As if he sensed the mortifying direction of her thoughts, he turned and captured her gaze. He did not speak, but only stared at her, an endless, disconcerting stare. She wanted to turn away, to close her eyes and seal her thoughts from him, for she feared he would discern things she did not want him to know. But she could not avoid those brilliantly dark eyes. They compelled her and seemed to raise her shameful remembrances even closer to the surface.

"You are ready for your lesson." Not a question, but a statement. As if he were still Reevius, his words seemed to carry a double meaning.

She swallowed hard and reminded herself sternly that he was not Reevius. He never had been. "No. I am not ready. Nor am I in the least interested. But I am here—as you ordered."

"So you are."

Beyond him Gandy and Linus took their bows to enthusiastic applause. At once several of the youngsters in the hall surrounded the pair, for despite everything that had happened, the dwarf and giant remained great favorites, as did their pet. People drifted into smaller groups, several men to throw dice, the few women to chat. Tillo was no longer anywhere to be seen, she noticed. Nor was Newlin, whose advice she could sorely use. But it was Rhys ap Owain who faced her now, and save for the several curious glances sent their way, the two of them were essentially alone.

"Come." He rose and she fell back a pace. His hard features

relaxed in a half-grin. "Be at ease, Isolde. So long as you are compliant, you need not fear my temper."

"How reassuring," she muttered.

"I would rather we speak in Welsh."

"Very well," she answered in sarcastic Welsh.

Again he studied her for a long, uncomfortable moment. Then he gestured for her to accompany him nearer the hearth. "Play that lullaby," he ordered once they were seated in the light of the fire. "The one you played down at the beach."

"I don't remember it."

"You do." He positioned the instrument on her lap, then circled her shoulders with one arm. "Shall I remind you?"

"No!" Isolde slid away from him, as far as the bench allowed, and took up the gittern as he'd taught her. Anything to avoid his wholly unsettling touch. She bent over the instrument, her heart hammering as she fought to regain her calm. But she would not meet his eyes, for he might then guess how distressed he made her.

And she was deeply distressed.

I hate him! she reminded herself. *He is not Reevius. He is Rhys ap Owain, my bitterest enemy.*

But as she recalled the several chords he'd taught her, and began to pick out the simple lullaby, she admitted to herself the awful truth. He had some power over her, some pull she was helpless to avoid. Was it because she had already succumbed to him once? Was she now destined ever to be haunted by her erotic memories of that night?

That night.

Her mother had explained the basics of the physical relationship natural between a woman and her husband. But Isolde understood now, as she had not then, that marriage was not a necessary component for such a relationship. In those same explanations, had her mother ever mentioned lust? Had she warned about the fiery consequences of innocence lost—the enduring consequences?

"Sing the words," Rhys said, startling her from her disturbing thoughts. She trembled at the dark quality of his voice, at the warm whisper of his breath against her cheek.

"You ask too much of me," she blurted out. "I cannot sing, not when I am so . . . so distraught." Too late she realized her mistake. For once she looked up at him, she could not look away.

"You were distraught when you drew the mural, or so you said. Yet despite that, your sketch vibrates with passion. The truth is, your art is improved by the distress you profess to suffer—for the passionate feelings it rouses in you. So play for me, Isolde. And sing the words to me. Relieve those furious emotions of yours with music, and we shall see what comes of it."

He strummed the strings, brushing her fingers in the process, and a shudder of awareness quivered through her.

"All right," she muttered. "All right. Just . . . just allow me some room to breathe."

He laughed, but he did lean away from her. He stretched out his long legs, crossing them at the ankles, and folded his hands contentedly across his stomach. It was truly astounding, the aberrant thought came to her even as she fought to ignore his proximity. She hated him—she always had. And yet she felt a terrible attraction to him, as well. How could she be so utterly perverse?

She bent to the gittern, beginning the lullaby anew. But when she felt sufficiently composed to sing, she did not sing all the words as she knew them. A few she altered and made up as she went along.

> *Faraway, faraway child of mine,*
> *There will come wolves, strong and fine.*
> *The fears of the night, they'll slay in time,*
> *And you shall be safe come morning.*

> *Faraway, faraway babe I hold,*
> *The dragons of night can seem so bold.*
> *But soon enough, their fire will grow cold*
> *And you shall be safe come morning.*

She slanted a look at him, to gauge his reaction, for she knew she once again courted his anger. To her surprise, however, his mouth turned up at the corners in a droll smile. Did he find her amusing? She bent to the gittern emboldened by anger.

Faraway, faraway child, you'll see.
Enemies one and all shall be
Draped on your father's mighty shield
And you shall be safe—

Rhys's hand came down hard on the strings, cutting her off mid-note.

"You don't like my song?" she asked with exaggerated innocence.

"The lyrics are unwise," he said in a cool tone. "But as I suspected, they do display your passion."

His big hand slid to cover hers and though she tried to free herself from his grip, she could not. His callused palm enveloped hers, hot and hard, while the gittern's neck beneath her hand was cool and smooth. Like the two sides of a dangerous man, she thought inanely. He was a man of beautiful words and music. But he was also a man of war. He was filled with rage, and one way or the other, it must be set free.

"I do not know any other songs," she muttered, averting her eyes. "I told you that before—"

"Then you will sing to my tune."

He took the gittern from her. It was a relief to be free of his touch, she told herself. The hall had gone quiet and she realized that everyone who had not yet sought their beds was staring. She grimaced at the spectacle he made of them. But it was plain that did not bother him one whit.

He began to play a traditional Welsh air that every Welsh child knew. With a dark look and the arch of one imperial brow, he commanded her. "Sing."

It was a simple song about the hills and rivers and the spirit of the wind. But Isolde was certain no one had ever sung it with less enthusiasm than did she. She sang in a flat, off-key monotone. He sang as well, though through teeth gritted in anger. Several of his men joined in with wine-fueled fervor, and on the last of the verses their voices drowned out all the others. But even they could not mistake the tension that seethed between her and their leader.

"I would retire," she said, lurching to her feet when the last note died in the air.

"You have tasks that yet require tending." He stood and,

still gripping the gittern, started for the stairs. "Come."

He did not look to see if she followed, and for several long seconds Isolde did not move. She was afraid to follow him, for he was not to be trusted. But neither was she—or rather, neither was her body to be trusted. For just the thought of going up those stairs with him had started a hot knot writhing in her stomach.

"What tasks?" she hissed, trailing reluctantly behind him.

What tasks, indeed? Rhys wondered, for what he wanted of her and what he *should* want of her bore no similarity whatsoever.

To the victor went the spoils. That was a truism of all battles. Both English custom and Welsh supported his claim to her. But he was no barbarian heedless of those he conquered. Though he did not like to acknowledge any honor on the part of the FitzHughs, one truth could not be ignored: rape of Welsh women had been strictly forbidden, and transgressions had always been severely punished. Rhys had no intention of appearing less honorable than a FitzHugh.

But it was difficult to deny the urgent burn of desire, this inconvenient fire she'd ignited in him. He heard her soft tread on the stairs behind him, and the beast inside him clawed for release.

"What tasks?" she demanded once more. Was that a quiver of fear in her voice?

On the third-floor landing he turned. She stood halfway down, backlit by a torchère mounted in the curve of the stairs. The flickering light cast a shimmering golden halo around her. But she was no angel, he reminded himself. More like a she-devil. Again he felt a rush of desire as heat pooled in his loins. She had but to come up a dozen more steps. The bed was just beyond the door.

"You are no longer the lady of the castle," he stated in a harsh tone. "You are my hostage. My captive. As such, you must earn your keep like any other."

"Is not the mural sufficient to earn my keep?" She stared resentfully at him. "Did I not serve the meal well enough? What else must I do?"

He did not answer, but his gaze on her was steady, and a vein throbbed in his neck. As the silence stretched out, her eyes grew wide with comprehension and fear, and she backed down a step.

"No. No! You cannot mean that—"

"You will fold back the bedcovers," he snapped. "And arrange the drapery." His voice sounded cracked and hoarse, even to his own ears. But he pressed on. "You will hang my garments and clean my boots, and tend to the soiled linens."

She shook her head. "I'll not go inside your bedchamber while you are in it."

He should not want her to. But her violent objection fanned some primitive fire inside him. She would take back those words; he would force her to. "What is it you fear from me, Isolde?"

She took a harsh breath. He saw the rise of her breasts against the bodice of her simply cut forest-green kirtle. When she only stared warily at him, he went on.

"Methinks it is not me, but rather your own passionate nature that you fear."

"Then you are wrong!"

"For you have lain with a man," he continued, "and taken much pleasure in it—"

"I did not!"

"Ah, but you did, Isolde. You filled with passion. You throbbed with it." He was the one throbbing now, but still he pressed on. "Though you know you should not want to experience such passions again, you nonetheless want to. Isn't that the truth of it? You fear not my lustful nature, but your own."

He was not certain how right he was, not until she turned to the side and the light revealed the high color in her face. It also outlined the tautness of her nipples beneath the soft wool of her kirtle.

Beneath his tunic, trapped within his braies, his manhood swelled to its full, demanding length.

Damnation! He fought down a groan.

" 'Tis you and your own lust that you fear, not me," he managed to get out. "Get you up to the tower room," he added, though it pained him to do so. "This night only will I absolve you of your responsibilities."

He stepped back and gestured up the stairs with one hand.

"Go, before I change my mind," he muttered, furious with the situation she'd put him in. "But think on what I have said, Isolde. Think on it and admit the truth, at least to yourself. 'Tis your lust that you cannot face."

She did not move, not for the longest time. Neither did he, for it had suddenly become imperative that she come up to him. She must pass within his reach in order to seek the privacy of her prison room. He did not intend to touch her—though the restraint might very well kill him. But he would content himself with forcing her up the stairs, with seeing the truth of his words in her huge gray eyes.

And when she finally relented, when she gathered her full skirt in one hand and came slowly, warily, up the steps, it was harder even than he thought—and more rewarding.

She advanced past the circle of light cast by the lower torchère and into the light of the one on the third level. Her face was soft and pink; her hair rich and golden in the irregular amber light. And her eyes were a dark, fathomless gray. In that moment she was more beautiful, more desirable, than any woman he'd ever known.

That was the hard part, to stand rock still—and rock hard—and let her go by.

But the rewarding part was the flush of arousal she wore. He sensed it as if it were a palpable thing, a signal she gave off, her body to his. A scent of desire and longing and regret.

She wanted him, just as he'd said she did.

She sidled past him, shooting him a quick, wary—guilty—glance. Then she scurried up the stairs, into the dark rising well that led to her tiny chamber just above his.

If he wanted her, he had but to go to her.

He knotted his fists until his arms trembled and he thought he might crush the slender neck of the gittern in his ferocious grip. Better for her to come to him, he told himself, though sweat popped out on his brow and his jaw hurt from clenching his teeth. She would not accuse him of rape. Better to wait for her to approach him, though it took every bit of his will to do so.

The time would come and soon, he told himself, when she would come to him. Then he would claim her in every way a man could claim a woman. He would lose himself in her softness, bury himself in her warmth, and fill her with his strength.

"Holy Mother," he swore and closed his eyes, fighting for control. He managed to turn on his heel and stalk toward his chamber. He managed to close the door without slamming it, and lay the gittern aside. When he came face-to-face with the mural, though, with the wolf lying beneath the rearing dragon, he let out a string of oaths, every foul word he'd ever learned, in Welsh and English and French.

She'd drawn the images he'd demanded, the symbolic domination of the FitzHughs by the Welsh. But in the dark and solitude he knew a bitter truth. As he leaned his fevered brow against the cold stones of Rosecliffe and pressed his hand against his aching loins, he felt less the victor and more the victim.

Of all the women to desire, why her?

Downstairs in the great hall, the last of the castle folk sought their beds. All but Gandy and Linus.

"I don't want to fight against her family," Linus complained. He looked mournfully at his friend. The dwarf patted his crooked knee, then cuddled Cidu when the little dog leaped into his arms. After a few seconds Linus continued. "If he keeps her, they will come and fight him. But if he lets her go—"

"They will still come and fight," Gandy interrupted.

"But I don't want to fight anymore."

"Then don't."

Linus scratched his head. "I don't want him to fight, either, Gandy. He should stop."

"I don't think he can. Anyway, 'tis not our business."

"But he is our friend."

At that moment a dark figure descended the stairs with movements slow and uneven. Gandy slid down from his stool and Cidu leaped at once into Linus's broad lap, as the ancient bard of Rosecliffe shuffled toward them with his odd sideways gait.

"Have you come from his chamber, or from hers? Or perhaps they are together," Gandy said, giving Newlin a knowing wink.

Newlin smiled at him, a sweet, benign smile. "They are apart physically, but not because they wish to be. Other mat-

ters separate them, though." Slowly he shuffled past them to
stand before the glowing hearth. He held his hands to the heat
and his beribboned cloak fluttered and moved around his squat
form.

" 'Tis cold, and 'tis certain to grow more so."

"Winter is nigh," Linus said.

"So it is." Newlin nodded and smiled at the simple fellow.
"So it is. It will be bitterly cold, I am afraid."

"Not particularly promising weather for mounting a siege,"
Gandy remarked.

Newlin turned to face him. "In truth, the bitter cold may
be of great aid to this siege."

Gandy smirked. " 'Tis plain you know little of warfare."

Newlin did not answer, except with another smile. He
stepped closer to the welcome heat in the huge hearth. *'Tis
not warfare I speak of,* he thought.

Gandy had turned away. Linus lavished Cidu with affection. Across the hall, sitting alone in the shadows, Tillo looked
up in dismay. Not warfare? What did Newlin mean? Then
Newlin turned and looked straight into the shadows, straight
into Tillo's eyes.

Alarmed, Tillo shrank back, pressing a trembling hand to
his chest. How had he heard the bard's thoughts? More importantly, did the strange little man hear Tillo's own dark
thoughts? Tillo shivered fearfully, for he did not want Newlin
to divine his thoughts or delve into his secrets.

But he knew somehow that Newlin *had* seen the truth. He
had seen Tilly, who for so long had been protected by Tillo's
façade. Would Newlin reveal that truth now? Would he expose
Tilly for who she truly was?

And if he did, what would she do then?

SIXTEEN

THREE DAYS PASSED. WINTER DESCENDED WITH ABRUPT FE-
rocity, and the mural progressed. Meanwhile the tension between Isolde and Rhys seethed with violent throes of repressed
emotions.

A relentless storm descended over the land, pushing snow
into high drifts and driving both men and beasts indoors. The
mural grew and developed with each added swath of dark
paint. Fiery rivers of blood red; vivid streaks of yellow and
purple and blue that brought to life a battle to the death.

It was because she fought just such a battle within herself,
Isolde fretted as she stared up at the nearly completed painting.
She'd not meant it to be so large, nor so compelling, and every
comment Rhys made on its progress infuriated her. But she
could no longer deny the truth. It was her best work, her most
ambitious and her most powerful.

The foul dragon, painted in blacks and blues, with glowing
nostrils and glittering eyes, was supposed to be hideous. But
somehow it had become magnificent.

She stood back and wiped the back of her wrist against her
brow. If the dragon was magnificent, it was because it sym-
bolized Wales, and through her mother, she was half Welsh.
But she could not allow the dragon to actually defeat the wolf,
symbol of the FitzHughs and the other half of her lineage.
After all, her mother had not defeated her father, nor had he
defeated his Welsh wife. They had struggled—she knew the
tales of those difficult first years. But once they'd joined to-

gether, once they'd wed, their union had made everything better.

Occasionally they still fought, but neither of them was ever defeated, and neither could Isolde allow the wolf in her painting to be defeated. So the wolf grew and became splendid. Her fangs gleamed; her claws fended off the mighty dragon.

And day by day, as the pair struggled across the wide plastered wall, Isolde refined the image she meant one day soon to destroy. With layer upon layer of paint, she added details: roses along a cliff; the hazy shadow of a distant castle. Painted people crept out from the shadows, watching the battle in awe. She wanted to stop, to call the painting complete. But she could not, and Rhys seemed not to begrudge her the long hours she spent working in his chamber.

That he stayed away during the day was a relief to her. At first. She left when the daylight faded. He returned once she was gone. He complimented her on the work while she served his meal, and all in all, she should have been reasonably well satisfied with the progress of her captivity. But sometimes at night she heard music from his chamber just below hers. The muted tones of the gittern; the muffled tones of a low male voice singing words she could not quite decipher.

She was drawn to those midnight songs—and repelled, as well. He was not Reevius, who sang so beautifully, she sternly reminded herself, but Rhys, her nemesis. But still it was a nightly torture.

Nearly a week had passed. By now her father should have received the dire news and be preparing for his return. In another week he would arrive and this ordeal would finally be done.

But a part of her dreaded that moment of conflict, for it could only end badly. Men like Rhys and her father and Uncle Jasper took warfare seriously. A fight over Rosecliffe—and over her—would be a fight to the death for someone.

The door creaked open and she whipped around, her heart thumping in alarm as it always did when she thought Rhys was near. It was not Rhys, though, but Tillo. Just as quickly as Isolde's pulse had leaped, so now did it droop in disappointment.

"He is in the stables, honing his blade," the old minstrel

said, shuffling in. He shot her a knowing look and she glowered mutely at her paint-stained hands. Then Tillo stared up at the mural that now dominated the chamber, and nodded. " 'Tis a rare talent you possess, child."

"I hate it," Isolde replied, with more candor than she usually expressed in the presence of those loyal to Rhys.

"You hate your talent?"

"I hate this painting."

Tillo squinted at her. "But it is magnificent."

Isolde tossed her paintbrush into the rinse bowl. Muddy water splashed over the rim and pooled on the table. She frowned as she mopped it up with a rag. "It was not meant to be magnificent."

"Ah. Yes." Tillo nodded. "I understand."

"Do you?" Isolde's voice was sarcastic.

"Yes. I do." Tillo stared at her a long moment, then sighed. "There are those women who seem destined to participate in their own downfall. I do not know why that is."

Did he speak of her? Guilt washed its hot color over Isolde's face. "I see Rhys has been boasting to you," she muttered. "Well, whatever he has said, it is a lie. I may have mistakenly succumbed to Reevius," she conceded. "But once I learned his true identity, I have done everything I can to defend myself from his overtures."

"Too late," Tillo said, staring up at the mural with the dragon rearing over the wolf. "Too late."

Tears of frustration stung Isolde's eyes. "It will be too late for him when my father arrives."

"Yes. And someone must die that day."

Isolde went still at those solemn words. They were no more than what she had thought. Yet to hear them expressed out loud was chilling, indeed. The minstrel studied her gravely, then continued. "You do not wish Rhys to die, do you?"

"I . . . I don't care what happens to him."

Tillo stamped his cane on the floor. "I have no time for lies!" Then his old face took on a startled expression, as if his own words were somehow a revelation. "There is no time for lies," he repeated more thoughtfully.

"It doesn't matter what I want!" Isolde cried. "Don't you see? They will fight no matter what I do."

But the old minstrel seemed lost in thought. He threw back his mantle, revealing his slight frame bent over with age, and his bony arms. He loosened the ties at the throat and let the garment fall. Then he drew down the snug-fitting cowl that covered his head and shoulders.

Isolde stared at such bizarre behavior. "Do you desire heated water to bathe?" she ventured. "The kitchen is far warmer than this chamber."

"I am a woman," Tillo announced belligerently.

A woman? Isolde did not immediately react to that startling statement. How could he be a woman? Then the old minstrel reached back to loosen the knot of gray hair at his nape.

At *her* nape, Isolde amended as amazement gave way to comprehension. Tillo was a woman.

"But . . . but why have you passed yourself off as a man all this time?" Isolde blurted out.

Tillo sighed and pushed back a wiry gray curl. In that movement Isolde saw everything she'd not seen before. "A woman alone is not safe," Tillo said.

"Yes . . . Yes, I understand that. But why do you choose to reveal yourself now? And to me? Does Rhys know?" Isolde added, searching Tillo's face. The features were delicate for a man's. His hands—her hands were slender.

"I need your help," Tillo admitted. "And you need mine."

"Rhys does not know?"

Tillo stared at her. "He does not need to know."

"Surely you do not fear him."

Tillo compressed her lips and shook her head. "Men look at women differently than they do other men. As a man—even as an old man—I have some value, albeit limited. As an old woman I have no value at all. Even as a young woman, like you, my use was limited." She stared sadly at Isolde. "Surely you know the one use Rhys has for you."

A little shudder snaked down Isolde's back and she hugged her arms around herself. She knew. But that was a subject she would rather avoid. "I still do not understand your purpose in revealing your secret to me. How can I possibly help you?"

Tillo stared up at the mural. "I do not believe you wish for your lover to die."

"He is not my lover!"

"But he has been," Tillo snapped. "We both know that." Then her voice gentled. "Do not fret, child. I do not wish for him to die, either, for he has been more than fair with me. I fear the only way he may be spared such a fate, however, is through your intercession. You must escape and go to your father."

Isolde's heart began to race. She glanced warily at the door, then focused back on Tillo. "Do you mean to help me?" When Tillo nodded, Isolde could hardly believe it. "But why would you do that?"

"I am old. I need a warm place to live."

"Have you no family of your own? No children to turn to?"

Tillo seemed to go gray in the face. But her back straightened, and her eyes glittered angrily. "I have never conceived a child. Two husbands drove me away because I bore them no sons. But that is of no import now," she added with a sharp gesture of her hand. "I need someplace to live out the remaining years of my life. Not here," she hastened to add. "Mayhap you will prevail on your uncle to allow me to join his household."

Isolde shook her head. "Why not here?" she asked, not understanding any of this.

"I have my reasons," Tillo answered peevishly. "Decide, girl. Will you accept my aid and save Rhys's life or not?"

"Why do you believe my escape will save his life?"

"Because you will plead for him."

"But I hate him!"

Tillo shook her head, and for the first time she smiled. "You do not hate him. You are too young to hate him, too on fire for the pleasure he brings you. And he is on fire for you. But when that fire burns out, then you will see how little a man truly values a woman. And then you may, indeed, hate him. But not yet."

Isolde was so confused. While one part of her vowed her hatred of Rhys, another part wanted to deny she would ever hate him. She turned away from the mural and its mesmerizing effect, and tried to think. "You are wrong. Not all men are as you describe. My father values my mother—and not merely because she has borne him children."

Tillo snorted. "Is she beautiful? Does she entice him still to her bed?"

"They love one another."

"If that is true, then they are the rare couple. Do not mistake my words, child. Rhys is not a bad man. He is better than most of his kind that I have known. But he is a man. He cannot help but be true to his nature." She paused. "And you cannot help but be true to yours."

Isolde looked over at her and their eyes held a long moment. "My true nature is to be loyal to my family above all things."

Tillo's face creased in deep lines. "And you think I am not loyal to mine, such as it is? I want Rhys to live, Isolde. That is why I will help you escape. I cannot dissuade Rhys from this reckless path he has chosen and the death that surely awaits him. But your father spared his life once, when his brother Jasper asked it. Surely he will do so again if the plea comes from his beloved daughter."

Rhys honed his blade with a fervor close to reverence. He'd been betrayed many times in his life, but never by a properly prepared weapon. The purest steel; the truest oak; the finest leather. All these he used and maintained with rigorous diligence. But today his focus was less on the perfect edge he honed, and more on the woman he avoided.

There was no point in denying the truth. He was avoiding her. For three days now he'd ignored her. Three agonizingly long days.

He wanted her with a ferocity that had become the overriding factor of both his days and nights. But he was determined that she be the one to come to him. It would sweeten his victory over the FitzHughs, he told himself. It would prove also that he was as honorable as any of them. Even more honorable.

He paused and wiped his brow with his sleeve and stared unblinkingly at the lantern that lit the bitterly cold stall where he worked. Again the unwelcome truth assailed him. His foremost reason for avoiding her—a reason that had grown out of control—was that he feared revealing the power of this insane desire she inspired in him. If she should discover just how much he wanted her . . .

He wiped his brow again. He could not allow that to happen. He would not allow it.

So he resumed the rhythmic motions of honing stone against glittering steel, and tried to take some comfort from the routine of his task. When he detected movement behind him, however, he started like a green lad and sliced a thin line down the fleshy base of his thumb.

"Gwrtaith!" He pressed his mouth to the wound even as he whipped the sword around. "Newlin!" He cursed again and stared balefully at the twisted old man. "Is there some reason you creep about like a thief in the night?"

" 'Tis not I who plot in the night," the bard glibly replied. "Besides, 'tis still day. Put down your weapon, lad. I wish you no ill."

"Would that I could be more certain of that," Rhys muttered. He frowned down at his stinging thumb, then picked up the stone and resumed his work.

"You may be certain," Newlin replied.

"What do you want of me?"

"Your companions have settled easily into life at Rosecliffe. Most of them."

"And why not? This is Wales; they are Welsh."

"I speak not of Glyn and Dafydd and the others, but of your traveling companions, your minstrel band."

Rhys did not deviate from his work. "Linus and Gandy have heretofore led difficult lives, badgered and mistreated. I deal with them fairly and so they follow me. They are loyal to me," he added with emphasis.

"I believe they are. But what of Tillo?"

"Tillo?" Rhys lifted his head and stared at Newlin with narrowed eyes. "Do you imply that Tillo is not loyal?"

Newlin smiled, so sweetly he momentarily appeared childlike. "I understand the great truths of this world. But people . . . People have wills of their own. How they use that will, ah well, even I am sometimes surprised." Then he rubbed his hands together. " 'Tis cold in here. Methinks even your great beasts of burden would appreciate a fire this day."

Rhys only grunted and returned to his work. But after a

few moments when Newlin turned silently to leave, he stopped him with a grudging question. "When will FitzHugh arrive?"

Newlin stared out of the stall, into the dim recesses of the stable aisle. "Soon enough."

"He has learned what has occurred here?"

Newlin nodded, then began to rock forward and back, a faint movement that Rhys found disconcerting. "Be careful of what you have put into motion, lad. You may achieve your aim and yet nonetheless never reach your goal."

"I am no lad," Rhys snapped, glaring at the old bard.

Other men would have quaked at the threat in Rhys's demeanor, but not Newlin. "No, you are no longer a lad, not in strength or in prowess with yon sword. But you are not so changed from the lad you once were. You are still Owain's son."

"And always will be!" Rhys stated, holding the sword up with a strong, steady hand.

Newlin blinked at the light glinting off the flawless blade. "Your will is your own," he finally said. "I pray you use it wisely."

Josselyn did not look up when the messenger approached Rand, except to sigh in dismay. Another summons or invitation or urgent request, no doubt. They'd been in London but three days and she'd already begun to tire of the endless round of private discussions, secret meetings, and political maneuverings. As two of the mightiest lords along the Welsh marches, Rand and his brother Jasper had been sucked into the maelstrom surrounding the strong-minded young king's ascension to power.

Added to that, they had learned only yesterday that John FitzHugh, Randulf's dissolute older brother, had died two weeks previously, leaving no known heir. That meant that Rand would now be invested as Lord of Aslin.

Josselyn wasn't certain how she felt about that. Despite their Welsh heritage, she and Jasper's wife, Rhonwen, already were being pulled into the social machinations of the female side of the royal court. As Lady Aslin, she feared the pressure would only grow stronger.

For the most part Josselyn found life in London pretentious

and oftentimes even silly. But the court of King Henry was new and not yet settled. Rand had assured her that court life would not always be this frenetic.

At least Henry's queen, the lovely Eleanor, was no milksop. Though Josselyn had not spent much time with her, it was plain to one and all that she was both intelligent and worldly. She would be a strong influence on her younger husband and his court, Josselyn decided. A woman's touch on the reins of power met with her complete approval.

"Something's afoot," Rhonwen murmured, nudging her with her elbow.

Josselyn looked up from the trio of ribbons she braided for Gwen to wear in her hair. Later today the girl would be presented to the queen. "What now? Could it be that someone has been seated at the wrong end of the tables?"

Her sarcasm faded, however, when Rand stiffened. And when he grabbed the messenger by the front of his tunic as if to murder the man, Josselyn leaped to her feet, the dainty ribbons forgotten.

"How can that be?" Rand hissed at the trembling man through gritted teeth. "I built Rosecliffe to be impregnable!"

"Yes, milord. But . . . but he tricked everyone—"

"Osborn is no fool to be taken in—"

"Rand!" Josselyn cried. "What is it?"

When he turned to her his face was devoid of all color. But in his pale visage his eyes glowed with fury. And with fear.

"Lady Isolde is . . . is unharmed," the messenger babbled, still choking in Rand's iron grip. "In truth there . . . there was little bloodshed. And no lost lives."

"Isolde?" Josselyn's heart seemed to stop beating. "Dear God, what has happened?" She grabbed Rand by the arm. "Tell me! What has happened at Rosecliffe?"

"Rhys ap Owain." He spat the words out as if they were foul. Then he abruptly released the hapless messenger. "That bastard son of a bitch." He swung his fierce gaze toward his brother Jasper. "I should have killed him ten years ago. I should never have listened to you!"

Jasper tensed and his hands tightened into fists. Rhonwen placed a calming hand on his arm. But Jasper's anger was not directed at Rand. "If he has harmed one hair on her head, I will kill him myself." Jasper swung toward the messenger who backed nervously toward the chamber door. "Tell us everything that has happened. Everything."

It did not take long, for there was little to tell. Josselyn listened intently, concentrating on every detail and trying to picture the events unfolding in her faraway home. She was horrified to think of her beloved Rosecliffe held by another now, and that so many of their people had been ousted from their homes. But her fears for Isolde were somehow not as desperate as Rand's.

"He held Isolde in his arms when she was but a babe," she tried to reassure Rand, trailing in his wake as he strode furiously for the stables. "He will not hurt her."

"He was but a boy then."

"A wild boy. An untried, angry boy! Yet still he was always gentle with her."

"You forget how much he hates me—and Jasper even more. He hates everyone of English blood. God in heaven, but I was a fool to think a knight's training would change him. That it would teach him honor. And now he has Isolde—"

He broke off and swallowed hard. Then he reeled off a list of orders to the stablemaster.

"When do we leave?" Josselyn asked.

He gave her a sharp look. "Jasper and I leave within the hour. You and Rhonwen and the children will go on to Bailwynn. Gavin is old enough to ride as your protection."

"I am going to Rosecliffe with you."

A muscle jumped in his jaw and he started to respond. Then he sighed and rubbed the back of his neck, and she saw how anxious he was. "We'll be traveling at a punishing pace, Josselyn. It will be impossible for you and the children to keep up."

She came up to him and looped her arms around his neck, unmindful of the stablemaster's sidelong glances. "I promise you, Rand, that I will not hold you back. Rhonwen and I are already decided, so there is no point in debate. We will ride with you, a family united in the defense of our home. We are a loyal bunch, we Welsh women. We love our men, our children, and our homes, above all else."

A faint smile eased the worried lines of his face. "I am glad to have you with me and not against me, my love. Your Welsh obstinance is a great comfort to me." He planted a kiss on her brow.

"But Rhys's Welsh obstinance is not so comforting," she said.

He pulled away from her. "Do not defend that thankless ruffian to me. If that is why you ride with us, better that you stay behind."

She bristled and glared at him. "I ride with you to rescue my daughter and my home."

They stared at one another a long moment. "Very well," he conceded. "But we waste time in this palaver. Let us go."

Yes, Josselyn thought. *Let us go. Let us go and see if our first-born daughter has tamed the wild Welsh-born knight whom no one else seems able to control.*

SEVENTEEN

ISOLDE HATED THE COMPLETED MURAL. SHE HATED IT. YET she seemed ever to find excuses to slip into the master's chamber, and there she would stand as she did now, staring up at the horrible rearing dragon and the battling wolf beneath it.

It was her best work, she conceded, albeit bitterly. In truth, she should have used a better mixture of paints to preserve it.

But soon she would scrub it off, she told herself. Soon she would cover it with an even better image. Next time, the wolf would beat down the dragon.

She shuddered at the thought. In a few more days she knew the real confrontation between dragon and wolf would begin. The relative peace of this last week would end and her father and uncle would arrive to finally confront Rhys. But instead of Rosecliffe Castle repelling outside invaders, this time the stout walls would stand firm against the man who had built them.

Isolde hugged her arms around herself and fought back the sting of unhappy tears. It was not fair, not to her father, or to Rhys. She gave a humorless laugh at such an insane idea. How ironic that she, who had hated Rhys ap Owain all her life, could fear for his well-being now, and could even understand what drove his rage.

Had one brief night of passion skewed her thinking so far? It was not just that, she vowed. In truth, it was much more. She'd always envisioned Rhys as an ogre, a monster who hated everyone. But in less than a week she'd witnessed enough of him to recognize the flaws in so simplistic an assessment. He was a good leader to his countrymen, and fair to those he'd defeated—so long as they did his bidding. He'd not ransacked Rosecliffe as she had feared. Indeed, he seemed determined to make it even more productive than it had been before.

Equally important, he'd made no further attempt to force her to his bed. Nor had any other woman of Rosecliffe been harassed or poorly treated.

What was she to make of a man like that?

She thought back to Tillo's strange offer to help her escape. There had been no further word on that front, perhaps because the weather was too foul. But Isolde had thought on it long and hard, and had decided it was the only opportunity she would have to avert a battle between Rhys and her family. Even then, her chances were slim. But so long as she remained a captive inside Rosecliffe, she had no chances at all of preventing it.

"So. Again I find you in my bedchamber."

Isolde gasped and whirled around. One of her hands pressed nervously against the base of her throat when she spied Rhys in the doorway. He leaned his shoulder against the door frame in a nonchalant pose. She, however, with hammering heart and flushed features, felt anything but nonchalant.

He glanced up at the mural, then grinned at her, a smug, slanting grin. "Admiring your handiwork again? Or is there something else you wanted?" This time he looked pointedly at the bed.

Isolde's face went scarlet. Of late he'd not referred to the passionate hours they'd spent in that bed, when she had believed him to be a minstrel. She'd almost thought he'd put it out of his mind. Ironically, that possibility had dragged it to the forefront of her thoughts. With every passing day her memories of that evening became clearer. With every passing night she remembered something else he'd done, some movement or caress or kiss that had roused a storm of passion in her—and did so again in shameful memory.

Even now, in the middle of the day, those memories did the same—especially when his eyes were so dark and hungry upon her. For days he had ignored her save to issue orders.

Bring fresh water to his chamber. Refill his cup with wine. Brush his tunic and hang it on a peg.

Why did he look at her now as if he wished to devour her?

She gritted her teeth, turned on her heel, and snatched a candle brace from a small chest. "You are just as crude as your man Dafydd, it seems. Not that I am surprised. I am tending your chamber as you ordered. That's all. There are wax drippings to be scraped from this."

She looked over her shoulder at him. He still blocked the doorway. "Will you let me pass? Or are you so bored that you have come here to torment me with your unwanted presence?" she added with a haughty sniff.

He pushed off from the deep door opening and approached her—stalked her. Considering her inflammatory words, what else could she expect? Why must she goad him so? Despite her determination not to appear the coward before him, Isolde retreated three steps, until she came up against the bed.

"Shall I push you backward, down onto the bed?" He took her by the shoulders, curving his big hands around them, and pushed, though not hard enough to make her tumble onto the mattress. He was forceful enough, however, that she had to fight to retain her balance. "Are you so certain my presence is unwanted?" he murmured, taunting her. He pressed a little harder, just enough that she had to catch the front of his tunic in her hands to stay upright.

"Cease this foolishness! Leave me alone," she ordered, though her voice quivered with emotion.

"Who's to make me?" He whispered the words, bending nearer.

Who, indeed? Her senses were so rattled Isolde could hardly think. "You . . . you do not condone rape," she finally stammered. "That's what you said."

"No. I do not. But seduction . . . Seduction is something else entirely. You liked it, Isolde. We both know that. And I liked it, too. Are you ready to be seduced again, sweetling? Is your heart racing? Does your belly grow hot?"

He reversed the pressure and pulled her unexpectedly against him, then rubbed his chest back and forth against her peaked nipples. Just a slight movement, but it inflamed all her senses. "Tell the truth," he went on in a husky whisper. "Do your breasts ache for my touch?"

Yes. Yes. Yes! she wanted to scream. But she bit her lips against the traitorous words.

Then one of his knees pressed between her thighs and Isolde let out a guilty little sob. She ached everywhere for him. That quickly. That completely. And it seemed he knew. He pressed more boldly against her so that she rode his leg, and the hot yearning in her nether regions turned to a melting desire.

"Damn, but that feels good. Doesn't it?" His voice was a hoarse caress in her ear.

Better than merely good. Isolde bowed her head against his chest and gamely fought the physical longing he roused in her. How could she want this man? How could she?

Oh, why could he not still be the minstrel she'd thought he was?

"You're not Reevius," she muttered in final opposition. She hit his chest with one fist, then with both. "You're not Reevius!" she cried, lifting a stricken face to him.

His face hardened in a scowl. *"Uffern dan!* I am he," he swore. "I am he." Then he drew her up and caught her mouth in a fierce and angry kiss.

He was not Reevius, she told herself as he dragged her deeper and deeper into the pure carnality of his kiss. He was not her minstrel, but rather the dragon she hated. The mighty dragon she feared. The magnificent dragon of her painting . . . of her tortured dreams . . .

When Isolde finally relented, melting against him and rising into their kiss, Rhys felt a surge of pure triumph, of primitive domination. It was like the best of battles: confrontation and struggle with a worthy opponent, and in the end, victory. He had her now. He'd won. He had but to tilt her back onto the bed and take his pleasure of her, his first reward for these hard days of waiting and wanting.

It had worked, though, for she'd been wanting him, too. Now she was more than ready to be taken.

He plundered her mouth, savoring his reward. But then her hand crept up to cup his face, first one small hand, then the other. She held his face between his palms in a way that felt at once both erotic and innocent, and without warning, Rhys felt everything change, as if the world shifted beneath his feet.

But it hadn't, he told himself.

He tangled his hands in her silky hair and thrust his hips roughly against her soft belly. She was a willing woman and he a lusty man. It was simple and basic.

With a quick movement he tilted her backward and in a moment he lay over her on the bed, just like before. His mouth crushed hers. He stroked deep with his tongue, possessing her mouth, proving to her and to himself that she was his for the taking. He meant to make her his, and to use her in every carnal way he'd ever learned to use a woman.

But then she sighed, and she circled his neck with one arm, as if intent on prolonging their kiss. Again he felt it, as if something kicked hard in his chest.

Guilt?

No. Not guilt. There was no reason for him to feel guilt.

He pulled a little back from her, but she rose with him and somehow took control of the kiss. Her tongue stroked into his mouth, rousing him with its tentative foray, while one of her hands stroked his ear in the most erotic fashion imaginable.

"Jesus, God," he swore, tearing away from her. "Don't do that!"

He braced himself on stiff arms above her, appalled by what he'd just said. Beneath him she lay breathless and beautiful. Disheveled, with her luxuriant hair spread about her. Her eyes were bright with desire; her lips were red from their passion. She wanted him and he wanted her. There was nothing complicated about it. So why did he hesitate?

Then she swallowed hard. He saw the smooth undulations of her pale throat. "What . . . What is wrong?" she asked in a faint voice.

God help him, but he did not know. How could he want a woman so urgently and yet hesitate when she urged him on? He was hard and ready. So hard he hurt. Yet something warned him away from her, some well-honed sense of self-preservation.

But that was ludicrous. She was no man of war with weapon raised to strike him. She was just a woman.

He stared at her, as if at a creature he'd never seen. He'd

had prettier women in this very position before, he reminded himself. Women with bigger breasts and far more experience. Women with clever hands and even cleverer lips. As he stared at this woman, though, the faces and names and physical attributes of those other women all disappeared. His heart that had been racing with desire began now to hammer with fear.

Fear!

God's blood, was he going mad?

He lurched up from her, then backed away from the bed and stood in the center of the room, staring at her like an idiot. Her confusion was apparent and he took advantage of that to compose his own rattled nerves. "So, 'tis Reevius alone that you desire," he taunted. "Apparently not. How fickle a lover you prove to be."

She sucked in a harsh breath at his cruel words, then turned her face away from him, and Rhys knotted his fists in an agony of despair. Why had he said that? He'd hurt her for no reason, none except this unreasoning panic she inspired in him.

Now, though, it was physical pain that tore at his gut, excruciating pain, as if some giant hand squeezed his heart. He watched her curl into a tight ball of misery and shame, and he felt sick to his stomach for making her feel that way.

"Isolde," he began, reaching a hand toward her—a hand that shook. When she flinched, he let his arm fall to his side.

The silence was awful. It was also accusing. She did not weep, nor did she rail at him. He would have preferred either of those to this rigid silence. But he had struck her a deliberately cruel blow and now he must suffer the only retaliation she could give. Still, he could not leave without saying something to her.

He gritted his teeth, unsure of himself and hating the feeling. "I was wrong to say that to you."

She did not move.

His chest hurt so hard it was painful even to breathe. "I was wrong," he repeated hoarsely. Then like a coward, he turned and he fled the scene of carnage—the carnage he'd inflicted because *she* had terrified *him*!

How fickle a lover you prove to be.

Isolde lay in the ruined aftermath of desire and heard those awful words over and over again. *How fickle a lover.*

He'd seduced her, then taunted her with his triumph. But that was not the worst of it. The worst part was that he was right.

A sob rose in her throat, hot and choking, the same sob she'd suppressed ever since he'd abandoned her to her misery. But she was determined not to allow it release. Bad enough that she was a silly, fickle girl. She would not be a weepy, idiotic one, as well.

Easy to say, she thought as she struggled to control herself. Nearly impossible to do when pent-up emotions burned in her chest for release. Slowly she rolled onto her back—only to be met by the sight of the demon dragon, looming over the embattled wolf. She gasped in renewed despair, and in so doing, lost her fight for control. The sob rose and broke, and her tears burst free. With a cry of fury and shame, she lurched from the bed—the scene of her pitiful capitulation.

"I hate you!" she screamed at the mural, at Rhys, and at herself. "I hate you!" She snatched up the pot of rinse water that still held her brushes, and heaved it at the wall. With a crack it shattered, and water and shards of clay flew everywhere.

But the dragon was unaffected by the violence of her emotions, and it loomed over the wolf as menacingly as ever. She faced it, chest heaving, tears streaming down her face. "I will destroy you," she vowed, swiping vainly at her eyes.

Her paints were there, the precious pots of colors she'd worked so hard to mix. And for what purpose? To paint ugly murals that dishonored her family? That glorified villains?

She grabbed the first paint pot and the nearest brush. Then she attacked the wall. Swaths of red—blood—in great wild strokes. She cared nothing for line or form or balance. She slapped paint on the wall in utter abandon, wanting only to obliterate the beastly dragon from the wall. To obliterate *him* from her head!

Two floors down in the great hall, Rhys sat stone-faced in the lord's chair. He heard Isolde's shrieks of rage—half the castle folk heard—and he wanted to go to her. But he knew he was the last person who would be able to calm her.

"What have you done to her?"

He jerked at Tillo's sharp words. The old minstrel stared accusingly at him—as did several serving maids and pages. Linus's big face was lined with worry; even Gandy looked concerned.

"What have you done to her now, Rhys?"

His hand cut the air in an abrupt gesture. "Nothing! I did nothing!" *Except toy with her. Seduce her. Then insult her.*

Tillo snorted in disbelief. "Considering your intentions, she has borne our presence in her home very well. 'Tis clear some new atrocity has befallen her."

Guilt drew him to his feet. "No atrocity. Just the unwelcome realization that she is no better than those who live outside Rosecliffe's exalted walls. She is no more deserving than any other woman. No more constant. No more trustworthy."

Rhys stood, muscles tensed, fists knotted, glaring his intent to silence Tillo with violence if the old man did not back off. But when Tillo did just that, retreating safely beyond the reach of Rhys's clenched fists, Rhys felt another surge of the same shame that had beset him upstairs with Isolde.

Was this what he had deteriorated into, a bully who threatened anyone who disagreed with him? Daffyd had become a bully since last he'd seen him. His own father had been the same—brutal, driven. He himself had been the recipient of that brutality often enough to have vowed never to behave thus. But here he was, wielding words like weapons to crush Isolde, and threatening physical violence on an old man half his size. It was not Isolde or Tillo who deserved his anger; that he should reserve for Rand and Jasper FitzHugh. They were his targets, not the others.

He unloosened his fists, then raised his hands and stared at them. He would never be like his father. Never.

He looked over at Tillo. "Of late I have let anger rule sense. In the future I will do better."

Tillo's expression was not forgiving. "A cold swim and a few hours on your knees in prayer—that is the cure for this ailment that plagues you."

Another crash echoed down from the second floor. "Perhaps you are right," Rhys conceded. "That will not ease her mood, however."

Tillo snorted. "Why should you care about her mood?" Another crash. "Save that she may demolish what it took her father twenty years to build." Then Tillo turned a shrewd gaze on Rhys. "You should have sent her on the ship with the others. You can still free her. Send her to Chester, or to her uncle's home at Bailwyn. You do not need her, for whether you hold her hostage or not, you still hold Rosecliffe. The FitzHugh brothers will return here to retake their castle. You will not miss the battle you crave."

Rhys realized that Tillo spoke the truth. But there was something in him not yet ready to release Isolde FitzHugh. "She is too vital a bargaining tool for me to send her away."

"Methinks there is another reason."

Rhys bristled. "My reasons are my reasons. You are free to leave Rosecliffe if you do not find my rule here to your liking."

"Mayhap I will leave this place," Tillo replied. "I would live out my remaining years in a place of peace and contentment. 'Tis what I sought when I followed you here. But you are not peaceful here, Rhys. Nor are you content. I wonder now if ever you will be."

Again Rhys's temper boiled over. "Go then." He gestured angrily at the door. "No one prevents your leaving."

Tillo glanced from Rhys to the door, then toward the stairs. "Let her come with me."

"No!"

The word burst from his lips of its own accord—vehement, final—and Rhys refused to examine its source. Tillo gathered his purple mantle close around him and Rhys had to remind himself again that this was no enemy he faced, but an old man. An old man who had been his friend these many years.

He let out a long sigh. "Seek you your rest, Tillo. There is no reason for us to quarrel. Soon enough the FitzHughs will arrive. Then I will defeat them and peace will return to this place. You will see."

Tillo stared at him unsmiling, and in his old face all the lines earned over a lifetime of tribulation showed. "It may be too late then. Too late," Tillo repeated, turning away.

Rhys watched him shuffle away. With an effort Tillo tugged the heavy iron-strapped door open, letting in an icy blast of winter. Then he disappeared into the bitterly cold dusk outside. A shiver marked its way down Rhys's spine, but he ignored it. Just as life must get worse before it could get better, so would the winter grow colder before the land warmed again.

He would survive both events, he told himself. One day he would be content, just as he would eventually be warm again.

He looked over the hall from his lonely place at the high table. "Stoke the fires," he ordered a passing boy. The lad jumped, all big eyes and fearful expression. "Stoke the big hearth, then see to the fire in mine own chamber," Rhys added.

Isolde would not vent her temper on an innocent lad, he reassured himself.

Then she is a better person than you, an unpleasant voice in his head pointed out.

"Never mind," he said, before the boy could run off. "I'll take care of it myself."

"Stoke the fire? You, milord?" the lad ventured, plainly amazed that the new lord would tend a page's tasks.

"You tend this fire," Rhys said. He stared over at the stairs that led to the upper floors. "I'll tend the other one."

EIGHTEEN

Rhys expected to find his chamber in a shambles. He did not expect, however, the total havoc she'd wreaked. The furnishings were unaffected. His belongings were untouched. But the mural . . .

Only one lamp yet burned, but it cast sufficient light to reveal the enormity of the destruction. He stared at it, stunned at the ruin she'd so swiftly made. Days of work to create a truly magnificent mural, but only a few minutes to destroy it.

"*Uffern dan,*" he swore. He frowned and raked his hands through his hair. "What in God's name has she done?"

Something shifted in the shadows to his left. Someone. Then she stepped forward and crossed boldly in front of him to stand before the smear of paint and water that now covered the wall. "Do you like it?" she sarcastically inquired. She swept her arms wide and stared at him, an odd combination of triumph and wariness on her face. "I think it a vast improvement."

"Damn you, woman!" He advanced on her and she fell back. But still her jaw jutted obstinately forward. Had it not been for the wild glitter in her huge gray eyes and the damp trails down her cheek, he wasn't sure what he might have done. As it was, he grabbed her by the arms, ready to throttle her for such idiocy. But her eyes and their silent testament to her distress affected him in a way he could not explain. Instead of punishing her, he wanted to comfort her.

He wanted to kiss her, he admitted to himself. Not wise at all.

He kept his arms stiff, holding her a safe distance from him. "How could you destroy your own art?"

"I hated it!"

"If you hated it, you would not have labored so long at it. You would not have created the images with such passion and fire."

She glared up at him. "It was hideous."

Outrage warred with understanding. Rhys's hands tightened until he felt the beat of her blood in his fingers. "You will have to repaint it."

Mutely she shook her head.

"You will do as I say, Isolde, else you will suffer the consequences."

Her eyes darkened at his threat, but still she opposed him. "Then I will suffer the consequences. I will not paint your disgusting murals. I will not tend your temporary household. Could I tear down the walls of Rosecliffe, stone by stone, to keep you from possessing it, I would do that, too!"

"*Gwrtaith!* I should have sent you away with the rest of them!"

"Why didn't you?" she cried, struggling finally to free herself.

"Because I wanted—" He broke off. Because he had wanted to possess his enemy's daughter. And because now he simply wanted to possess *her*.

But to tell her that was to reveal how desperate his obsession with her had become.

"You will repaint the mural or suffer the consequences," he repeated, angrier at himself than with her. For he'd underestimated her. She was a worthy opponent, he now saw, far more dangerous than any mounted knight he'd ever battled.

True to form, the stubborn wench answered him. "Then I will suffer the consequences."

Isolde could not explain what drove her to make such a reckless declaration. The same demon that had driven her to ruin the finest work she'd ever done, she supposed. A part of her knew the mural had been exceptional. But though it was beyond the ordinary, it was nevertheless obscene and an insult to everything she believed in. She been right to destroy it. Now, though, she must prepare herself to suffer his retaliation.

"Uffern dan," he swore again, his black eyes glittering. "God save me from—" He broke off. "Any other man would beat you for your defiance."

Isolde felt an undeniable quiver of relief. At least he did not mean to beat her.

"Any other man would make quick use of you, then discard you for the pleasure of his men. Ah, I see that draws a response from you," he added when she sucked in a fearful breath.

So it did. "But you are not like other men," she prompted, unable to bear the suspense of what he had in mind for her.

Again she felt his hands tighten around her arms. But this time an emotion other than fury seemed to drive him. It was desire, she realized. A purely carnal desire for her. She recognized it because she too felt the same emotion.

She shuddered, appalled by such perverseness in her nature. She desired a man she hated. She made a masterpiece of a mural she despised. But she had destroyed the mural, she reminded herself, and she would destroy these inappropriate feelings, too. Then she would help her father destroy Rhys.

But was that truly what she wanted to do? She knew it was not, and once more she shivered.

"No," he said in a rough whisper, pulling her nearer. "I am not like other men. I am more the fool than they." He stared down into her eyes, not blinking. Not moving. He was all tension and muscle and more dangerous than he had ever been. Yet Isolde was afraid to move, afraid to break the spell that held them together this long, tenuous moment.

He held her so long she thought surely he would kiss her, as he'd done before. What would she do then?

She did not have the opportunity to find out, for with a groan he suddenly thrust her away. "Get up to the tower room," he ordered in a voice raw with emotion.

She stumbled, then caught herself on the sturdy table beside the door. "Gladly!" she flung back at him. "Anything to be out of this room—and to be rid of your unbearable presence!"

But she did not leave. She stood in the doorway, caught between right and wrong, between duty and desire. She wanted to hate him—and she did. But something prevented her from hating him as completely as she should. On impulse she said, "Leave here, Rhys. Leave here before anyone has to die. 'Tis not worth it."

Whatever emotions he felt seemed to harden at her words. His lips twisted cynically. "Who are you afraid for, Isolde? Your father? Your uncle?" He waited, a grim expression on his face, and she suspected he wanted to keep anger as a buffer between them. But she was done with anger. She'd spent her anger destroying the mural.

Who was she afraid for?

She answered with the truth. "Yes. I am afraid for them. But I am also afraid for you, Rhys. For you." Then she turned and she fled. Up the dimly lit stairwell. Up to the tower, and away from the tumult of feelings he roused in her.

Rhys stared after her a long while, long enough to slow the thundering pace of his heart and bring his breathing under control. But his muscles remained tense. His entire body remained rigid. It was the only way he could prevent himself from following her.

Why had she said that?

Did she mean it? Was she afraid for him?

With a grimace he tore his gaze from the empty doorway. When it lit upon the mural, however, he let loose a curt oath. He spun on his heel, only to face the massive curtained bed. This time he let out a groan.

She was twisting him into knots, and he seemed unable to stop her. When she was furious he wanted to tame her. When she was distraught he wanted to comfort her. Those perverse responses to her were bad enough. But that admission of concern she'd made, that small expression of worry . . . Had she not fled the room, he feared he might have been sucked body and soul into the comfort he'd seen in her eyes.

He had desired many women through the years, and most of them had professed to worry about him when he rode into battles or tournaments or melees. But their concern had been more for themselves than for him. Every woman wanted her lover to be champion, to defeat the men he rode against. It increased a woman's standing to have a powerful lover. He'd understood their concern for him, and he'd used it to his advantage.

Before them he'd not known any woman's concern—save,

briefly, for Josselyn's. But she'd betrayed her people for a FitzHugh, and later his friend Rhonwen had done the same. Their worry for him had not been sincere. As for his mother, she'd died when he was but a babe.

Now there was Isolde expressing concern for him. Was he supposed to believe her?

He rubbed a hand over his eyes and grimaced. He'd be a fool to believe her. A witless fool. But a part of him wanted to do just that, and he was afraid to wonder why. So he turned away from the bed and the mural and the door, and he crossed to the narrow window. It was cold outside and he pressed his overheated brow against the rare panes of glass, trying to clear his mind.

He pounded one fist against the window frame. It was the waiting that was addling his brain. He needed to confront his foes and strike them down. Waiting for their return was driving him mad.

But waiting was all he could do. Wait and prepare, and learn every secret of the enemy fortress he had seized.

The next three days he did just that. No passage or storeroom was too insignificant for his study. From the cranking mechanism of the mighty bridge, to the postern gate behind the kitchen, to the steep descent to the beach below, he examined everything—everything except the tower room. He avoided the tower room and its maddening occupant. Instead of confronting her, he confronted every other person now under his rule.

He goaded the woodcutters to increase their efforts, demanded that the fishermen and hunters remain long hours at their tasks and ordered all their game smoked or salted, cured and packed for future use. He demanded that the armorer and all his men-at-arms labor just as diligently repairing weapons, stockpiling arrows and spearheads, and oiling the leather straps and lacings that kept both weapons and armor in their best working order.

A battle was imminent, as was a siege, and Rhys prepared for both, using every bit of planning and cunning he'd learned during his years as both a Welsh rebel and an English knight. As the days passed, his confidence increased. This was the test he'd prepared all his life for. He would not lose Rosecliffe. He could not.

Unfortunately the days occupied but half of Rhys's time. The nights were another matter altogether. Another form of torture. He spent those long and grueling hours alone in his chamber, lying in the giant bed, staring up at the violent smear of color that dominated the room, and thinking of her. By day the ruined mural was just that, a magnificent image lost forever. By lamplight, however, hidden images revealed themselves. And by the erratic flicker of the niche fireplace, Rhys could almost believe that shadowy figures moved in its depths. He scoffed at such fanciful imaginings. If images on that wall moved, it was because of late he'd been drinking more than was his wont. Still, a sane man would have had the wall whitewashed, or would have hung a tapestry over the ruin Isolde had wrought.

But therein lay Rhys's problem. For he'd come to the morose conclusion that he must not be a sane man.

On the night of the third day of Isolde's confinement, Rhys entered his chamber later than usual, and drunker. The castle was asleep save for the guards posted along the walls. He'd sat the whole evening in the lord's chair, scowling into his ale while Linus and Gandy entertained the castle folk. But it was hard to achieve a jovial mood. With each passing day the tension mounted, for everyone knew a battle was inevitable. So Linus and Gandy had abandoned their routine, and people had drifted quietly away. Now, in addition to the bitter cold, the night wind was heavy with the wet scent of snow. They'd had two days of warmth and thaw, but now another winter storm approached.

Removing his girdle, Rhys hung his short sword on a wall peg, then unstrapped his dagger sheath and tossed it on the bed along with his hood and gloves. He stood there a moment and scrubbed his hands over his weary face. Then he stared at the heavily draped bed. His chamber was cold, but not bitterly so. A brazier filled with hot coals had only to be slid between the linens to warm the bedclothes, and once he was beneath the coverings with the hangings drawn, the bed would warm up nicely.

But there were other ways to heat a bed, other ways far

more appealing than hot coals in an iron brazier.

"Damnation," he swore and sent a killing glare toward the mural. Like a dark devil tormenting him, it merely stared back at him—the hulking mess that had been the dragon, the prone swirl that had been the wolf. He fancied the wolf still stared at him, the yellow eyes a clear gray now, though shielded behind the muddy shadow of paint.

Damn her!

He snatched up an ewer and flung it against the wall. It crashed high against the mural, drenching the painting with water that streamed down the wall in streaks of gray and red.

Rhys raked his hands through his hair, conscious that he was shaking. She had done this to him. His plan to take Rosecliffe had been daring but it had succeeded. Now she was wreaking havoc with that success. He took a deep breath, willing himself to a hard-fought calm.

As a boy he'd held her—an infant—in his arms, he reminded himself. As a youth he'd fought her family and, for a short while, held her hostage. Now she was once again his hostage. Yet perversely it felt more like he'd been imprisoned by her. She haunted his thoughts and his dreams. She tortured him waking and sleeping. And why?

Because he was frustrated. It was that simple, he told himself.

Like a randy youth, his body craved hers. He spent half the day fighting down his desire for her. Only when his body was fully engaged in physical effort—when sparring with his men or laboring beside them—did he defeat the demon in his braies. But at all other times he was sore beset. Especially here, in the chamber where he had lain with her.

He felt it now, the urgent desire to possess her, and for just a moment he did not fight it. He wanted her. And she wanted him. He'd tasted desire on her lips and felt it in the arch of her soft, supple body against his.

Why had he denied himself and her? What foolish point of pride had he been trying to make?

The beast inside him raged and he pressed a hand to his aching groin. Damn her for besting him in this private war they waged!

He spun abruptly on his heel and stalked to the door. He

took the narrow stairs two at a time, and before good sense could stop him, he stood on the fourth level facing the thick oak door to the tower room. Three days of agony. It must end now.

But what was he going to do?

End this torment she caused. Assuage this hunger that gripped him. Take what was his to take.

To the victor went the spoils. He was the victor; she was the spoils. He'd had enough of waiting. He placed his hand on the door latch, then froze when he heard a sound. Holding his breath, he pressed his ear to the door. She was speaking out loud.

". . . help me to do what I ought . . ."

No. She was praying.

". . . 'tis a sin. I know it is," she went on in a low voice laced with emotion. "I am a sinner." Then she moaned and Rhys swallowed hard. She was praying and yet that little sound she'd made incited him even further. God, but he was no better than his coarse, rutting father—to want a woman even as she was at her prayers.

He started to back away. When he heard the soft sound of her sobs, however, he froze. By the rood! She was weeping. But why?

Idiot! he chastised himself. You've taken her innocence and her freedom and have vowed to kill her family. What else could any woman do but weep?

What he was to do—that was the real dilemma. His hand tightened on the latch. He wanted to flee, but he could not. Then she moaned again, and without pausing to think, he pushed into the small chamber.

A single candle flickered in a flat dish and it nearly guttered when he swung the door open. The tiny flame nonetheless lit most of the small room with a faint golden glow, enough for Rhys to see Isolde jerk upright on her small pallet. Tears sparkled on her cheeks—her flushed cheeks. They glinted in her eyes as well, dark and wide and staring. Her hair was loose and long, a wealth of silken tangles, and she wore only her chemise. Her feet were bare as were her legs, until she hastily pushed the hem of her chemise down to cover them.

He stared, mesmerized. She was woman at her most basic,

hidden only by a single layer of thin linen, and he reacted as man at his most basic. If he'd wanted her before, now he was rabid to possess her.

"You . . . you came," she murmured. "I was just thinking of you and . . . and you came."

"You were praying." Idiot words, he immediately thought. But his mind seemed momentarily disengaged. For some reason, however, his comment caused her face to go scarlet.

Isolde licked her lips and averted her eyes. She had indeed been praying, but it had done no good. Or perhaps it had. For he had come. She'd been thinking of him—dreaming of him— and remembering all the ways he'd touched her. And as if he were there, touching her again, her body had become inflamed. Though she knew it was wrong, she'd lain there upon the pallet and let her fingers find the places that most ached for him. She had touched herself, then hated herself for doing it. Then he'd appeared, the answer to her prayers.

Slowly she raised her gaze back to him. "You overheard what I was saying?"

He nodded. "But if you are a sinner, Isolde, I am ten times more so."

She stared up at him from her place on the low bed. She saw how his wide shoulders filled the doorway and his powerful personality cast an aura over her. Had he come to sin with her? Her heart leaped with joy. Though she knew she should disdain him and send him away, she simply could not. He'd come at a moment when she most wanted him. For three days she'd pictured him in that doorway, filling the space with his warrior's body, bending slightly to enter . . .

As if he divined her thoughts, he did just that. He bent his head slightly, then entered and closed the door behind him. It creaked and shut with a solemn thud.

Isolde swallowed hard. Like a creature with a life and will of its own, her body reacted to his nearness, to the sensual spell he cast over her. She had destroyed the mural he admired. But in the three days of her confinement for that transgression, she'd thought of nothing but that dragon looming over the wolf. The wolf she'd painted had not been afraid, and she was not afraid now either. At least, she was not afraid of him. Rhys would not hurt her, not physically. But her heart . . . That he could shred—and would.

For a moment she hesitated. If she gave in to these fierce longings, she would regret it. Not tonight, perhaps. But someday.

But you will regret it far more if you deny him. You will regret it every day for the remainder of your life. Though it was wrong, though it was a sin, Isolde knew what she must do.

He advanced toward her. Three strides and he towered over her. His night-dark eyes burned into hers, then raked her thinly clad form. She shivered with rising desire. He knew what she felt. He'd known from the very first.

"I've come for you," he said, his voice low and hoarse. "You'll not deny me."

"No."

"Do not say me nay, Isolde. 'Tis a useless gesture."

She let out a sound that was half sob, half hysterical giggle. "I meant no, I will not deny you."

If possible his gaze grew even more torrid. Isolde felt like a pagan offering, a virtuous maid given up to appease a vengeful God. Except that she was no longer virtuous. Certainly her thoughts prior to his arrival had been anything but virtuous. Without thinking she murmured his name. "Rhys . . ."

Like the dragon warrior he was, he swooped down upon her. As if her weight were nothing, he lifted her high and she let him. Held in his arms, his powerful enemy arms, she resigned herself to her fate, and chafed with impatience for it. Down the stairs they flew, the dragon and his captive. Into his lair, into the heavily draped shadows of the massive bed.

Then he loomed over her, the hot-blooded demon of her dreams, and she welcomed him.

His clothes were few; hers practically nonexistent. Something ripped but neither of them cared. They struggled; it was very nearly a battle. His strength was greater and he pressed her deep into the bedding. But Isolde's strength was of another sort. She pulled Rhys into her and forced him to be gentle. He dominated her, but she tamed him.

And when his straining manhood pressed against her belly, at once both threatening and promising, Isolde arched her body against him, heedless of that threat. She wanted the promise he held, the promise of relief and pleasure and unimaginable joy.

This time there was no pain, only heat and fullness and an inexplicable sense of connectedness. It felt good and right, and without warning, the sob she'd suppressed broke free.

"Rhys," she gasped, clinging to him.

He answered her with a kiss, hard and demanding. He claimed her mouth even as he claimed her body. He wanted everything from her, and meant plainly to take it. But she wanted everything, too.

As he began the fierce rhythm of possession, Isolde met each powerful thrust. He was the dragon, to be feared. To be fought. But she was the wolf and she had her own strengths. Their bodies wrestled, sliding slickly together. Their breath mingled—gasps, groans, and long, low sighs of pleasure. He was driven on and on, tireless and desperate, and he lit her with fire.

Isolde clung to his wide shoulders, damp now from their exertions. Her arms circled his neck. Her fingers tightened in his hair. Her legs circled his hips. Then, as if all his power were suddenly vested in her, she felt the monumental wave begin.

He must have felt it, too, for his thrusts grew faster and even deeper than before. Suddenly she was afraid. It was too much for her. He must stop—

"Isolde," he panted. "Isolde—"

Then with a fearful cry, she succumbed to the wave. It crashed over her, sucking her down, lifting her up. It washed over her, leaving her gasping, shaking. Practically insensible. But still, she heard his shout as the wave caught him, too. She felt every wonderful, terrifying shudder, both his and her own. And when he had flooded her with passion, then collapsed spent upon her, she hugged him as tightly as her trembling arms could manage.

In the shattering aftermath, however, she refused to think. Instead she lay beneath him, damp and hot, despite the winter cold. He had slain her with his passion, and enslaved her, it seemed. But for now he was hers, and right or wrong, she would not let him go.

The room cooled around them. The small fire died to embers. The one candle sputtered, then drowned in its own pool of melted wax, so that they lay in a comforting darkness. Then Rhys groaned and pushed up from her, and Isolde took a deep, greedy breath.

"My pardon," he murmured, rolling at once to the side. But his arm stayed tight around her so that he took her with him. Lying atop him was an astounding experience. He was big and hot and hard. Yet they fit so well together. When she shivered from the chill, he tugged a thickly woven wool blanket over them, and though it was scratchy, Isolde did not mind. Her skin felt excruciatingly alive to every touch and every texture. Yet each sensation felt good. She felt good and sated and so utterly exhausted.

When she awoke she lay on her side with her back to Rhys who curled around her. His arms were strong and safe, and she could easily have succumbed again to the lulling security of sleep. But she blinked and forced herself awake.

What had she done?

He was naked against her, so the answer was more than clear. But why had she done it? That was less clear. How could she have lain so eagerly with her enemy?

Behind her Rhys shifted in his sleep and his knee insinuated itself between her legs. He sighed and his warm breath heated the back of her neck. Then his right hand moved and the knuckles grazed the bare peak of one of her breasts. At once Isolde's body tightened in arousal. Every part of her from breast to belly, as well as the entire surface of her skin, shivered into readiness. He brushed the taut nipple again, a deliberate, provocative movement—

He was awake.

The heat in her belly became an inferno.

"Do you like that?" he whispered into her hair.

Isolde could not answer, not with words. But the breath caught in her throat, and she grew warm all over. Hot. He seemed somehow to understand. His knuckles kept up that slow stroke, a faint grazing of first one rigid peak, then the other.

"I can continue this all night, Isolde. All night. All day. Would you like that?" He nuzzled through her tangled hair and kissed the nape of her neck, and all the while kept up the tortuous, seductive movement of his knuckles.

"I . . . I like it," she confessed, hardly aware she'd spoken the words out loud.

He pulled her closer, pressing against her naked backside. She felt the clear outline of his rigid manhood against her and she shivered with anticipation. Was he going to join with her again? Heavenly Mary, but she hoped so! She should be ashamed to feel that way, but to herself, at least, she could not lie. She wanted more of this man. This one and no other. She needed more of him.

His knuckle gave way to his thumb and when a small excited groan slipped from between her lips, he groaned, too. Without warning, he flipped her onto her back, and suddenly he lay between her legs.

In the darkness she could see little enough. But she saw his eyes and the faint glitter of light and heat in their midnight depths.

"How I would like to keep you forever, Isolde. Hidden away in this tower. In this room. Away from all others. Just keep you for my own pleasure. And for yours."

Then his mouth found her peaked nipples and she cried out in pleasure, gripping his shoulders. She dug her fingertips into his flesh as she lifted her hips in silent supplication. She was hot and ready. In truth, she was frantic to have him inside her.

But he was far more patient than she. While she panted and cried out and bucked beneath him, he concentrated on her breasts, cupping them in his hands and teasing them with his lips and teeth and tongue. He wet them, blew upon them, then nibbled and drew them deep into his mouth. It was a torture and a pleasure, an unbearable delight.

But though Isolde tugged frantically at his shoulders, trying to draw him up and over her to relieve this terrible need he roused, he would not relent. Only when she truly thought she could bear no more did he finally move lower, pressing those same kisses and erotic caresses down her ribs to her navel and belly. But his hands continued to stroke and tease her nipples and breasts.

Then his mouth moved to the place between her legs and Isolde gasped. Momentarily panicked, she tried to twist away from his seeking lips. But he caught her by the waist and kept her still. "Don't fight me, Isolde. Don't fight what you feel. Let me caress you. Let me show you how sweet it can be for you. How powerful."

"But . . . But I can't—"

"You can." And he swiftly proved he was right. For at the touch of his lips to the hidden place between her legs, Isolde's struggles died a swift, sure death. Every fiber of her being focused instead on the unthinkable things he was doing to her. The unimaginably exquisite things he was doing to her.

Her heart thundered in her chest; blood roared in her ears. And when she erupted beneath him, it was with a cry of utter capitulation.

At once Rhys covered her body with his, thrusting deep into her. That only magnified the ongoing tremors further still. Like a man consumed by a furious passion, he moved in and out with long, hard strokes. Taking her. Marking her. Making her cry out with the force of her passion. On and on, until Isolde thought she must die of the pleasure. Then with a last, final plunge and a cry of his own, he found his release.

In the stunning aftermath, they were hot and damp and entwined so completely Isolde felt as if there could be nothing else. Nothing further. Not another day or night. No future at all. Only forever, just as they were. A perfect completion. A perfect union.

NINETEEN

RHYS SLEPT AND HE DREAMED, AND IN EVERY DREAM HE WAS content. He was not hungry or cold, or lonely. He did not have to fight for survival or for any other purpose. He was content. He was happy.

He felt the woman at his side. She snuggled against him, soft and warm, damp and fragrant with their lovemaking. He sighed, more satisfied than he had ever been, and he slept more soundly than was his wont.

Once he shivered, but he was quickly warm again, and it was easy to let down his guard for once, easier than it had ever been after a lifetime of wariness. "Isolde," he mumbled, reaching out to her, wanting to hold her close. "Isolde?"

When he awoke it was abruptly. The room was cold, the fire dead, the candle spent. "Isolde?" he called once more. Then in a rush his dreams dissipated into bitter reality. The bed was empty.

She was gone.

"Bitch!" he swore as he tore from the bed. He yanked on his braies and grabbed his dagger. Then like a maddened bull, he was after her.

Ignoring the icy air on his bare torso, Rhys charged barefoot up to the tower room. Empty. Down to the hall he rushed where the silence was broken only by the occasional snores of the several servants rolled in rugs near the hearth. He pressed on, out into the freezing cold of the bailey.

Where was she?

He halted and forced himself to slow his raging, blind pursuit of her. In the dark, oppressive night, his breath showed in cold, pale puffs. He thrust one hand through his hair. She could not have gone far. He would have to collect his wits, however, if he expected to find her.

But he found it nearly impossible to be sensible. She had betrayed him. She had given herself so sweetly to him. So completely. She'd curled into his arms like a lover and lulled him to complacency. But he should have known better than to trust her. She was a FitzHugh, after all, and in the end she had reverted to her true nature. She was his enemy, born and bred to oppose him—as he must oppose her. He should not be surprised at what she'd done.

But he was.

He stared around him, up at the sheer walls, across to the stables and laundry shed and kitchen, and he gripped his dagger so hard his hand shook. Though half-hidden by clouds, the moon was full. He wanted to howl his rage into the sky. To howl his pain. Somewhere in the distance a dog or wolf did howl, a cold, lonely sound.

But Rhys had no time to pander to his emotions. She thought she'd escaped him. She thought she could use her body and his raging desire to dupe him. But she was sorely mistaken. He would hunt her down. He would bring her back.

And she would regret forever the day she'd thought to deceive Rhys ap Owain.

Isolde flattened herself against the base of the outer wall. Someone else was there!

Someone else stood outside the castle walls, motionless, silhouetted against the sea, blocking the cliff path down to the beach. A guard? Pray God it was not that wretch Dafydd!

The wind blasted against Isolde, damp and bitterly cold from its long journey across the northern sea. She shivered. Her skin was still damp and the mantle she'd taken was not adequate. She had snatched it up as she'd fled the tower, driven by fear and shame, and confused loyalties. Now she hugged it close around her and tried to think. Perhaps if she sidled away from the postern gate and hid in the shadows. Perhaps the man would not detect her there and she could wait until he eventually left. Please, God, let it be so, she pleaded as she inched silently to the left.

As if in answer to her fragmented prayer, the guard silently turned and slowly limped toward the gate. It was too dark to see his face, and too dark for him to see her, Isolde hoped. But as the fellow gingerly moved nearer, Isolde squinted into the darkness. He was small and old, and not a guard at all.

And not a man, either.

"Tillo?" Isolde spoke without meaning to, she was that relieved.

The figure halted. " 'Tis I, child," the old woman said, as if Isolde's presence was no real surprise. "I have been worried about you."

"You needn't have worried. I am . . . I am all right," Isolde said, hunching down into her mantle.

"I am told you have not been down to the hall." Tillo drew nearer. "Not in three days."

"No."

"Not of your own choice, I'd wager."

Isolde did not respond to that. If she had not ruined the dragon and wolf mural Rhys so admired, he would not have held her hostage in the tower so long.

Tillo let out a grim chuckle. "Not allowed down to the hall. Kept locked up in the tower. Yet now you roam outside the castle walls. 'Tis a curious thing, indeed. Do you flee him?"

Again Isolde did not reply. She could not. Yes, she was fleeing Rhys. But not for any reasons Tillo could understand. No one could possibly understand, for she herself could not explain her feelings. "I do not want there to be a battle here," she finally muttered in explanation. "You said you'd help me escape."

"Ah, child. Where once I thought you might be able to prevent it, now I am not so certain. 'Tis fated, I fear." Tillo sighed then lowered her frail frame onto a rough limestone block beside the gate. "Men will fight. That is the long and short of it. They are bred for it. Men will fight and women will weep for them."

Isolde began to pace, wringing her hands together. "But women can fight, too. Not in the same way as men. Not with swords. But sometimes we can force men to our will."

The old woman laughed, a thin, high crackle in the gusty night. "So. You think you can force Rhys to abandon his life-long goal by fleeing from him?"

"No. No." Isolde shook her head miserably. " 'Tis my father I seek. If I can just find him, I can convince him . . ." She trailed off, recognizing the flaws in that plan, too. She gestured hopelessly with her hands. "What else can I do?"

"I wonder," Tillo mused "I wonder what is the right thing to do. Oftentimes, when the decision is hard, we overlook the simplest of solutions. You must do what is right, Isolde. But then you must be willing to suffer the consequences."

"But what is right? Who is right?"

Tillo was silent a long time. When she stood, she faltered and Isolde reached out to steady her. Up close the old woman's face looked weary, and sad. "I have no answers for you, Isolde. I have not always been right in my own choices, so I am perhaps not the best person to guide you in your journey. But hear this one thing, child. Search your heart. Search it, and do not fear the pain you dredge up. To live in this world is to feel pain. That much I know is true."

Tillo moved toward the gate in the wall, and Isolde let her hand fall away from the old woman. Search her heart? What was she to make of that? If anything it confused her even more.

She turned her head and stared out into the darkness, to where the sea beat its steady rhythm against the land. She had fled Rhys and the bed they had shared, for she'd been so afraid of the emotions he'd forced her to reveal. He had found her out, all her secret passions and desires, and she was afraid to face him in the light of day. So she had taken a chance on escape, and she had succeeded. She had only to get herself down the cliff to the beach, then make her way past the castle, toward Carreg Du and the road her father must take.

But then, what would that accomplish? Her father would never relinquish Rosecliffe Castle without a fight, no matter what she said to him. And he had right on his side.

But Rhys felt he was right as well, and a small part of Isolde understood why. These had always been Welsh lands. For a hundred years. For a thousand. The hills, the valleys, the cliffs, and the rocky shoreline. To Rhys her family was the usurper. But she was half Welsh, as were her brother and sister. One day Gavin would sit as lord of Rosecliffe. If only Rhys could be patient. If only he could understand that the FitzHughs wanted good things for the Welsh marches, the same good things he wanted. If only she could convince him.

She turned to face the castle again and let her eyes roam up the massive stone wall, up from the base and the sturdy postern gate to the stones set too evenly for anyone ever to climb very far. She tilted her head to see all the way up to the battlements at the crest. This was her home. But the rose cliffs were part of Rhys's home, too. He remembered the cliffs before the castle was here. While her earliest memories were of ongoing construction and walls rising ever taller, he remembered a bare promontory, a long rocky hill covered with wild roses, then a rugged fall down to the sea. And yet he admired the castle and its mighty fortifications. She had watched from the tower as he explored it, trying to learn all its secrets.

Her father and Rhys both loved Rosecliffe. Was there truly no possibility of compromise, or of peace?

She pushed her wind-whipped hair back from her brow. If she left here now, she would never have the answer to the question.

Isolde turned abruptly on her heel. It was becoming clear what she must do, and it would be painful, just as Tillo had warned. She walked to the edge of the cliff and stared down toward the beach, straining against the dark to see the path she had meant to take, but now would not. She would never convince her father to abandon Rosecliffe to Rhys. But maybe she could convince Rhys that her family loved this part of Wales as much as he did. In his own way Rhys was as honorable and brave as her father. Perhaps she could search out enough common ground between them to forge a compromise.

An unlikely occurrence, she knew. But as she turned back to the castle, Isolde knew she must try. There were no true villains in this tragedy. She was beginning to see that now. Even Rhys was not so dreadful a person as she had imagined all these years. He was not dreadful at all. At times he seemed to actually care for her. Perhaps she could become the connection between him and her father—

"What do you think you are doing?"

Isolde gasped and froze in mid-stride. "Rhys?" But of course it was Rhys.

For one insane moment Isolde's heart thumped in glad recognition. He had come after her because there was some strange sort of bond connecting them, a bond that could be the beginning of a real and lasting peace between them.

Then he crossed the narrow ledge and caught her arm in an unforgiving grasp, and her gladness withered to doubt, and then to fear.

"You deceitful bitch."

She flinched at the coldness in his tone. "No. Wait." She tried to hold him off with her hands. His chest was bare where her palms rested, however. He wore only his braies, she realized, further disconcerted.

"Wait for what?" he growled. "For you to summon your countrymen? To lead them inside Rosecliffe so they can murder us in our sleep?"

"No! Listen to me, Rhys—"

"No!" He shook her hard. "No, I'll not listen. I'll not listen to any further lies from you!"

"But I'm not lying—"

"All women lie," he coldly bit out. "That is how they get along in the world."

Isolde gasped and recoiled at the pure contempt in his voice. Better that he had struck her full in the face than to have said that to her. The fact that he was so wrong spurred her from desolation to fury.

"Yes. You're so right, Rhys ap Owain. So knowledgeable. So wise. You know everything about everything—especially women."

Again he shook her, then shoved her up against the wooden gate. "I know what I see. And what I see is a woman who will lie beneath a man, who will spread her legs for him and take her pleasure with him, then ruthlessly stab him in the back."

His face was but inches from hers and though the darkness hid his expression, she nonetheless felt the full blast of his disgust. He was so wrong! What she sought was peace, not revenge. Yet she had no voice to tell him—none that he would hear, anyway.

A sob caught in her throat, a cold lump of bitter emotions. Why must it be this way between them? Why? She shook her head and fought to control her breathing, and to prevent bursting into tears. Her fingers splayed against his solidly muscled chest. The surface was rigid and prickled with the cold. Beneath the surface, however, was warmth. If only she could reach beyond his unyielding surface to the good and passionate man at his core.

"Rhys—"

He slammed his fist against the gate just beside her head, and she shrieked.

"If you value your pretty little neck, you will push me no further, Isolde." Then he yanked her to the side, jerked the gate open, and shoved her into the narrow passageway. "Get to the tower. Now."

Isolde did not wait for a second order. She fled blindly through the passage, guiding herself through the black tunnel with her fingers along one wall. Back to the tower. Back to her prison. Back to an even more hopeless situation than before.

Rhys waited until she was gone, praying all the while that she'd done as he had ordered. If she wasn't in the tower and he had to seek her out again, he did not think he could control himself.

He locked the postern gate, then leaned stiff-armed against it, breathing hard. He had wanted to hurt her. He hadn't done it. He'd restrained himself. But he'd wanted to.

But why?

The answer was simple. Because she had hurt him.

He wanted to deny it was true, but he could not. She'd struck him a blow more painful than any wound he'd ever received in battle. Blood could be stanched. Bones could be mended, and flesh stitched together. But he had a hole in his chest now, a huge, gaping wound—at least that was how it felt. And all on account of her. She'd ripped something apart inside of him, and he ached now with every fiber of his being.

She is not wrong to defend her family.

Rhys closed his eyes. It was painful to acknowledge that truth. It was harder still to admit that he wanted that loyalty of hers directed toward him, and him alone.

"Jesus God!" he swore. He pushed away from the door and started down the dark passage through the massive stone walls. Taking Rosecliffe castle had been a Herculean task, perhaps an impossible one, he had often feared during his long years away. Yet he had succeeded in his quest. With perseverance and determination and daring, he had succeeded. Though it should bring him great satisfaction, however, it did not. *She* was the reason for that.

If conquering Rosecliffe had been a farfetched idea, however, he now saw that conquering its fiery mistress was even more so. But he would do it. He would bring her to heel, if only on the strength of her naturally passionate nature.

As he strode into the silent bailey, he firmly quashed the possibility that it was she who might yet conquer him.

Josselyn and Rhonwen rode side by side. Contrary to their husbands' fears, their presence did not slow the progress of the small army the FitzHugh brothers had raised. Indeed, the two women were as driven as any of the men to return to Rosecliffe. Josselyn worried for her daughter; Rhonwen worried for her niece; and both of them worried for Rhys. Rebel he might be, a rogue knight who threatened everything they loved. But he was also their countryman, and he fought his battle for the sake of their country.

Josselyn could not help remembering a motherless little boy she'd tried to befriend, a child mistreated by his father and loved by no one. Rhonwen recalled the friend of her youth, an idealistic lad who'd always seemed to draw misfits to him.

"He has no family of his own," Rhonwen said.

"But an abundance of friends," Josselyn responded, knowing instinctively to whom Rhonwen referred. "He travels with a band of minstrels."

"Yes. A giant and a dwarf, the messenger said. He always had the talent to draw others to him, to inspire their loyalty. Especially those with no other place to turn."

"Lonely souls like himself," Josselyn mused.

"Like I once was," Rhonwen added.

They rode a while in silence. When the column of riders approached a long trench that snaked across the countryside, the women shared a smile. "Home," Rhonwen said, breathing deeply. They had reached Offa's Dyke, the meandering border dug during ancient times between England and Wales. "Only two more days at this pace."

"We cannot allow this to become a full-scale war, Rhonwen. No one will win, and everyone will lose."

"But what can we do?"

The older of the two women stared past the heavily armed men ahead of them, to where her husband and Rhonwen's rode together. What a magnificent pair they were. Strong. Handsome. Dedicated to their families. "Would he make a good husband?"

Again there was no reason to explain who "he" was. "For Isolde?" Rhonwen asked. "Politically, yes. There is much to be said for a match between them."

"It would solve a multitude of problems."

"But would Rand agree?"

Josselyn sighed. " 'Tis not Rand who worries me. Isolde has been headstrong in the matter of a husband."

Rhonwen nodded. "And she hates Rhys. She always has."

"What of Rhys? Would he agree to such a thing? And would he be good to her?"

Rhonwen chewed her lower lip. "He is not a bad man, you know."

"Yes, I believe that. But he has been gone from here for ten years, and his reputation is fierce. Rhys the Wroth. Rhys the Enraged. He is called that and more."

"Our husbands also had fierce reputations. But that was in battle. They have ever been gentle with us. Except for when we wish them to be rough," Rhonwen added with a saucy grin.

Josselyn rolled her eyes. "You make a good point. But Isolde is my child. My firstborn. I must be sure before I suggest a marriage between her and Rhys. After all," she added, her face turning grim. "He is the son of Owain ap Madoc."

"When he weds he will not be like Owain. Of that I am certain," Rhonwen vowed.

They guided their horses down into the trench, then up onto Welsh soil. "Then I suppose we are decided," Josselyn said at last.

"In truth, it seems to be the only way to achieve a lasting

peace," Rhonwen agreed. "Enemies wed to one another." Then she laughed. "An unusual situation, to be sure. But we have, both of us, found happiness in that very same manner. Why should it not be so for Isolde and Rhys?"

TWENTY

THE SNOWS RETURNED. THE WIND HOWLED IN FROM THE SEA, bitterly cold and with a dampness that cut to the bone and pierced to the soul. No place in Rosecliffe Castle was warm enough, especially the small tower room. Higher than the castle's outer walls, it was unprotected and exposed to the rip and claw of the winter squall.

Despite the hideous weather Isolde sat outside the tower room on the side of the walkway opposite the wind. She could not bear another minute of confinement inside the tiny room. Yet being outside was little improvement. Despite three pairs of stockings, two chemises, two kirtles, a heavy mantle, a thick shawl, and a wool blanket covering her, she could not get warm enough. Worse, however, there was nothing for her to see from her frigid perch, save the castle yard, still and frozen beneath the shrouding silence of the snow.

What she would give for a few minutes of company. But there was no one about. Even the guards were inside. The only movement visible was the gusting swirls of snow piling up against the walls in the bailey She breathed into her cupped gloved hands and tried unsuccessfully to retain the heat against her cheeks and nose. Her ears were freezing and her fingertips were numb. Her toes were beyond numb.

Stubborn fool! Go down to the hall.

She drew the blanket over her head, burrowing into the darkness, and again breathed into her cupped hands. She was being childish, she knew. Rhys would not deny her the warmth of the hall. In truth, he'd sent several of his lackeys to bring her downstairs. Gandy had been the first to come, though he had been so muffled as to be nearly unrecognizable. "He bids you come down," the dwarf had said.

She'd sent him swiftly on his way and, later, had sent Linus away as well. Then Tillo. At least Tillo had understood Isolde's obstinance. Still, the old woman's parting words had been sharp. "What does it gain you to win this war of wills if you freeze to death, or else succumb to a fever of the lungs?"

But Isolde had resisted every urge to descend to the great hall where a huge fire fought back the cold. Rhys would be there and she was too sick at heart to be anywhere near him. She hated him; she desired him. She wanted to protect him; she wanted to escape him. It was utter lunacy. Yet after hours of pondering her behavior, she'd been led time and time again to only one miserable conclusion. She was falling in love with Rhys. It was madness. It was self-destructive. It was a curse. Yet what else could this confusion of emotions be?

She curled her feet closer under her legs. Better to freeze to death on the overlook than let the awful wretch see how cruelly he tormented her. What a delight he would take in such knowledge.

She peered unhappily out from her blanket tent and stared at the oppressive sky, then shivered when a cold gust of wind billowed the blanket. She could not hold out very much longer, she glumly realized. Soon she would have to descend to the warmer hall, for she did not think she could bear another night like the last one, shivering too violently to sleep.

Why was she being so obstinate?

"Why must you be so obstinate?"

Isolde peeked out from beneath the blanket. Had someone spoken? Or was she beginning to hear voices in the icy wind?

"Isolde!" A large hand shook her shoulder and she let out a shriek. "Come along. I'll not allow you to freeze to death on account of stubbornness." In a moment she was lifted up, blanket and all, and cradled in a pair of strong arms. Rhys's strong arms. "You're practically frozen," he muttered.

"I am not," she countered. But her voice was muffled by the blanket. She started to struggle against his high-handedness. But in truth he was so warm and strong that she could not muster any opposition. She was so very tired of fighting him. Besides, he'd come for her himself, instead of sending one of his cohorts. Her anger dissipated, she let out a sigh, and sank contentedly into his embrace. It would be warmer in the great hall and the food would be hot. How good it would feel. How good he felt.

As he strode down the stairs, Rhys cursed himself for a fool, for an idiot. For a selfish, single-minded bastard. She'd rebuffed everyone he'd sent up to her. But instead of giving orders that they drag her down anyway, or doing the job himself, he'd fumed and cursed her, and vowed to let her freeze if that was what the hardheaded wench wanted. He'd sat there in the chilly hall, sullenly nursing a mug of heated ale, and tried to convince himself it was anger he felt, not pain.

But it hadn't worked. He did not know why she was being so stubborn, but he knew why he was. Because he had begun to care for her. It was the worst thing he could do and the last thing he wanted to do. But try as he might, he could not deny the feelings she roused in him. She was his enemy. She hated him and she would betray him at every opportunity. He knew all that. He knew also that he could make her want him. But that was not enough. He wanted her loyalty for himself. Ludicrous as he knew it was, he wanted her to choose him over her family.

Was that love? No, he told himself. He had begun to care a little for her, but that was not love. He did not love her. It was only that all this confusion and frustration was driving him mad.

So he'd broken down and taken the stairs to the tower, three at a time, intending he knew not what. When he'd burst into that mean chamber and not found her, his anger had immediately turned to fear. When he'd pushed out onto the overlook, however, that fear had turned to horror and his heart had stopped.

She'd been huddled in a pitiful heap, practically frozen beneath a pile of clothes and blankets, and he'd thought at first that she was dead. Even now his heart thudded with dread for she was so still in his arms. And so cold.

But she was alive and he meant to keep her that way. Down the stairs he went with his precious bundle in his arms. He kicked open the door to his chamber. It was not warm, but it was a vast improvement over the tower room. He was loath to release her, but he had to put her down in order to build up the fire. When she moaned as if in objection, he cursed under his breath. She needed him and his body warmth.

In a trifling he stirred up the embers and piled wood over them. Then he stripped off his leather hauberk, kicked off his boots, and climbed into the bed with her.

She was cold, so cold that when he wrapped his arms around her, he shivered. But he was undeterred. He burrowed beneath her mantle and pulled her close, tucking her within the curve of his body. Even her hair was cold as he pressed his face against it.

"Damn you, woman," he muttered. *If it was your wish to strike back at me, then you have succeeded very well.*

A harsh shudder wracked her body and then another. But Rhys held her close, sharing his warmth and absorbing her violent shivers. It seemed to take forever. But slowly she warmed. Slowly her body lost its tension. The shivers eased and she relaxed against him.

But as she relaxed, Rhys grew more tense. He had her in his bed where he'd wanted her all along and his body reacted accordingly. Then she sighed and shifted against him, and he bit back a groan. This was no longer a good idea.

"Isolde? Isolde, are you awake?"

Isolde heard the low voice so near her ear. She felt it rumble against her back and blow warm through her hair. But she did not want to respond. It was so nice lying in his arms, pretending all was right with the world. She had but to close her eyes and go to sleep beside him and not think of anything else. She had been so cold, but he made her warm.

"Isolde." His voice was more urgent, dragging her unwillingly from the pleasant fantasy she wove. "Do you hear me? If you do, answer me, sweetling. Please."

Sweetling.

Beneath the heavy coverlet she smiled and stretched. Rhys had called her sweetling. And he sounded so sincere.

Then her backside came up against the ridge of his manhood, and she let out a little gasp.

His arms tightened around her. "So. You are awake."

She slowly nodded. She was awake all right.

"Are you warmer now?" he asked.

"Y-yes." Her voice was husky, and she nervously cleared it.

There was a long pause and every added second made her more and more aware of him and the intimate position they shared. He held her so close, in a lover's embrace. At least they were clothed. At least she was.

What chamber had he brought her to?

With one hand she tugged down the marten coverlet that muffled her face. The air in the room was cold, but not nearly so bitter as the tower room. A quick glance confirmed what she'd already guessed. They were in the master's chamber. Beyond the bed hangings the ruined mural loomed, reminding her of all the reasons she must hate him.

She tried to shove his arm away from her. "I cannot stay here."

"You cannot leave," he countered, tightening his hold. "I'll not have you freezing up in that tower."

"Then let me go to my own bedchamber. Or down to the hall."

" 'Tis too late for that, Isolde. You are here now and I will not let you go."

Isolde hated that part of her that found such great pleasure in his words. But still she could not help asking, "Why?"

He moved and drew her onto her back. In the dim room his face was nevertheless close enough to be distinct. "Because I want you here. And I want that to be sufficient reason," he added, so softly she barely heard him. But she did hear, and the honesty—the vulnerability—of his words stilled her objections. He wanted her to stay. She wanted to stay. Her mind spun with indecision. Would it be so terrible to remain with him a while? If she ignored the myriad problems that complicated their lives, everything became so simple. They wanted the same thing: to be together, shutting out the rest of the world.

Would there ever be another time when they could do that? Was now the only chance they would ever have?

The terrible answer was yes. What was it Tillo had said? "Search your heart and do not fear the pain you dredge up. To live in this world is to know pain."

There was no future for Rhys and her, only the present, and Isolde knew she must accept that unhappy truth. There would be no future for them save one filled with pain. But there was now, this moment. If that was all she could have, then she must not waste it.

She stared up into his eyes and for once she forced herself not to hide her emotions from him. "When you found me outside the postern gate . . ." Her voice wavered. "I . . . I was not running away from you. I was coming back to you—"

The rest was lost in a kiss. It stole her breath; it stole her thoughts. It stole her heart. He pressed her down into the thick mattress, kissing her. Devouring her. Did he believe her? He must. Exultant, she rose to his kiss. His mouth took possession of hers and she gave in. His tongue demanded entrance, and she allowed it. His body moved to cover hers, and she moaned her acceptance.

At once he lifted his head. "I've hurt you."

"No."

"You are ill from the cold."

"No." She circled his neck with her arms and pulled his head down to hers. "I am not ill. I am not cold, either. Kiss me."

It was his turn to groan. But he did not argue, and he did not hold back. As if some barrier between them had finally collapsed, he kissed her deep and long and hard. Her lips, her cheeks and eyes and ears. He found the tenderest skin of her throat, the most sensitive spot beneath her ear. It was heaven and Isolde gloried in the frenzied eroticism of it. Her hands slid along his back and arms and shoulders. Her fingers tangled in his hair. She wanted him closer. She wanted his hot skin against hers.

He heeded her desires. Though they were swaddled in blankets and bed linens, his clothes and hers, they managed to strip the primary barriers away. His chainse, her mantle and a pair of kirtles. His chausses and braies, her chemises and stockings. The bed drapery kept out the cold while their passions heated the small enclosure.

Then they were naked, the two of them beneath the heated sheets, lying face-to-face with no impediments to their joining.

Rhys slid one hand slowly down her side, tracing the slope

of her waist and the curve of her hips. She mirrored his motions, exploring the hard ridges of his chest, the trail of hair that thinned as her fingers followed it down. In the dark she could not see, but she could feel and she could tell how eager he was.

"Damnation," he groaned, catching her wrist as her hand moved lower still. He pushed her onto her back.

"Let me," she protested.

"I fear you will unman me," he said, beginning a new exploration, but with his lips this time. "You do things to me"—he kissed her mouth—"that rob me of all reason." He moved his lips down her cheek to her throat and along her collarbone. "And bring me too fast to the brink." He caught one of her nipples between his teeth and she gasped, arching up to the pleasure of it.

"You bring me to the brink," he murmured, the hot words alternately against one breast and then the other. "You bring me to the brink, Isolde, but I would bring you there first."

"We can . . . we can go there together," she panted.

"We will." He slid up over her, allowing his full weight to press down on her, and it was such an arousing feeling she nearly swooned. His weight, his heat, his strength. They were all focused upon her and it made her breathless with desire.

"Rhys—"

One of his knees parted her legs and the hardest, hottest portion of him burned against her belly. "I cannot wait," he whispered roughly in her ear. His mouth claimed hers again and he drove his tongue deep, stroking in and out, until she was on fire.

"Rhys," she pleaded, arching up against his greater weight.

"Damn, but I burn for you." He lifted her knees and positioned himself, but when their eyes met, he hesitated.

If she bade him stop, he would. She saw it in his eyes and that knowledge banished whatever might remain of doubt in Isolde's mind. She loved him. And if he did not love her in return, at least he cared about her. He cared, and her heart swelled with that knowledge. It grew and swelled until it filled her up and spilled over to him—and filled the entire room.

"Don't stop now," she said with a trembling smile. "For I shall die if you do—"

She broke off with a groan when he came fully into her. This was right, she told herself as he began. This was right.

They were right.

I love you, she thought as they moved in tandem. *I love you . . .*

They rushed to the crescendo. Frantically. Feverishly. They catapulted to it. Then it came, the shuddering peak. The shattering joy. He thrust over and over, prolonging the exquisite agony of it. "I love you." She gasped the words out loud. But then, what reason to hide the truth when surely she must die from this pleasure he brought her?

In the aftermath they were hot and damp. He lay heavily upon her, his heart thundering against hers. As their breathing slowed, as they cooled, he rolled to the side, pulling the snarled bedcovers over them both. But he kept her close and she held tight to him.

Had he heard her confession of love? She did not know, but she vowed not to fret about it. He'd proven that he cared for her. That was enough. She would not think about anything but him and the time they had left together, Isolde told herself. Just him and her. The bed would become their world, and this night the sum of their years. She buried her face against his neck, knowing how pitifully flimsy this little world was. But it was all she could contrive. There was no other way.

Rhys held Isolde close. He felt her breathing slow. He felt her body relax against his. They did not speak with words, but they communicated clearly.

Why had he waited so long to go to her? Why had he wasted so much of this week? There was so little time left. His arm tightened around her and he breathed deeply of her womanly scent. She was his now, at least until her family returned. He clenched his jaw. Once they returned—once he faced her uncle and her father and slew them as he must— then he would lose her. This bond they'd made would never endure that. And the words she'd said in the midst of her passion . . . She would never say them again to him.

"Damn," he muttered. He did not want to think about the future. He wanted only to think of now.

So he pressed his face into her hair and breathed deeply, and he drew her over to lie across his chest. She wriggled into a more comfortable position, then sighed as if she were asleep. Then he felt her hand moving slowly up his arm, each finger stroking lightly. His skin tingled wherever she touched, and despite his weariness, he felt revitalized.

"Are you awake?" he asked.

"No." She breathed deeply, and her softness—her breasts and belly against his chest and loins—was amazing to him. They fit, the two of them. "I am asleep," she continued in a warm, husky voice. "And I'm having the loveliest dream."

Rhys's arms tightened around her. God, but he loved her—

His entire body tensed. No. This was not love. It was just desire. Just passion. It was a stronger passion than he'd ever before felt, he admitted. But that did not make it love. He wouldn't let it be love. And anyway, he knew nothing of love. He did not truly believe it existed. So he focused on his physical desire for her and shoved any other emotions into the background.

"I believe I may be having the same dream," he replied when she shifted again so that she lay fully on him. "Some angel has come down from heaven to drown me in pleasure."

She chuckled and he felt her lips move against his chest. "Some angel has rescued me from the cold."

"Come here, angel," he murmured.

She came over him so sweetly, with such earnest intent to give him pleasure, that Rhys could easily believe he had died and some angel had indeed carried him up to heaven. Except that he was more likely to wind up in hell.

But he was in heaven now. And he could not deny himself the pleasure of it.

So he let her make slow love to him. They slept, then he pleasured her again. They pleasured one another. Rhys did not fear that Isolde would try again to escape, though he could not say why. He just knew that this time she would not flee.

Only one thought marred the perfection of the long night they shared. Eventually he knew he must let her go. And when the time came, it would kill him.

TWENTY-ONE

Snow fell, alternating with sleet and sometimes just a bitterly icy rain. For four days the castle lay as if in siege, only it was the winter, not an army, that held Rosecliffe in its iron grip.

As she sat in the great hall, Isolde tried not to think of her father and uncle, caught somewhere in the relentless storm, struggling with their men to reach Rosecliffe. She worried endlessly for them, but she could not help them. The best she could do was to keep the people of Rosecliffe warm and well fed, and to remind them by her presence that the FitzHughs had always valued the well-being of their people as highly as they did that of their own families.

So she had abandoned the tower room. It was too cold, and it was selfish of her to wallow in her own private misery. Besides that, Rhys would not allow it.

Isolde paused now, her needle poised half the way through a torn seam in one of her aprons. Rhys had been so different these past few days. Since that night he'd carried her down from the tower room, something had altered between them.

She swallowed hard and blinked, and bent back to her stitching. But her thoughts remained fixed upon him, as was more often the case than not. He had installed her back in her own chamber on the second story, and without dissent she had resumed her role as chatelaine of the castle.

By day she supervised the workings of Rosecliffe, as her mother had taught her to do. With outdoor activities severely curtailed by the storm, it fell to her to find suitable activity for the many idle hands. Every repair that had been postponed during the busy harvest season was now performed. Buildings, furnishings, tools, and garments—no item was too small to escape her notice. Near the front door a group of men crafted new fish baskets, ropes, and leather harnesses. A sewing circle of women worked near the pantler's cabinet, its membership ebbing and flowing through the day. The hall fairly hummed with activity, becoming workplace, dining hall, and sleeping accommodations to twoscore additional workers. Better to heat one larger space than numerous smaller ones. Even Rhys's men-at-arms abandoned their barracks for the warmer quarters of the hall. And it seemed all of the folk turned to her with their questions.

For their disputes and quarrels, however, they turned to Rhys. Or rather, he interceded in those matters before they could deteriorate into brawling matches. Had he not been a constant presence in the crowded hall, Isolde was certain several of those disagreements would have gotten out of hand, for with little to do, his men-at-arms had turned to drinking and gambling. Had he also not been a constant presence in the hall, Isolde might have been better able to compose herself. At least she hoped she could have.

But Rhys was constantly there, working at his own tasks, but nevertheless always within sight. She had but to lift her head and glance about, and without fail she would spy him—and without fail he would look up and meet her gaze.

Though she tried to stop herself, Isolde looked up now and found him, his dark head cocked as he listened intently to something Gandy said. Her heart began to drum in her chest, an insistent beat that pumped awareness into every portion of her body. What was it about him, about this one particular man? He'd even begun to look natural sitting at the high table in the lord's chair. Her father's chair.

At that moment he looked up directly into her eyes, as if he knew instinctively where she was and what she was thinking.

Not much longer until we retire for the night. Were those his thoughts or her own?

Isolde blushed and averted her gaze to the needlework in her lap. By day they kept apart and tended the tasks they must.

But by night . . . By night he became her lover, and she his. She went up the stairs first, and he allowed her sufficient time to let down her hair and make her evening ablutions. Then he came into her chamber—no knock to warn her. But she was always ready. He came into her chamber and she did not protest.

By day she recounted all the reasons she must end this shameful liaison. She knew she must put a stop to the duplicitous life they shared.

But by night . . . Oh, by night she could no more send him away than she could will herself to cease breathing. By night he was the man she'd always wanted, and always would want. Tender. Demanding. Possessive. Generous. He could be rough and forceful, but he knew, somehow, to stop just short of hurting her.

She felt her stomach clutch now, and a wicked warmth began down low in her belly, where the pleasures of the body all centered. Did he feel this all-consuming passion when he gazed upon her from across the room? she wondered. Did he feel faint with desire as she did? Did he wonder whether she loved him?

She had never said those words to him again, not after that night. If he'd heard them he had not acknowledged them. That alone should tell her something about the nature of his feelings for her, she told herself. And if he had not heard her confession of love . . . Well, it was just as well. Naught could come of her feelings for him.

She stared at the well-worn apron and the row of neat stitches she'd sewn. The best she could hope for was that her father would regain Rosecliffe without killing Rhys, and that he would find it in his heart to spare Rhys's life once more. Her hand tightened on the softened cloth she held, twisting it into a knot. She feared her father would refuse to spare him. But she meant to plead for Rhys's life. She would beg her father on her knees, if necessary, and promise to wed whomever he chose, if only he would not pass a death sentence on Rhys. Isolde could not bear the thought of Rhys's death, especially at her own father's or uncle's hand.

"What a picture you make, milady."

Isolde looked up, startled, and pricked her finger with the needle. It was Dafydd.

He grinned, then took a long noisy drink from his cup, all the while staring at her. "You better be careful. Don't want to go bleedin' all over your lover's shirt. Or is that somethin' you're making for the babe he's tryin' so hard to get you with?" As before, his eyes fastened on her chest.

Isolde had to fight the urge to cringe from his repulsive stare. But she refused to show any fear. "Get away from me," she ordered him through gritted teeth. She glared up at him. "Get away or I'll—"

"Call Rhys? He just left for the stable," the odious wretch gloated. "That wench from the dairy is waitin' for him," he chortled. "And anyway, what d'ye think he'll do? He's had you now. He's had FitzHugh's daughter enough times to plant ten babes in your belly. A Welsh bastard from a cold English bitch."

He laughed at her stunned expression. "Fitting revenge considering that it's Rhonwen he's always wanted, a Welsh cunt who's given your uncle his own pair of English bastards. But Rhys has found another Welsh cunt in Emelda. So if you get lonely, Isolde, I can take your mind off him quick enough."

Isolde lurched furiously to her feet, her fists knotted, ready to launch herself at his awful grinning face. But Dafydd backed away and with a leer and a wink he turned and sauntered away.

One of the pages looked over at her, as did Gerta who labored near the hearth. But after a moment they returned to their tasks, leaving Isolde to stand there alone, trembling in impotent rage. How could Rhys call that disgusting man his friend? How could he think Dafydd a better man than her father and uncle?

Then her anger dissolved to fear. Dafydd was lying. He must be. He was a vengeful, evil man—and a drunkard—who sought revenge because she'd embarrassed him before the other men. He was wrong about Rhys and Emelda. Wasn't he?

Her eyes swept the hall, searching for Rhys. He was not there, though, and the implication of that suddenly seemed ominous. Was he in the stable with Emelda? She spied that wretch Dafydd near the pantler's closet, refilling his cup with

ale. She knew he hated her and he would not be above lying
to her. But what if it were not a lie? What crueler way to
torment her than with the truth?

After all, Rhys had loved Rhonwen all those years ago. But
she'd wed Jasper, the only man he hated more than Isolde's
father. Now Rhys made love to her, the daughter and niece of
those men. Every night they came together. How could she
not expect a child to result? How could he not?

Was Dafydd right? Was that all Rhys wanted from her,
another form of revenge against his foes? For should he not
survive the coming conflict, his child born of a FitzHugh
would provide him the final revenge against her family. Meanwhile, did he turn to another woman—a Welsh woman—to
spite her?

Isolde's hand went to her throat as she fought down such
awful suspicions. Yet that was a more likely truth than the
simple one she preferred to believe: that he was beginning to
love her and would eventually abandon his revenge on account
of that love.

Devastated, Isolde sat down hard, staring blindly across the
hall to the upper windows with their muntins lined with snow.
Only when Gandy approached did she drag her emotions inside and tamp them down. Even then, however, the little man's
expression was curious.

"Is aught amiss with you, Isolde?"

She shook her head and grimaced, for she could not make
herself smile. " 'Tis this confinement to the keep. That is all.
I grow impatient to be outside again."

"I've spent many such a night in the wildwood. This keep
is stout and warm, and I, for one, am glad to be inside it." He
gestured with one hand toward the hearth. "The meat is done.
Will you begin the meal soon?"

"We await Rhys," she answered, swallowing hard at the
thought of where he might be. "And Tillo. Where is he?"

Gandy shrugged. "Of late he has been out of sorts."

"Has he?" Isolde sighed. The little dwarf was so clever, yet
he could not recognize the elderly woman beneath his friend
Tillo's garb.

Was she just as blind to the truth about Rhys?

"Tillo has been out of sorts. Then Newlin arrived earlier

today, and Tillo has been absent ever since." Gandy crossed his short arms over his chest. "Does Newlin have the second sight as everyone claims?"

"He is very wise," Isolde admitted, setting her needlework aside. She smoothed a loose curl back from her brow. Had Newlin deduced the truth about Tillo? Could he tell her the truth about Rhys? "Where is he?"

"Who, Newlin or Tillo?"

"Both of them," Isolde replied, wondering if the two might be somewhere together. " 'Tis nearly time for supper and, besides, they are old. They should take a place near the fire."

Across the room Cidu began to bark, a high-pitched, excited yammer, and a group of little children began to laugh. "They'd best not be feeding him fat," Gandy grumbled. As he toddled off, Isolde's gaze once again swept the hall. Newlin and Tillo. Was something afoot with those two? Even it were, however, Isolde knew neither of them would do anything to hurt either Rosecliffe or Rhys. Still, they were both wise and they both wished for peace. Mayhap together they could help her sort out the truth. Meanwhile, she must put aside Dafydd's insinuations for now.

Rhys entered the hall on a burst of frigid air and snow flurries. But Isolde did not look over at him. Once he took his seat at the high table she signaled for the meal to begin.

Tillo and Newlin did not appear until after the meal had begun, and then they entered separately and sat apart. Isolde stood near the hearth, supervising the serving maids. When she spied Tillo, she approached her at once.

"Come sit near the fire. You are frozen!" she exclaimed when she touched the woman's shoulder. "Where have you been?"

"Do not fuss over me," Tillo grumbled. "I have not yet reached my dotage."

"You told me once you wanted only a peaceful and quiet place to live out the remainder of your days. 'Tis my intention to help you find that place—and to increase the number of those days. I cannot do so if you freeze to death, Tillo, so do not argue with me."

With an arm around Tillo's shoulders, she steered her toward the hearth. "Here, sit and eat. And after the meal," she added, "I would speak with you a while."

Tillo looked up at her and a faint smile passed over her lined features. "You have a good heart, child. But that ofttimes makes for a harder life."

Perhaps so, Isolde thought as she turned and searched out Newlin. But it was too late to alter the direction her heart had taken. And too late to protect it.

Still avoiding Rhys, she found Newlin sitting in a squat heap along the side wall, holding a trencher of brown bread filled with stew. Three of the castle hounds sat in an expectant half-circle facing him, their mouths lolling open in anticipation of his generosity, their tongues slurping in eagerness.

"Ah, good-hearted Isolde," he said, smiling more widely than was his wont. "Be of good cheer, my child. From the coldest winter still comes the hope of spring."

Isolde stared gravely at him. "I am grateful to hear as much. Would that I could be more certain precisely what that means."

But Newlin only smiled and tossed a bit of bread to one of the patient hounds.

Isolde sighed. "I bid you come and sit where it is warmer." He shook his head. "Tillo will leave if I come too near."

Isolde arched her brows. So. She was right. "Why would she do that?" She barely stifled a groan when she realized her verbal slip. She had referred to Tillo as "she."

It was plain from Newlin's steady gaze, however, that he already knew. "She does not trust me. Yet."

Isolde smiled in relief. "Do you intend to change her mind?" she asked, curious about the old bard's interest in Tillo.

Newlin took a bite of stew and stared intently at Isolde as he chewed. "We must each of us do what we must do, even if it is outside the bounds of the life we have heretofore lived—or the life we have expected to live."

A furrow creased Isolde's brow. The urge to confide in the old man was overwhelming, but this was neither the right time nor place. "Do you speak now of my life, or of yours?" was all she asked.

"Perhaps of both. Perhaps of everyone's," he added, gesturing to the crowded hall with his one good arm. "Go along with you, child. I have no advice for you this evening, save that you too should look outside the boundaries you set yourself."

Dismayed, Isolde nonetheless obeyed his dismissal and retreated. But her mind could not let loose of his words. The boundaries she set for herself? She'd already broken all the bounds of acceptable behavior. If the world knew of her sin, she would be widely vilified. A ruined woman. Unmarriageable.

Doubly so if she bore a child.

And yet she seemed unable to prevent herself succumbing to that same sin night after night. She shook her head in dismay. So far as she could see, there were no bounds left for her to breach, save to renounce her family, and that she would never do.

Confused and preoccupied, Isolde returned to the hearth. Everyone had been served. She could sit and partake of her own meal now. But for a moment she just stood there, cold despite the roaring heat from the freshly stoked fire. Rhys would expect her to join him at the high table as she did at all the meals now. Once her work was done, she always sat in her mother's chair beside him. But tonight she hesitated. It would not be much longer. This storm would break; her father would arrive with an army of men; and then this brief idyll would come to a violent end.

A sudden wave of panic overwhelmed her, and Isolde pressed a hand to her belly. What if she did indeed grow Rhys's child within her? Though it was too soon to know, it was easily possible—and more reason than ever to prevent a confrontation between Rhys and her father and uncle. For if Rhys despised the men who had killed his father, how would a child of hers feel toward the men—family though they might be—who killed its sire? By the same token, she could not bear the idea of Rhys's demise, even if he'd only bedded her for sport. Oh, God, but she was so confused.

Isolde turned, searching instinctively for an answer and for Rhys. She found him staring at her.

Their gazes met and held, and Isolde was mesmerized. For whatever reason—and she would never know what that reason was—Rhys ap Owain was the man for her. The man meant to possess her heart. Hiding it was useless. Repressing the words changed nothing. She loved him and she always would. But did he care for her at all, or was he merely using her?

The meal was a torture. Isolde needed to be close to Rhys, yet conversely she could hardly bear his nearness. She needed to speak honestly and openly with him, and yet she was terrified to do so. So she picked at her meal and made small talk as needed. Soon enough they would be alone. Then she must confront him. Then they must determine what they truly were to each other.

For his part Rhys was conscious of a new tension in Isolde. But Glyn sat on his opposite side, and it proved easier to converse about falcons and peregrines than to probe the dangerous territories of Isolde's mind. He knew what to do with her body; it was her emotions that confounded him, and her motives. Of late she had been exceedingly sweet and unbearably passionate. Did she hope to lull him to some complacency, to change his mind and alter the course he was set upon? If so, she was destined to fail. So he ate and he spoke with Glyn and he waited for her to make the first move.

The meal finally ended, though the drinking did not. While the clearing away began, Gandy and Linus performed a skit, aided by two of the pages and little Cidu. Isolde excused herself from the table to oversee the last of the evening chores. Rhys stayed her with a hand to her wrist. "I will be delayed a while tonight."

She met his eyes briefly before nodding, then turning away. But Rhys's eyes followed her. What would he do with her once this bitter fight with her family was done?

It was a question with no good answers. In bedding her, in wreaking that particular revenge upon the FitzHughs, Rhys discovered too late that he'd made a grave error. For he could not avoid being burned now by his own revenge. She would spurn him once he killed her uncle and father. Even if he forced her to stay with him, she would hate him. And though a week ago he would not have cared, in the last few days something between them had altered.

Still, he could not change any part of his revenge. Nor, he vowed, did he wish to.

He stared at the skit, neither hearing nor seeing the antics below him. Only when the laughter subsided and Glyn nudged him did he rouse from his gloomy thoughts.

"Those blades should be cool by now. Let's go check their balance."

With a nod Rhys pushed up from the lord's chair. There were weapons to amass and defenses to perfect. The pleasures of the flesh could wait—as could these morbid contemplations of his future.

So he flung his mantle over his shoulders and strode from the hall, once again bracing himself for the winter's frigid assault. He did not feel Gandy's concerned gaze upon his back, or Tillo's worried stare.

Nor was he conscious of Dafydd's resentful glare.

On the next floor up Isolde stood in the doorway of her bedchamber. Not so long ago she'd shared it with her sisters. Now, like her parents chamber one flight above, it had become the scene of so many erotic episodes with Rhys. A frisson of anticipation shivered up her back. Soon enough he would seek her out here.

Was she a fool to await him again?

Was he even now cavorting with another woman?

She shook her head, certain that was not true. She could not allow Dafydd's ugly lies to ruin what little she and Rhys shared.

But soon enough it would be ruined anyway. Meanwhile, every time she lay with him she betrayed her family and her people.

A sob rose in Isolde's throat but she brutally stifled it. She would not feel sorry for herself. Anything she'd done, she'd brought on herself. Still, she could not await him here tonight. Nor in his chamber with the disfigured mural looming over them, the dragon and the wolf muddied and ruined.

So she climbed further, past the lord's chamber to the lonely tower room, dark and cold. Fitting, for her heart felt dark and cold this night. The whole world felt dark and cold, with no hope for dawn's light or spring's warmth to sustain her.

Her wool kirtle and heavy shawl were inadequate to the cold, but Isolde nevertheless braved the overlook. The snow had ceased, and the unrelenting wind had whipped the overlook clean of any gathered drifts. Below her the dark world lay silent and deceptively peaceful. But the snow was simply a cold blanket that disguised a festering wound, one that Rhys sought to expose.

Isolde bowed her head and gripped the ice-cold edge of one corbel. "Please, Lord, find some way out of this horror, some way that we may all survive." In her desperation she was oblivious to the cold. "Please help me," she prayed into the night. "Please help us all."

As if in answer a light flared in the bailey far below. A man strode from the armorer's shed, and though the night sheltered his identity, Isolde knew at once that it was Rhys. She leaned out, the better to see—then abruptly was spun around. A man thrust her rudely against one of the corbels.

"Milady Isolde." Dafydd's awful grin loomed before her face. "Pining for your faithless lover?"

Isolde twisted away, but not fast enough. He caught her shoulders in a cruel grip, then slammed her once more against the wall.

Three terrifying thoughts flashed through her head. He was drunk. He meant to rape her. And no one would hear her cries until too late.

As if in confirmation, he did not bother to muffle her mouth, but instead yanked her skirt up. "I'll make you forget about him." He ground his hips against hers so that she could feel the stiffened obscenity beneath his braies. "Thinks he's so high-and-mighty now, fucking a FitzHugh. Well, I can do that, too, better'n him."

"No!" She fought him, scratching, biting, trying to knee him in the groin. But he was too strong and too soaked with alcohol to feel any pain.

"Rhys!" she screamed. But the biting wind threw his name back in her face.

"He can't hear you. And he can't help you, neither." Dafydd shoved one of his knees between her legs. "You owe me," he hissed, then bit her neck in a repulsive parody of a caress. "You owe me for that shovel, and for everything you been givin' him—Ow!"

He jerked to the side when she boxed his ear, but he did not let go. "You owe me and I aim to get it."

"Rhys will carve your heart out for this!" Isolde sobbed.

"No he won't. He needs every man here, if he expects to win. Besides, him and me go way back. We've hunted together and fought together. We've shared many a fire and a meal—and many a woman."

He yanked her shawl off and his fingers fumbled for the neckline of her kirtle. Isolde twisted and fought, striking at him wherever she could. But he was unfazed. He wrapped one hand around her neck, pinning her against the wall with a suffocating grip. The more she struggled, the harder he squeezed, until she had no strength except to fight for breath.

He chuckled then, and his obscene lips pressed against her ear. "Me and Rhys, we shared plenty of women an' you're no different—"

A roar cut him off mid-word. Dafydd's hand ripped away from her throat. His body flew back from hers.

Isolde sagged to the frozen walkway, sucking in great gasps of air. She could breathe. Dafydd had stopped—

Rhys had come! She looked up dizzily to see him towering over the other man.

"You bastard!"

"What do you care?" Dafydd spat out. "She's just another whore, one you're supposed to hate. Or are you turning into one of those cowards from Carreg Du?"

Rhys's face contorted in rage. "Those cowards don't rape women!" His nostrils flared with disgust. "It takes a special kind of coward to do that." He dragged Dafydd to his feet and held him by the tunic, then glanced over at Isolde. "Are you all right?"

At once Dafydd struck. Only lightning-fast reflexes saved Rhys from a disabling knee to the groin. As it was, however, he was thrown off balance, and the other man took swift advantage. He yanked a dagger out of his boot and lunged, only missing Rhys by a hairsbreadth. He swung again wildly as Rhys rolled away.

Isolde gasped and slid along the wall toward the door. She must get help! But Dafydd saw her movement and slashed out at her. She leaped back, but even so felt the tip of his blade catch the cloth of her sleeve.

Before he could strike again Rhys tackled him. They fell

together, a writhing mass, cursing and struggling for possession of the deadly dagger.

Isolde wanted to help Rhys. But she was afraid her interference might make matters worse. Again she darted for the
door. But as she swung it open, the two men rammed into her.
She fell over them with a cry of alarm, cracking her head
against the wall. Before she could right herself, Dafydd tore
away, heading for the stairs. Rhys was fast after him, and she
followed them down, her heart constricted with fear.

"Leave off, Rhys!" Dafydd's voice echoed up the stairs. "I
didn't want anything more from her than what you been get-
tin'."

"You bastard. You tried to rape her!"

"An' you didn't?"

Isolde halted, hugging the wall as she stared at the scene
below her. Dafydd backed slowly down the curving stairs,
holding the dagger on Rhys who followed step by step, just
beyond the reach of the blade. When Dafydd spied her, his lip
curled in disdain.

"Are you forgettin' how many times I covered your back?"
he said. "She's your enemy, man. Not me." Then his face
hardened when Rhys did not respond. "But you don't care
about any of that, do you? No. That juicy cunt of hers has
you forgettin' just who your friends are—"

Rhys leaped. Isolde screamed. And they went down, a roil-
ing ball of legs and flying fists. The dagger skittered away and
Isolde swiftly snatched it up. But the men fought on, tumbling
down the stone stairwell, cursing and grunting all the way.

"Be careful, Rhys!" Isolde cried, helpless with fear for him.

Then somehow Rhys got the upper hand. On the landing
just outside the master's chamber he stopped their bone-jarring
descent. There was blood on his face and his hands, but whose
Isolde did not know.

He straddled Dafydd and punched him, once, again, and a
third time. Blood squirted from the man's nose. Teeth flew.

"Uffern dan!" he swore. "You unholy bastard!"

"Rhys, stop. You'll kill him!"

"I want to kill him."

"Rhys!" This time it was Linus and Gandy chorusing the
alarm as they scrambled up the stairs. "What are you doing?"

Linus grabbed his arm, while Gandy's worried gaze sought out Isolde. She shook her head in response to his questioning look. She was not harmed. Not really.

Meanwhile Linus had a bearhold on Rhys and dragged him off the unconscious Dafydd. Others crowded up the stairs, but Gandy swiftly took matters in hand. "You two. Take Dafydd belowstairs. Linus, put Rhys in there," he ordered, gesturing to the bedchamber. "Isolde." He studied her a long moment. "Go with Rhys. He may be injured."

Isolde was already on her way. She shut the door against the onlookers and turned to face Rhys. Linus had released him and backed toward the door. Rhys paced the room now, his rage barely controlled. When he saw her he halted. "Did he hurt you?"

She shook her head. "No. But what of you?" Blood drenched one of his sleeves. "Let me see to your wounds."

Rhys stared at her, not blinking, not hearing her words. She was unharmed. Dafydd had not had time to do any real harm. That was all that mattered.

Then she crossed the room, her worried eyes running over him. "Fetch water," she told Linus. "And bandages. Also, soap and a cleansing salve—and a needle and thread. Gerta will know what I need."

Linus left and they were alone. Only then did Rhys understand how afraid he'd been for Isolde—and how enraged he'd been by Dafydd's vicious attack on her. She was not hurt. His relief was so profound Rhys felt light-headed. He steadied himself against the bedpost, only then realizing his hand was bleeding.

"Uffern dan!" he swore, wincing at the sudden pain.

"Let me take care of it," she said, gently cupping his hand in her own. "I'll take care of you, Rhys."

She studied his wounds, a slash in the fleshy part of his right thumb, another on his left forearm. Then she looked up at him, a long steady connection of their eyes, and it was as if she made a vow to him. A private, personal vow. I'll take care of you. Had sweeter words ever been said to him? He knew they had not.

Linus and Gerta came in and set the supplies on a small

table, then departed. Although Isolde thanked them, she never looked away from him.

She loved him and though that should not matter to him—though he'd never wanted that from her—Rhys's heart swelled with the knowledge. No one had ever loved him. No one had ever promised to take care of him. He'd never needed to be taken care of, and he didn't need it now. But she wanted to do it, and he wanted to let her.

"I'll try to be gentle, but this may hurt," she murmured, her hands still holding his. Were those tears sparkling in her eyes?

"I am fine. Do your worst," he jested. "I will survive."

"I will do my best," she vowed, her face solemn.

Whether solemn or gay, angry or even weeping, Rhys knew that hers was the one face he'd rather gaze upon than any other. In that moment he was glad he'd been cut. The pain meant nothing, for Isolde was here to tend his hurts.

She led him to the table and pulled his sleeves up. "Hold your hands here," she instructed, "while I pour water over them."

"Damn," he muttered when the water stung the two cuts. Now that his rage had eased, he was able to give her a crooked grin. "My apologies. I should not curse so in your presence."

"Please, Rhys. Do not apologize to me. 'Tis I who . . ." She faltered and looked away, pressing her lips together a long moment. She blinked several times and he marveled at the movement of her long dark lashes upon the delicate skin of her cheeks. Like butterfly wings against rose petals.

He almost laughed out loud at that sentiment. She was turning him into a besotted fool, a poet spouting inane words of love and admiration. But he didn't care. Her cheeks *were* like rose petals, soft and pink and fragrant.

Hardly aware of his movement, he leaned nearer to her. At the same moment she lifted her head up again, so that their faces were mere inches apart.

"Thank you," she whispered. But though her voice was soft, it quivered with emotion. "Thank you, Rhys."

He loved the way she said his name. That was the only coherent thought in his thoroughly besotted brain. He loved the sound of his name on her lips.

"I . . . I am so sorry you are hurt," she continued. "I should not have gone up there alone. I should have guessed . . ." She shook her head slightly. "Thank you."

"You owe me no thanks, Isolde," he finally managed to say. "Nor any apologies. You did nothing wrong."

She looked down, sheltering her emotions behind the heavy curtain of her lashes. She poured fresh water over the wounds, then pressed clean cloths over both cuts. "Does that hurt?"

"No." So long as her warm touch remained upon him, he could feel nothing else.

She took a deep breath. They were so close. He could see the rise and fall of her breasts, and he felt the immediate rise of his own manhood. Be done with ministration to his wounds. He had far more urgent needs!

"Isolde," he began.

"No. Be still, Rhys." Her small hands tightened on his. Then she looked up at him and he knew she'd read his thoughts. "First things first. Let me see to your injuries. Afterward . . . Afterward I will tend to your other needs."

TWENTY-TWO

ISOLDE FELT LIKE ANOTHER PERSON, AS IF ANOTHER PART OF herself had decided to take over both her thoughts and her actions. No. Not her thoughts, she amended. This was not the first time she'd imagined being the aggressor in her relations with Rhys. But always before she'd been too shy, too awed by the powerful emotions he raised in her. But not tonight.

He had saved her. Had it not been for his quick response to her peril, Dafydd might have done anything to her. The very thought made her shudder. That Rhys suffered now in her stead only strengthened her feelings for him.

She was right to love him, for he was a good man.

And she was right to tend to him in all ways tonight. He wanted her, despite his injuries. She saw that clearly in his midnight eyes.

Gingerly she patted his cuts dry, then prepared the needle and thread. She could have called for the village healer, but Isolde wanted to do this herself. So she braced herself and concentrated. Rhys was silent as she took three stitches in his thumb and five in his arms. Afterward she dabbed a soothing ointment of thinned beeswax and ground hyssop and black poplar buds on his wounds, as well as on his skinned knuckles. Then tenderly she wrapped everything in soft strips of linen.

"Does it pain you very much?" she murmured, sitting back and wiping her hands clean.

"No."

She raised her eyes to his. "Later, when you are quiet in

the night, they may throb. But I can give you a draught of vervain to help you sleep."

"I do not wish to sleep right now."

Isolde's pulse began to race in anticipation. In spite of Dafydd's brutal attack—or perhaps because of it—she wanted desperately to be close to Rhys. "Very well, then." She stood, then glanced up at the ruined mural. This might be their last night, she realized. Their last. And if it was, she wanted it to be perfect. She wanted to see approval and desire and love shining in his eyes. Especially love. She could manage the remainder of her life without any of those things, she told herself, just so long as she could have them this one night. But not in this room.

"Come," she said. "I will bring the ointment and more bandaging to my chamber." She felt his avid gaze upon her, but she was suddenly too shy to meet his eyes. So she gathered what she needed onto a platter, and started for the stairs.

He followed her. Step by step, down the stairs they went, she leading, he close behind. And with every step they drew nearer her private chamber—their private domain—and nearer the moment when he was bound to recognize her love. She was so fearful her legs trembled beneath her.

In her chamber she fidgeted with the medications, arranging and rearranging everything upon a table. Finally she turned away, only to kneel before the small hearth to feed fresh logs to the fire. She felt him near her, though, and she was aware of his every movement.

When he grunted in pain, she turned to find him sitting on the bed. He'd tried to grab one boot to remove it.

"Let me do that." She hurried to his side, then knelt before him and swiftly removed one of his tall leather boots. But she did not look up at his face. She was too overcome with shyness.

Then she felt his hand on her head, a light caress as his fingertips moved gently through the waves at her temple. "Be careful," she said, looking up at last. "Don't hurt yourself."

Their eyes connected and held. "My hands are but one part of me. There are other ways for us to touch. And know this, Isolde. I want to touch you everywhere." His eyes were so dark, yet they seemed alive with light. Isolde could not breathe. She did not have the ability to draw air into her lungs, and as their gazes clung, her chest ached. His hand moved to cup her cheek. She felt the rough glide of the linen bandage against her skin.

"I love you." She whispered the words without realizing she had done so. Once said, however, they relieved the tightness in her chest. "I love you, Rhys. I did not want to, but nevertheless, I do."

His hand stilled. But when she closed her eyes and bowed her head, he forced her face to tilt up again. "I don't want your gratitude." His voice was harsh.

" 'Tis not gratitude I feel."

He frowned. "No? Mayhap it is merely desire and gratitude mixed up together."

She shook her head. "No. I wish it were merely that, for it would be . . ."

He leaned forward when she trailed off, and cupped her face with his uninjured hand. "For it would be what, Isolde? Finish what you began."

"I wish it were simply desire and gratitude," she said in barely a whisper. "For it would be far simpler, far easier."

She felt the shudder that went through him. He closed his eyes—just for an instant—and she knew then how much her words meant to him. Then he released her face and sat back, not speaking.

Isolde took a slow, shaky breath. She'd told him the truth of her heart. If he was not ready to hear her yet, she would be patient. But a part of her feared she would never hear those same words back from him. She wanted to hear them with an intensity that was truly terrifying. And in time she thought he might find the words within him—if only they had time.

She would not think about that, though. She would not ruin this night by worrying about what was to come. So she bent to his other boot and removed it. Then operating on instinct alone, she began to unbuckle his girdle.

He let her undress him, bending and twisting, raising his arms, but letting her take charge. When he was naked she backed away. He was aroused. His manhood stood upright, drawing her eyes. She forced herself to look elsewhere, for in truth, he was beautiful everywhere. A delight for her eyes.

Broad shoulders, thick arms. A muscular chest covered with a light layer of dark hair. Thighs, calves, every part of his body proclaimed him a warrior. By comparison, she was a weak creature, indeed. But all his power and strength was there for her use, she reminded herself. At least for now it was. He was hers to use and take pleasure from.

As she stared at him, at his magnificent body limned with gold in the fire's light, it occurred to her that the greater part of her pleasure came from pleasing him. And he seemed to take great pleasure in pleasing her. She licked her lower lip. That was the true perfection of their joining.

She vowed to make pleasing him her only goal this night.

His eyes burned over her as she began to remove her heavy clothes, mantle, girdle, then kirtle. She peeled them away, layer by layer, slowly and with great deliberation. " 'Tis my intent to make love to you," she said, astounded by her own boldness. But she went on, her gaze never wavering from his face. "For once I have the upper hand with you, and I intend to take full advantage of it." She paused. "To take full advantage of you."

Where such brazen words came from, she did not know. He'd transformed her into a wanton these past two weeks. But when he sucked in a harsh breath, then let out a groan, she was gratified. She might be a wanton, but he clearly approved.

He reached out with one hand. "Come to me, Isolde."

"I will. When I am ready."

Again he groaned. "Do not torture me, woman. I am an injured man. Have mercy on me and hurry, else I might die."

Isolde laughed, heady now with the power she wielded over him. "I dearly hope not, for I plan to have my wicked way with you." She stepped out of her shoes and removed her hose, then stood before him clad only in her chemise. Though the room was still cold, between the leaping fire and her own leaping desire, she was anything but chilled.

"Damn you, woman. Look what you do to me." He exhaled then stroked himself awkwardly with his bandaged hand.

Isolde watched the movement of his hand, then mirrored it on herself. She stroked down her chest slowly, past her breasts to her belly, then lower still.

"Damn," he muttered, his eyes fixed on her movements.

She stroked back up, tugging the chemise above her knees in the process, and her breathing grew shallow. To have him watch her that way was more arousing than she would have guessed. Her hand did not feel like her own, but rather like his, like an extension of his eyes and his will.

"Touch your breasts," he ordered hoarsely. "Use both hands."

Isolde did as he asked. She was embarrassed, yet not enough to stop. Her breasts felt heavy and warm when she cupped them, the nipples taut and extended—and so sensitive.

"You are beautiful," he murmured. "So beautiful. Show yourself to me, sweetling."

She raised one hand to tug down the shoulder of her chemise. The other she flattened against her belly. She was on fire for him.

"Hurry," he rasped out.

But she had no intention of hurrying. For once she was in control—at least somewhat. She meant to impress upon him how good it could feel to let a woman take charge of him. So she bent forward, allowing her hair to fall in front of her like a thick curtain as she let the last of her garments slither to the floor.

"Come here," he pleaded. "Isolde . . ."

Instead she began to finger-comb her hair, reveling in the feel of it moving against her naked shoulders and breasts. The waving ends tickled her belly and hips. "Would you like me to slide my hands and my hair over you?" she asked, advancing a step nearer.

"Yes."

She quivered from the raw intensity of that one simple word. She stepped nearer still, running her hands down her own body as she'd done before.

"Isolde." He lurched to his feet, the perfect picture of virile masculinity, a warrior ready to battle and defeat the demons of desire that gripped him. But those same demons had a merciless hold on her, and Isolde knew that only he could defeat them for her. She was done with teasing him. She was too aroused to go on. So she closed the final distance between them. She stepped into his embrace, bare skin to bare skin, with only the strands of her hair separating them.

He wrapped his arms around her, pulling her into full contact with him. She wound her arms around his neck and stood on her toes. But to her surprise, he did not kiss her, not at first. He bowed his head until their foreheads touched, and for a moment they simply stood that way. The desire was there; his arousal scalding her belly was proof enough of that. But there was as much emotion between them as there was physical longing.

Isolde clung to him, filled with love and with hope that he would confess his true feelings to her. Do you love me? her heart silently cried out to him.

"When I saw him on you—" His arms tightened even more. "I was so afraid for you."

She smiled. Say the rest, she prayed. Say it.

"But you are all right."

She nodded slowly. "You are not, though. You came to my rescue at great risk to yourself." She paused, waiting still. But when he said nothing, she added, "No one else. Only you." Still he said nothing and she felt a twinge of disappointment. But she pressed on. "He was your friend for many years."

He took a deep breath; she felt his chest expand against hers. "That was long ago. He changed. Or perhaps I have." He paused. "I could never stand by and not offer my aid to you. But enough of that. If you would thank me, you know how best to do it."

He pulled her back onto the bed.

He was not going to say it, she realized. He cared for her. She was certain of that. But he was not going to respond to her confession of love with similar words of his own. Had they not been naked and lying upon a bed, and she already aroused, the keen disappointment might have overwhelmed her. But his eagerness for her buoyed her hopes.

I will make you love me, she vowed as she kissed him. *I will make you love me.*

Something was different between them. Rhys felt it in the way Isolde moved over him. Her kiss was fierce and yet tender. Her body was sweet and hot, and she used it very well to arouse him. He closed his eyes and she slid up and down him, just a few inches of friction, but it had a powerful effect on him.

He groaned with pure pleasure. If she seemed different, he told himself, it was only that she had learned what he liked during their past few nights together, and that she was grateful to him. Her profession of love had nothing to do with anything.

Though a part of him had wanted to believe her words, he'd since regained his perspective. She desired him. That was not love. She might think it was, but she was wrong. And even if she did love him, he did not feel the same way about her.

But you do!

"No." He said the word out loud, breaking their kiss, and abruptly rolled her over. But when he tried to move, he grimaced at the immediate pain in his hands.

"Just lie back," she ordered, pushing him to the side. Her face was flushed with passion; her eyes were bright with it. "Lie back and let me do this, Rhys."

Frustrated, gasping for breath, Rhys did as she ordered. But his emotions were in a turmoil. She knelt over him, her pale skin showing through the heavy curtain of her hair, and he knew he'd never beheld such a beautiful sight. Pink lips ripe for passion; equally pink nipples protruding through the rich silk of amber tresses. His eyes drank in the delicious view. God in heaven, but he wanted her.

"Be still now," she told him. "I'll do all the work."

But it was almost impossible for him to lie still. She straddled his thighs, her womanhood open and so near his aching arousal. Though his hips thrust upward in blatant demand, she only smiled. "Be still," she crooned, as her palms slid up his rigid belly to his chest. "I want only to give you pleasure."

"You know how best to do that, Isolde. No need to play games with me."

She leaned over him and swept her hair back and forth over his face and chest and shoulders. "I am curious. I want to explore a bit. There's no need to rush," she added. "We have all night."

One of her hands moved down toward his arousal and he groaned. No use to fight her. It felt too good to resist. So he lay there and let her use her fingers and her lips and every other portion of her body to please him.

She slid up and down him again, her weight a hot stroke down the entire length of his body. She kissed him everywhere, beneath his ear, along his collarbone. When he swallowed she nipped his throat. When he groaned she moved her sweet lips and lethal teeth to his chest and hardened nipples. And when he thrust his hips up convulsively against her belly, she slid lower still.

He thought he would explode.

He thought he would die from the pleasure of it.

"Enough," he muttered, trying to grab her and pull her up. But his bandaged hands had him at a disadvantage and she knew it.

"Do you like that?" she whispered, gasping for breath.

"Yes. Too much. Come here, Isolde."

"Wait." She wet one finger, then watching his face, ran that finger up the straining length of his manhood. "I want to be certain you are fully aroused," she said, smiling down into his eyes.

"I've never been more—Damn!" He gritted his teeth, trying desperately to restrain himself.

"Never? No other woman has ever done this to you?"

"No."

"Are you certain?"

He shook his head, his jaw still clenched. "Don't speak of other women."

"But there were others," she persisted.

He stared at her flushed face and winced at the vulnerability she could not quite disguise in her eyes. "There has never been a woman like you, Isolde. Not for me."

He hadn't meant to say that, to reveal so much to her. But when her lips trembled so that she could only still them by pressing them together, he was glad he had. The vulnerability disappeared from her eyes, replaced by a shining joy. "I love you," she said once again, so faintly this time that he hardly heard.

Then, not waiting for a response from him, she took him in hand and sheathed him within her.

Rhys shuddered, his relief was so profound, and it took every bit of his control not to erupt. But he knew he could not long withstand her sensual assault. She rocked over him, holding him so tight, and he wanted to hold her tight also. But when he tried to grip her waist, he could not. Wherever he tried to hold her or caress her, he met with the same barriers of pain and the bulky linen bandages.

She must have sensed his frustration, for she paused and pushed his arms down onto the mattress. "Can you not just lie here and let me give you pleasure, Rhys? Must you always be the one in control?" She ran her fingertips down his chest in the most provocative manner. He could see in her eyes that she understood what she was doing to him.

She continued. "For this night, at least, I am stronger than you and more adept. Tonight I am in control, not you."

A feeling akin to panic rushed through Rhys, nearly over-powering passion. Had he ever allowed anyone that sort of control over him? No. At least not since he had become a man. For giving up control, whether in battle with another man, or in bed with a woman, was a sign of weakness. He had vowed never to be weak.

But where Isolde was concerned . . .

She resumed a slow, sultry rhythm and his hard-fought control began to slip. "Damn you," he muttered as she began, oh so gradually, to increase her pace. "Damn you, Isolde . . ."

She went faster. She held him tighter and tighter. Then abruptly, in a flash of light, in an explosion of all darkness, he lost control. It blinded him. It ripped him apart. It exposed his guts and threw every secret part of him out for her to see.

He grabbed her despite the pain in his hand and held on as he poured himself into her. "Isolde," he chanted as he filled her with himself over and over again. "Isolde."

I love you.

BOOK III

Wolde God that it were so
As I coude wishe betwixt us two!

—Anonymous medieval verse

TWENTY-THREE

THE ALARM CAME AT MID-MORNING. BY THEN ISOLDE HAD cleaned and redressed Rhys's injuries. She had also made love to him again, and whispered words of love in that exquisite moment when they'd found their release together.

As before, he had not responded with the words she so wanted him to say, but by now she thought she understood why. She'd heard enough of the life he'd lived to know that love had never been a part of it. He knew nothing of love, save the physical side of it, whereas she had grown up surrounded by love, but only the emotions.

He'd taught her the intense pleasures of making love; she meant to teach him the utter joy of being in love. But it would not be easy, nor would it happen quickly. But he did care for her. She had felt it in the reverent way he'd awakened her, kissing up the length of her body. She'd been surrounded by it when they'd curled together, enjoying the steamy aftermath of their early morning love play. For him to admit to himself that he could love her went against everything he'd believed, for she was a FitzHugh. For him to say the words to her might take him a very long time. But she was convinced that in his own way he did care for her.

In time he would come around.

If only they had time.

But she refused to let the threat of the future ruin the happiness of the present. So she had closed her eyes against any shadows over that happiness, refusing to let them in. And she'd succeeded. She'd presided over morning prayers and a warm, filling breakfast. There had been a few breaks in the cloud cover, and an occasional ray of sunshine had fallen brilliant upon the pristine snow. The world was beautiful today. Why could it not always be so?

But then the alarm had come, first a shout from somewhere along the walls outside. Then the bell had rung. The telltale creak of the castle bridge rising and the heavy thud of the cross bar in the gates had been the final blow for Isolde. She did not need to see Rhys's face to confirm the grim news.

The FitzHughs had returned. Her father and her uncle Jasper had arrived.

By rights she should have been relieved. She should have exulted. At last the captured Rosecliffe Castle would be liberated. But instead Isolde wanted to cry. Not yet. Not yet!

Though she knew it would change nothing, Isolde wanted to pretend just a little longer that Rhys was not her enemy, that he was not intent on destroying people she loved. She wanted time to soften his need for vengeance and teach him how to love.

But the alarm bell dashed her hopes; the cold expression that descended over Rhys's face killed them.

The fact that he met her eyes for but an instant before turning to hear his man's report buried her hopes forever. This was it, the day she'd once hoped for and now dreaded. The beginning of the end of her life. The day someone she loved must die.

Rhys strode from the hall, as did most of the Welshmen— men-at-arms and servants alike. The women and others who remained in the great hall turned at once to Isolde, watching for her response. She rubbed her hands together anxiously. They probably knew, or at least suspected, what had passed between her and Rhys. They could not know, however, how completely her heart had become engaged.

What did they expect now, for her to renounce him? Or renounce her family? Or did they watch her to see if she would fall apart?

She pressed her lips together to prevent them trembling and glanced around. Worried faces. Troubled faces. One or two, however, stared hopefully at her.

Hopefully?

Isolde wove her fingers nervously together. What did they hope for? Did they think she could bring peace between these knights who hated one another? While it sometimes had seemed possible, Rhys's harsh expression this morning shook her confidence. Still, she could not stand idly by while the world collapsed around her. So she snatched up her mantle from a hook in the pantler's closet. But as she hurried toward the door to the bailey, she was halted by Tillo's call.

"I fear they will break your heart, child. The two of them, father and lover. They will break your heart." The old woman hobbled out from behind a square stone column. " 'Tis what men do best," she added, shaking her head.

Quick color flooded Isolde's cheeks. "You don't understand any of this," she snapped in reply. "How could anyone possibly understand?"

"I understand that you love them both." The old woman broke off when Newlin came toward them.

"She loves them both," the misshapen bard echoed. "And they have both brought her great joy."

"But no longer," the old woman warned.

Newlin faced Tillo, and with his one good hand he caught her by the wrist. "That is a choice her heart must make. If a person turns away from a love that is freely offered, 'tis not the love that inflicts the pain. 'Tis a choice, Tilly. A choice."

Isolde stared at Newlin, puzzled. He wasn't speaking of her now. Those words were for Tillo—except that he'd called her Tilly—and they sounded suspiciously like a declaration of love. Isolde heard it as clearly as she'd heard the alarm bell sound. Here, in the midst of a war for possession of Rosecliffe Castle—at the unlikeliest moment possible—could the ancient seer of these hills be declaring his love for an old woman who disguised herself as a man? Despite her own fears and confusion, Isolde's lips curved in a bittersweet smile. Perhaps one bit of goodness would emerge from these dark days.

No other good possibly could.

"Be wise in your response to him," she said to Tillo. She touched their hands, which were still joined. "And be brave. There is much to gain and time is running out."

"I might give you the same advice, girl," Tilly muttered. But her tone was not so caustic, and when her faded gaze darted toward Newlin she seemed less sure of herself.

"The pair of you would both be wise to heed the advice

you give each other," Newlin remarked with a soft smile. "Go, child. See what peace you might bring out there."

Isolde stared at him a long moment before she turned to go. Everything was so uncertain. Did Newlin believe she could insert herself into this mess and somehow ease the tensions? Linus stood near the door, his expression as friendly as ever and yet worried, too. He opened the door when she approached. Outside Gandy stood on the top step, wrapped in a doubled-up blanket as he stared out at the busy yard. She hesitated beside him, searching for Rhys.

The dwarf looked up at her. "I do not like this."

Isolde gave a short, unhappy laugh. "Nor do I."

"He cannot fight. He is still injured from the fight with Dafydd."

Isolde stiffened. That was true. He would not be able to grip his sword well enough to fight. A little part of her began to hope. Perhaps there would be no battle after all. But she knew better. She knew that was not possible. Rhys had prepared his whole life for this day. He would let nothing stop him. Not his pain. Certainly not her love.

Unaccountably, memories of the Welsh children's chant rose in her mind.

> *When stones shall grow and trees shall no',*
> *When noon comes black as beetle's back,*
> *When winter's heat shall cold defeat,*
> *We'll see them all 'ere Cymry falls.*

She pulled the mantle close around her neck. The first two predictions had already come to pass. Twenty years ago a stone fortress had begun to grow on the rocky rose cliffs. Then ten years later the midday sky had blackened to night. She remembered it well, the panic, the fear that it was the end of the world. But it had not been the end of the world and the darkness had saved her uncle Jasper from sure death. And it had led to Rhys's first defeat.

But the third prediction, winter's heat . . . She pondered what it might mean. Would God come and melt the snow just like he'd darkened the sky back then? Would He save Rhys as He'd saved Jasper? But then, saving Rhys would mean sacrificing Jasper or her father. Isolde wrapped her arms around herself. She believed in the chant; she was too afraid not to. But she had no idea how to interpret it.

She forced herself down the steps, consumed with guilt. If Rhys could not defend himself sufficiently because of his injuries, it would be her fault. He'd hurt himself in her defense. In spite of her need to protect her family, she also wanted to protect Rhys.

Dear God, but she did not want him hurt!

She started across the silent, snow-packed yard, but at the steep stone stairs that led up to the wall walk her path was blocked. A grim-faced Welshman stared her down. "Go back to the hall. This is no place for a woman."

"Let me pass," she ordered, glaring at him. "I have business with Rhys."

"You'll have to wait. You'll have to wait," he repeated, though in a less confident tone.

Isolde planted her fists on her hips. "Perhaps you forget that I am the bargaining point between him and my father. What I have to say to Rhys is vital. His life—and yours—may hang upon it."

When his gaze darted away from hers then returned, only to dart away once more, Isolde knew she'd won this contest of wills. But that was of small comfort. Rhys and her father were the ones she must try to divert from a disastrous confrontation, and that task seemed hopeless.

She sidled past the guard and clambered up the cold steps, never looking back. Up on the wall walk the wind was bitter. Beyond the castle the land lay still and white. The forest crouched in the distance, dark under its mantle of snow. The river Geffyn showed, edged with boulders and brush. Had the entire surface of the water frozen over, or did an icy center yet rush headlong to the sea?

How Isolde wished she could that easily be washed away from here, removed from this battle that could have no true victor.

But she could not float away. And anyway, this was her home. So she squared her shoulders and headed toward the gatehouse parapet and the men clustered there.

The looks sent her way were a mixture of wariness, suspicion, and gloating. She was the enemy they all expected to defeat. But Isolde cared nothing for anyone's opinion but Rhys's, and he stood beside Glyn staring out to the road that ended on the far side of the moat. The other half-dozen Welshmen there grudgingly parted as she advanced through them.

"Come to see your father's defeat?" one of them laughed.

"Give 'em a wave. They'll get no nearer than that," another burly fellow jested.

"Let her through!" Rhys barked. He stood in the open space between the crennels, his arms resting on the walls framing it. He scowled down at the knot of horsemen at the edge of the moat.

"Come here, Isolde." Still he did not turn toward her. "Your father and uncle would see you."

With a lump in her throat, Isolde made her way to his side. It was cold and quiet on the wall walk. No bird wheeled through the winter sky calling out. No hound barked in the bailey. Even the men were silent behind her. The wind's moan along the high walls was the only sound, and it added to the chill that gripped her.

"Rhys, please," she whispered when she stopped beside him.

But his jaw was clenched tight, and when she touched his arm, it was rigid with tension. "Rhys—"

He turned, abruptly shaking off her hand, and grabbed her by the arm. If it hurt his sliced hand to propel her forward, he gave no indication of it.

"Here she is, FitzHugh. Unharmed, as I said."

Isolde tore her eyes reluctantly from Rhys's hard profile. Below them, so near and yet so impossibly out of reach, sat her father and her uncle Jasper, along with four other mounted men.

She leaned out, overwhelmed by a rush of love for her family who she knew loved her so much. On impulse she waved, and one of the knights waved back. Isolde squinted. Was that her younger brother, Gavin?

It was. Quick tears stung her eyes, and though she brushed them away, she could not so easily brush aside the fierce emotions that lodged in her chest. Even her young brother, not yet fully a knight, had come racing to her rescue.

"I . . . I am all right!" she called to them past the lump in her throat. "Do not worry over me."

Her father separated himself from the others, riding alongside the moat. He pushed down his cowl then raised a hand in salute to her. Isolde felt almost as if he'd touched her cheek.

"Papa," she whispered, stretching her hand out to him.

"I am relieved to see you," Randulf called up to her. "We have, all of us, been worried." Then his voice grew strident. "Release her! She is innocent of our dispute!"

"I am not harmed!" Isolde cried before Rhys could answer. "Nor am I afraid. Is Mother here?"

"Yes."

"Enough." Rhys pushed her aside, and at his signal one of his men quickly took her in hand. "I am a man of my word, FitzHugh. She will come to no harm in my care. But neither will she be freed until I have my vengeance."

"Vengeance for what? I spared your life. I provided for your education—"

"You stole Welsh lands. Your brother murdered my father!"

"Then meet *me* in battle!" Jasper threw out. He rode up beside his brother, his massive steed snorting and pawing. "Meet me in battle. But do not hide behind a woman."

"Done!" Rhys snarled.

"Then come. Come on, then." Jasper shook his fist at him.

"The battle is mine!" Isolde's father roared. "She is my daughter and this is my home!"

"I'll fight him, Father. Let me," Gavin shouted.

Isolde's blood turned to ice. "No." She struggled against the man who held her. "No, Rhys. Please, no!"

He flinched. She was sure of it. But he did not otherwise acknowledge her words. "Decide among yourselves. It is no matter to me whom I fight. I'll fight all of you. Just come, tomorrow at midday. I'll slay Jasper FitzHugh first."

"No, no!" Isolde cried.

"And once I have dispatched him," Rhys continued, "I will take on all comers."

"Tomorrow. At midday," Jasper answered in steely tones. "I'll be here."

In the awful silence that fell, Isolde heard the hoofbeats of her father's small band leaving the moat and returning to the village. She heard the harsh sound of her own breathing and the boastful mutterings among the Welshmen on the wall walk. But the man who'd set this whole tragedy into motion made no sound at all. He only watched his enemies depart, then slowly—slowly—turned his head toward her.

His expression was fierce, the coldly determined face of a man raised on war, conditioned in battle, and not afraid to die in pursuit of vengeance. But there was a bleakness in his eyes, a flat finality that frightened Isolde even more than the revenge he sought. He stared at her across the gulf of twoscore years of hatred, and she heard the silent truth in his eyes. What little comfort they'd found together—what passion and even, perhaps, the beginnings of love—could never make up for a lifetime of rage, a lifetime of waiting for this confrontation. She held no sway with him; she saw that with a sickening clarity. She could change nothing of his intent; nor could she ever forgive him for it.

They stared another long moment. Isolde did not struggle against the man who yet held her in his grasp. What purpose was there for struggle now?

"Take her to the tower," Rhys ordered after a moment. "You will remain there until this matter is done," he added to her. Then he turned and stalked away, and Isolde finally understood.

His hand was damaged and his arm, but they would heal. But he bore other scars of a deeper damage, hidden scars upon his heart and upon his soul, and they would never heal. Never. Though he had begun to care for her, he could not love her. And he understood, as she was now learning to, that the absence of love must leave them only with hate.

Randulf and Jasper were furious, as much at each other as at Rhys, it seemed. Josselyn and Rhonwen shared a look when their husbands returned, but they wisely kept their distance.

"The battle is mine!" Randulf thundered.

"But I am the one he has sworn vengeance on!" Jasper countered.

" 'Tis my daughter he holds and my castle he has stolen!"

Josselyn caught Gavin by the arm and dragged him into

the kitchen of the small cottage they'd taken in the village. "What news of Isolde? Did you see her?"

Gavin's young face was pale, but his eyes were bright with youthful outrage. "I saw her. We all did. She waved and she said she was not harmed. But he would not let her go."

From behind them Rhonwen nodded. "I told you Rhys would not hurt her."

Josselyn just arched one brow and turned back to her son. "What has transpired?"

Once Gavin had explained about Rhys's challenge to meet each of them in battle, beginning with Jasper, Josselyn let the lad go. When they were once more alone, she said to Rhonwen, "There must be no battle. Not tomorrow. Not ever."

"But how can we prevent it?" Rhonwen threw her hands up in frustration. "Oh, why must men turn first to their weapons when talk can accomplish so much more?"

Josselyn stood there, her arms crossed over her waist, thinking. "It is up to us, Rhonwen. You and I—and Isolde. We are the ones who must forge a peace here, else someone we love will die."

They were quiet a moment. Then Rhonwen asked, "Do you think he has seduced her?"

Josselyn pursed her lips a moment, then nodded. "Yes. I am almost certain of it. What I am not certain of—what I hope is true but cannot say for sure—is whether *she* has seduced *him*. Whether she has cracked the surface of his hard heart."

"How can we know?"

Josselyn peered through the doorway at her husband, whom she dearly loved but who was too old to face a young man like Rhys in battle. Even Jasper was not so keen with his weapons as he'd been in years past.

"We cannot know for certain. But I believe time is our ally. Yes. Our ally." She faced Rhonwen with determination shining in her eyes. "We must use any reason we can find to delay this battle they plan for the morrow. We must at least do that, and then trust in Isolde to manage the rest."

Isolde paced the confines of the tower room. Four paces across the tiny chamber. Four across, four back. It was not as cold now as it had been earlier in the day. The clouds had increased

again, but instead of snow a dull rain fell, melting the snow
and ice and turning the world to a wet and gloomy gray. It
well suited the gray gloom that had settled over her soul.

Someone would die tomorrow. Someone she loved.

She halted her nervous pacing and pressed her hands
against the sides of her head. She could not bear the thought;
she simply could not.

On impulse she dropped to her knees. "Dear God, sweet
Mary, Lord Jesus. I have been a sinner. I know I have. But
please, I beg you. Do not punish me by hurting one of them.
Spare them, all of them. Oh, please . . ." She trailed off, head
bowed over her tightly clasped hands. She needed an answer,
she needed some assurance from God, some sign from above
that He heard her prayer.

But there was none. How could there be? she asked herself.
Mere mortals could not make demands of God, no matter how
sincerely motivated, and expect a quick answer. Still, she remained on her knees a long while, searching her heart for a
solution.

When she finally rose, she had made no progress, save for
knowing that she could never fully hate Rhys. Even should he
fight her uncle and her father, and strike them both down, even
then she would hate what he had done, but she would not hate
him. She only hoped beyond all reason that it would not come
to that.

Restless, she made a circuit of her tower prison, rattling the
locked stair door, then moving to the other door that led to
the overlook. It was not barred, but it was raining outside, a
cold blustery rain, and she retreated from it. With nothing else
to do, she took up her charcoal stick and stared at the bare
wall.

Rhys had been so tender of late, especially last night and
this morning. It was hard to align that Rhys with the man
who'd vowed death to her family just hours ago. She reached
out with the piece of charcoal and drew a tentative line on the
stone. The slope of a nose. The angle of a chin. At first her
hand trembled. She did not want to draw him. She did not
want to memorialize him on the walls of Rosecliffe.

But she kept on. The dark slash of his brows—he was
smiling. She shivered and turned away, then began afresh.

This time the brows lowered in anger. His eyes sparked with vengeance. She drew in great arcs of movement, swiftly. Faster and faster. The charcoal scratched across the uneven stones. Then it splintered in her hands and fell in useless shards to the floor.

"Why!" she screamed. Then she attacked the drawing, smearing the charcoal image with her hands as she raged at the injustice of it all. Why? Why?

"Isolde."

With a gasp she spun around. Rhys stood in the doorway, and for a moment she was frozen in shock. She had not heard him remove the bar. But he had heard her, and now he stared at her two frenzied sketches. The good Rhys and the bad one.

She turned away from him. "What do you want?"

He sighed and that small indication of his weariness reverberated through her.

She blinked back the sting of unwanted tears. "What do you want of me, Rhys?"

He did not answer, but instead studied the first sketch. "Is this me?"

She shrugged. "Sometimes."

"Sometimes?"

She stared down at her hands, grimy from the charcoal. "Sometimes you are easy to be with. Kind. Thoughtful."

"And this other sketch," he said after a moment. "Was that also of me, sometimes?"

Isolde nodded.

"Sometimes. When I am cruel? When I am angry?" Another pause. "When I vow to kill your family?"

She closed her eyes. "I cannot speak with you about that," she said in a strangled voice. "If that is why you have come, then I wish you would leave."

But he did not leave. "I am neither of those men, Isolde, but rather a portion of both. Can you not see me as both? Not wholly good; but not wholly bad, either."

She turned half the way toward him. "I know that."

He held his arms open. "Then draw me that way. Draw me as I am."

It was the oddest experience, drawing Rhys. Odd, with a feeling of unreality about it. He seated himself upon a stool beside the window so that the meager light through the stretched skin fell upon him. A solitary candle on the windowsill increased the shadows across his face, and Isolde stared solemnly at him. His was a handsome face, a man's face, strong and stubborn, and she wanted to draw him. Her hands fairly itched to make his image.

She sighed and pulled out a precious piece of sheepskin, one she'd been saving for something special. This was special, though not what she'd imagined using it for. Tomorrow would her drawing be all that remained of Rhys? She did not want to think about that.

She sat cross-legged on her pallet so that she was positioned lower than he, then stared up at him. "Turn your face toward the light."

He studied her a long moment before doing as she asked. "Like this?"

"Yes." It was not as difficult as she thought. Without his dark observant eyes upon her she was free to stare at him as long as she liked. The wide brow and strong nose. The full, curving lips that neither smiled nor frowned. His chin jutted out, determined. His jawline was straight and firm. His neck was thick with muscles and disappeared into the opening of his quilted hauberk.

She drew it all without rushing, dipping a goose quill into the ink as she created his image on the sheepskin. It would be all she would ever have of him, no matter what tomorrow brought, so she wanted it to be perfect. His raven-black hair. His midnight-dark eyes.

But she could not depict him wholly dark. There was a darkness in his soul, but she had discovered that there also was light, and she wanted that to show, as well. So she labored carefully over his image, and when she was finally satisfied, she pushed the ink aside and sat back on the pallet.

"Will you show it to me?" he asked, looking down at her.

She held it up. "You are a good subject. Much more so than my sister Gwen. She squirms and . . ." She trailed off. The subject of her family cast a pall over them both. She knew how he hated them.

He stood, a faint crease marking his brow. " 'Tis good work. As I have said before, you have a rare talent." He cleared his throat. "You may come down to the hall for the evening meal," he added.

She stood also, setting the drawing aside. "Am I commanded to appear, or is the choice mine?"

Their eyes held and her heart raced of its own accord.

"The choice is yours."

Then he left and she had only the echo of his words for company. The choice is yours. She wanted to laugh, except that she feared she might cry. The choice had never been hers. Not to leave him, or to love him.

Some decisions the heart made all on its own.

TWENTY-FOUR

IT DRIZZLED OFF AND ON THE WHOLE DAY AND INTO THE night. When the bells of prime pealed over the cold, bedraggled countryside, Josselyn had already been awake two hours, worrying, praying. Plotting. She would not allow her husband to fight Rhys—nor her brother-in-law, Jasper, either. They were men—angry men—with a need to strike back at anyone who threatened them, their loved ones, or those they were sworn to protect. But though they were angry, they were not stupid. If she could just convince Rand that waiting would aid their cause . . .

But how could she be certain? What if she were wrong about Rhys? What if he vented his anger on Isolde?

Josselyn hugged her arms around herself, afraid for her firstborn child, but afraid also for Rhys. Did she dare take such a chance?

A figure moved in the muddy street, not huddling against the damp wind. A child? But when Josselyn squinted she recognized Newlin.

Newlin! She pressed her tightly clasped hands against her mouth. Newlin would know what to do. The fact that he came directly toward her convinced her all the more. She held open the low door for him, and giving her a sweet smile, he entered with his familiar sideways gait. For all the rain, he was not excessively wet and he declined her offer of a warming tea.

"It has come round to us, my child," he said. "Winter's end is nigh. Do you remember when I taught you those words in the foreign tongues of Norman French and Saxon English?"

Josselyn nodded. "It has been more than twenty years. But those lessons, they have served me well."

"Yes, with a Norman husband and a lengthy sojourn in the lands of the Saxons."

"But I am back in Wales. In *Cymry*," she said, growing more serious. "And now I am forced to face a countryman as my enemy, when I would rather face him as my friend."

"Winter's end is nigh," the old bard said, blinking.

"Winter's end? But it is not even Christmastide."

He only smiled and that more than anything encouraged Josselyn. Did he mean that the end of the discontent at Rosecliffe was nigh? She knelt before him and took his twisted old hands in hers. "He will not hurt her, will he? I cannot believe Rhys would allow any harm to befall Isolde, no matter how angry he might be."

"No, he would not," the old man agreed.

"Not even if no one faced his challenge this day? Even if his revenge upon Jasper and Rand was somehow foiled?"

The ancient little man patted her hands and for a brief moment both his good eye and the one that wandered focused together on her. "You cannot delay this confrontation forever. Indeed, it may be that only in their confrontation can one season die and another finally be born."

" 'Tis not the death of a season that worries me, but the death of someone I love!" Josselyn stood and began to pace, then stopped. "Tell me this. Does he love her? He has held Rosecliffe for two weeks and in that time he has not hurt Isolde, or so she says." She paused, pinning her wise old friend with her eyes. "Has he taken her to his bed?"

The bard's eyes twinkled. "So some believe."

Josselyn pursed her lips thoughtfully and considered that news. She was too practical to be very upset about her daughter's loss of virginity—if she had been willing.

"She was." Newlin answered her question before she could ask it. He turned away and stretched his hands to the fire. "But now, Josselyn, I would make a request of you."

Josselyn's mind was still circling the fact that Isolde had accepted Rhys's affections, so it took a moment for Newlin's words to sink in. "A request? Oh, but of course."

Newlin stared into the fire. "There is a woman at Rosecliffe. She arrived with Rhys. An old woman named Tilly—though she goes by Tillo and disguises herself as a man."

Josselyn's brows arched in curiosity. When Newlin's wizened face pinkened ever so slightly, however, she could scarcely believe it. Was the solitary Newlin enamored of a woman? "Her name is Tilly?" she asked, dumbfounded by the possibility.

He nodded. "She is in need of a home, and though she denies it, I know she likes Rosecliffe."

Josselyn's senses came immediately alert. "Are you saying I will soon be in a position to decide who may or may not reside at Rosecliffe?"

The bard glanced over at her and grinned. "I had not meant to reveal that. I see the years have not dulled your mind."

Josselyn chuckled, pleased beyond measure by both his remark and his revelation. "Nor has time dulled yours, though perhaps someone has distracted you?" Then she waved her hand. "Never mind about that. We are in agreement, then. Tilly will have a home at Rosecliffe. But what of Rhys?"

Newlin sighed. "Some things are clear to me, Josselyn. Others less so. And remember, Rhys has a will of his own. His choices are his to make, not mine. Only time will reveal to us what those choices will be."

"But he will not hurt her," Josselyn murmured under her breath as Newlin turned to leave. "He will not hurt her," she repeated as she watched her old friend depart. That was enough for her to know. Now, she could turn her energies toward convincing both Rand and Jasper that to decline Rhys's challenge was not cowardice, but rather, a strategic decision. No easy feat, she knew, for they were both angry and impatient. She would have to find a way to distract them.

Thunder boomed and rolled across the land, rattling the doors and windows, and a fresh wave of rain beat down on the sturdy thatch-roofed cottage. Though the snow was fast melting, it was still not a fit day to be out-of-doors. She tapped a finger against her chin. Better to stay abed.

Then she smiled to herself. A day spent abed, that was one way to distract Rand, and surely Rhonwen could do the same with Jasper.

Feeling better now, she added a few logs to the fire then turned for the stairs. First she would speak with Rhonwen. Then she would search out her magnificent, hardheaded husband and teach him a thing or two about strategic warfare.

Rhys stalked along the wall walk, clenching and unclenching his fists. Where were they? Where in God's name were they!

He glared down at the village that spread beyond the castle walls. It was strangely still for this hour of the morning. After the heavy snowfall, then the melting rains of the past few days, the village folk should be taking advantage of the break in the weather. There was livestock to tend, wood to be collected. Hunting to do.

But the village was as still as death. Only the numerous spumes of chimney smoke gave evidence of any life there at all.

He stopped his pacing and leaned forward between the crenellations, ignoring the pain to his stitched wounds. "Show yourselves, you bloody cowards," he muttered.

From the corner of his eye he saw Linus huddled in the shelter of the gatehouse. Like Linus, every warrior at Rosecliffe was on alert, battle vestments donned, weapons honed, and senses attuned to any movement from the village. Though the battle was rightly between Rhys and Jasper, the revenge of a son directed at his father's killer, there was more than that at stake. These were Welsh lands; they deserved a Welsh ruler. If he should die on the point of a FitzHugh blade, Rhys hoped Glyn and the others would carry on the battle.

How would Isolde react to his death?

He closed his eyes, fighting off any thought of Isolde. Thinking of a woman during battle was deadly, a mistake he'd never before made, and one he refused to make now. But ignoring his memories of Isolde was impossible. His head was filled with them. His body fairly thrummed with them.

She'd been incredibly attentive to him yesterday and this morning, as well. She'd removed his bandages twice, checking his injuries and spreading a soothing ointment over the wounds. Then she'd rebound his wounds, and all the while she'd spoken of subjects far away from the one uppermost in both of their minds. Music. Art. Sculpture. At her urging he'd described the town of York, the great castle at Richmond, and the Abbey of Whitby on the German Sea. He'd explained how the Scottish pipes worked and she tried to explain her need to create art. She'd practiced again on his gittern. In time she would be very good.

But neither of them had mentioned politics, family rivalries, or their conflicting loyalties.

At the evening meal she'd played her role as lady of the castle one last time. One last time, for whether he won or lost this battle today, he would lose her forever. She would leave. He would have to return her to what was left of her family.

He stared blindly at the village below him. He should return her to them now.

But he could not.

He pounded his fist against the stone parapet, reveling in the stabbing pain. "*Sceat!* Show yourselves!" he roared. Then breathing heavily, he turned away from the deceptively placid village. He strode to the stairs. "Bring my horse," he ordered the first man he saw. In the bailey he gestured to Glyn. "You will hold Rosecliffe while I ride out with three men."

The lanky Welshman looked astounded. "But they have not shown themselves. If you ride out with but three men they will take you. Did you not see the size of their army?" Glyn shook his head. "Our strength lies in these walls, Rhys. Out there we are outnumbered." Then a sly look came into his eyes. "Except, of course, that you hold the girl. They will not risk her, I think."

Nor will I risk her.

The response was nearly out of Rhys's mouth before he caught himself. He would not risk Isolde, either. But her family could not be sure of that. Though the idea left a bad taste in his mouth, he knew he must use their fear for her to his advantage.

He fixed his gaze on Glyn. "I hold Isolde FitzHugh. But I am not craven enough to do her harm. Nor will any man harm her if he expects to live out the day."

Glyn met Rhys's warning glare and he stiffened at the implication. But he gave a curt nod. "I am not Dafydd. I know our battle is with her menfolk."

Rhys nodded as well, but he was not totally appeased. If

he should fall to the FitzHughs, could he trust his Welsh countrymen to safeguard Isolde when their own lives were in danger? He watched his second in command climb the steps with a sinking certainty. He could not trust Glyn no matter what he said, nor any of the others.

But he could trust Linus and Gandy and Tillo.

Isolde watched from the tower overlook. It was strange to observe from afar the preparations for the conflict to come. Today men would pit their lives for possession of Rosecliffe Castle, men like Rhys and her father and uncle. Good men all, they were honorable and brave, and were their loyalties not so squarely in opposition, they would all respect one another. She was certain of that.

She shielded her eyes against the light, stinging rain. The village was still, as was the castle. Only the Welsh men-at-arms moved about the bailey and wall walk. Everyone else hid and waited. But she could not hide.

Then she spied Rhys descending the stairs from the wall, conversing with one of his men. Tall and bareheaded, he was nonetheless dressed for battle. He wore his padded hauberk, and his long sword swung at his side. He signaled several men and in short order four horses were led out from the stables. Her heart began an uneven thudding.

"Please don't fight them." She leaned out between the crennels, needing Rhys to look up at her and hear her plea.

But he did not look up. He spoke to Linus. He gave orders she could not hear and men dispersed at his command. Then he mounted a huge destrier and positioned his weapons: his long sword, a mace, a pike in its sheath. He raised his chainmail cowl and placed his helmet on his pommel. Then at his gesture the bridge creaked down, the gate screeched open, and he and the three others started forward.

She reached out a futile hand to him as he disappeared beneath the gatehouse, a powerful, broad-shouldered figure bent on his own destruction. Then she turned away, consumed with a grief that was as illogical as it was overwhelming.

She did not see him emerge on the road beyond the wall. She did not see him turn once as if to scan the castle defenses for any weakness.

But it was not weaknesses in Rosecliffe's walls that Rhys searched out. He knew already the weakness in his plan, and it lay not in the mighty fortress walls, nor in the meager number of men left to defend the castle. The weakness was one he carried inside him—in his heart, if one could believe the love-struck words of the minstrel balladeers. He loved Isolde FitzHugh. That was his weakness. And he sought one last sight of her. He needed to see her, to know her eyes were upon him no matter that her loyalties lay with her family.

But she was not there. On the tower overlook he saw nothing, and in his chest something hard seemed to turn over. As he turned his attention back to the road and the hostile village, he told himself he was glad she was not there. It was better if she kept herself apart from this day's doings. A man did not need a woman lurking in the background when he faced another across the raised length of his sword. His jaw clenched in a grimace. In truth a man did not need a woman at all, save to vent his lust upon.

As they made their way down the wet, rocky road, however, he knew he was a liar. He had never needed a woman in his life—until he met Isolde. And though he had made her his captive and could keep her as long as he wanted, that was no longer enough. She'd said she loved him, but more than that, she'd shown him her love in so many little ways. That was what he most wanted from her, he now realized. The small, everyday expressions of her love.

But it was too late for that. After today he would either be dead or she would hate him for having killed her uncle and perhaps her father.

"Will they attack us?" one of the men asked, breaking into Rhys's morose thoughts. The man who spoke was a burly fellow, the best of the Welsh swordsmen. But the best fighter could stand only so long against greater numbers. He understood that and so did Rhys.

"I go to goad the cowards to a confrontation, but not a confrontation between the four of us and them. This fight is between the FitzHughs and me."

He drew his mount to a halt in a wide place in the road just before the enclosure of the first of the village cottages. The clouds hung low and heavy, a cold blanket over an even colder ground. The village was silent, but he saw faces behind the shutters, and shadows behind doors opened a margin.

"Show yourself, Jasper FitzHugh. I am Rhys ap Owain. You can run from me no longer!"

A fierce gust of wind howling around a corner was his only answer, that and the excited bark of an unseen hound.

"Damnation! Is your fear so great that you would shame yourself before all these people, English and Welsh alike?"

He tensed at the sound of angry voices. Then the door of a large cottage halfway up the street crashed open and two men emerged. The FitzHugh brothers! Both of them wore only their short swords and daggers, still sheathed at their hips.

Rhys's grip on the reins tightened unconsciously and his horse backed up and half reared before he eased his stranglehold on the leather straps. He stared at the two men. His entire life had been altered by these two, directed in ways no one could have predicted when he was but the young son of the fierce Welsh warrior, Owain ap Madoc. His father had lusted after the lands of the rose cliffs, and also after the woman, Josselyn, who went with those lands. He'd not lived to possess either of them. Now twoscore years later, here he was, Owain's son, in possession of both of those treasures, the land with its newly built castle, and the woman who belonged to it, though it was the daughter now, not the mother.

All in all, a heady feeling, but disconcerting also. For though he fought to retain possession of the castle and lands, he knew he could not possess the woman for long. But he brutally shoved those thoughts aside.

"So. You show yourself at last." He leaned forward nonchalantly and the leather saddle creaked beneath him. "Who will be the first to die beneath my blade?"

Though their expressions were murderous, they did not rise to his baiting. "How fares Isolde?" Randulf FitzHugh demanded. He strode boldly forward, one of his hands resting on his sword hilt. "How fares my daughter?"

"She fares well. Are you prepared to face me?"

"There will be no battle. Not today," Jasper FitzHugh said, coming up beside his brother.

Rhys stared at them in disbelief. Despite the insults he'd

hurled at them, he did not truly take them to be cowards. Did they delay in the hope of raising more men?

"Face me now or suffer the consequences," he bit out.

Randulf FitzHugh tensed and started to jerk his sword out. But his brother's hand on his arm stayed the movement.

Rhys could not believe this. "Are you spineless? Must I dismount and throw my gauntlets in your face before you will respond like men instead of craven worms?" The words struck home. He saw that much in their furious expressions. But something held them back.

"We are but four men," Rhys continued, determined to prod them to action. "I know you are nearly twenty. And yet you fear me." He shook his head, deliberately taunting them. "Look at them," he said to his nervous men. "Twenty Normans do fear four Welshmen. Are we not the sons of dragons? Are we not the fiercest warriors on this isle?"

"So fierce you hide behind my daughter's skirts!" Randulf roared.

Rhys observed him coldly. "She is but enticement to force your return."

"Rescuing my home is enticement enough to hasten my return. No, you did not keep her to entice me here. Rather, it is you who are enticed by her. That's the only reason you keep her. And though I would happily strike you down this very moment, until she is returned to the safety of her family, I cannot risk it. I cannot risk her."

Rhys stared contemptuously at him. "It is not you I want to fight, but rather my father's murderer. If it pleases you, though, I will take you on once he is dead."

"Neither of us will fight you until Isolde has been released," Jasper stated. "That is the only way we can be certain your men will not retaliate against her upon your death."

Rhys bristled and his mount stamped one massive hoof. "That will not happen." He'd already made certain of it. "Welshmen do not wreak their vengeance upon women," he added.

"Your father did."

Rhys sucked in a sharp breath and glared furiously at Jasper FitzHugh. He wanted to deny the man's charge, except that a part of him knew it was true. Owain had fought to keep Wales free of Norman invaders, a noble goal. But he'd also not hesitated to trample upon anyone weaker than himself—women, children. His wife. Even his own son. It didn't matter who.

For that reason, Rhys silently conceded, FitzHugh had every right to be suspicious of his treatment of Isolde. His mind swiftly weighed his choices. If reinforcements were coming, he needed to fight the FitzHughs as soon as possible. And if they would not meet him in battle until Isolde was freed . . .

He steeled himself for what he must do. "Very well, I will free her."

In the distance thunder rumbled, low and long, as if it traveled from a faraway place. But Rhys ignored the threat it carried. He'd always known he must someday free her. That time had now come.

"Don your battle garb and meet me in the field beside the moat," he clipped out. "The two of you come alone, and I will come with Isolde. Then we will fight. Then we will end this, once and for all."

Then I will die, if not my body, then most assuredly my heart.

TWENTY-FIVE

SHE HEARD HIM COMING. A DEAF WOMAN WOULD HAVE heard him coming. Thundering horse's hooves on the bridge. Angry voices in the yard. But Isolde did not turn away from her task. A flash of lightning lit the shadowy room. The crack of thunder that followed rattled the shutters. But still she did not break her concentration.

From the moment Rhys had disappeared beneath the massive gatehouse, she had been compelled to paint. Unlike the careful portrait she'd done of him, this was a burst of wild energy, a hurried and passionate effort. Almost without conscious thought the work took form on the bare wall before her. A rearing dragon faced a charging wolf. Two magnificent creatures locked in battle. Or was it an embrace?

She suppressed a sob and dipped her brush in a pot of pale gray paint. The dragon's eyes were black, like Rhys's. The wolf's would be gray, like hers.

A door slammed. Footsteps, heavy and purposeful, were coming up the stairs. To her little tower room?

The door crashed open without warning. She only bent more intently to her work. She heard his harsh breaths. He was angry. But then, when was he not?

The answer came easily: when they were alone. When it was only them without the intrusions of the outside world and the weight of the past, then he was not angry.

"I am come to set you free of this place."

She flinched, but refused to look at him. The dragon's

claws were sharp. His breath was searing. But the wolf's fangs were equally sharp, and she was fearless.

"Damn you, Isolde! I am releasing you from this prison. Go! Go now to your family."

She shook her head. "You will not put me out of my rightful home." She swung her head around to face him, an obstinate light in her eyes. "This is my home, Rhys. I will fight to keep it just as fiercely as do you. You of all people must understand that."

He stood there in his battle array, dwarfing her, dwarfing the chamber. She pressed her lips together. He was more magnificent than she could ever depict. So strong. So driven. His sense of honor was a thing to admire, no matter that it demanded vengeance upon her family. She sucked in a deep breath then slowly turned back to her painting. The dragon was not right. It did not do him justice.

"You have to go to them," he said, his voice quieter now. " 'Tis time."

"No."

"Yes. If you will not go willingly, then I will force you."

"You told me that it was not your way to force a woman—"

"Uffern dan!" He yanked her upright and spun her around. Brush and paint went flying, but Isolde paid them no mind. Her dragon lover meant to rid himself of her, and her heart simply could not bear it.

His midnight eyes burned into hers. "You will go. They're waiting for you."

"Why are you doing this now?" She tried to grab his chain mail in her fists but she could not. The hard links bit into her palms, but still she tried. "What will happen if I go out to them?"

He didn't have to say the words; she could see the truth in his eyes. But still he said them. "When you are safe again in the bosom of your family, only then will Jasper meet me on the field of honor."

"Do not do this, Rhys. I beg you. Do not."

He shook his head. "It has been too many years since I have made this vow to possess again what should have been mine all along."

"You can have it without this fight, without anyone dying."

Their eyes held so long that Isolde felt hers sting, for she feared to blink and break their tenuous bond. It was he who blinked. "You are a woman; you don't understand. But I am a man, as are they, and we fight for what we must have."

"I *am* fighting, Rhys. I'm fighting as a woman fights. Not with your weapons, but with mine. I think you love me." She trembled as she said the words. What if she were wrong? But she pressed on. "I think you may love me, and I know I love you. So wed with me. A marriage between us will end forever this feud between our families. Let us be wed, Rhys. I am the firstborn—"

He thrust her away and then stared at her as if she were mad. "Your brother will inherit." Then his hand sliced the air. "Besides, a union between us cannot change the past."

"It can if you will let it. If you will choose me over vengeance."

But he only shook his head and Isolde felt panic rise in her chest. "Please, Rhys. I love you."

His face twisted in torment. Every muscle in his hard warrior's body trembled with violent emotion. It was a fearful sight and yet Isolde was somewhat heartened. She reached out a hand and rested it lightly upon his chest. "Do you not see how blessed we are—"

"Do not work your ploys on me!" His voice was angry. But he clasped his hand over hers, pressing it against the chain mail links. "If that is how you feel, then you must accept me as I am. I cannot change my destiny now."

Isolde's heart ached for him. He wanted her love, something he'd never had from anyone before. But at what price? Could she pay it? Could she love a man who would happily slay her family?

Something inside her seemed to break. "I cannot be with you, Rhys, if you would destroy my family. For I love them, too."

He threw off her hand so fast she stumbled backward.

"Then go to them," he snarled. "You cannot love me and also love my enemies. Go!" he bit out through clenched teeth.

Isolde backed away from him, hugging her arms around herself. "I am staying here." Her voice trembled; her entire body trembled. "I am staying here. In my home."

"No. You are not."

Operating on instinct, Rhys grabbed Isolde and tossed her over his shoulder. His chest constricted with pain as he closed off the part of him she had just managed to touch. She had made him love her and she'd nearly made him confess to it. But when he'd reached out to take what she offered, she'd yanked it back. She had put a price on it, a bounty. And it was too high.

"No, Rhys! No! Don't do this," she cried, struggling against his rigid grasp. But Rhys steeled himself against the desperation in her voice. He knew what he had to do and he could not allow her to deter him. She kicked and squirmed, and pounded her fists against his back, but he was immune to her blows. He strode from the small chamber, ignoring Linus's worried look, while Isolde fought him all the way.

He had known from the beginning that his attraction to her was foolish. He'd known it was madness. But even he had not guessed that it could be so dangerous. Or so painful.

By the time he reached the bailey she had ceased fighting. But that only made his task more difficult. To ignore Isolde when she struggled against him was hard enough. To ignore her when she lay warm and soft across his shoulder, with the ends of her silken hair flying up against his neck and her unique scent of lavender and paint invading his senses, was nigh on to impossible.

"Rhys," she beseeched him, bracing herself against his back. "Put me down. Think what it is you truly want."

"I know what I want," he retorted, striding across the bailey. "I've always known."

He ignored the raised brows and startled faces of both castle folk and Welsh men-at-arms. From the gatehouse the guards stared down on him, but no one dared stop him, for he was lord of Rosecliffe now, and he meant to hold that position. Beneath the gate he strode, and across the bridge. In the field beyond the moat his three men waited. From the village he heard a shout and knew word of Isolde's appearance would carry swiftly to the FitzHughs. They would have to fight him now.

When he put her down she stumbled back three paces. Her loosened hair whipped like a fragrant pennant in the wind, but she swept it aside with one hand. Gasping for breath, she glared at him. "You think that because you fight you are brave. But it takes more courage to love than to kill. You are brave with your body, Rhys, but you have no courage of the heart. None!"

He tried not to wince, but her words struck home with excruciating accuracy. So he raised the only defense he could: denial. "It was lust we shared, not love," he growled, hating himself for the lie and the way she blanched in response.

One of her hands pressed against her chest in the vicinity of her heart. "No, Rhys. No." But her voice wavered and he knew his words had shaken her.

"Go." He pointed down the road to where two women stood staring at them. Josselyn and Rhonwen, he realized. How perversely fitting, for these three women were the only ones he'd ever truly admired. Each of them had at some point offered him comfort: Josselyn, that of a mother; Rhonwen, that of a friend; and Isolde, that of a lover. And he had wanted what they'd offered. He'd gladly accepted it. But in the end each one of them had betrayed him. Each one of them.

He took a harsh breath and drew himself up. In time he'd learned to hate the other two. He turned his eyes back to Isolde. In time, God willing, he could learn to hate her, as well.

Josselyn grabbed her husband's arm. "Do not fight him. I beg you, Rand."

But he shook off her hold. "He has stolen our home and done God knows what to our daughter. Now he vows to kill my brother. No, Josselyn. No. I have delayed this confrontation long enough. I understand your affection for him. But he is a man now. He's not the boy you once knew. And he must bear the weight of the choices he has made."

So saying, he strode toward the two figures standing in the open field.

Josselyn clasped her hands against her chest. Rhonwen came up beside her and, clinging to one another, the two women watched Rand and Jasper advance on foot toward Rhys. Someone would die this day. Someone they loved. And though they'd done everything they could to sway their husbands from their grim task, it seemed they had failed.

Rhys stood his ground as his adversaries approached him. His three men, still mounted, formed a defensive half-circle behind him. Rand called out to Isolde and after a moment's hesitation, when her eyes clung to Rhys, she ran into her father's arms. But Josselyn and Rhonwen had seen that hesitation, and now they shared a look.

"She loves him," Josselyn murmured

"As well she should. He is a good man still. I know he is."

"Would that our husbands thought as much."

From behind them three of their own knights rode out to back up their lords. From overhead the heavens rumbled discontent.

"Let it rain," Josselyn prayed aloud. "Let the heavens yield their bounty now. Rain, snow, sleet. Please, God, prevent this battle. Please, Mother Mary, intercede for us. Stay these hot-headed men of ours."

But the only response was more thunder. Then Rand pushed Isolde gently toward the village. "Go to your mother," he said, his voice carrying to them.

"Isolde!" Josselyn cried out to her child and held her arms wide. She could not prevent what these men would do. But at least she could prevent her beloved child from witnessing the carnage sure to come. "Isolde. Come away from them."

Isolde spied her mother and her aunt. The urge to run to them was overwhelming, but she was afraid to leave the men, for then the fighting would commence. "Mother!" she cried out. "Oh, Mother, please make them stop. Stop, Father. Stop, Uncle Jasper!"

"We have tried! We have tried!"

Isolde shook her head and looked back at Rhys. Her father had stepped between him and Jasper, and he was defining now the rules of the fight to come. A fight to the death, she feared, and all for possession of a castle.

She looked over at Rosecliffe, the home that she loved. Yet she did not value it nearly so much as she valued the lives of these three men she loved. Then a figure stepped beyond the shadows of the gatehouse. Two figures, Newlin and Tillo. They stood close together, a united front, it seemed. They were shoulder to shoulder, and it gave her courage.

Without pausing to consider her actions, Isolde turned away from her mother and started back toward the castle. She did not run, but neither did she hesitate. Lightning cut a jagged streak across the sky and thunder crashed over her head, but she did not flinch. "I am returning to the tower," she announced as she marched past the three tense men. "To my home. Do not come to me, Father, if you or Jasper harm Rhys. And do not come to me, Rhys, if you spill the blood of either my uncle or father."

If they looked her way, she did not know. It was enough that the three mounted Welshmen stared at her as if she were a madwoman. The guards at the gatehouse did the same. But Newlin smiled at her, and Tillo briefly clutched her hand.

"Please," Isolde begged them both. "Please do something to end this madness."

"Take yourself off to the tower, child," Newlin said. "You have done the best you can do. What is left lies in their hands." He turned to face Rhys and the two Englishmen. "In their hands, and in God's."

It was the hardest thing Isolde had ever done, to turn her back on the impending disaster and march resolutely across the bailey. No one in the castle yard spoke to her, though she felt the weight of their stares. Some were stunned. Others confused. But one or two of the women wore expressions of compassion, as if they understood.

Isolde pressed the fingers of one hand to her temple. If only she understood. But she was reacting on instinct now, so she crossed the empty hall and mounted the stairs with a steady tread. Up past her old chamber. Up past Rhys's chamber on the third level, the room that had been her parents', until she reached the chamber that had, of late, become hers. The tower room.

It was darker in the close quarters than it had been minutes before. The storm blocked out the sun, and the unsettled clouds seemed to frown disapproval upon the foolish mortals beneath them. She stared at the mural she had begun. A splash of watery gray paint streaked across both dragon and wolf. Uniting them?

No.

Isolde turned away. It was doomed. All of it. The painting.

Her love. Her family. Her future. Outside the three men would kill one another, and in so doing, they would kill a part of her, as well. She could not stop them. Nor could she watch them.

So she righted the overset paint pot. She retrieved her paintbrush from the floor, and though tears clouded her vision, she found a rag and began to mop up the spilled gray paint. But continue to paint? She could not. Despite her dread, she strained to hear the clang of steel weapons, but she was not reassured by the silence.

Then she pressed her finger into the wet gray paint and impulsively drew a cross in the space between the dragon and the wolf. "God protect them, Welsh and English. God protect them."

TWENTY-SIX

Rhys focused on Jasper FitzHugh, the man he'd hated longer than he could remember.

His hand clenched around the sword hilt. One enemy at a time. He knew from having faced innumerable foes, in tournaments, melees, and actual battlefields, that to think beyond the adversary at hand was to court disaster. Disable them one at a time. That was the surest path to victory. First he must kill the younger FitzHugh brother. Then, if Randulf FitzHugh was bent on fighting, he would face him, too.

And when will you face Isolde?

His hand shook at the thought. Just a tiny tremor, but it transmitted up the mighty longsword he held before him. He saw the razor-edged tip of his favorite weapon waver. So did Jasper FitzHugh.

"Do you hesitate?" the man asked. "Is that fear? Or is it, perhaps, doubt that causes your hand to shake? For mark my words, Rhys, they are not the same thing."

Rhys's grip tightened, and a wave of sharp pain immediately shot out from his sliced hand. But that was good, he told himself. The pain would galvanize his fury. He glared at the man. Jasper FitzHugh might be past his prime physically, but he had not gone to fat. He was big and strong, and he would comport himself well on the field of battle. He met the man's stare without blinking. "I cannot fear a fight I have anticipated these twenty years gone by."

"Ah, but the stakes are considerably higher now than they were before. Perhaps what you feel is doubt."

"Nothing has changed." Rhys swore, then he lunged forward. At once Jasper leaped back and their swords clashed. But it was only the tips of the blades, just the beginning of their confrontation.

Was Isolde watching?

Again Rhys's hand trembled. The sword wavered.

"She must be in love with you," Jasper said in a reasonable tone. " 'Tis the only explanation I can see for my niece's curious behavior. She must love you."

"Not enough," Rhys muttered. With a burst he attacked once more, and this time he beat Jasper back with the fury of his blows. He was dimly aware of the other men around them, of the dozens of people from the castle and village who had crept out to watch this fight between lifelong enemies. He knew that Randulf FitzHugh waited, eager to take his brother's place when Jasper fell beneath his blade. And he would fall, Rhys vowed, pressing his attack.

But though Jasper gave ground, it was a strategic move, not a retreat, and Rhys was not foolish enough to interpret it otherwise.

"Think on why you fight me," Jasper continued, slashing back now. "Your father died at my hand that day. But Jossclyn was saved. He meant to kill her, to murder her. But I saved her life by killing him first. Do you think he deserves your loyalty? A man who would slay a woman? Do you think your father would have done as much for the Welsh people of these hills as she has? Healed them. Fed them. Kept the peace and made their lives better?"

"Save your breath for the fight. You will need it," Rhys snarled. He did not want to hear any of this. He thrust forward but Jasper turned the cut aside. For a moment their blades locked together. They were close enough to touch. Close enough to glare into each other's eyes.

How like Isolde's eyes his were, Rhys saw with a shock. The same clear gray shade, somewhere between falling rain and the deep, luminous color of quartz.

"No!" With a surge of raw strength Rhys threw the man backward. He did not want to see Isolde's eyes in his enemy's face.

Jasper stumbled back and his heel caught on a stone. Tilted

suddenly off balance, he went down on one knee. He was up in an instant, before the gasp from the onlookers had dissipated in the air. Still, it was enough time for Rhys to make his move.

But he did not.

He hesitated, then when it was too late, he cursed himself for a fool. Would he forfeit his life for a pair of gray eyes? For a woman who would never put him ahead of the rest of her family?

"Uffern dan!" he swore, and attacked with renewed zeal, slashing, thrusting, pushing FitzHugh farther back, and forcing the man to defend himself.

Neither of them had a spare breath to speak or taunt; they probed and parried and tried to make no misstep on the cold, slippery ground, soaked from the melted snow and earlier rains. Dimly Rhys heard the threatening roll of thunder. He heard the shouts and grunts of encouragement.

"You have 'em, lad"

"That's it. That's it."

"Careful. Take your time."

Sweat streaked down Rhys's face and arms, and stung his healing wounds. His muscles clenched and stretched as he hacked at the other man's defenses. He was operating on instinct, the smooth connection between his brain and his body that had brought him safely through a hundred such battles. A thousand, it seemed. Although he had a worthy opponent in Jasper FitzHugh, Rhys knew he was younger and more fit. Eventually he would prevail.

Sure enough, as the fight wore on he began to sense the oncoming victory. It showed in little ways. Jasper FitzHugh was tiring. His arm was slower to raise the heavy longsword. His thrusts were not as sure, nor as powerful. He was a canny fighter; Rhys would grant him that. But he was older and therein lay the difference. Jasper had but to endure a little longer.

Then without warning a shriek of light rent the air. A violent jolt of sound and light. Like a giant fist from the sky, thunder crashed over them. It seemed to roll right through them. The combatants both fell back at the abrupt onslaught. Horses reared and bolted, and screams of alarm sounded faintly in Rhys's deafened ears.

The hairs stood up on his arms and the back of his neck, and the air smelled fiery and rank. "Holy Jesu!" he exclaimed, momentarily stunned. What had happened? But he knew at once. Lightning had struck very near, and around him everyone scrambled for cover. Even his opponent was disoriented. FitzHugh had staggered back and he held a hand over one of his ears.

Rhys shook his head, trying to clear his senses. Now was his chance! Jasper's guard was down. His sword tip had fallen enough to allow Rhys a clean thrust to the man's chest.

Rhys steeled himself. It was no dishonor to take advantage of the confusion occasioned by the lightning strike. Had FitzHugh recovered first, he would do the same.

So Rhys tensed to strike. He focused on the vulnerable spot between the man's neck and shoulder, where the protection of the mail was weakest. Twenty years, he reminded himself. Twenty years of plotting revenge, of hating this man and all his kin.

Twenty years.

Jasper frowned and rubbed his ear. He still could not hear, Rhys realized. Rhys's own hearing was returning, though. He heard screams from somewhere beyond and the maddened snorts of horses and other cattle. But Jasper was still deaf.

Strike now. Now! the voice of revenge demanded—a voice that sounded suspiciously like his father's, hard and cruel and demanding. But Rhys hesitated and he could not say why. He raised the sword. He had but to swing it down and his revenge would be complete.

Then he heard it. A thin cry, yet shrill and piercing. "Fire. The tower, it's on fire!"

It carried over the din of panic and utter confusion, and it froze Rhys with his weapon upraised to deliver the killing blow.

"Fire in the tower. Fire!"

The tower. Isolde was in the tower.

A fear like nothing he'd ever known turned Rhys's blood to ice. Isolde! He spun around to face the castle and, horrified, saw the unreal glow of fire high up against the leaden sky. Had Isolde fled to the tower as she'd said she would? Was she up there now inside the burning top story?

Rhys forgot his revenge. He forgot his adversaries, both of them still partially deaf from the lightning strike. He even forgot the sword he yet held as he turned and sprinted for the castle. For him there was but one thought: if Isolde was in the tower, he must get her out.

He must get her out!

He tore across the clearing, over the bridge, and beneath the gatehouse. Around him utter pandemonium reigned, dogs barked, people screamed, staring, pointing in the directon of the tower. The place to which Isolde retreated.

He fought his way up the steps of the great hall, pushing past those fleeing the fire. Across the hall to the stairs, with the grim reek of the conflagration growing stronger in his nostrils.

"Isolde!" he screamed. "Isolde!"

But his only answer was the echo of her last words to him, just minutes before. "Do not come to me if you spill the blood of my uncle or father." And earlier she had pleaded so fervently with him. "Choose me over revenge."

But he had not. He had not.

God in heaven, was this his punishment for being a fool? A blind and heartless fool? "Save her," he prayed out loud as he took the steep winding steps three at a time. "God, I beg you, do not use her to punish me. Of us all, she is the only one innocent of wrongdoing. Save her. Save her."

Isolde heard a roaring sound. She felt heavy and her head hurt. But she was warm. She had not been this warm since . . . since when? Despite the pounding in her head and the oddest pressure in her ears, she smiled. She had not been this warm since she and Rhys had lain together, entwined in his big bed—

Rhys.

With a painful rush Isolde's memory returned. At this very moment he did battle with her uncle Jasper, and he meant to fight her father, as well. She gasped, then nearly choked on smoke.

What was happening?

She struggled to push herself upright and opened her bleary eyes, yet still she could not at first comprehend what she saw. Above her part of the roof had collapsed, while other parts of it were on fire. In places the flames leaped high above the roof, up into the sky. But how could that be?

Then she remembered an unholy sound, a streak of light and the unearthly crash when it struck the tower. Lightning! Lightning had struck Rosecliffe. Suddenly terrified, Isolde sat all the way up. The air was hot and thick with smoke, and she blinked back the burning sting of tears. She must get out!

But a shaft of pain shot down her back and into one leg, and sitting upright made her head spin. She stared around, disoriented. One wall of the tower had caved in. She could see the sky beyond and feel the wind. She pressed a hand to her head to stop the spinning. Where was the door? Where were the stairs?

She started blindly to crawl over rock rubble and splintered wood. Burning embers rained down on her. Ashes and charred wood. It was a nightmarish vision of hell, so hideous and terrifying that panic nearly overwhelmed her.

"Rhys!" she called out as she slapped at a smoking spot on her sleeve. "Rhys, help me," she cried, hardly aware of her words. She coughed and swiped at her eyes. Where was the door? Again she coughed, then lowered her face to the floor. The smoke was not so thick there, and she greedily gulped the blessedly cool air. As long as she could breathe, she could keep her wits about her.

But where was the door? Half-hidden by the rubble of the collapsed wall, she saw at last. And the top portion of it was already engulfed in flames!

In the castle yard one form of panic gave way to another. The castle folk fled the bailey, seeking respite from the angry God who saw fit to destroy Rosecliffe Castle rather than allow the claimants to battle for it. But others poured into the yard: the FitzHugh brothers and their men. And also their wives.

A still dazed Jasper FitzHugh managed to start a water brigade, shouting orders and grabbing men to do his bidding. His brother, Randulf, meanwhile frantically scanned the bailey, searching hopefully for the sight of his daughter.

"Where could she be? Surely not up there," Josselyn cried, running to catch him. "Rand, we must find her!" When she spied Newlin, however, she abruptly changed direction. "Newlin, help us. Help us! We must find Isolde!"

"He has gone for her," the bard answered in a calming tone. "Rhys ap Owain has gone for her. His will is strong, you know, and I had feared for him. But now it is come," he said with a glance at Tillo. "The third prediction is upon us."

The third prediction. Josselyn blinked at that sudden revelation. Of course. Winter's heat. And Rhys had gone to save Isolde. Did that mean this madness would finally end?

She spun about and dashed over to Rand, who had started toward the hall. She grabbed his arm. " 'When winter's heat shall cold defeat.' That is what this fire is. When it ends—"

"It will only end only when Rhys ap Owain is rendered powerless. But first I've got to find Isolde."

"She's in the tower, Rand, and Rhys has gone to save her. Don't you see?" she exclaimed as she followed him up the steps. "He could have killed Jasper, but Isolde's safety mattered more to him than revenge!"

His face was grim as smoke swirled around the hall he'd constructed with such care. "He is our enemy and I cannot underestimate him. I'll find Isolde." He caught her by the arm and shoved her back toward the door. "Get you to the yard. Organize our people and save what you can."

Josselyn started to protest. She started to say that she needed to find her child herself, and hold her in her arms. She wanted also to prevent her husband from reacting in anger when he found Rhys, for she was convinced he loved Isolde. He must.

But as Rand sped up the smoky stairs she said nothing. She must trust her husband. He had never let her down before. He would not now. After all, he loved his daughter as fiercely as did she. And he was nothing if not a fair and just man.

Rhys must pay for his crimes eventually, she knew. But who better to exact the appropriate punishment on the headstrong Welsh knight than Rand and Isolde?

TWENTY-SEVEN

THE SECOND LEVEL WAS EMPTY; SO WAS THE THIRD. THAT left only the tower room on the fourth floor. Rhys's heart turned to lead at the thought of Isolde trapped inside that conflagration, but he did not slow in his mad climb upward. The smoke grew thicker, as dense as river fog, only it was hot and made it nearly impossible to breathe. He had ripped down the curtain to the pantler's closet, and now he held the fabric over his mouth and nose to keep out the worst of the smoke.

"Isolde!" Where was she?

At the top of the stairs the door to the tower room was closed. But smoke seethed between the frame and the door itself. Without pause Rhys shoved at the thick oak panel. The top gave a little, letting out sheets of a choking black smoke. But the bottom held.

"Isolde? Isolde!" This time he threw his shoulder into it. She was there. He knew it!

The door gave, but only a little. Still, it was enough to see some portion of the hell inside the tiny chamber. Smoke poured out. Flames burning already on the inside of the door frame, licked out into the stairwell.

"Isolde!"

Ducking down to avoid the flames, he threw his whole weight against the door this time. Once. Twice. Again. Then something gave and the door sagged open enough for him to see the pile of fallen stones that blocked its inner swing. God in heaven, the lightning had shattered the very walls of Rosecliffe!

He coughed and stumbled back, overcome by the heat and smoke billowing into the stair hall. He wiped at his tearing eyes but that brought no relief. So he stooped down, took a breath, then charged the door once more. It shuddered and gave, just enough so that he could squeeze into the hell the room had become. "Isolde—"

"Rhys!"

She was huddled in the corner behind the door, struggling to drag the rubble away from the blocked entry, trying to escape even as he'd been pounding down the door. For a moment their eyes held, just one fleeting moment. But so much passed between them. Then she held up a hand and he grabbed it and pulled.

Above them the roof rafters groaned. The fire hissed and spat a shower of embers and sparks and burning ashes. Rhys pushed her through the door, then squeezed out after her.

Already the stair hall had filled with smoke and Isolde slumped over, her slender frame wracked with coughs. Despite his enormous joy at finding her, watching her fight for breath panicked Rhys anew. He had to get her outside away from the fire. She needed fresh air and water. And if she'd been burned—

"Rhys," she whispered, and only then did he realize the true depths of his fear for her, his terror and now his overwhelming relief. He scooped her into his arms and started for the stairs, but she struggled against him.

"Wait." She coughed as she reached out to grab the wall. "Wait. The door. Close it—" She broke off, coughing so violently he could not bear it.

"First I must get you to safety."

"No. Please, Rhys. Close that door, else the entire castle may catch fire."

Then let it burn, he almost replied. It was a tempting thought, the complete destruction of Rosecliffe, and a part of him would have rejoiced in the destruction of this symbol of Norman English aggression in Wales. If he could not possess it, then neither would the FitzHughs.

But what of the FitzHugh in his arms? If he hurt those others, then he hurt her. And one truth he had faced in the terrifying moments just past: he could never hurt Isolde. Never again.

Despite the blinding smoke and unbearable heat, Rhys set Isolde down and turned back to the fire. Somehow, crouching low, he found the door handle. It was hot but he wore gloves, and with a grunt he jerked the thick panel shut. It would not stop the fire, but it would slow its spread.

Then fighting for every breath and blinded by the hellish smoke, he groped his way back to Isolde. Though she protested, he lifted her into his arms. Then down the stairs he staggered, both of them sucking in great draughts of air, cold and sharp and healing.

"Are you hurt?" he asked when he could speak. He paused below the third floor, leaning against the outer wall as he looked down at her.

Isolde's face was pale from shock and smudged with soot. Her eyes were red from smoke and tears, and charred spots caused by the sparks and embers pockmarked her kirtle. But her gaze was steady and her voice, though hoarse and cracked, was not weak. "I am not burned. Not badly. I . . . My leg . . . I will be sore. But I am not hurt. Not really."

Then she wound her arms around his neck. "Once again you have saved me, Rhys. I can never repay you."

Rhys shook his head. He did not want her gratitude. In truth, he could not bear to speak of this at all, for he could not abide the thought of how close she'd come to death. He trembled to even imagine it.

But she persisted. "Once more you have saved my life." Her face was very close to his. Her eyes were serious and dark, yet very, very clear, and he was suddenly aware of his heart pounding in his chest. He wanted to look away from her. The fire seethed two floors up, a raging inferno such as only the devil could relish. But outside in the bailey another sort of hell awaited him. For he must now face her family, his avowed enemies.

Yet he did not fear either of those hells nearly so much as he feared the power this slender, disheveled woman held over him. God held his soul in his hands; the FitzHugh brothers held his life in theirs. But Isolde . . . Isolde held his heart. He did not fear death, neither the death of his body nor his soul.

But if she did not love him completely—if she should turn away from him and go to them—then his heart would break. It would stop beating and he would cease being a man. He would cease being anything.

His hold on her tightened, and unable to contain his emotions, he squeezed her against his chest. "I cannot live . . ." His voice faltered. "I cannot live without you."

Isolde heard the anguish in Rhys's voice, and she recognized the battle he fought inside himself. Had he been any other man, the pain his admission caused him would have sent her into a downward spiral of despair. Why could he not love her with joy instead of regret?

But Rhys was not like any other man. For him to admit his feelings for her was to let go of a lifetime of hate. It was that which was tearing him apart.

Yet he had said it. He could not live without her.

Her arms tightened around his neck. "I knew you would come for me. I knew you would. Though I could hear the fire eating away at the roof, and the stones creaking and moving in the walls—" She broke off as a coughing spasm struck. Then she smiled up at his dear, smoke-smudged face. "Even with all that, I knew you would come."

Their eyes held, and she saw him swallow hard. He did not respond with words, but then, Isolde did not need words to know the truth in his heart. He started down the stairs once more and Isolde relaxed into his strong embrace. Whatever would come, they would face it together. She laid her head against his shoulder and smiled, for despite the fire and chaos, and the problems that beset them from all sides, she felt the first blossoming of a tremendous happiness. "I cannot live without you either, you know. So I suppose we must either agree to stay together, or we both must die." She smiled and rubbed her hand along the neckline of his mail shirt, seeking the touch of his warm skin. "I know which of those two choices I prefer."

He looked down at her. "As do I—"

He broke off when her anxious father met them midway between the second floor and the main hall. Randulf FitzHugh rushed up, blanching at the sight of his daughter in Rhys's arms. "Is she hurt? Isolde—"

"I am unharmed, Father. Truly. Rhys has saved me—"

" 'Twas he who put you in this danger," Randulf countered. He drew his sword out with an ominous slither and held it at the ready. "Put her down." Then, to Isolde, "Can you walk?"

Rhys started to lower her to her feet, but Isolde clung stubbornly to his shoulders. She glared sternly at her father. "No. I cannot walk." She turned a smile on Rhys. "Please, will you bring me to my mother?"

At that very moment Josselyn scurried up the smoky stairwell, a *couvrechef* held across her mouth. She dropped it when she spied the trio. "Oh, my! Isolde! Rhys, you have her!" Her eyes met with her daughter's, and though they did not speak, Isolde somehow knew that her mother understood. Gesturing urgently with her hand, Josselyn said, "Bring her into the yard. Hurry, Rand. We must fight the fire. Jasper has formed a water line."

Isolde saw her father's fury at Rhys. But her mother had reminded him of the fire. Though the threat to Isolde had eased, the threat to Rosecliffe had not, and his eyes turned anxiously up toward the tower.

"The door is closed but the fire has consumed most of the roof," Rhys told him as he came down three steps. "Unless you intervene swiftly, it will soon burn through the door."

It was their turn to share a look. The two men were eye to eye, with Isolde in Rhys's arms between them. She was the only thing that stood between them, preventing their mistrust of one another from spilling over into violence. Very likely she would have to play that role for a goodly while. But not forever, she vowed.

She reached out and caught her father's hand. "Be careful, Papa. I do love you so."

"As I love you, child of my heart," he gruffly responded.

"Come," Josselyn urged. But she was smiling at Isolde when Rhys hurried past. And she kept smiling at her husband when they were alone. "Yes. Be careful, my dearest heart, for I love you very much."

The bailey was in complete chaos. Yet amid all the frenetic activity, there was some semblance of order. At the well a team of boys hauled water just as fast they could. Women rushed forward with every bucket and pot and pail to be found.

Men streamed into the hall, ferrying the precious water to the source of the fire. And above it all, the sky rumbled and groaned. Lightning lit the gloomy sky and crashed in the forest beyond the walls, causing everyone to jump.

Was the world coming to an end? Isolde had been so grateful to be rescued, so happy to hear Rhys's grudging admission of his feelings, and so relieved to know he and Jasper had not completed their battle, that she'd not recognized the true gravity of the situation. Now, when Rhys set her down on a keg near the gatehouse, she looked up and gasped.

Flames leaped from the roof of the tower, tall and brilliant against the dark sky. Burning embers showered down upon the castle walls and yard and ancillary buildings. A trio of women with wet rags ran about, stamping out the burning splinters, crushing the seething embers. A small blaze had started in the kindling barrel near the kitchen, but two youths swiftly doused it. But the fire in the tower raged on, so hot she could feel the blast of it against her cheeks.

When winter's heat shall cold defeat.

The children's verse sprang suddenly into her head. The third prediction. Was this what it referred to, a fire so large it chased the chill from winter itself?

"Will you not help them?" It was Newlin who spoke, startling Isolde. But he stared at Rhys, and for once the bard's wandering eyes focused together. "Will you not lend your strength to saving Rosecliffe Castle? 'Tis a fine and worthy place. Strong and well built."

Beside him Tilly stood, and for once the old minstrel was unmistakably a woman. Her wiry gray hair appeared softer than usual; her expression was gentler. " 'Tis the people within that make a place fine and worthy, be it castle or a humble cottage." She smiled at the young man with whom she'd travelled so long. "Help save it, my boy. Keep it fine and worthy."

Isolde told herself she would understand if Rhys chose not to assist the efforts to save the castle. The fire was not of his doing. Indeed, he'd already done more than could be expected, for he'd risked his life to rescue her. And he'd not yet recovered from his own injuries.

When he looked down at her, however, and when he sighed, then gave her a wry half-smile, her heart leaped with joy. "I will return to your side," he said. "There is much that yet remains unsettled between us." Then he was gone, racing to the well, grabbing up a pair of buckets and plunging back into the smoke-filled hall.

Another streak of lightning split the sky and Isolde flinched. But there was delay before the thunder shook the ground, and even then it was muffled by the fat splattering of raindrops.

Rain!

Within seconds the heavens let loose a torrent. With a roar it came down, a cold, stinging onslaught, yet nevertheless gladly received. Once again the people in the bailey scampered for protection from the elements, into the kitchen and alehouse. Into the stables. They peered from beneath the laundry shed and shrank back against the outer walls.

Beneath the gatehouse, Isolde rose to her feet and joyfully held her hands aloft to catch the rain on her fingers. A swirl of wind blew the cold downpour in her face, and the rain mingled with hot tears of gratitude.

"Was it you who caused this?" she shouted to Newlin above the drowning drum of the rain. "Did you bring the rain—and the lightning before that?"

The bard smiled his old sweet smile and shook his head. "I have powers of observation," he demurred. "I see things that others are prone to overlook, and on occasion I share my opinion or, perhaps, impart a little advice. But command the weather? This I do not do. No more than I direct the actions of others."

Isolde was not certain she believed him, but at the moment it did not matter. She stared up at the tower and saw the fire sputter and falter. Then suddenly it disappeared in a dark circle of smoke. Her smile was huge when she looked back at Newlin. "Perhaps it is as you say. But you knew how this would turn out. I am certain of that. And now, I have only to bring peace between Rhys and Jasper and my father."

Newlin smiled at Josselyn's special child and began to rock forward and back in the faint rhythm that gave him such comfort. Beside him Tilly reached out and gently took his gnarled hand in hers. His rocking slowed as she drew him back to the moment. But then she began to rock in a rhythm that matched his own, and he sighed contentedly. Together they watched

Isolde limp across the yard, her arms upstretched as if beckoning the rain down from the sky and urging it never to cease. She was heading for the great hall, searching for the man she loved and the beginnings of the life she would create with him.

"Winter's end is nigh," Newlin murmured.

" 'Tis barely begun," Tilly replied. But then, understanding what he meant, her old fingers squeezed his. "Winter's end is nigh. But I am cold, and hungry. Come, old man. Let us seek our fire."

A twinkle sparkled in Newlin's faded eyes. "I wager 'tis not in the *domen* that you wish to weather this storm."

She harrumphed. "That hard, frigid hole? You have but to ask and any of the villagers will offer us shelter. They fear to tell you no."

"They have no reason to fear me," the ancient bard protested.

"No," Tilly agreed, smiling warmly at him. "No, they most assuredly do not."

In the hall Isolde found her mother and her aunt Rhonwen. "Where is he?"

"Upstairs. They're all three up there," Josselyn said. She waved a cloth, trying to fan the smoke out through the open doorway. Rhonwen had already opened up two low windows while a manservant opened the higher ones, and the damp wind had begun to seep the air clear. From the stairwell the smoke still swirled as if uncertain whether to rise up, sink down, or simply drift away. But it was already thinner than before, cooler and paler, as well. The rain had come none too soon.

Isolde started up the stairs.

"You're limping," her mother cried, hurrying behind her.

" 'Tis nothing."

"But Isolde—"

"Mother, please! I must find Rhys."

"Yes, yes." Josselyn gave her a quick hug. "Of course you must." But she followed in Isolde's wake, as did Rhonwen.

They found the knot of men on the fourth level. The door to the tower room stood ajar now, smoking still. Beyond it the roof had collapsed. The massive timber beams were charred and smoldering. But the rain was heavy and the fire had no choice but to surrender to it.

Though smoky and sodden, there was an oddly triumphant feel to the disparate group gathered there. When Isolde appeared, however, their joint triumph over the fire faded, and everyone turned to look to Rhys. One problem had been resolved. However, another, more difficult one remained.

But Isolde knew how this must end and so she crossed directly to her father. "You have fought together, you and Jasper and Rhys. You have fought together to save me, and to save Rosecliffe. Can you now not abandon the need to fight against one another?"

Her father scowled down at her, but he was no proof against the earnest entreaty on her face, as she had hoped. With a muttered oath he opened his arms to her and she rushed gladly into his embrace.

"I am willing to forgive the past," he conceded, staring beyond her to Rhys. "But he cannot persist in his efforts to attack me or any other of my family."

"If you mean me," Isolde began, "You need not fear—"

"I mean Jasper," he interrupted.

Isolde turned within her father's protective embrace and leaned back against his chest. Jasper stood beside them, as did two burly English knights. Across the small shambles of the tower room Rhys stood alone. His expression was hard. The rain beat down through the open roof, plastering his hair against his head. He was all muscle and bone, she thought, a dark, virile man, beautiful in his own harsh way, yet vulnerable all the same. All the muscle and anger in the world could not truly disguise the pain he hid in his heart.

Determined to banish that hurt from him forever, she disentangled herself from her father's arms. For a moment he tried to hold her back. But when she looked him straight in the eye, smiled, and said, "I love him," his hands fell to his sides.

"I love him." She repeated that simple statement to her uncle Jasper. Then she took three steps and stood directly before Rhys. They were close enough to touch. "I love you."

He said nothing. But his eyes, dark as night, searched her face.

"I love you, Rhys. And I love them. We must come to a peace among the three of you, else you and I . . ." She trailed off, shaking her head. She was unable to speak such an awful thought aloud.

He struggled. She saw the turbulence in his face and in his heart. "I would have you, Isolde, despite the name FitzHugh that you bear. I would have you to wife." He paused, and she knew that concession had been hard for him. "But we cannot stay here," he added. "I cannot be near this place, knowing an Englishman rules where a Welshmen ought."

There was a commotion near the door, and everyone turned to look. Josselyn stood there, staring intently at her husband with a pointed expression on her face. Isolde's brow creased. What did that look mean?

But if Isolde did not know what it meant, Randulf obviously did. He cleared his throat, then addressed Rhys. "Jasper holds sway at Bailwynn to the south. His rule there has been just, as any honest man of that district will attest. His wife is Welsh and his children are as much Welsh as English. The same is true of myself. I have worked diligently to be a good lord to the people of these lands, and in this my Welsh bride has been a great aid." He glanced again at Josselyn. "But times change. There is a new king in England, and a new demesne for me there. Aislin," he said in answer to Isolde's questioning look. "Our family's ancestral holdings, passed down to my eldest brother, John. With his death, it has passed to me."

"You're moving away, to Aislin?" Isolde cried. Though she'd never been there, she'd heard stories of her father's childhood home. "But I don't want to live in England."

With one hand her father cupped the side of her face. "Then live here. With your husband."

Isolde stared up at him a long moment. Was he saying what she thought he was saying? Then he smiled and shrugged, and she turned abruptly to Rhys, her heart pounding with sudden joy.

Rhys heard the same words Isolde did. He understood their meaning in the same moment as she. Yet still he stood, disbelieving. Could this be true?

The older man went on. "I am now Earl of Aislin, and Gavin is heir to that title." He glanced toward the door, then continued. "My beloved ladywife has requested of me that our Welsh estates pass through our eldest daughter." As if to emphasize the importance of his words, the sky rumbled.

Rhys wiped the rain from his eyes. The storm still lashed them as they stood in the ruined tower of Rosecliffe. But Rhys knew the castle remained strong. What had been ruined could be rebuilt.

Rosecliffe Castle had been well sited, and with its wide moat and mighty walls, it was as fine a fortress as any in England, Scotland, or Wales. Certainly it was finer than anything his father might have constructed, he realized. For twenty years now, Rosecliffe Castle had served as shelter and protection to all people of good heart, Welsh and English alike. Randulf FitzHugh had done that. And Jasper FitzHugh had aided him.

But for once it was not the need to possess Rosecliffe that prodded Rhys. Nor was it his need for revenge against the FitzHughs. For the first time in his life another emotion ruled all those others, an emotion tied wholly to the woman standing so bedraggled before him. His brave and beautiful Isolde.

He looked down at her, with her upturned face wet with rain. Her hair was drenched and disheveled, her gown was ruined, and yet she was the loveliest ceature his eyes had ever beheld. But more important than that, her heart was beautiful and her soul was pure.

Randulf FitzHugh had done that, too. He and Josselyn had raised their child that they loved into a woman whom Rhys could love. The only woman he could ever love.

She blinked. Were those raindrops or tears in her eyes?

He reached out a hand that trembled and cupped her face as her father had. She wrapped her slender fingers around his wrist.

"Will you have me as your husband?" The words came out of their own volition, unplanned. But he did not regret them. Indeed, a huge weight seemed to lift away from him. "Will you consent to be my wife, Isolde?" he asked, staring intently into her serious gray eyes.

"Yes."

The single word seemed to quiver between them. Then she launched herself into his arms, nearly unbalancing him, and

Rhys's heart swelled with joy. She was small, but she was strong, this woman of his. She was gentle but she could also be fierce. And though a lady, she had enough of the wanton in her to keep him eternally content.

"You will marry me?" he murmured into her soaked hair.

She nodded, and only then was he aware of clapping. With his arms still wrapped tightly about her, Rhys looked up to see that they were all clapping. He was momentarily nonplussed.

Then Randulf FitzHugh approached him with hand extended. "I would have a true peace between us," the older man said. It felt right for Rhys to take his hand, and he did so without hesitation.

Then Jasper FitzHugh came forward, his hand offered in friendship as well. "There has been enough ill will between us. If you wed Isolde, you become my nephew."

Rhys felt Isolde tense in his arms. When he glanced down at her, however, he saw nothing but love in her eyes.

"I love your niece," he answered the man, though he stared still at Isolde. "If you are her uncle, then you must be mine, as well."

Then he grasped the man's hand in a pledge of peace. He could feel in Jasper's strong grip the empty place where one of his fingers was missing—the finger Rhys's father had cruelly severed. How long ago those awful days seemed. But this was a new age. He shook Jasper's hand, then turned to face his Isolde.

"I would have a private word with my bride."

He held her before him, a hand on each of her shoulders, staring deeply into her eyes as he waited for everyone to leave. Then they were alone, just he and her in the smoldering ruins of the tower, with the weight of twenty years echoing around them.

"I love you." The words came hard. They were foreign to everything he'd ever known. But they were the only words that came even close to revealing the emotions in his heart. "I love you, Isolde. I . . . I wished to tell you that in private." He took a shaky breath. "I have been a fool not to have recognized that simple truth long ago. I tried to give it another name. But . . . I love you," he repeated, gratified by the glitter of emotion in her eyes. "And you should know that I would want you for my wife, with or without Rosecliffe Castle."

She had listened solemnly and now she nodded. A smile trembled along the edges of her lips. "Would you have made peace with Jasper for me alone?"

Slowly he nodded. "For you, it seems, I would do anything."

"Even walk through fire," she said with tears in her eyes. But they were tears of happiness, the only tears he hoped ever to see in them again. Then laughing through those tears, she flung herself into his arms, sealing their love and their vows with a kiss.

Rhys wrapped her in his arms then, picking her off her feet, began slowly to spin in a circle. How had he come to possess so perfect a creature as she? What had he ever done to deserve her?

"We will be so happy here," she whispered, and he knew it was so. From this ruin they would raise new walls. Strong walls.

Good walls.

EPILOGUE

When stones shall grow and trees shall no',
When noon comes black as beetle's back,
When winter's heat shall cold defeat,
We'll see them all, 'ere Cymry falls.

—ANONYMOUS

EPILOGUE

ISOLDE SPUN IN A SLOW CIRCLE. HER EYES WERE HALF-closed, deliberately unfocused so as to better visualize the mural she worked on. Above her on the roof, the leadfitter hammered, using heavy mallets to seal the new lead sheets into place. This time the tower roof would be impervious to fire.

She had been waiting to begin this project for nearly a year. But the long winter had delayed rebuilding the tower room walls. Then had come the spring plantings and the sheep shearing. During the summer, however, the workmen had finally turned their efforts to the tower repairs. Even Rhys had labored at it, laying stones and muscling the massive timbers into place before winter's first snowfall.

But now spring was imminent and the final work on the roof was nearly done. It was a point of pride with Rhys that the tower be completed before her parents came for their first lengthy visit to Rosecliffe.

But Isolde wanted more than merely the walls and roof and parapet finished. She wanted the mural complete, as well, the endless scene she envisioned enveloping the entire room.

Rhys had been gone these past two days, attending to business at Afon Bryn, and during that time she'd worked feverishly from the first pink light of dawn through the lengthening evening hours. Today she'd had even more cause to hurry. She rubbed her hands in slow circles around her extended belly. Baby Alan—or Alana—was growing impatient, it seemed. He'd settled a little lower, and all day her back had ached. Whatever part of the mural she did not complete today would go unfinished for several months to come, she suspected.

She made the complete circle once more. The trail of roses was finally right. And the silhouette of the mountains to the east and the profile of Rosecliffe Castle pleased her now. The wolf was better. But the dragon . . . She squinted. Something about the dragon was not yet right. His eyes, she decided. They were as dark as Rhys's, but they did not sparkle as his did. She smiled to think of that sparkle, sometimes heated by passion, other times simply by love.

The door creaked open as she worked on them. "Lady Isolde, you must stop now," Magda scolded. "If not for your sake, then for mine. You know how fussy Odo becomes when the meal is delayed. And he refuses to serve without you, so 'tis no use to tell him to commence while you are still up here."

Magda waddled farther into the room, her stomach almost as large as Isolde's, and Isolde let out a chuckle. "We are quite the pair, aren't we? But I think, Magda, that I shall regain my waistline before you do."

"Oh, milady, has your time come?" Magda's eyes widened as she anxiously scanned Isolde. "We must get you to your bed. I knew you should not have been allowed to climb all those steep steps. Lord Rhys will have my head if he should hear of it."

"You climb them," Isolde pointed out. "And you're nearly as far along as I am. Don't fuss, Magda. Rhys fusses enough for both of you. My labors have not yet begun, but I do feel different today. Perhaps the babe will not greet us this evening, but soon. Quite soon."

" 'Tis a good thing Lord Rhys has returned," Magda grumbled.

"He has returned! Oh, why was I not notified?"

"But that's precisely what I'm doing, milady. Osborn spotted him coming up the old road from Carreg Du. I came up to fetch you so you can greet him in the bailey when he arrives."

"And so he won't know what I've been up to, eh?" The baby kicked and Isolde laughed. "Let us be on our way, then."

They started down the stairs arm in arm. The mural was nearly done; her parents would arrive within a matter of days; and Rhys was home. To Isolde's mind her life could not be more perfect. Rhys loved her, he'd made peace with her family—and himself—and soon she would present him with the ultimate proof of her love for him. She could hardly wait to see him.

A half league from the castle, Rhys rode like a man possessed. Around midday he'd had a sudden premonition. A baby in the village had cried out and he'd felt the hair on the back of his neck rise. Within the hour he had left Gandy and Linus to finish his business at Afon Bryn. He had to see Isolde. He had to be with her. He should never have left when she was so near to her time, even though she'd assured him she had several weeks to go. He should have listened to his heart and remained at her side.

Up the hill his game steed labored. He passed Carreg Du, then made his way through the cleared fields that surrounded Rosecliffe. The field workers were returning home from their daily labor, some to Carreg Du, others to the village below the castle. Everything looked as it ought; but until he saw Isolde, he would not be content.

As he rounded the turn near the *domen*, he lifted a hand in greeting to Newlin and Tilly. But he did not slow his pace. Then he saw the castle and its newly finished tower. He was home.

A figure in the gatehouse spied him and waved—but did not signal any distress. Rhys took a deep breath of relief, then on impulse reined in his weary mount and simply gazed upon Rosecliffe.

Home. How strange for him to feel such a powerful connection to the one place he'd always hated. In the past year, however, there had been many such alterations in his feelings. And all because Isolde loved him.

A hard lump of emotion rose in his chest. Isolde had seen something in him worth loving. But even more amazing, she'd made him look deep into his own heart and discover his ability to love in return. It sometimes terrified him, how desperately he loved her.

Now she must suffer the wrenching pains of childbirth on

account of his love, and that terrified him anew. Some women died in childbirth.

He leaned forward and urged his steed forward once more. He must get to her. He must be certain she was all right.

Newlin watched Rhys fly up the hill to the castle and smiled. "There is magic in the tower," he murmured to Tilly, who sat beside him on the *domen* soaking up the last of the day's sunshine. Soon the sun would be gone, but for now it warmed the land, and gleamed upon the noble walls of Rose-cliffe Castle.

"Magic?" Tilly asked. "Is the babe to come tonight?"

"Methinks so," he murmured, patting her hand.

"Speaking of babes. I have heard of a child, born in Afon Bryn. Its face is misshapen, and one of its feet, as well. The villagers believe it is cursed. But of course it is not. It is only very small and defenseless."

Newlin was quiet a moment. "And you wish to raise it?"

"I do."

Newlin smiled and again patted Tilly's hand.

"Winter's end is nigh," he said, and everywhere the signs said as much. Buds swelling in the forest. The pintails beginning their mating rituals. A child would soon be christened in yon castle—and another brought home by Tilly to his little abode.

His old heart swelled, for he was happy.

"I have heard a song," he said, beginning to rock back and forth. Tilly rocked with him. "It came to me in a dream."

> *When stones shall grow and trees shall no',*
> *When noon comes black as beetle's back,*
> *When winter's heat shall cold defeat,*
> *We'll see them all, 'ere Cymry falls.*
>
> *But what is ruin when next comes June*
> *To rise and gro' what 'ere we sow?*
> *Pick wise the seed and heaven heed,*
> *Then pure of heart, seek your reward.*

The last ray of sunlight kissed the highest portion of Rose-cliffe, then melted away, leaving lavender to claim all. As darkness crept over the land, candles were lit, and torchères and lanterns, then as the hour grew late, those lights slowly winked out—save for one.

In the tower room the candles burned a long while. A man paced the overlook, sweating despite the cold night, for his ladylove suffered to bring their child to life, and he could hardly bear it.

Her words came back to him, words from the hardest part of their past. It *was* far easier to fight than to love. He believed her now, for his heart was breaking at her every cry of pain.

Then there was a new cry, a baby's thin, trembling wail, and a dam broke in Rhys's heart.

"Rhys?" Isolde called out to him. "Rhys? Come and see your son. Come and see him."

And with tears of joy streaming down his face, Rhys went to her.

Haywood Smith

"Haywood Smith delivers intelligent, sensitive historical romance for readers who expect more from the genre."

—*Publishers Weekly*

SHADOWS IN VELVET

Orphan Anne Marie must enter the gilded decadence of the French court as the bride of a mysterious nobleman, only to be shattered by a secret from his past that could embroil them both in a treacherous uprising...

_____ 95873-0 $5.99 U.S./$6.99 CAN.

SECRETS IN SATIN

Amid the turmoil of a dying monarch, newly widowed Elizabeth, Countess of Ravenwold, is forced by royal command to marry a man she has hardened her heart to—and is drawn into a dangerous game of intrigue and a passionate contest of wills.

_____ 96159-6 $5.99 U.S./$7.99 CAN.